Just
Tell Her

by

NICOLE PYLAND

Just Tell Her

Chicago Series Book #2

Charlie Adams has two best friends. Ember Elliot and Hailey Grant, the woman she's secretly been in love with since the moment they met over a decade ago. She has watched Hailey date all the wrong women and never said anything about how she wanted to be Hailey's forever love.

Hailey Grant had a first love that she was comparing every other woman to. When that woman comes back into her life, Hailey has to get to know her again after all this time. As Hailey tries to figure out if her first love is actually her forever love, she sees something is different about Charlie.

When the two women embark on new relationships, they'll have to finally confront their growing attraction for each other and decide if they can be brave enough to risk the most important friendship they have for possibly something more. Charlie might just be the girl who gets the girl after years of watching Hailey be miserable with other women who didn't deserve her, and Hailey might have just had the right woman by her side this whole time.

To contact the author or for any additional information, visit: **https://nicolepyland.com**

You can also subscribe to the reader's newsletter to be the first to receive updates about upcoming books and more: **https://nicolepyland.com/newsletter**

BY THE AUTHOR

CHICAGO SERIES:

- Introduction – Fresh Start

- Book #1 – The Best Lines

- Book #2 – Just Tell Her

- Book #3 – Love Walked into The Lantern

- Series Finale – What Happened After

SAN FRANCISCO SERIES:

- Book #1 – Checking the Right Box

- Book #2 – Macon's Heart

- Book #3 – This Above All

- Series Finale – What Happened After

TAHOE SERIES:

- Book #1 – Keep Tahoe Blue

- Book #2 – Time of Day

- Book #3 – The Perfect View

- Book #4 – Begin Again

- Series Finale – What Happened After

BOSTON SERIES:

- Book #1 – Let Go

- Book #2 – The Right Fit

- Book #3 – All Good Plans

- Book #4 – Around the World

- Series Finale – What Happened After

SPORTS SERIES:

This series is related by a sports theme, not by characters.

- Book #1 – Always More

- Book #2 – A Shot at Gold

- Book #3 – The Unexpected Dream

- Book #4 – Finding a Keeper

CELEBRITIES SERIES:

- Book #1 – No After You

- Book #2 – All the Love Songs

- Book #3 – Midnight Tradition

- Book #4 – Path Forward

- Series Finale – What Happened After

HOLIDAY SERIES:

- Book #1 – The Writing on the Wall

- Book #2 – The Block Party

- Book #3 – The Fireworks

- Book #4 – The Sweet Escape

- Book #5 – The Misperception

- Book #6 – The Wait is Over

- Series Finale – What Happened After

ANTHOLOGY:

- The Meet Cute Café

FIRE UNIVERSE:

- The Fire
- The Disappeared

STAND-ALONE NOVELS:

- Reality Check
- The Show Must Go On
- Future Wife

YOUNG ADULT / NEW ADULT:

- The Moments
- Love Forged
- Pride Festival

EROTICA:

- Once a Month

CONTENTS

CHAPTER 1

"CAN you believe it? I mean, seriously," Hailey asked of Charlie as they sat off to the side at their best friend's engagement party. "Everyone's pairing off and getting married. I'm including Ember in that group. *Ember* is getting married!"

"Alyssa and Hannah will probably have a kid in, like, a year," Charlie added.

"And we're still single, with none of that on the horizon. Alyssa and Eva are both younger than us and, somehow, ahead of us. Ember and Hannah are both around our ages."

"It doesn't have anything to do with age, Hails. It's about finding the right person and taking those steps with them. They all just found their person."

"And we still haven't," Hailey stated.

"Right," Charlie muttered to herself more than to Hailey.

"Well, where's my damn person already?" Hailey questioned, exasperated.

"No idea," Charlie replied halfheartedly.

Charlie had already met her person, or at least it had felt that way. It had for the better part of a decade. Charlie and Hailey had known one another for more than ten years. They met at Ember's family restaurant, which is where they also met Ember and formed their bond of friendship that had gotten them through all their major life events so far. Despite life getting busier the older they got – with the new jobs and promotions, with additional responsibilities and new relationships – they had always kept their Thursday coffee meetings. They made sure to stay involved in one another's lives. That had sometimes been a problem for Charlie, because she had been madly in love with her best friend, Hailey Grant, for a very long time. Hailey, herself, had a habit of dating all the wrong women, and Charlie had to watch the woman get burned time and again, all the while imploring Hailey silently to just pick her.

"I'm glad Ember and Eva stayed here. I would've hated Ember leaving Chicago. I know it wouldn't have been that far away, and we would have still seen each other, but we would have missed out on so much." Hailey waved at a very excited Ember, who was standing next to Eva, laughing with expressive eyes. Then, Ember held up a finger, indicating she would be right over. "God, look how happy she is. I want that."

"Hails, you'll get it someday. You just have to find the right woman first."

Charlie gave Hailey the same mantra over and over. She was getting more and more frustrated that she had to continue to deliver it, because she wanted Hailey to see *her* as that woman, but she hadn't ever told her best friend how she felt. Charlie had only revealed her feelings to Ember accidentally, while intoxicated. Ember had kept her secret, though, only revealing Charlie's feelings to Eva – because you do that when you enter a relationship with someone, apparently. Charlie had been in several relationships in the past, but none had ever come close to resembling what Ember and Eva had found.

As time went, they had formed a new group of six, with the addition of Hannah and Alyssa. The longer that went on, the more Charlie wanted someone like that for herself. It got harder, not telling Hailey how she felt, but Charlie also knew that she wasn't that brave. She had never been brave where Hailey had been concerned. Well, that wasn't exactly true. When the three of them first met at the restaurant, Charlie had nearly asked Hailey out on a date.

Unfortunately, Hailey hadn't known that the reason Charlie had approached her was to ask her out. Hailey had started in on how hot Ember was and that maybe she would ask her out. Charlie then told her to go for it and walked away with a lowered head. They had all only known one another for a few months at that time, and Charlie had used every minute of those months working up the courage to ask the girl out, only to hear her talking about Ember. Ember, of course, was still in her date-every-woman phase, and she never asked Hailey out. Hailey met someone else, and then someone else.

***

"Why are you two over here?" Ember approached and sat down in the booth next to Hailey and across from Charlie. "The party is going on all around you. You're missing it."

The party was being held in Ember's family restaurant, which was always closed on Sundays. There were about sixty or so people moving around the space, enjoying food, drinks, and the sound of the soft music playing from the overhead speakers.

"We just needed a break from the lovefest," Hailey explained. "I'm so happy for you guys, though."

Ember laughed and slid her ash-blonde hair behind her ear, allowing Charlie to catch another glimpse of Ember's new engagement ring, which seemed to fit the woman so well.

"She's totally happy for you," Charlie echoed and earned a wry grin from Hailey. "What?"

"Okay... So, here's my problem." Ember leaned over the table. "I have a lame older brother and no sisters. I do happen to have two best friends, though. And I was hoping that you guys would be my bridesmaids."

"Of course, Em," Hailey returned with a smile. "Whatever you need, we're there."

Charlie took a moment to glance at Hailey while she was engaged in a moment with Ember. Hailey's blonde hair had been put into a braid that the woman wore down one shoulder. Her green eyes were as magnificent as ever. They flickered a little with the light from the small candle in a red holder on the table. Hailey's hands were small, with long fingers that Charlie just wanted to hold. There were other things she wanted to do with them, too, and many a night, she had touched herself picturing Hailey doing it with them, instead. But mostly, though, Charlie thought about how it would feel to hold Hailey's hand. She wanted to be the only one that got to intertwine her fingers with Hailey's and lift their joined hands to her lips to kiss Hailey's soft, flawless skin. Hailey's lips were full. Charlie had to constantly remind herself not to stare at them.

"Charlie?" Ember's blue eyes were on her.

"Huh?" Charlie had zoned out and had no idea what she was being asked.

"Bridesmaid?"

"Oh, yeah. Of course," Charlie agreed. "You know that."

"I don't really know what to do about the whole maid of honor thing... You two are both my best friends."

"We can both do it," Hailey suggested. "It would make things easier." She lifted one shoulder and looked at Charlie. "We're both really busy at work right now. We could share the responsibilities. It could be fun."

Planning a friend's wedding with the woman *she* wanted to marry one day? *'Yeah, that could be fun,'* Charlie's internal voice rang with sarcasm.

"Sure," Charlie then agreed again and took a long drink of her gin and tonic.

Ember squinted her eyes in Charlie's direction, as if she was considering something. Ember was always on her case to tell Hailey how she felt. The problem was while Charlie had always been the dry, sarcastic one of their three-some and the necessarily assertive one at work, when it came to relationships, she had never been brave. Every day that passed, she felt less and less so, because it meant that she and Hailey had known one another for yet another day. Their friendship had lasted so long and was so important to Charlie, that the thought of any awkwardness, arising when Hailey inevitably told her that she just wanted to be friends, made Charlie sick sometimes. The thought that she could lose Hailey from her life was enough to not tell her anything and live with the pain she felt every time Hailey met someone new.

At least *that* hadn't happened lately. Hailey had finally taken her friends' advice and hadn't just fallen for another woman that was just trying to get her into bed or who was bad for her. She hadn't had anyone to talk about at coffee for over three months, and those were three blissful months for Charlie Adams.

"When were you two thinking about having the ceremony?" Hailey asked. "That kind of tells us when we need to start working on things."

"Well, here's the thing…" Ember glanced over at Eva, who was talking to Hannah.

Charlie watched as Eva somehow felt Ember's glance and smiled when their eyes met. Ember didn't even say or do anything, from what Charlie could tell, but Eva excused herself and headed over.

"You rang, Ember Elliot?" Eva sat across from Ember and next to Charlie.

"They want to know the date," Ember shared.

"Oh." Eva smirked at Ember. "So, we were going to wait for a while, since we just got a house, just got engaged, and that's what everyone thinks we should do… But we don't want to wait a while."

"My mom is also concerned because my aunt isn't well," Ember explained. "She's had some heart problems recently. She's Mikey's mom, so she's basically like my second mother." Ember's cousin, Mikey, was the chef at the restaurant and was essentially another brother to her. "We thought about doing it next February – since that's the anniversary of when we met and when we proposed, but I don't know if she's going…" Ember began to fade.

Eva reached her hand over the table, and Ember slid her own into it. Charlie thought back to Hailey's hands.

"Em, I'm sorry," Hailey consoled.

"We want to get married this summer," Ember stated and lifted her eyebrows up in concern at her friends' reactions.

"This summer?" Charlie nearly choked down another sip of her gin and tonic. "It's March, November."

"That's confusing," Hailey pointed out.

"I used her full name for emphasis," Charlie remarked.

"I know it's a lot, but I'm presenting at that conference in June. We had already planned to take a two-week vacation after that. We thought we could have the wedding before that and fly to Miami. I can present my article, which will only be about three hours of work at the stuffy event, and then, we would have two weeks together to celebrate," Eva explained.

"It's fast, we know," Ember continued. "But we don't want anything big. Honestly, we're looking for something small. It shouldn't take too much work."

"The only thing that might cause some problems is the location," Eva added.

"You want to do it here, right?" Charlie presumed.

"Not exactly…" Eva looked to Ember to reveal the information to her friends.

"We're going to do it in Iowa." Ember smiled. "It's in Eva's hometown. All of her siblings have been married in this barn on one of the neighboring farms. It's like this tradition."

"And I'm not always one for tradition, but it's important to my parents, and–"

"It's where we first danced," Ember interjected. "And we kissed for the first time in that tree house and slept to–"

"Gross, Em. We don't need to know that." Charlie waved a hand to get her to stop talking.

"We slept, Charlie. That's all, remember?"

"I want to do this for them, because we don't go there very often. It's not too far away from here, so getting Ember's side there shouldn't be difficult."

"I think it's cute," Hailey joined in. "I'm sure it won't be a problem. Do you guys want separate bridal showers or together? Do you want to do one bachelorette party or two? Oh, there's this place that makes amazing cupcakes in Evanston. I used to get them for professors when I was at Northwestern."

"Because you were a kiss-ass," Charlie pointed out.

"Because I liked my teachers," Hailey corrected with a glare in her direction.

"She's a weirdo," Charlie offered the group.

"You realize I am a professor, right?" Eva delivered to Charlie with a smirk.

"I'm sure you're the only one that deserves the cupcakes," Charlie returned with a smile.

"We don't know that stuff yet," Ember told Hailey, returning them to their original conversation. "We haven't really talked about the other stuff that comes along with weddings. We just thought June and Iowa."

"Well, you'll want to figure it out soon, because it's, like, three months away, Em."

"I know. We will," Ember said.

"Alyssa and Hannah will be my duel maids of honor. Is that how you say that?" Eva checked with Ember. "Or is it duel maid of honors?"

"You're the one with a Ph. D in English, babe."

"Literature. There's a difference," Eva corrected her. "We thought it might be fun for the four of you to work together. We've all been spending so much time together lately. There would be four of you to handle things, but we don't expect anything. We're not hiring a wedding planner because my sister wants to do that instead of being in the wedding."

"It's true. She's already asking us for a guest list. It's kind of cute." Ember smiled at Eva.

"We were thinking we would all get together when Ember and I are on a break from school in a couple of weeks. We could start figuring things out officially then. We could have lunches or dinners and maybe do dress stuff on the weekend."

"Sounds good to me."

"Sure," Charlie echoed and finished her drink.

"Thanks, guys. I know it's soon... But, honestly, it's about more than just my aunt. I want to marry this woman like crazy." Ember continued to hold on to Eva's hand on the table.

"We just bought a house together, but she doesn't seem to think that's enough of a commitment," Eva joked with them but never took her eyes off her fiancée.

"I'm locking you down, girl." Ember lifted her eyebrows.

"Okay... We get it. You like each other," Charlie joined in on the joking. "I have work tomorrow, and I am exhausted. I'm going to head out." She went to move out of the booth.

"I'll go, too," Hailey offered. "I'll drive you home."

"I can walk," Charlie stated as Ember and Eva slid out of the booth so that Hailey and Charlie could get up.

"Why? I can drive you. I have my car."

"You live in the opposite direction of where I'm going."

"Ember, give her the math, please." Hailey crossed her own arms over her chest and glared at the stubborn Charlie while she asked Ember to do something they'd both started to do the moment they found out their best friend was a math genius.

"Well, Charlie is right. You live in the opposite direction."

"Thank you," Charlie matched Hailey's playful yet stern posture.

"But, Hailey's more right. Or is it righter?" Ember glanced at Eva, who just smiled. "She only lives fifteen

8

minutes that way," she said of Hailey and then turned to Charlie. "You live five minutes from here by car. It makes more sense for her to drive you, given the traffic patterns at this time of night in combination with the freezing weather you would have to walk through. You've also had at least two gin and tonics, which isn't good for a nighttime solo walk in the city. The ice would likely make you walk slower, so it's more, like, a fifteen-minute walk home in the dark, in a major city rife with crime."

"Rife?" Charlie rolled her eyes at Ember. "Your fiancée has expanded your vocabulary there, Em."

"Math holds, Charlie," Ember retorted. "She should drive you home. It will take her only five minutes. Then, she can take Lakeshore back home, which will be deserted this time of night."

"See?" Hailey uncrossed her arms. "Come on."

"Fine," Charlie acquiesced.

"Thank you for coming." Eva hugged a smiling Hailey.

"Sorry," Ember said and embraced her friend. "Not sorry," she added as she pulled back and offered Charlie a wink.

They exchanged partners, offered more hugs, and said their goodbyes to the other guests they knew, including Hannah and Alyssa, before they headed outside.

"I'm over here." Hailey pointed at her new Lexus.

She had bought it about six months ago, when she started traveling more for her job in the PR department at a major Midwestern bank. Charlie followed her to the car and climbed into the passenger's side, as had been her habit now for years. Charlie didn't have a car herself, since she lived and worked in the city. If she needed one, she could either borrow Hailey's or now Eva and Ember's. Almost a year prior, she had started working at an architecture start-up that focused on modern design and also redesigning and re-modeling old warehouses and other historical buildings in the city, to make them work for today's companies. Charlie was a Senior Manager of her department, initially, but had recently been promoted to Director of the Renew and Recycle team. That was more of an external title. Internally, they called her team the Historians, which still sounded funny to her, but they had earned that moniker due to their primary focus on old buildings. While everyone else in the company was striving for modern and trendy, her team focused on updating the older structures while maintaining much of their old-world vibe. The combination of the two elements was something her firm was known for and something Charlie really enjoyed about her job.

"Thanks for the ride," she told Hailey when the woman pulled up and parked in front of Charlie's new apartment.

Charlie had moved in only about three months prior, when her promotion came with more money and she could afford the building with a doorman, concierge service, and other amenities she had never dared to hope for when she was a mere city planner and on a government salary.

"Sure," Hailey replied. "Hey, would you mind if I just crashed here tonight? I'm kind of tired. It would be easier than driving home. I have to be on this side of town tomorrow for work anyway."

"You planned this, didn't you?" Charlie pointed a finger at her. "You wanted to drive me home just so you could crash at my kick-ass apartment."

"So, can I crash at your kick-ass apartment?" Hailey checked.

"Of course, you can. But you don't have anything–"

Charlie stopped herself abruptly when she watched Hailey reach in the back seat and pull up a small overnight bag that Charlie recognized.

"Thanks." Hailey smiled at her and turned off the car.

"You did plan this!" Charlie laughed and opened the car door. "You're just lucky Mondays are not street cleaning days, Hailey Jean Grant," she chastised.

"You know I hate that middle name," Hailey retorted as they made their way to the front of the brand-new building and the doorman opened the door for them with a nod.

"That's why I used it, obviously."

"Smart-ass," Hailey replied and hit the button for seven before Charlie could.

"Maybe you should just get a kick-ass apartment, too. You make enough money. Why are you still in the hole?"

"It's not a hole," Hailey argued as they stepped into the elevator. "It's a nice studio, and it's rent-controlled."

"You had termites last year. You had to stay with me for a week while they fumigated."

"It's been fine since."

"Yet, you've stayed here, like, ten times since I moved in."

"I'd ask if I was being an imposition, but I don't care enough to worry about that tonight." Hailey stepped out of the elevator first, and Charlie followed her down the hall until they reached a black door with a giant number painted on it in block lettering.

Charlie pulled her wallet out of the back pocket of her jeans. She had been glad the engagement party was not a formal affair, since it enabled her to wear simple jeans and an argyle sweater she often wore to work, with a collared shirt beneath. She pulled out the RFID key card all the apartments used, went to swipe it in front of the reader, but then, she saw Hailey's wide eyes.

"Go on." Charlie passed Hailey the card.

Hailey waved it in front of the reader, heard the beep, and smiled before passing it back to Charlie.

"Still so cool," she said and walked inside.

Eddie, Charlie's chocolate lab, met them immediately and began licking Hailey's outstretched hand.

"He likes you better than me," Charlie joked and closed the door behind them.

"Probably," Hailey teased and dropped to her knees to take Eddie's face in her hands. "You like me better, don't you?"

"I'm going to take him out. I'll be right back." Charlie

grabbed Eddie's leash off the table next to the door. The dog instantly chose her over Hailey. "Come on, buddy." She attached the leash to his collar and opened the door back up to take him outside.

***

When Charlie returned and allowed Eddie to run through the expansive living room, as he always did when he got back upstairs, she found that Hailey was already in the shower. Charlie liked the openness of the apartment. It was the main reason she had leased it. Eddie had a lot of space to move around, and he even had an area toward the side window that was his domain with toys, his food and water, and his giant bed that he loved so much, he often tried to drag it from place to place in the apartment. She didn't want him doing that, though, so she got him a blanket. Her precocious little man would take the blanket with him around the apartment instead. Sometimes, he'd encourage Charlie to drape it over him, and he'd wander around like that. It was one of his little eccentricities that she adored about him so much.

She let him run around for a few minutes while she sorted the mail she had picked up on her way back in. She found most of it was junk, and she tossed it aside before moving toward her room to change. She quickly found the sweats she'd slept in the night before, on her unmade bed, and exchanged those for jeans before finding a shirt in a drawer and tossing her dirty clothes into the hamper in her walk-in closet. Then, Charlie lay down on her comfortable plush mattress and turned on the TV.

"I forgot the pants." Hailey had finished in the shower and now stood in Charlie's bedroom doorway, wearing a Northwestern T-shirt and a towel under it around her waist.

Charlie knew the woman probably had underwear on, but they hadn't ever been the kind of close friends that had seen each other naked or even close to it.

"You what?" Charlie laughed at the image of Hailey standing there half-dressed, with wet hair that was dripping onto the light gray shirt.

"I brought a shirt to sleep in and clothes for work tomorrow, but I forgot to pack the pants to sleep in," Hailey explained her previous statement.

"Oh. Bottom drawer." Charlie pointed to the dresser that was on the wall opposite her bed.

Her fifty-two-inch flat screen hung on a wall over it. Other than the two bedside tables that she had bought merely so that she could put these matching lamps on and maybe a phone and some water at night, there was no other furniture in the room.

"Thanks." Hailey bent over, careful to hold the towel as she did.

Charlie told herself she could glance for a second before returning her eyes to the TV. It would only be a second. It was more than a second, but no more than five, she convinced herself. Hailey's legs were bare and freshly shaven, it appeared. Her skin glimmered. The towel Hailey had chosen had been a large one, unfortunately, and that meant that even when she bent over, Charlie didn't get much of a look. That was a good thing. For one, she shouldn't be torturing herself like this. But she also didn't want to objectify her best friend like that. She pulled her eyes back to the guide she had just put on the TV, clicked it to her DVR list of recordings, and watched Hailey slide on a pair of her flannel pajama pants before dropping the towel on the bed for a moment to pull her shirt down correctly.

"This TV is way too big for this room." Hailey pointed at the flat screen.

"This TV is the perfect size for this room."

"Charlie, it's massive, and this is the bedroom. Why didn't you get a smaller one for in here? You should sleep in your bedroom; not watch a giant TV right before bed. There have been studies done on that kind of thing." Hailey headed back toward the bathroom – which was just outside the bedroom – as she lectured, causing her voice to fade out toward the end.

"I heard you the first time you complained about it." Charlie selected an episode of Chopped and tossed the remote next to her on the bed.

If Ember was the genius in their threesome, Hailey was the one that always knew about the recent discoveries or studies. She had no particular area of interest. She merely read about anything and shared it with people in her life. She would be the first person to tell someone to decrease their salt intake because it was bad for them and then read a second study and tell them the exact opposite. Somehow, Hailey always managed to make it okay, though. She was never annoying about it, or even forceful or judging. It felt to Charlie as if Hailey just wanted people to know these things so that they could make their own decisions.

"What are you watching?" Hailey returned to the room and sat on the edge of the bed.

"Chopped. You want to watch it with me, or will that interfere with your precious REM cycle, Hails?" Charlie teased, but she knew the answer already and moved the remote control to her table so that Hailey could climb up next to her.

Hailey did just that and quickly slid her legs under the large light-gray comforter that matched the soft sheets beneath. Charlie made it to the entrée round commercial break before her eyes closed after several moments of her trying to combat sleep, with Hailey still sitting next to her, engrossed in the episode.

CHAPTER 2

HAILEY finished the episode of Chopped on her own, since Charlie had fallen asleep beside her. She used all the stealth she possessed – which wasn't much – to reach over Charlie on the queen-sized bed for the remote that was on the table. Once she nudged Charlie's shoulder and felt the woman somewhat beneath her begin to turn, Hailey recognized her mistake. She should've just gotten up and walked around the damn bed to do this. She grabbed the remote, though, turned the TV off, and didn't risk putting it back in place. Once it was settled on the table on her side, she considered going out to the sofa to sleep for the night. That was her spot. She claimed that sofa two years ago, when Charlie bought it from this local furniture store. The first time she fell asleep on it, she woke up completely rested. From that moment on, it was love. In all their years of friendship, Hailey had fallen asleep in a bed with Charlie maybe a handful of times. And it was only because they were in the hotels with Ember when they were young and couldn't afford separate rooms.

Their trips were few and far between and were also not to some glamorous places, like most college students seem to flock to over spring breaks or summer vacations. Hailey was not from a well-to-do family, and neither was Charlie. It was one of the reasons they'd both ended up at the restaurant where the three of them met.

Hailey could see Charlie's peaceful expression in the

dim light of the room, caused by the hallway light that was visible through the open door. Charlie always slept with the hall light on. The woman was thirty-one years old and was still somewhat afraid of the dark. Hailey had confronted her about it years ago, and when Charlie denied it, Hailey went to the nearest store to buy one of those self-activated night-lights, that stay off until the room or space is dark and then turn on, giving people enough light to be able to see in the dark. Hailey had been proud of the purchase and of her demonstration of their greatness, since this would save electricity and solve Charlie's problem. The next time Hailey stayed over, though, the lights were still there, but they never turned themselves on because Charlie still used the light in the hall.

That was when Hailey determined Charlie was not a fan of the darkness. She hadn't brought it up since, but they'd had many conversations over the course of their friendship. Hailey had managed to piece together a theory. Charlie had once lived in a bad neighborhood in the city. Her neighbors had been robbed, people did drugs in the open, and there were mentions of some peeping Tom type situations. Hailey guessed the light was a comfort, more than anything, because Charlie was a single woman, living in a big city on her own. Her new apartment was definitely much more secure, but anything could happen, since nowhere is 100% safe. By the time Hailey finished her thoughts about bed or sofa, she found herself lying down next to Charlie. Then, as if on instinct, her eyes closed, making the decision for her.

Hailey woke up to an empty bed. Charlie had always been an early riser. It used to drive Hailey and Ember crazy, because even when they did take those trips, Charlie was up by six at the latest, ready to start the day. The two of them wanted at least three more hours, to nurse the hangover or get the sleep they hadn't gotten the night before because they'd been up talking.

In high school, Hailey had a friend or two. She wasn't

a leper, but she never tried to fit in or be popular, either. She wasn't a joiner who participated in extracurricular activities. She tried track in middle school but found running in an endless oval to be boring and gave up on sports. She also tried the spelling bee once, at a teacher's coaxing because her grades were good, but she didn't really like speaking in public. And when one has to spell difficult words in public, it may not matter how great their spelling skills actually are. At one point, her guidance counselor suggested she run for class office. Hailey had thought it a joke, at first, until the reaction to her laughter made her realize it was not a joke. Her guidance counselor thought she should stand up in front of the entire school and make a speech about why she should be in charge of things.

Hailey didn't want to do it. She really had no intention of going through with it, but her mother thought it would be a good experience for her and would help make her applications to college look better. Hailey wrote a speech, had her mom review it for her, and then she practiced it in her bedroom while standing in front of her mirror, like a total tool, or at least that was what a seventeen-year-old Hailey thought she looked like.

When the day for the speeches came around, she tried to fake being sick, but her particularly astute mother knew what she was trying to pull and forced her to go to school by driving her there herself and then sticking around for the actual speech. Hailey had seen her mother standing at the back of the auditorium while the students all filed in. She waited backstage with clammy hands and with sweat forming in all the places sweat forms. Hailey had decided to run for class secretary, because she honestly had no idea what that person did and had determined it wouldn't be nearly as important as the president or vice-president of the student body. It also meant she'd be running unopposed, since no one else wanted that position. She had hoped, not so secretly, that she wouldn't have to give a speech after all, but because technically, students could write in names on their ballots, there was always a chance they'd do just that, and she'd lose to someone who didn't even want the damn thing, to begin with.

That day turned out to be a pretty important day for Hailey, though; for two reasons. One, she had been able to get over her inability to speak publicly. It didn't happen all at once, of course, but after no one booed her, she had gained a little confidence. It led to an entire year of her working with other seemingly confident students who had no problem speaking in front of others. Hailey had observed them carefully, and by the end of the year, she had actually asked for opportunities to speak in front of the students. The second thing that happened that day was that Hailey met someone, and therefore, made a very important realization about herself.

After delivering her speech, walking off the stage, and practically running toward the bathroom because she thought she was going to puke, the door opened. There was another girl standing there. She went into a stall and emerged a few moments later while Hailey was standing over the sink, attempting to gain her composure. She had seen her around a few times, but the two of them didn't share any classes. Hailey didn't know her name, what year she was in, or anything about her other than the fact that she was gorgeous. She had this dark-colored hair that she had pulled back into a tight ponytail. While she washed her hands at the next sink, Hailey watched her in profile. Her nose was strong, as was her jaw. Her eyes were brown and matched her hair along with her somewhat pale skin. Her hands were sliding back and forth with a soapy lather, but Hailey could make out strong, long fingers. Her eyes followed up the girl's arms to see some toned muscle there. She was clearly athletic.

"You were great, by the way," the girl spoke up and moved to the hand dryer to push the button and dry her hands.

"Sorry?" Hailey moved her eyes back to the mirror to

try to cover up the fact that she had been staring at her.

"Your speech; it was good. I'm going to vote for you." The girl continued to hold her hands under a barrage of hot air. "I don't exactly know what the secretary does, but the speech sounded nice."

"I don't either." Hailey lifted an eyebrow.

"Well, I hope you figure it out, I guess." The girl shrugged her shoulders, took a step toward Hailey, and held out her hand. "I'm Emma. I'm a senior. I think I've seen you around. Before today, I mean. You're a junior, right?"

"Yeah." Hailey shook the soft and now completely dry hand in front of her and prayed that the clamminess on her own hand had been dealt with appropriately.

"Cool. So, if you don't know what you're doing, why'd you run for it?" Emma asked as their hands disconnected. Two girls entered the bathroom laughing and disappeared into stalls, leaving Emma standing in front of Hailey, with Hailey having no idea what to say. "We can go out there." Emma motioned backward with her thumb, seemingly reading Hailey's thoughts. Hailey nodded.

Emma held open the door for her. Hailey walked through it past her until Emma was next to her. The hall was pretty packed, considering it was between classes. Hailey had a free period and, therefore, had nowhere specific to be. She usually spent her free period in the library, though, so her legs naturally pointed her in that direction, which would take her past her locker to get her things. Emma kept stride with her as she walked the twenty feet to her locker, proceeded to twist the padlock, and pull open the locker door.

"It was because my guidance counselor suggested it," Hailey finally answered Emma's much earlier question. "I needed more activities or something."

"Not in a lot of clubs or sports?" Emma leaned confidently against the locker immediately next to Hailey's.

She was so close. Hailey could smell something like coconut and suspected it was either the girl's lotion or shampoo, until she glanced at the top shelf of her own locker and remembered her lotion, which was coconut and mango and had, apparently, been left uncapped inside. She was losing her damn mind. Why did she care what this girl smelled like? That was creepy. That was most definitely a thing creepy people do.

"No, not really," Hailey answered Emma's question honestly, pulled her bag out of her locker, and dumped two textbooks inside it along with some other study supplies.

She couldn't tell anyone what textbooks exactly or even if she had work to do in those subjects, because she kept feeling how close Emma was to her. She closed the locker and hefted the bag onto her shoulder.

"I'm on the dance team, myself." Emma continued walking alongside Hailey.

Hailey wondered two things. She wondered what class Emma was clearly going to be late for, as the rest of the students seemed to be in that patented high school *'hurry and beat the bell'* pace toward their classes; and two, she wondered why Emma was still talking to her.

"Dance?"

"Yeah, I've been doing it forever. It's pretty fun most of the time."

"Cool," Hailey replied.

"We perform at the games. You haven't seen us? With the cheerleaders?"

"Games?" Hailey turned her head to get clarification.

"Football," Emma returned with a lifted eyebrow, and Hailey wanted to marry that eyebrow.

It had this somewhat thin point when it was arched. Hailey thought it was possibly the sexiest thing she had ever seen. What? She was then nearly toppled over by a large boy who was trying to run past her, but in all her lack of focus on anything other than that eyebrow, Hailey had failed to notice.

"Jake, calm the fuck down! You could have killed her," Emma half-yelled at the boy in the football jersey and jeans.

"Sorry, Emma and–"

"Hailey," Emma told him.

"Hailey. Sorry, Hailey." He rushed off.

Hailey returned her bag to the proper spot on her shoulder and regained control over her body, only to finally discover that Emma's hand was on her back. It must have been there for a minute, because Hailey knew that if it had only just appeared, she would have definitely felt the touch.

"You okay?" Emma asked her sweetly.

"I'm good. Thanks," Hailey replied and then motioned with her finger toward the library. "This is where I'm going. Don't you have a class to get to yourself?"

"I'm a student aid this period," Emma explained. "I have to go to the office and file stuff, so... I'm good. But, have fun in the library." The girl smirked at her, and Hailey nearly died.

"Thanks."

"Are you going tonight?"

"To what?"

Emma laughed.

"To the game? Sorry. To the football game. It's at home tonight, in that giant stadium behind this building."

"Oh, I don't usually."

"You should. They're pretty fun. Maybe if you do, we can hang out. I have warm-ups right before half-time, and then the performance, but before and after that, I'm pretty free."

"Hang out?" Hailey queried.

"Yes. Like teenagers do sometimes." Emma was finding Hailey's questions funny, but not in a rude or condescending way.

"I might," Hailey offered. "I don't know."

"Well, if you do, just find me. I'm usually either around the concession stand or at the bottom of the bleachers, with the rest of the dance team." Emma turned to walk off and then quickly turned back. "Nice to meet you." She gave Hailey a shy smile.

That smile was all it took for her to fall endlessly in love with Emma Colton. Hailey went to her first-ever football game that night and happened to catch Emma in an almost private moment. The girl had been on the phone with someone and had, therefore, been separated from the pack of girls she'd just been surrounded by. Truthfully, Hailey had seen her and watched for about ten minutes before approaching. The thought of walking up to her, when she was around all those other people, was a little too much. Hailey hadn't ever had a boyfriend, that was true, but she had never been asked out, either; so, that explained that part. The thoughts she was having about that eyebrow – and the eyes under it, and the hair and the hands and the lips and the fingers, and how the shirt this girl had been wearing at school seemed to fit her perfectly in all the right ways –had Hailey's head spinning. She had never been attracted to a girl before, and she needed to not be attracted to this one; because Emma was nice, but Emma wasn't gay. She knew that much. Hailey also knew she was feeling something more intense than friendship, but friendship would be all that was offered in return. She gulped back at the thought of how Emma looked in that dance team uniform.

"You came?" Emma smiled at her and placed a hand on Hailey's elbow. "I was just talking to my dad. He was checking in, as usual. Did you just get here? It's after half-time. Did you see the performance?" That was rattled off quickly, and Hailey didn't know which question to answer first.

"I got here a few minutes ago, and yeah, I missed it. I got here earlier, technically, but I had to park on Shallows, because I was late. I walked all the way here, tried to get in, and they told me I needed my student ID. So, I had to walk all the way back, then here again, and wait in the entrance line to get the ticket, and–"

"That seems like a lot of work. I hope you didn't just do that for me." Emma's smile was still plastered on her face.

"Oh, I–"

"I'm kidding," Emma saved her and removed her own hand from Hailey's elbow. She then looked past Hailey to the girls on the dance team. Hailey heard one of them call for her. "Do you want to walk around a little? It's your first game. We can check everything out."

"I don't want to take you away from your friends."

"It's okay. I do this with them every week," Emma pressed. "Come on."

They walked around the stadium on the outside. Hailey didn't see a single second of the game that night. What she did see was the outside of the stadium from every angle as they continued on, and Emma regaled her with stories about herself and peppered Hailey with questions, too. There was laughter, and some serious topics were shared between them as they continued around for the second time. There had been cheers from both sides of the stadium, so Hailey didn't know who was winning. Their school butted up against about an acre of woods, and she noticed a couple walking in that direction. She had never thought to even go back there before, but then she saw another couple proceed down what appeared to be a path.

"What's back there?" Hailey pointed in that direction and watched Emma's eyes follow her hand.

"Oh, that's where people, you know…" she stated vaguely.

"They…?"

"They mostly make out. I'm sure some of them go further… But, thankfully, I've never encountered that."

"You've been back there?"

"Not to do anything, no," Emma pointed out as if she needed to defend something. "There's this little pond back there. There are these frogs or toads or something that croak. It's kind of cool at night. Do you want to go back there? I can show you."

"The pond?"

"Sure. Why not?"

Hailey was seventeen when she was kissed for the first

time, and she was kissed by a girl. Emma walked them down the path. Before Hailey knew it, they were holding hands. It wasn't like the friend hand-holding she had seen gaggles of girls do, either. It was the fingers linked together kind of hand-holding that after only a few minutes had escalated to Emma's head on Hailey's shoulder. And Hailey knew it then. She knew it. She liked girls. She liked the softness of Emma's hand in her own. She liked the head on her shoulder, and the feeling of a warm body pressed against her side, and the warm breath, and the giggles against her neck as they continued to walk and talk.

When they sat in front of the pond and were completely alone, Emma confidently sat between Hailey's legs and encouraged Hailey's arms around her own waist. Hailey had it figured out by then. She had never felt comfortable talking to boys. She could talk to a guy as a friend with no problem, but the moment it could possibly turn into something more, she would make an excuse to end the conversation.

Hailey felt completely normal for the first time in her life. It was because her arms were wrapped around a girl, and she could rest her chin on Emma's shoulder. There were more words exchanged, but none of them had to do with orientations or what they were doing at that moment. Hailey was afraid that if she brought it up, it might stop. And she did not want this to stop. In fact, she wanted more. She didn't know if Emma wanted more, though, so she kept holding her as they had minutes of sporadic yet comfortable silence. Then, Hailey felt Emma's head begin to turn. It was just a small turn, at first, but Emma began slowly inching her head to the side. Her lips were so near Hailey's. They hovered there for a moment, and each girl stared at the other. There was just a gentle press of lips, at first, and they both pulled back, but not far and not long before they rejoined. Hailey managed to open her mouth just slightly, enough to indicate that she wanted to take the kiss further. Emma, apparently, did as well, because her lips parted, and she took Hailey's bottom lip between her own. Then, Emma's tongue was inside Hailey's mouth, and Hailey's body was on fire. She was being pressed backward to the ground. Emma was hovering over her in an instant. Their lips remained attached as their limbs began to entangle themselves. And it was only after an announcer's voice boomed through the loudspeakers of the stadium that someone had done something worthy of cheer, that they broke apart. Emma remained where she was, still on top of Hailey, staring down at her with expressive dark eyes. And Hailey felt right. She felt happy.

They started dating in secret that night, because neither of them was sure what it all meant yet. It took them some time for each to determine how they'd identify themselves when they came out to their respective parents. Hailey was happy to have Emma there when she had told her mother about not only the fact that she was gay, but that she had a girlfriend and that they'd been together for three months. Emma's mom had died when she was young. She only had her father left. And he was great about the whole thing.

When graduation came, Hailey cried. Emma had gotten into Rutgers and planned to study veterinary medicine there. That meant they only had three months left before Hailey would only see her girlfriend on breaks from school, when they could make it work. Hailey knew she wouldn't follow Emma to Rutgers, and she also had no intention of applying to schools out there merely because her girlfriend was there. They had a great summer together and managed to make it until Emma's spring break her freshman year before things ended. It wasn't a horrible break up. There was no yelling or cheating. And that might have made it worse for both of them. They were still in love. There were tears during and after the breakup on both sides. For about an hour after, Emma just sat up in Hailey's bed right next to her. They were both silent, save sniffling and tears that flowed every so often. And then, Emma got up, walked around to the other side of the bed, reached down to take Hailey's hand, squeezed it, and then kissed the top of her head.

"A part of me will always belong to you. You know that, right?" she uttered as her lips hovered over Hailey's head.

"Yes. For me too."

"I should go." Emma released Hailey's hand, and they said their goodbyes.

She saw Emma for the first time three years later, at her father's funeral. She found Emma in the church for the service first, but she had been unable to approach and wouldn't have, anyway. It wasn't the time. When they arrived at the cemetery, the crowd was smaller and sat in white wooden chairs in front of the casket. Emma was one of the last to arrive. That was when Emma's eyes found Hailey's. Hailey hadn't yet sat down, because she wasn't sure where to sit, if at all. Emma let go of her uncle's hand and hurried in heels and her requisite black dress in Hailey's direction. She wrapped her arms around Hailey's neck, pulled her in, and Hailey knew she needed her own arms around Emma's waist. They held on to one another like that for several minutes, Hailey guessed, as she heard sniffs and felt warm wet teardrops land on the sweater she had worn over her own dress. She squeezed Emma as tightly as she could, as if that would somehow bring her father back or stop this pain. Emma pulled back and wiped her eyes. She let out something about thanking Hailey for coming, to which Hailey said words she no longer remembered. Then, she felt Emma's hand pull her in the direction of the front row of chairs. Hailey sat there next to her, holding Emma's hand for the entirety of the rest of the service; even daring to offer Emma a kiss to her temple while moving the hair away from her neck.

That was years ago now. They had been friends on and off since then. It seemed as if they both found it easy to be in contact when they were single, but the moment one of them started dating someone else, the other disappeared. They would speak via text until there was a breakup.

***

As she sat up in Charlie's bed that morning and pulled the blankets off of herself to head into the kitchen, where she knew she would find Charlie making cereal and coffee, Hailey wondered why she'd been thinking about that one real time she had been in love so much these past few months.

CHAPTER 3

WHEN Charlie woke up to find Hailey lying asleep beside her, she had a moment of panic rush over her. She knew she had fallen asleep while watching the show, and that Hailey had been next to her, but Hailey always slept on her couch, despite Charlie offering her the bed time and again, and even offering to sleep on the couch herself, if Hailey wanted. But Hailey liked that thing.

This woman had been in her bed this morning, though, and she looked so beautiful. Her eyelashes were long. Charlie could picture the light-green eyes under the closed lids, and she smiled. She rarely got a chance to just stare at Hailey, because that would make it pretty obvious that she wanted her. When Hailey slept on the couch, she always managed to be turned facing the back of it, revealing only her back. Charlie had stared at that a few times. She knew she was pathetic. She worried, for a moment, that maybe she'd done something while asleep, like, try to hold Hailey, or maybe she'd just drooled. She had shaken that out of her head, climbed out of bed slowly, so as not to wake her sleeping friend, and made her way to the kitchen to make breakfast.

"Morning." Hailey ruffled her already messed hair as she made her way into the kitchen and sat on the stool in front of the island.

"Hey." Charlie pushed an empty bowl, the half-used gallon of milk, and the fruity cereal she knew Hailey liked over toward her, and then sat beside her.

"Sorry, I crashed next to you after the show."

"I noticed. No big deal." Charlie took a bite of her somewhat soggy cereal. "Coffee?"

"No, I'll get some on the way to work. I'm going to grab a muffin or something, too. But, thanks." Hailey pushed the cereal and other items back toward the center of the island.

"You never turn down sugar cereal. What's up?" Charlie questioned with a sip of her own coffee.

"Nothing," Hailey offered in reply. "I just feel like hitting up Sally's on the way in. I've got to head that way," she said, referencing their local coffee shop.

"Well, you can have the bathroom first. I'm working from home this morning and going to a site later."

"Cool. Thanks." Hailey stood and made her way to the bathroom to ready herself for work.

Something was off with her. Whenever Hailey stayed over like this, it was the same routine. She slept on the couch; Charlie would inevitably wake her when she went to the kitchen to make her breakfast. Hailey would join her, pour her favorite kids' cereal, and eat alongside her while they sipped on coffee neither of them managed to finish.

Charlie finished her cereal and coffee and found Eddie standing near the door, doing his outside dance. She had tried to take him out as soon as she'd woken up, but he had been uninterested and was instead busy playing with his toy rope by himself. Charlie took the dishes to the sink and attached his leash to his collar, which was a mistake because she had yet to put on her shoes or coat, and Eddie was now whining.

"Where was this sense of urgency when I tried to take you out, like, ten minutes ago?" she questioned the animal who didn't understand or care.

She finished getting dressed and thought about yelling to Hailey that she was taking him out, but Hailey would figure it out when she noticed them both gone. Eddie was picky about where to do his business, and he had already grown tired of marking his territory on the nearby trees, posts, and sidewalks, so it was a solid twenty-five minutes before Charlie returned to her apartment to find that Hailey was gone. That girl had always been quick at getting ready. Part of it was because she wasn't the kind of woman that spent forty-five minutes on her hair, and the other part was that Hailey was naturally beautiful, so she wore only a small amount of makeup.

Charlie let Eddie off the leash so that he could run around, as usual, grabbed another cup of coffee, and went to her desk that was against the side wall of the wide apartment. She had thought about dividing up the space with panels or shelves but hadn't gotten around to it in the beginning, and then, liked the open feel of it after all. The couch faced the wall with her living room TV. The kitchen was in front of the living room, and then there was the space behind the couch, which was an office and Eddie's play area. She didn't have a dining room table yet, but when she got one, that would be where it would go. It would cut down on Eddie's runaround space, and because he was cooped up in an apartment for most of the day, especially during the winter, Charlie felt she owed it to him to have a place to call his own. Her office was really just a desk with a few shelves on either side, but it worked for her. The desk faced the wall, but she had put it directly in front of a window. She often took brain breaks as she worked, and she found having something to stare at was helpful for her process.

As Charlie opened her work email, she noticed the same picture she'd had in a frame on her desk since college. The photo and the frame had been the first gift she had received from Hailey. Ember had gotten the same gift for Christmas that first year they met. It was a picture taken at work one night. Charlie and Hailey each still wore their aprons, while Ember had on her manager garb, including her nametag. The restaurant had been closed early that night, and Francine, Ember's mother, held the staff holiday party for everyone. There had been food and even karaoke. That was the night their friendship had been cemented. They had been work friends up until then but hadn't spent time together outside of the restaurant. That night was the night they all shared their coming out stories with each other. Ember told them about how her parents reacted with some difficulty, and how her relationship with her father was particularly strained due to her sexuality among other things. Hailey revealed her tale of her first girlfriend and how they'd come out together. And Charlie told her own story to fit in. Problem was, that story was a lie. Charlie hadn't officially come out yet, but she didn't want to tell her new friends that, because things were going so well, and also because Charlie wanted Hailey to think she had the courage to come out. Charlie's lack of overall courage in her personal life continued to be a major theme.

The truth was that Charlie had known she was different than her friends since she was in middle school. She had grown up in Elkhart. Elkhart was a small town in northern Indiana. Her family relocated to Chicago during her junior year of high school – which is, of course, the worst time to relocate for any teenager. Charlie had never said anything during her early years. They were not a well-to-do family by any means. Her mother worked two jobs, while her father commuted to a factory job in Gary before he passed away in a work-related accident when Charlie was fourteen. There was some insurance money that helped her mom keep Charlie and her brother with food and clothing, but not much else. Charlie never really felt like she was poor, though. Her mom always made an effort to make sure they went to secondhand stores to get day to day items, but they also had a few new items in their wardrobe that they could pull out for special occasions.

The one thing Charlie's mother always seemed to have, though, was at least a dollar in her pocket for a scratch-off lottery ticket. While the woman had won a few dollars over the years, she'd definitely spent more than she had brought back in. Until one day, when Charlie was seventeen. Her mom, Nancy, bought a scratch-off while getting gas, and she had won $150,000. When the taxes were taken out, it left them with around $80,000. Nancy used that money to move them out of Elkhart to just outside of Chicago, where she had a cousin they could stay with until they found a place of their own. It was a very fast move, the way Charlie remembered it. JJ, her brother, was eighteen and in a technical school as opposed to a regular high school. He chose to remain behind to finish up and then planned on joining them, but he never did. Charlie had no choice. It wasn't that she loved Elkhart or anything. It was just that she knew what to expect there. She knew the score. She knew by then that she was gay, that she was likely the only lesbian in her small class, and that if she told anyone, she would never hear the end of it. Charlie knew how to blend in. She knew how to lie about having crushes on boys and how to pretend she enjoyed kissing them at parties. She even had a boyfriend for about three months once, until the move happened and they broke up. It was probably for the best, Charlie remembered telling him, and she was silently thanking her mother at that moment that she wouldn't have to lose her virginity to Harry, when she really wanted her first time to be with a girl in her class named Stacey.

The money didn't last. Charlie's mom hadn't ever had that much money in her life before, and she had no clue how to spend it. The woman had also failed to plan for the fact that Chicago was much more expensive than Elkhart. For her first day at the new school, though, Charlie's mom made sure to buy her a closet full of new clothes so that Charlie could fit in. When she arrived that first day, Charlie went into her 'hide at all costs' mode to protect herself from anyone finding out she liked girls.

It went like that for the rest of Charlie's junior year. By summer, Nancy was worried that she wasn't making any friends, so she signed Charlie up for a church youth retreat. Charlie prepared herself to be bored for three solid days, as there would be no technology of any kind allowed. It was a weekend to celebrate God and her relationship with Him. She had no relationship with God, despite her mother's coaxing toward attending church on Sundays.

On that first day, though, Charlie had been paired up with a girl named Julia. Julia was a little shorter than Charlie's 5'6", and she had the skin the color of rich caramel. She had dark hair and dark eyes, and these round cheeks Charlie found adorable, with plump lips she found to be very sexy. She and Julia had been tasked with an icebreaker, and by the end of their exchange, Charlie had a major crush. By the end of the weekend, she had also lost her virginity.

The morning after Charlie's first time was also their last one at the retreat. Julia seemed to be ignoring her. She didn't sit next to Charlie at breakfast and didn't want to pair up for the last activity. By lunch, they were all packed into a bus that would take them back to the church where their parents would pick them up. When they got off the bus, Charlie saw her mother waving wildly for her, but her eyes went to Julia, who was hugging her parents. Julia turned back to see Charlie staring and gave her an expression that said so much without words. It told Charlie that she couldn't. That was all Charlie needed to know.

Charlie never told her mom about that experience. What she relayed to Ember and Hailey that night was the story of Julia and how it ended with Charlie being heartbroken for a few days, before coming to realize that the experience they had shared wasn't about Julia. It was about finally confirming what she'd always known to be true. She was gay. Charlie also added that she'd told her mom about Julia a few weeks after it happened and that her mom had taken it well when she talked to Ember and Hailey. That was her coming out story. Except that it wasn't. About two years after meeting Hailey and Ember, Charlie finally confessed to Hailey that she had never told her mother she was gay. Nancy had later moved out of Chicago to a town in southern Illinois, so Charlie had been able to keep that part of her life away from her.

Once she confessed to Hailey, though, Hailey gave her the courage to come out to her mother and to her brother, who was still in Elkhart. Hailey wasn't forceful or even upset that Charlie had lied to her. She had understood. Hailey had always been able to understand her. She even accompanied Charlie to her mom's house to tell her, and then to JJ's place with his new wife, to tell him. Charlie fell a little more in love with Hailey on that trip, because the woman had cooked breakfast for everyone, sat next to her at the table, and carried the entire conversation before Charlie told them, so that Charlie could warm herself up to the idea of her brother and sister-in- law knowing her biggest secret.

***

Charlie arrived at the site at precisely 1 o'clock to meet her contact from the Health Department, who would walk her through the project. The Chicago Health Department had recently purchased an old building in the government quarter of the city that had been vacant for the past several years due to some structural concerns. After a bidding process, Charlie's company had been hired to create the plans to bring it up to code, and also to modernize the building for use without disturbing the inherent historical value.

Charlie arrived first, it appeared, and decided to just get to work. Her contact would arrive when they arrived, and then they could discuss, but she didn't want to waste any time getting started. She took pictures of various elements of the first floor of the building and made notes as she did. Then, Charlie made her way up to the second floor and continued. The building itself was four floors and was basically crushed between two other buildings, as if they had been built first, and then someone had inserted this much smaller building between them, when the opposite had actually been true.

"Hello? Sorry, I'm late. Are you Charlotte Adams?" A brunette woman was about Charlie's height and age, with her hair pulled back and light-brown eyes that bordered somehow on a dark-green.

"Charlie is fine," she said and reached out her hand

for the woman to take. "Are you with the Health Department? I was expecting a Lloyd Montrose." Charlie read from the name on the clipboard she was holding out with her free hand while the other shook the woman's hand.

"Sorry, Lloyd couldn't make it," the woman began. "I'm Emma. I'm the Head of Special Projects. Lloyd works for me, but his wife went into labor about an hour ago. So, I'm here instead."

"I guess, congratulations to Lloyd and his wife, then," Charlie returned. "I've been through most of the building, and we've done the initial inspection already. I have the plans for you to review. If you approve them, we can get the contractor in here to get started on the necessary demolition work. Once that's done, we'll have a better idea of what's behind some of these walls. We need to determine the condition of electrical and plumbing before any real work begins," Charlie delivered her routine speech. "I'll have a member of my team on site for the beginning of the work."

"Okay," Emma said.

The woman was more or less just staring at Charlie expectantly while she rubbed her gloved hands together for warmth.

"We'll notify you if we need to go beyond the initial budget that was discussed, based on what we find."

"You used to work in the city planning office, right?" Emma asked her.

"Yeah. Why?"

"People in government agencies talk. I have a friend that knew you. Scott?"

"Scott Sans?"

"He mentioned that you worked for this firm, but that you also used to work with him. He said you would likely be great at sticking to a government budget, since you were used to adhering to one before."

"That's true. I can't guarantee the building will cooperate with the budget, though. I will make sure we don't do anything without approval."

"Thanks."

Charlie's phone rang in her pocket.

"Sorry, just…" She faded as she checked the screen. "Never mind. It's just a friend." She looked back at Emma.

"You can take it."

"It's my friend, Hailey. I'll call her later." Charlie tucked the phone back into her pocket.

"Wait a minute…" The woman took a step back unconsciously, and her hand went to her chin, as if she was thinking. "Your name is Charlie, and you have a friend named Hailey?"

"Um… yeah. Why?" Charlie stared at her, confused.

"Hailey Grant?"

"How do you know Hailey?"

"I knew it couldn't have been a coincidence." Emma let out a laugh. "I'm Emma Colton. I don't know if–"

"Her ex-girlfriend?" Charlie interrupted with shock.

"Oh, yeah…" Emma seemed to take a moment. "I guess I am her ex. It's just been so long that I don't really think of it like that, but… Yeah, I'm her ex-girlfriend, Emma."

"Small world," Charlie expressed.

"Apparently," Emma returned.

CHAPTER 4

HAILEY knew Charlie was at work, but she had finished her last appointment of the day early and thought that maybe they could get a late lunch. She sent her a quick text, instead of leaving a voicemail, and decided to go home and work from there the rest of the day. By the time she arrived, Charlie had texted her back. Hailey read the message while sorting through her mail. Her eyes went wide, and she called Charlie immediately.

"You what?" Hailey questioned.

"I met Emma today. She's in charge of the new building I'm working on."

"You met my ex-girlfriend Emma?" Hailey repeated. "Emma Colton?"

"Yes. Brown hair and matching eyes? I met her."

"Wow!" Hailey sat down on her small sofa.

"Yeah, wow. How is it that you've never introduced Ember or me to her before? You two are friends, right?"

"I haven't talked to her in a while; maybe a year. She was dating someone."

"She said she'd call you."

"Oh," Hailey replied as she thought about the last time she had seen Emma.

They'd had dinner and shared stories of their most recent failed relationships. Hailey had wondered if maybe they would rekindle their romance, but Emma spoke about how she was ready to be single and have some time to herself. Hailey hadn't brought up her thoughts about how beautiful Emma looked or how she still got those butterflies every time she saw her.

"Okay. Well, you're being weird," Charlie pointed out. "I'm on my way home now. Do you want to grab dinner tonight?"

"Sure. I'll call Ember and see if she and Eva are free," Hailey stated.

"Eva has a class on Monday nights, remember?" Charlie supplied.

"Right. I'll call Ember anyway, and see if she wants to come."

"Okay," Charlie agreed, but Hailey heard a sigh. "I'll go wherever. Text me where you pick."

"You okay?" Hailey decided to check. "Now, you sound weird."

"I'm fine. I'm going to go check on Eddie and finish up some things. Six tonight?"

"Yeah," Hailey replied and heard Charlie hang up.

Hailey shook her head, trying to figure out what had caused Charlie's mood. She hated when Charlie was in a bad mood. When Charlie was in a good mood, everything was right in the world. When she was in a bad mood, the woman would usually go reclusive. She would spend more time alone than usual and would only see Hailey or Ember for their weekly coffee dates until the mood passed. Hailey did not like when Charlie was in a bad mood. Her phone rang again, and she smiled when she saw who was calling.

"Hey, bride to be," Hailey greeted Ember. "I was just about to call you."

"Yeah?"

"Charlie and I are grabbing dinner tonight. Wanna come? You're without your other half tonight, right?"

Ember laughed and said, "Yes, Eva is working. I was calling for the same reason. It's weird, but you get used to having dinner with the same person each night. When she's not around, you just kind of stare into the fridge, wondering what you can make just for yourself."

"I wouldn't know about that," Hailey returned. "But we're going around six. Want to try that new Indian place?"

"Not really. Eva and I went there on Friday. How about our Japanese place?"

"Oh, yeah! That sounds good." Hailey loved that place.

"Meet you two there." Ember hung up.

Hailey took her time finishing up her tasks and started getting ready for dinner. She pulled out an old pair of jeans and a cream-colored sweater, but before she could change out of her work clothes, her phone rang again.

"Hey," she greeted.

"Long time, no talk," Emma replied.

"I know. I heard you ran into someone I know today." Hailey sat down on the bed and listened to the sound of Emma's voice that still managed to take her back to high school.

"The mysterious Charlie you've mentioned in the past, yes."

"How is she mysterious?" Hailey laughed.

"Because you never introduced us. And if I remember correctly, you two are close."

"She's my best friend, yes. And I didn't *not* introduce you. It just never happened."

"Whatever you say, Hails." Emma laughed a little. "Hey, when are you free? We should get together. It's been too long."

"Yeah, it has," Hailey agreed and had an idea. "I'm going to dinner with Charlie and Ember tonight. You should come. That way you could meet Ember, too. Are you free?"

"I was planning on making a frozen pizza and eating it alone while scrolling through Pinterest, but I think I can cancel my plans for you."

Hailey smiled.

"I can pick you up. You're on my way there."

Emma agreed, and they said goodbye. Hailey hastily shoved the old jeans and a sweater she had chosen earlier back into the drawers and walked to her closet, where she found the dress she was looking for. It was a short red and somewhat tight number, with spaghetti straps. It was totally inappropriate for the weather, but her long black dress coat would keep her warm. Hailey took a look at her messy hair and didn't think she had time for a shower and a complete redo, so she just put it back up and braided it simply in its ponytail.

She pulled up to Emma's building to see her standing outside, waiting, and before Hailey could get out to greet her, Emma was climbing inside the car.

"Hey." Emma reached her arms across the center console and hugged Hailey.

Hailey hugged her back and smelled something like vanilla mixed with cinnamon. She breathed the woman in before they had a chance to pull apart.

"It's really good to see you," Hailey told her.

"You too. I don't know why we keep losing touch like this. We live in the same damn city. We should be talking more."

Hailey knew the answer to that. She was pretty sure Emma did, too. There was just something about seeing the person you fell for first, fall for someone else. That was especially true when that relationship didn't end in anger or because someone fell out of love with the other. It ended because of distance and circumstance.

"We'll work on it," Hailey promised. "You still like Japanese, right?"

"Of course," Emma replied and faced the front. "Where are we going?"

"You know the answer to that question," Hailey told her and looked over to see Emma smile.

A few days after Emma's father's funeral, she and Hailey went to Japanese for dinner, and they both really liked the place. Hailey had later recommended it to Ember and Charlie. It had become one of their regular spots over the years.

***

"Hailey, over here," Ember called from their usual table and waved Hailey over.

"That's Ember." Hailey pointed, and Emma followed the finger.

"She's pretty."

"She's engaged," Hailey returned as they walked.

"I didn't say I wanted to date her, Hails." Emma laughed.

They undid their coats as they walked toward the table in the semi-crowded restaurant.

"Ember, this is Emma. I invited her along," Hailey introduced as she placed her coat over a chair and then watched as Emma did the same in the chair next to her.

"Emma? *The* Emma?" Ember's eyes were huge as Hailey sat down in front of her and Emma sat next to Hailey.

"Yes, *the* Emma. And thanks for embarrassing me." Hailey glared at her.

"Nice to meet you, Emma." Ember turned to look at the woman.

"Nice to meet you, too." Emma nodded and then glanced in Hailey's direction.

"Hey." Charlie stood in front of the table. "Nice to see you again, Emma."

"Again?" Ember questioned as Charlie took the empty seat next to Ember.

It felt a little strange to Hailey, because Charlie always sat next to her when the three of them were out together. Ember was usually the one sitting on the other side alone.

"I met Charlie today. Her company is in charge of a project that I'm the lead on."

"What a coincidence," Ember shared and looked back at Hailey.

"Hailey told me you're engaged," Emma tried to start a conversation.

Ember's smile went wide.

"I am. My fiancée is at work tonight, or else she'd be here."

"Congratulations," Emma offered.

The waitress approached and took their drink orders. When she departed, Hailey took a look in Charlie's direction. She knew instantly that her best friend's bad mood was still very much in effect.

"Charlie, you okay?" she asked.

"I'm fine," Charlie lied.

Hailey squinted with concerned eyes at her.

"Em, do you want to split the steak and shrimp with me?" Hailey asked.

"Which Em?" Charlie spoke up over her menu.

"What?" Hailey retorted.

"Ember or Emma? Which Em?"

"Oh, yeah." Hailey looked at Ember and then Emma. "I guess I do call you both that."

"I'm getting sushi," Ember pointed out, apparently not noticing or caring that Hailey gave them both the same nickname.

"I'll split it with you." Emma smiled at her. "But only if we can get that awesome ginger sauce with it."

"I love that stuff."

"I know. I remember," Emma told her, and Hailey smiled back at her.

Over the course of the dinner, Ember talked about Eva and the upcoming wedding in Iowa. Hailey tried to engage Charlie a little more in the conversation, but the woman seemed to be off in her own little world. And Emma seemed to fit in with most of the group well enough.

***

"Hey, I know you're not okay." Hailey pulled Charlie back from the other two as they walked outside the restaurant. "What's going on?"

"Nothing, Hails," Charlie told her for the millionth time.

"That's crap, and you know it."

"Hailey, I'm tired. I just want to go home."

"Then, why did you even come out tonight?" Hailey asked her.

"Because I thought it was going to be you and Ember."

Hailey stopped them and asked, "You don't like Emma?"

"I don't *know* Emma," Charlie reminded. "But I also didn't expect to bring my work to dinner tonight, Hails. I'm leading the project for the Health Department. I don't usually socialize with clients."

"Shit," Hailey stated and then noticed a particularly large snowflake land on Charlie's forehead. She watched it melt for a moment and then used her gloved hand to wipe away the leftover water. "I'm sorry... I didn't think about that when I invited her."

"It's fine. I'm just going to go home. I am tired." Charlie started to walk again, and Hailey kept up with her while glancing at Ember and Emma, who were a few yards ahead of them.

"You weren't in a good mood earlier, either. And that had nothing to do with me inviting her to dinner with us," Hailey recalled.

"This is me." Charlie pointed at the Uber she had ordered, apparently, with no one noticing. "I'll see you on Thursday, Hails," she more or less sighed out.

"Charlie..."

"Good night," she said, then climbed into the car, gave Hailey one more look, and closed the door before the driver took off.

"Hey, are you coming?" Emma turned around to check on her. "Bye, Charlie." She took a few steps back toward Hailey and waved in Charlie's direction as the car drove off.

"Yeah, bye." Ember waved awkwardly at her friend that hadn't said goodbye, and then looked confused at Hailey, who just shrugged. "My car is on the next block. Where are you?"

"We're up there," Hailey pointed. "Want us to drive you to your car?"

"No, I'm going to stop at the store on the corner. They have that candy Eva likes. We can't find it near the house."

"You looking to get laid tonight?" Hailey teased.

"Every night." Ember winked at her. "It was nice to finally meet you, Emma."

"You too." Emma laughed at their exchange.

"I'll see you Thursday, Hails."

"Yeah," Hailey returned.

Ember looked at Emma, then back at Hailey, and winked at her before she about-faced and headed down the street. Emma laughed again and turned to face Hailey. She took a step toward her and then tugged on Hailey's coat, causing Hailey to smile.

"Still works."

"What?" Hailey laughed.

"If I pull on your coat like that, you still smile," she replied.

"I guess I do." Hailey noticed that the hands were still on her coat before they slid into her pockets, where Hailey's hands also were.

"Can I ask you something?" Emma asked.

She was close, and her breath was visible in the cold.

"Sure."

"Why didn't we ever try again?"

Hailey wasn't expecting that question. "You mean, try us?"

"Yes," Emma told her, and Hailey felt Emma's hands do their best to link their fingers while still inside her pockets.

"Em, the last time we dated, we were teenagers."

"I know. But, Hails, we broke up because I was in New Jersey, trying to figure out college life, and you were still in high school in Chicago. It wasn't because we stopped wanting to be together."

"But, Em, we've seen each other since then. Why now?" she asked.

With their proximity, Hailey was having a hard time

talking at all. Emma's lips were so close to hers, and it had been so long since she'd touched them.

"Do you remember last year, when I told you I needed to be single for a while to figure some things out?"

"Of course."

"I did that. I've been single since then. I've focused on work. I've got some great friends now. I go home alone every night, make dinner for myself, and I think about you." Emma then paused and made sure she met Hailey's green eyes with her own. "I compared everyone else to you, Hails. You and I were good together. I thought about calling you the other day. But I decided to wait because I'm going to Milwaukee tomorrow through Friday, for a conference. I figured I'd call you when I got back. But then, I met Charlie today, and I thought it must be fate or something."

"You want us to go out?" Hailey checked.

"Yes, Hailey." Emma laughed. "I would like us to go on a date and see if there's still something there between us, because it feels like there is." She pressed her forehead to Hailey's and closed her eyes. "Does it to you?"

Hailey closed her eyes as well and recalled the last time they'd been this close.

"Yes, it does."

"Go out with me on Saturday night?" Emma asked her.

"Yes," Hailey told her.

Emma pulled back, and they smiled at one another for a long moment before they broke apart and headed toward Hailey's car.

CHAPTER 5

CHARLIE hated that she'd been rude to all of her dinner companions Monday night, but there was just something about seeing Hailey with Emma – the legendary perfect first girlfriend, that made her feel incredibly pissed off and also incredibly sad. Ember had always questioned Charlie about why she never revealed her feelings about Hailey. In turn, Charlie had given her completely valid reasons, but there had been one she left out. No one, in Hailey's mind, would ever compare to the best girlfriend in the world, Emma Colton. Charlie had heard every single story about Emma and how they never should have broken up in the first place. Then, Charlie had to see them sitting next to one another at dinner that she thought would just be her with her best friends. Emma had even taken *her* seat next to Hailey, which Charlie did not appreciate. They'd sounded like an old married couple all night, despite the fact that they hadn't spent much time together at all since they'd broken up over a decade ago.

Charlie didn't talk to Hailey or Ember on Tuesday or Wednesday. She considered not going to their Thursday morning coffee, but she thought better of it, because that would only make Hailey harass her more about what was going on. She had arrived at Sally's earlier than normal and sat there, sipping on her coffee. She had made a decision over the past two days. She was going to finally move past Hailey Grant. Hailey would never see her as anything more than a friend. Charlie decided she'd have to be okay with that, and she would have to start actually trying to date women that she didn't compare to her, or only date to see if Hailey got jealous, or even just to see if the woman was worth putting her whole heart into. New leaf, Charlie told herself. She was turning over a new leaf.

"Jesus," she muttered into her coffee when Hailey entered the coffee shop, looking sexy as hell in skinny jeans, black boots, and a black button-down Charlie could see because Hailey was already unbuttoning her coat. "Not fair." She sipped her coffee.

"Hey. You ordered already? It's my turn." Hailey hung her coat over the back of the chair next to Charlie.

"I got here a while ago," Charlie explained.

"I'll get you another one, then." Hailey looked up. "Hey, Em."

Charlie looked up to see Ember approaching their table.

"Morning, ladies."

"You're one minute late. You were doing so well, too," Charlie commented on Ember's tardiness.

Since meeting Eva, their friend had been early to just about everything, correcting her previous bad behavior of being late to everything.

"It was for a good reason," Ember replied.

"Sex?" Charlie suggested, and Hailey walked off to get their drinks.

"Yup," Ember replied with a smirk. "My gal loves morning sex. I am happy to be of service."

Charlie laughed at that. She'd missed Ember. They had always had their coffee, but it hadn't been the same since Ember found Eva. Charlie was extremely happy for her friend and was so glad that she had found someone that understood and appreciated her. Charlie only hoped to find that person for herself one day.

"How's school, Em?" Hailey asked as she set down three coffee cups.

"Same," Ember replied and slid her coffee toward herself. "Still liking it. Is it weird that I'm on my second semester and I'm almost done with a year of grad school?"

"Yes, yes, it's weird," Hailey replied. "You're, like, a million years ahead of the rest of the world, because you're a damn genius."

Charlie smiled at her without looking over at her.

"She's right. We both only have bachelor's degrees. You've been in school for less than a year, and you're about to finish a master's. We kind of hate you a little bit," Charlie offered.

"Are you growing your hair out?" Hailey's hand was at the back of Charlie's neck, playing with the short hairs there.

"No, I just need to get it cut," Charlie answered about her pixie cut that she had an appointment to get cut in a week.

"Oh." Hailey's hand went back to her own lap, and Charlie caught Ember's lifted eyebrow aimed at her.

"So, Emma was at dinner the other night," Ember stated the obvious.

"Yeah. So?" Hailey took a sip of her coffee.

Charlie looked away toward the barista, who was steaming milk for a drink.

"So, what's with that?" Ember queried.

"I don't know. We talk every so often. She met Charlie that day, called, and we went to dinner."

"That's all?" Ember asked, and Charlie's attention returned to the conversation.

"She asked me out," Hailey said with a smile Charlie almost couldn't stand to see.

"She did?" Ember asked.

"For Saturday."

"And you said…" Ember continued.

"She said yes," Charlie answered for her and stood. "I have to get going. I have an early meeting."

"We just got here." Hailey glared at her as Charlie picked up her coat and slid it over her shoulders.

"I know. But it's across town, and I'm taking the train."

Charlie nodded at Ember and then picked up her bag

to go. She almost made it to the door when she felt a hand on her arm.

"Hey, I'm sorry," Ember told her.

"For what?" Charlie looked to Hailey, who sat staring at them, looking confused.

"I shouldn't have brought up the Emma thing. I didn't mean to–"

"It's fine," Charlie proclaimed. "I think it's about time I move past this whole thing. Don't you?"

"Charlie, it's–"

"She's never going to see me that way, Ember. Seeing her with Emma, the other night, just confirmed it. I used to pray she'd look at me how she looked at her, but if they're going out, that's it. And I need to move on."

"I am sorry."

"I know. I'll see you later, okay?"

"Yeah, okay." Ember let her go.

Charlie headed out into the cold toward the train station, climbed aboard, and got off several stops later to then walk to her office. When she arrived, she passed by the members of her team and said her good mornings. She then dropped her things at her desk, pulled her computer out of her bag, and headed to the conference room for a meeting with a potential client. Her boss and a couple of the other executives joined her. One of the assistants walked the potential client into the room. There was a man of about fifty, with salt and pepper hair, wearing a black suit with a navy-blue tie, along with the woman he was with, who looked to be about thirty-five, wearing a gray business suit with an unbuttoned jacket that revealed a white shirt underneath. She had blonde hair that went down to her collar, and it had clearly been straightened. The cut made her appear intense and in control. She also had blue eyes that appeared almost turquoise. Charlie wasn't sure if that was even an eye color a person could have, but it was the word that came to mind when the woman's eyes connected with her own. The two newcomers shook hands with the rest of the group, and then Charlie realized she should stand to shake their hands. She shook the man's hand first, as he introduced himself as Oliver Brody, VP of New Market Development for O'Shea's Grocery Mart.

"Charlie Adams," she supplied him, then turned to see the woman standing to his left, and held out her hand.

The woman's hand slipped into her own. Charlie felt like maybe they were shaking hands a little too long without either of them saying anything.

"Lena Tanner, Director of Operations," the woman introduced herself.

"Charlie," Charlie repeated her first name.

The woman sat down in the empty chair next to her. Charlie stared at her computer, but her eyes wanted to move to the woman beside her. She did her best to focus on the presentation she wasn't really a part of, since her team wouldn't be working on the project. Her boss had just asked her to sit in on it anyway. Charlie thought they had a good pitch, and Oliver seemed to agree. The woman remained somewhat stoic and hard to read. Charlie found herself wondering if she would get in the car with Oliver and tell him to go with the pitch or go with another company. Charlie also wondered if the man would take Lena's recommendation, and guessed that he likely would.

The pitch finished, and there was some light small talk. Charlie didn't engage in small talk a lot and felt like since this wasn't her meeting, she should really be seen and not heard. She closed her computer and began to head out with the rest of them. Then, she turned to walk toward her desk, when she felt a hand on her arm.

"Sorry," Lena said when Charlie turned around with an expression that must have said she was frustrated.

"Oh, it's okay," Charlie returned.

"I was just wondering if you could point me in the direction of the bathroom." Lena lifted a shoulder.

"Oh, sure. It's down the hall and on the right." Charlie pointed past Lena in the direction of the hallway.

"Thanks," Lena replied and gave her a smile. "You didn't say a lot in there," she added.

"It's not my project. I was just sitting in," Charlie explained.

"What do you work on?" she asked.

"We do the historic renos, mostly."

"Renos?" Lena lifted a confused eyebrow.

"Renovations," Charlie explained. "We take old buildings and make them new again, basically."

Lena smiled at her.

"That sounds interesting."

"It can be, yeah," Charlie agreed and set her laptop down on her desk.

"I may be totally off-base here and definitely a little forward, but... Do you want to grab a drink sometime?" Lena questioned just as Charlie's eyes returned to meet her blue ones.

"Oh." Charlie was in shock as she stood in her workplace, with her co-workers around, and was being asked out by an attractive woman that may also be a client.

"I was wrong. My apologies. I'll just—"

"No, you weren't wrong," Charlie returned. "I am," she stated. Everyone in the office knew she was gay, so she wasn't worried about being outed unexpectedly. "I just don't date clients."

"We're not clients yet." Lena smiled and then lowered her head for a moment. She had been so unmoved in the meeting. This was a different side to her, a lighter side. "And it's not your project even if we become clients, right?" she added.

"That's true, but—"

"I understand. I thought I felt something in there, but I'm still getting used to this whole thing. I'll see myself out." The woman turned and began walking toward the hall.

Charlie followed behind until she caught up to her.

"New to this stuff?" Charlie asked.

"It's a long story," Lena provided and continued walking but slowed her pace. "You're technically the first woman I've ever asked out. And that went really well…"

"Really?"

"Late bloomer, I guess," Lena told her. "I only came out a year ago." She paused. "You don't need to hear this. I, uh, sorry for all this."

"We're here." Charlie pointed at the door to the women's bathroom and stopped.

"Oh, I didn't really need to go. I just needed an excuse to talk you. Oliver's waiting with the car," she explained and moved to stand in front of Charlie. "Sorry, again."

Charlie noticed her soft expression and decided she liked it. She also liked the strong, assertive expression this woman had had in the meeting just moments ago.

"Let's get that drink," Charlie suggested.

"You're pitying me because I told you the thing about-"

"I'm not pitying you," Charlie interjected. "I want to get a drink with you."

"Why?"

"Because I felt that thing too, earlier," Charlie admitted and felt her cheeks blush slightly.

"Yeah?"

"Yeah. So, let's get a drink."

"Tomorrow night?" Lena proposed.

"I'm free tomorrow night," Charlie returned.

Lena reached into her bag and pulled out a business card.

"My number is on that. Call me later, and we can arrange it?"

"Sure." Charlie smiled and took the card.

"I have to go. Oliver's waiting."

"Okay. I'll see you tomorrow," Charlie said.

Lena smiled again, turned, and left.

Charlie had a date. She had a date with an attractive, successful woman. She had been on many dates in her time, and none of them had worked out in the long-term; so, she shouldn't be excited yet, but she was. She had felt something when she shook Lena's hand. She wasn't sure what it was, at first, but as her eyes kept trying to find the woman on their own, Charlie had pieced it together. She had glanced at Lena's legs under the table and then at her hand, trying to see if there was a ring. She never thought about asking her out, though, and she never expected Lena to do the asking.

***

Charlie arrived home from work on Friday, walked Eddie, and then went about readying herself for her date. They were meeting at Windy's, because she knew Windy's like the back of her hand; she was comfortable there. Charlie couldn't wait to get ready, so she picked out her clothes, laid them on the bed, and then heard the front door unlock and open. She walked out to see that Hailey had let herself in with her key.

"Hey, I need your help," she said immediately after seeing Charlie. "Hey, buddy," she greeted Eddie, who was sniffing the garment bags she held.

"What's wrong?" Charlie questioned, remaining near her bedroom door.

"I need your help," Hailey repeated and hung the garment bags over the couch so that she could remove her coat.

"You said that already, Hails. I need new information now."

"I need you to help me pick out what I'm wearing tomorrow night."

"Tomorrow night?" Charlie walked into the living room.

"My date with Emma."

"Oh." Charlie lowered her head. "I can't right now, Hailey. Can you ask Ember?"

"What? No, she's out with Eva, Zack, and Grace tonight. Double date with the brother and sister-in-law. Why can't you help me?" Hailey sat on the couch.

"Because I have to get ready myself."

53

"For what?"

"Hailey, it's Friday night. I have plans." Charlie grew frustrated.

"Oh, sorry. I didn't know."

"You didn't ask."

"How could I ask? You've been avoiding me, Charlie. You practically ran out of coffee yesterday. I thought we could hang out tonight."

"You should have called. I have a date." She met Hailey's green eyes.

"You have a date?" Hailey seemed surprised.

"Yes, Hailey. I have a date. I do date."

"I know you date," Hailey replied softly. "I didn't mean it like that. I just didn't know you were dating someone."

"It's a first date, actually," Charlie shared. "And I need to start getting ready."

"So, you want me to go?" Hailey checked and seemed hurt. "I can help you get ready tonight, and you can–"

"Hails, I just–" Charlie stopped herself for a second. "I need a break."

Hailey stood and walked toward her.

"A break? From what? From me?"

"From all of this, yeah." Charlie motioned a finger between the two of them and hated herself for it.

"From our friendship? From our near twelve-year-long friendship?" Hailey was definitely hurt now.

"It's not like that, Hails. I'm going through some stuff. I think I need to be on my own to do it, and–"

"Are you asking Ember for a break from your friendship with her, too?" Hailey's voice grew louder.

"I haven't talked to her about it."

"But you will? Or is it just me that you need a break from?"

"Hailey, you're my best friend."

"I *am* your best friend. So, why can't you go through whatever it is with me?" Hailey's voice grew soft again as she stood in front of Charlie. "Let me help you."

"You can't, Hails. I'm sorry, but you can't."

"Are you sick or something?"

"What? No, I'm not sick."

"Then, what is going on?" Hailey pressed.

"Can you just give me some time, please? We can laugh about this sometime in the future. But, right now, I just need some time."

Hailey turned and walked in a huff back toward the couch, where she put her coat back on and then grabbed her bags.

"Fine." She paused. "I don't know what is going on with you, but I do love you, and I hope you're okay. I'm a little upset right now and will likely go cry my eyes out, because my best friend in the world can't talk to me about something that is clearly wrong or important or, maybe, both – I don't know. Just call me when you figure it out." She avoided Eddie's attempts to play and left the apartment.

Charlie just stood there, worrying that maybe she'd made a mistake.

CHAPTER 6

"HEY there," Emma greeted Hailey's call.

"Hey. I'm sorry to call you. I know you're traveling. I just needed to talk to someone, and Ember's busy, and—"

"It's fine. I just landed back in Chicago; like, ten minutes ago. What's wrong? Are you okay?"

"You're here?"

"I took an earlier flight. The conference wrapped. I headed to the airport and got on standby. I was going to call you later, when I got home, to firm up plans for tomorrow. What's wrong, Hails?"

"I had a bad fight with Charlie. Or maybe it wasn't even a fight. I don't know."

"Let me get my bag, and then I can meet you somewhere."

"No, you don't have to do that. I'm fine," Hailey said.

"I can meet you at your place if you want. I can be there in an hour."

"You haven't been home all week, Emma."

"So? I don't care," Emma returned, and Hailey heard the background noise of an airport. "Are you hungry? I haven't eaten. I can stop by and get us something."

"Em, that's too much."

"No, it's not, Hails. I'll be there in an hour, okay?"

"Okay," Hailey relented.

The strangest part of that conversation wasn't that she'd had it with her first love. It was that Hailey normally had conversations about her problems with Charlie. She realized, as she stared down at her phone, that this was the first time she'd had to have a conversation with someone else about a problem *with* Charlie.

***

An hour later, Emma was standing at her door, holding up a bag of take-out, with her luggage beside her.

"You really didn't have to come over," Hailey greeted the woman.

She then opened the door wide, grabbed the bag handle, and rolled it in. Emma walked past her and stood still while Hailey closed the door behind her. Hailey smiled at her, took one of the bags Emma was carrying from her, and walked toward her small kitchen.

"I wanted to see you, anyway. So, it's win-win."

"You're seeing me tomorrow."

"I can't see you two days in a row?" Emma replied and sat the other bag on the counter next to where Hailey placed the first one. "I got burgers. I hope that's okay."

"It's great."

"And I got you your favorite," she added and pulled a large container of ice cream from it.

"Neapolitan?" Hailey nearly cackled, she laughed so hard. "That was only my favorite ice cream because you like the vanilla, and I liked the chocolate part."

"We split the strawberry; I know. I'm sure your tastes have matured since we were teenagers, but I thought it would be fun to reminisce."

Hailey laughed some more as she removed the food from the other bag, grabbed the plates and napkins, and placed the ice cream in her freezer so it wouldn't melt while they ate. They sat on the couch next to one another and dug into the food. Hailey asked Emma about her conference. Emma asked Hailey about her workweek. Both avoided the real topic until they'd finished the burgers and had moved on to their shared ice cream. Hailey placed the carton on the couch and opened it. She then passed Emma a spoon and watched her slide it along the top of the vanilla section of the ice cream. Hailey did the same with the chocolate.

"Thank you. I needed this." Hailey took a bite of her chocolate ice cream.

"You want to talk about what happened?" Emma questioned softly.

"I went over to Charlie's place. She was getting ready for a date, I guess. I didn't know she had a date. But then, she said she needed some time alone."

"Alone?"

"Away from me, I think. She said she was going through something and wanted some time to deal with it herself. But, Emma, we don't do that." Hailey dropped the spoon into the ice cream. "We've been friends since college, and we don't do that. We deal with things together. We help each other figure stuff out."

"Maybe it's something she has to figure out on her own," Emma suggested.

"Like what?"

"I don't know. But, sometimes, people have to be alone to get stuff done. Look at me; I took a year to figure some things out. I barely saw the friends I did have, up until recently, and I just reached back out to you. It doesn't mean I didn't care about them or that I didn't want them around. It was just something I needed to do."

Hailey squinted at her.

"You're being logical. I don't like it." She tried to keep her squint going, but Emma smiled, and Hailey couldn't hold it. "I haven't been without her for my entire adult life. Ember would drift in and out of our friendship, based on her crazy work schedule, or because she has Eva now, but not Charlie. She's been the one constant in my life."

"I'm sorry, Hails."

Hailey noticed Emma's spoon sticking in the ice cream and figured they were both done. She grabbed the spoons, closed the lid, and took it over to the kitchen. When she returned, she saw Emma facing the TV. Hailey sat beside her and relaxed into her body, resting her head on Emma's shoulder.

"Is this okay?" she asked.

"Sure. But I bet I smell like an airport," Emma replied.

Hailey laughed and burrowed farther into her. Emma wrapped her arm around Hailey. Hailey pressed her face into Emma's neck.

"You smell like you."

"How do I smell?" Emma laughed lightly.

"Just like Emma, I guess."

"Hails, I missed you," Emma said. "This week, this past year, this past decade, even. I've never managed to get beyond you. I tried. When I got back to Rutgers, I tried to stop thinking about you. I couldn't. I dated, and not one kiss could ever match any of our kisses. When you were at my dad's funeral, I thought about how much I wanted us to get back together, but I couldn't back then. I was dealing with losing him. When I got back to Chicago permanently, I thought about it. When we'd hang out, I'd think about asking you out, and then, I'd worry that you'd say no." Hailey felt Emma's free hand take her own and move it to her lap. "I don't know, Hails… This feels so good right now. Maybe this is how it was supposed to be: we met all those years ago and had to get here later."

"I was so nervous that night."

"Which night?"

"That first night, by the pond."

"So was I."

"You didn't act like it," Hailey told her. "You seemed so confident."

"I wasn't," Emma revealed as she laughed. "I'd seen you around school. I thought you were beautiful. I wondered why I was thinking about that. And when I saw you in that bathroom, I got nervous, because I was actually talking to you. I thought I would invite you to the game, and we could be friends. But I couldn't just be friends with you. I actually remember thinking that if I tried to kiss you, and you freaked out and told everyone, I would only have to deal with it until graduation."

"You did not!" Hailey exclaimed and lifted her head to look at Emma.

"I did, I swear." Emma placed a hand on Hailey's cheek. "I felt like I had to kiss you then, Hailey. I think you were always destined to be my first love. Now, I feel like I have to kiss you again." Emma's hand slid to her throat, and Hailey swallowed.

She hadn't kissed this girl in so long. No, Emma wasn't a girl anymore. Emma was a woman. She was definitely a woman now. Hailey hadn't kissed her in so many years, but she wanted to kiss her again. She wanted to feel the press of those lips against her own, because all of their kisses back then had been so special and felt so important. She leaned in, to let the woman know she wanted her to keep going. Emma's eyes were boring into Hailey's as if waiting for a second layer of permission. Then, Emma understood that Hailey wanted this, too, and leaned in to connect their lips. It took Hailey a moment to register that this was the same Emma Colton she was kissing. But, as soon as that hit her, she pressed herself farther into the kiss, allowing Emma's tongue to play with her top lip in the way that she liked and that, apparently, Emma remembered. When Hailey felt Emma's tongue request entrance, she opened her mouth to allow it inside. That caused her to moan audibly, and her hand went to Emma's cheek and then her neck. She moved her body to straddle Emma on the couch before she pulled her lips away only so that Emma would attach her lips to Hailey's neck, which Emma did. With her arms around Emma's neck, she pulled her in closer and felt Emma's hands on the small of her back, just resting there.

"You know what's different from then to now?" Emma questioned before pressing a light kiss to Hailey's neck.

Hailey worried about what Emma might say. Was she

a bad kisser now? Did Emma not like her as much as she had when they were younger?

"What?" she managed out.

"We're not sneaking around, trying to avoid teachers or our parents, this time."

Hailey laughed, and her head went back as she did. Emma's lips kept reaching for her skin, though. They stayed in that position for a long while, sharing soft kisses that turned heated and then soft again, before they finally broke apart.

"I know this is lame, because we have done this before... But, I think we should maybe wait to take this further," Hailey suggested.

"I think that's a good idea," Emma agreed.

"You do?"

"Yes, I do. Just because we've had sex before, doesn't mean we should dive right in. I think we should work back up to it. Let's wait until we're both ready, like last time."

Hailey smiled at Emma and kissed her again.

"I missed you," she shared after a moment.

Emma kissed her again. A few minutes later, they said their goodnights and finalized their plans for their first official date.

***

Charlie got to Windy's a little early and sat at her usual table toward the back. Out of habit, she took the seat she always took, nearest the wall, because, typically, Hailey sat in the one next to her, and she didn't like the seat next to the wall. Charlie shook herself out of it, and she immediately felt weird, sitting against the wall when she was alone. So, she moved over to Hailey's normally occupied chair.

Lena arrived in that moment and approached the table with a smile. Her look was much more relaxed than the first time Charlie had seen her. She was wearing comfortable, fit jeans and a collared shirt under a teal cardigan, and had already removed her coat, which was hanging over her arm.

Lena's hair was also more relaxed and clearly hadn't been straightened, so it fell into light, natural waves around her face. The woman's eyes were bright in the dim bar lighting, and she appeared slightly awkward, which Charlie thought was adorable.

"Hi," Lena greeted unconfidently.

"Hey," Charlie replied. "Is this place okay?"

"Oh, yeah. Sure." Lena hung her coat over the back of the other chair and placed her purse on the seat before sitting down herself. "I've never been here."

"It's owned by a friend of mine." Charlie opted not to try to explain to her that Windy's was owned by Ember's sister-in-law's family, because that just seemed overly complicated.

"Really? That's nice." Lena clasped her hands on the table. "So, I'm sorry. I really don't know how to do this. I've..." She lowered her head and her voice.

"How about I get us some drinks, and we can just talk?" Charlie suggested.

"Yeah, okay." Lena lifted her head.

"What can I get you?"

"Anything with alcohol in it." The woman laughed. "I'm trying not to be nervous, but I think the alcohol would help."

Charlie laughed as well and then stood.

"They have a house drink here. It's rum-based."

"That sounds good."

"Give me a minute." Charlie went to move past Lena, but stopped next to her instead. "And, you can relax. I'm not worth getting all nervous for."

"How can you say that when you look how you do?" Lena stared at her.

Charlie swallowed. She had worn black slacks and a white v-cut sweater that she thought she looked pretty good in, and, apparently, was right.

"I'll be right back," she returned with a coy smile.

She headed to the bar and ordered their drinks. Then,

she carried them back with her and placed one in front of Lena before sitting back down.

"So, how long have you worked at your firm?" Lena asked and then took an immediate drink.

"About a year. Or a little more, I guess," Charlie replied. "What about you?"

"Three years at the company and one in my position as Director."

"Do you like it?"

"I do. It wasn't what I'd planned for myself, but I like how it ended up." Lena gripped her glass tightly with both hands.

"What did you have planned?" Charlie watched her eyes flit around the room.

"Well, I went to school for business administration, but I ended up getting married my senior year and then left a few credits shy of graduation."

Charlie wasn't expecting that.

"Married?"

"My ex-husband's name is Damon. He and I had known each other for years and started dating in college. I didn't know back then."

"That you were gay?" Charlie chanced a guess and took a sip of her drink, tasting the rum on her lips.

"I thought I would feel more in love with him after the wedding – which I know is stupid, but it's what the twenty-one-year-old me thought. We stayed together for about eight years before we separated and then divorced officially about five years ago. It was mostly amicable. I told him I thought I was gay. He was pissed for a while, told me that didn't make any sense. And then, we got to a place where we could tolerate each other, but the marriage was over. I haven't talked to him since. I found out from my sister that he got married again, a couple of years ago."

"Wow."

"I just kind of told you my whole life story there, huh?" Lena laughed.

"It's okay." Charlie laughed back.

"I took a few years to sort myself out. And then I finally just admitted to myself that I liked women and came out to my family last year."

"That's pretty amazing," Charlie complimented.

Lena laughed and took another drink.

"Amazing? I'm a thirty-five-year-old lesbian who's just now on her first date with a woman."

"Not everyone realizes it at the same age, or even takes the risk to come out to their family. I think it's pretty remarkable that you took the time to figure out how you felt and who you are, and that you told the people you love. Not everyone does that. It took me some time, too."

"It did?"

"Not the dating women part, but the coming out part. I didn't do it right away. It took me some time to work up to it. I'm glad I took that time. Because, the way it happened, it all worked out. I don't know if it would have any other way."

"I guess you're right."

"What made you ask me out yesterday? If you've never done it before, why now?"

"I signed up for online dating a few months ago. I just kept clicking past women, and if they expressed interest, I turned them down no matter how good they seemed. I just couldn't get up the courage to take the chance. And then, yesterday, I saw you when I was outside the conference room. I thought you were… beautiful. Then, I shook your hand, and it felt nice. I had to keep myself from staring at you during the meeting. I don't know… I just got tired of not taking action. So, I took the chance."

Charlie's cheeks were red.

"I'm glad you did," she replied. "You got lucky, because you were on the side of the table and, therefore, in front of me. I was behind you, so I couldn't help but stare."

It was Lena's turn to blush.

"Really?"

"You're gorgeous," Charlie admitted. "I had a hard time focusing on the pitch."

Lena looked down again, and Charlie found it endearing.

"You sure you don't mind putting up with this whole first everything? I've never done any of this. It's all new to me." Lena's eyes got big, and then they lit up. "That's presumptuous. It's a first date."

"I don't mind at all," Charlie replied and sipped on her drink.

They chatted about their upbringings. Lena told Charlie that she had been born and raised in Connecticut and had gone to school at Yale. She had moved to Chicago for her current job and loved the city. Her family was fairly well-off, as a lot of families in Connecticut were, and her ex-husband was from old money.

"I didn't work. Damon didn't want me to. We didn't need me to, either. We had his family money. He was going to law school and later, became a corporate attorney and brought in more than enough to support us. I wanted to work, though, so I volunteered at various organizations. And that's where I met her. I later found out we were neighbors. She started coming over more and more. When her husband left her for another woman, it made me think that if I just left Damon, I could be with her. We could have our own house and our own life together." Lena took a sip of her second drink. "That was naïve. She was very much straight and started dating shortly after her divorce was final. I knew that needed to be the end of my crush. It was an important first step for me, though, and it got me to where I am now."

"We've all had that straight girl crush. Mine was Stacey. Later, there was Christie. And after that, I think, came Laurie."

"You've had a few, it seems." Lena laughed.

"I wasn't out in high school, so I had a lot of friends that didn't feel uncomfortable or awkward around me. And

I had a lot of straight girl crushes as a result."

"I guess that's a first I can check off my list, then." Lena raised her glass in the air at Charlie and then finished the drink.

"Hey, do you want to get dinner? I know it's late, but I didn't eat earlier. There's this place down the street that's pretty good," Charlie proposed. "I'd suggest here, but they only have appetizers and bar food. I'd like to have an actual dinner with you."

"That sounds nice, actually. But, it's my treat. You bought my drinks."

Charlie smirked at her and then replied, "No, I didn't. I tried to, but Grace wouldn't let me pay." She motioned with her head, and Lena turned her head to see a woman behind the bar. "That's my friend."

"Oh, I see." Lena turned her attention back to Charlie, who had moved to stand in front of her. Lena was sitting facing Charlie now, and since she was in her chair, Charlie essentially hovered over her, but she was also about a foot away from her so as not to appear intimidating to the still nervous woman. "Hi," Lena said as she realized how close Charlie was to her.

"We can walk there if you want," Charlie told her. "It's close."

"Okay."

Charlie took a step back so that Lena could stand. She leaned around her and grabbed the woman's coat. Then, she held it out for Lena, taking a play out of Ember's playbook. Lena slid into it before reaching down to pick up her purse. Charlie put on her own coat in the meantime and started walking them toward the bar to say goodbye to Grace. As they made their way toward the door, she held it open for Lena and allowed her to walk past her. She noticed Lena was waiting for her, not sure which direction to walk. Charlie held out her hand for her to take, which Lena did, after she revealed a shy smile. Then, Charlie walked them hand in hand toward the restaurant.

CHAPTER 7

HAILEY sat with Ember in the living room of Ember and Eva's house, while Alyssa and Eva worked on lunch in the kitchen.

"I can't believe she said that," Ember expressed. "She needs time away from you?"

"She hasn't said anything to you about it? She hasn't asked for time away from you, has she?"

"No, she–" Ember seemed to need to take a moment to consider something. "She hasn't said anything to me."

Hailey wondered what that pause was about, but they were interrupted when Eva came into the room.

"Okay… I tried to make the sauce, but I think I burned it. Can you check, babe?" Eva placed a hand on Ember's shoulder.

"I'm not marrying her for her cooking skills," Ember told Hailey and then stood, giving a wink to Eva.

"I have no retort for that," Eva admitted and sat in Ember's place.

"Alyssa, what did she do?" Ember asked Alyssa as she walked toward the kitchen.

"So, how are you?" Eva asked her.

"I'm good," Hailey replied.

Hailey liked Eva for Ember, but she was also glad that she just liked Eva as a person outside of her relationship with her best friend. Hailey had yet to spend a lot of time alone with her, though, and she still hadn't shared anything real with her beyond what she'd shared when Ember was around.

"Em said you had something you needed to talk about. Did you get to, or did I just interrupt?"

"You did, but it's okay. She can't help, anyway," Hailey replied in a defeated tone.

"She's pretty good at a lot of things. You sure she can't help?"

"Charlie's going through something, and she doesn't want me around while she tries to figure it out."

"Oh." Eva's eyes widened.

"You know something, don't you?" Hailey accused.

"What? No, I don't know anything," Eva answered. "Really."

"Sorry. I feel like she's hiding something from me, and that's not like her. We tell each other everything. Last night, I called Emma, and she came over. We had this really good night together, and we're going out again tonight. The first person I wanted to tell was Charlie, but I didn't want to disrespect what she asked for."

"That's probably a good idea."

"And she had a date last night. I wanted her to call me, and tell me all about it, but she didn't." Hailey covered her face with her hands. "Normally, she tells me everything about the women she dates and then debriefs me afterward, but she didn't call. That worries me."

"Hailey, it's good that you let her figure whatever it is out. If you try to interfere, it will only backfire," Eva suggested.

"I know. It's just strange. I miss her when I don't see her. Is that weird?"

"Why would that be weird?" Eva asked her. "She's your friend."

"I don't miss Ember like that." Hailey then looked sheepish. "No offense."

Eva laughed at her.

"I'll say, none taken on her behalf."

"I just mean that, even though the three of us have always been best friends, Ember was usually on her own, and okay with it, while Charlie and I always stuck together. It's been like that forever. The longest I've gone without seeing her, was a week when I went on a business trip, and I talked to her nearly every day the whole time. The longest we've gone without talking has only been a couple of days, I think. It's now been less than twenty-four hours, and I don't know how long it's going to last, but I miss her."

"Hey, Han's stuck at the hotel, so she's not going to be able to make lunch," Alyssa explained as she stared at her phone and walked into the living room. "Ember says you didn't burn the sauce, she's just added salt. The pasta's almost ready. I'm going to go call Han, and see if she wants me to run to the store on my way home."

"You two are so married," Hailey teased her.

"Hey, don't knock it. It's pretty great." Alyssa put her phone to her ear. "Hey, baby." She then walked out toward the dining room to talk privately.

"She's right. I know I'm only engaged, but it is pretty great," Eva suggested. "I get to come home to the same super-genius hot chick every night, that pulls out chairs, helps me put my coat on, and opens doors, like we're in an old movie. She cooks, too." Eva smiled at Hailey. "And she's the best thing that's ever happened to me."

"Charlie does that stuff, too," Hailey shared. "It's sweet, isn't it?"

Eva glanced over at Ember, who was walking a giant pot of pasta into their dining room.

"It is, yeah. Does Emma do that stuff?"

"I don't know," Hailey returned. "We last dated when we were kids. I don't know that I remember that stuff."

"What *do* you remember?" Eva asked.

"I remember how she kissed me, and held me, and made me laugh. I remember how it felt when she held my hand that first day at school, after we were out." Hailey smiled at the memories. "She was the perfect first girlfriend. I was so lucky I found her."

"And she wants to try again now?"

"It's not like we broke up because we hated each other, or even fell out of love. It doesn't feel like it's trying again. It feels like we're just picking up where we left off."

"But, it's been a long time. Are you sure you're both

the same people? I know I'm not the same person I was when I was in high school."

"I don't think we're the same people, no. I think we both grew up. But I like who she is so far. I've spent time with her over the years. And I don't know what's going to happen, but it felt really good to kiss her again."

"You kissed her?" Ember questioned as she reentered the room.

"Yes, Em. I kissed her. And it was great."

"Lunch is ready. And I cannot believe you kissed her, Hails."

"Why not? We've done it before."

"Hailey–" Ember started and stopped. "I'm getting the drinks."

"Hey, when are we wedding-planning again?" Alyssa walked back into the room.

"We start next weekend." Eva smiled and stood. Then, she grabbed Ember's waist. "And I can't wait." Eva pressed her lips quickly to Ember's, causing the woman to smile, before they all headed into the dining room for lunch.

Hailey was left, once again, wondering what Ember was about to say but felt it might be wrong to ask, since Charlie was Ember's friend, too. If Charlie couldn't talk to her about something, maybe the woman could talk to Ember about it. And that had to be enough for right now.

***

Charlie was laughing. No, Charlie was cackling. Lena stood in her kitchen, with her back pressed against the refrigerator, while Eddie was up on his hind legs, trying to kiss her in that dog way that seemed to make them so happy. It also made Charlie happy, to watch her dog seem to like this new person so quickly.

"Eddie, leave her alone." She laughed and then helped him off of her. "Sorry, he gets a little excited."

Lena was laughing, too, as she straightened her now

rumpled clothing.

"It's fine. He's cute. How old is he?"

"He's five, but he still acts like a puppy. I secretly love that, but don't tell him." Charlie leaned back against the island in front of the refrigerator. "I was nervous there for a minute. I thought my dog might get to first base before I do," she teased.

"Oh, God! There's a thought. I assume there's a different base system for women... Do I need to learn that?" Lena questioned with a reddened face.

"Why do you keep thinking you need to learn things?" Charlie reached her hand out, lightly touched Lena's stomach through her shirt, and then returned her hand to her side.

"I don't know... I just feel like there's a lot for me to learn. I lived with and had sex with a man for over a decade, and he..." Lena did that thing where she lowered her head again. "He was the only..."

"The only person you've ever had sex with," Charlie finished for her.

"It's kind of embarrassing."

"Why is that embarrassing?" Charlie asked and took a small step forward.

"Because I'm thirty-five. I've been with one person. And that person is a man, because I wasn't ready to accept or even to understand that I was gay back then."

"But, Lena, there's nothing wrong with sleeping with one person. Sometimes, I look back and think that I wish I would have waited a little longer. I don't regret what I've done, necessarily, but I don't think having a high number of sexual partners is important. I think each person should be with who they want to be with. It's not my place to judge, but I don't think you should be embarrassed about having one partner."

"So, you'd be okay with us going slow? I mean, this is a second date..."

"We can go slow." Charlie smiled at her, then closed

the distance between them, and placed her hands on Lena's hips. "I like you. And I had a really good time with you last night, especially when you almost made our waiter cry," she mocked.

"I did not almost make her cry."

"You gave her a serious glare when she got your order wrong."

"I'm allergic to nuts. I told her, 'no walnuts on the salad.' She almost killed me," Lena exclaimed, and Charlie knew her distraction worked when Lena's arms went around her neck.

"I thought I saw her tear up," Charlie continued.

"She did not tear up. Really? Did I really…"

"No." Charlie laughed, then placed her head on Lena's shoulder, and pulled her in for a tight hug.

"This feels nice," Lena shared after a moment, pulling Charlie in closer.

Charlie pressed a gentle chaste kiss to her shoulder and pulled back.

"Pizza and a movie; that was the deal. I'll order. You go pick out a movie."

Lena just nodded and let out a deep breath. She let go of Charlie and made her way toward the couch, while Charlie walked to her laptop and ordered their food. She then sat down next to Lena, who was scrolling through a list of movies on the screen, and made sure to leave enough space between them so that the woman wouldn't feel uncomfortable. They decided on a movie and started it, while Eddie lay at their feet. When the pizza came, Lena insisted on getting the door, and Charlie smiled at the thought until she remembered that Hailey usually did that when they would hang out and order food. She would have Charlie's legs in her lap, most times, and she would still insist on getting their food for them. Charlie shook her head as Lena asked her where the plates were and then started putting their meal together to bring it back to the couch.

They ate in relative silence. When they were finished,

Charlie took their now dirty dishes into the kitchen. By that time, Eddie was doing his dance, so Lena paused the movie and accompanied them on their walk. When they returned to the apartment, they were both slightly frozen. Charlie grabbed a blanket off the back of the couch and draped it over both of them. She glanced over at Lena, who appeared to be less nervous after their shared evening. Charlie risked putting her arm around Lena's shoulder. Lena smiled and turned her head toward Charlie for a moment, before resting her head against Charlie's shoulder and continuing to watch the movie.

***

"Well, that was fun," Emma expressed as she took Hailey's hand and walked them toward her car.

"Yes, it was," Hailey agreed. "I don't think I've ever seen a movie with subtitles in the theater before," she confessed.

"Me neither."

"You haven't?"

"No."

"Then, why did you suggest it?" Hailey questioned. You seemed all into it."

"I don't know. It seemed like a good idea at the time."

"You hated it, didn't you?" Hailey laughed and swung their hands.

"Yes," Emma shared. "I'm not sure I even understood the story. There was a goat involved… And what was that woman doing, carrying that bucket of water up a hill like that?"

Hailey laughed and pulled Emma closer to her.

"Why did we go?"

"Because I'm stupid," Emma stated. "I guess I thought that we should do something we never did before. We're older and supposedly more sophisticated now. I thought we'd like a more sophisticated movie."

"Em, you're cute," Hailey told her.

"Sorry. I promise, I'll take you to a good old-fashioned Hollywood blockbuster next time. It will be a terrible rip-off of some other movie that came before it, but at least we'll understand it."

"Pretty confident that you're getting another date, Miss Colton."

"Am I?" Emma stopped them and pulled Hailey back a little to face her. "Am I getting another date, Hails?"

"Yes." Hailey let her off easy.

"Yeah?" Emma smirked.

"Yes. But no more movies with subtitles."

"That's easy. Come on, I'll take you home."

***

Charlie knew it was getting late and that she should probably be checking in to see if Lena wanted to go home, but the woman wasn't saying anything, and Charlie didn't want her to go. However, she was falling asleep on the couch and worried she'd pass out there, with Lena still pressed against her side. They'd started the second movie, and then watched a couple of episodes of some comedy show that Lena had recommended and Charlie had enjoyed. But, by the third episode, Charlie was having a hard time keeping her eyes open.

"Hey, I hate to say this, but I think I'm about to fall asleep on you," Charlie finally admitted and hated doing it because Lena sat up and looked at her.

"Sorry. I should go. It's really late." She looked at the clock on the cable box under the TV.

"You can stay if you want." Charlie placed her hand on the small of Lena's back. "You don't have to, obviously, but you can."

Lena considered it for a moment and then looked down at herself.

"I'd like to, but I don't have anything with me here."

Charlie smirked and ran a hand across Lena's cheek, pushing the hair back from her face.

"I do."

"Right. Dating a woman about your size means you can share clothes, probably."

"It does, yes. I have other stuff, too; like an extra toothbrush and stuff like that."

"For your other lady guests?" Lena lifted an eyebrow.

"It's complicated to explain, but here I go. One of my best friends, Ember, is engaged to a woman named Eva. Eva is best friends with a woman named Alyssa. Alyssa is married to Hannah. They both work for Camden Hotels, and they recently changed suppliers for their complimentary kits that they give out when you forget stuff. They had a bunch of extras, so they gave them to me and my other friend, Hailey."

"That does sound complicated."

"Anyway... I have a bunch of that in the bathroom, thanks to my *lack* of lady guests," Charlie explained.

"And if I stay..." Lena looked concerned, but Charlie wasn't sure if she was concerned that something might happen or that something might not happen.

"We sleep, wake up tomorrow, and I'll make you coffee," Charlie said and stood.

Lena stood and smiled. When Charlie held out her hand for the woman to take, Lena did, and they proceeded toward the bedroom. Charlie got her set up with clothes and toiletries, took Eddie out one last time before taking her own turn in the bathroom, and climbed into bed next to the sitting Lena.

"You okay?" Charlie asked as she pulled the blanket up to her waist and looked over at Lena, who had her hands clasped in her lap.

"I wasn't sure if this was your side or if that was, so I just took this one."

"This is my side, so you're good." Charlie placed her hand over Lena's clasped ones. "Do you want to turn the

TV on? It won't bother me. Maybe it will help you relax a little," she suggested.

"No, I'm okay."

"Do you normally sleep sitting up?" Charlie lifted an eyebrow.

Lena turned to look at her, rolled her eyes at herself, and then slid down on the bed to lie next to Charlie.

"No, I don't." She turned only her head toward Charlie. "Do you think that you could hold me?"

Charlie nodded and lifted her arm. Lena slid over, pressed her cheek against Charlie's shoulder, and placed an arm over her stomach.

"I can hear your heartbeat," the woman said after a few moments.

"I can feel your heartbeat," Charlie returned and ran her hand up and down Lena's back. "It's very fast."

"Sorry," Lena said.

"Nothing is going to happen until you're ready, or *if* you're ever ready," Charlie shared. "This is our second date. It may not be with me when it does happen, but I'm not the kind of person who will pressure you into doing anything. If it's not me, I hope that whoever you find won't pressure you, either."

"Do you normally go slow with stuff like this, though? I feel like making anyone wait for things at my age is so… lame."

"You're not making me wait for anything. I don't mind a natural progression of things. And yeah, I tend to go slow." Charlie thought of Hailey for a moment, and then again, found herself pushing the woman out of her mind. "Slow can be good. It builds anticipation."

"Anticipation is nice," Lena agreed.

"Yeah, it is." Charlie closed her eyes, and after a few minutes, she felt Lena's heart rate slow down and her breathing even out.

CHAPTER 8

"Do you realize that this is the first time we've woken up together?" Hailey professed as she took in Emma lying beside her.

"Oh, I guess it is." Emma laughed a husky morning laugh. "We had to sneak around back then, and you never visited me at the dorm."

"Like my mother would have let me," Hailey replied and ran a hand down Emma's back over her shirt.

"True," Emma said. "I had a roommate, anyway. She never left the room, so... We would've been able to wake up together, but we wouldn't have been able to do anything else."

"Yeah, I definitely would not have had sex with you on a top bunk with her under us," Hailey told her, causing Emma to laugh deeply.

"She would've freaked the hell out. She was not a fan of rooming with a lesbian. Now, I almost wish that would have happened; just to see her reaction."

Emma was lying on her stomach, with her head turned to Hailey. Hailey placed her hand under Emma's shirt and ran it up her back.

"So, you didn't see her reaction with any other girls?" Hailey tried not to sound shy or hopeful, but she was sure she hadn't pulled it off.

"Hails, it took me a long time to start dating after you. I was in my own off-campus apartment by the time I went on another date. And even then, I was still into you, and it went nowhere." Emma closed her eyes as Hailey's hand dragged back down.

"I didn't want us to break up," Hailey revealed.

"I didn't want us to break up, either," Emma said only moments later.

"Why did we, then?"

"Because we thought we should," Emma stated and opened her eyes to see Hailey's green ones looking back at her. "It felt like everyone around us, who was trying the same thing – doing the long-distance high school to college romance, was failing and breaking up. I just don't think we had the faith that we'd be the couple that actually made it through all that."

"Well, that was stupid." Hailey lifted Emma's shirt enough to see the small of the woman's back and pressed her hand to it before running her fingers over it from side to side.

"I know. We were young, though. We didn't know that it could work. People always say it can't, but we should have known better, I guess."

"But, Em, this feels good. Don't get me wrong – it does. But we still need to get to know who we are today. I've loved going through old memories with you. I want to keep doing that. But we also need to know who the other person turned out to be. I feel like I only know that old version of you that I fell in love with. I know you're not that person anymore. You're this person. And this person is someone I like and want to know more about."

"I know. I understand," Emma agreed. "We will. We should have a whole day or something, where we don't talk about the past and catch each other up on the stuff we missed and what we want out of our lives now, to see if it's still real."

Hailey smiled and stopped moving her hand against Emma's skin.

"I'm going to make coffee. Want some?"

"I'm more of a tea girl these days," Emma admitted.

"Tea? Did you become British since we dated?" Hailey joked but thought about her weekly coffee dates with Ember and Charlie. And then, she thought about how Charlie always made her coffee when Hailey stayed over.

"No, I just found a kind that I liked, and I drink it now. But I don't abstain from coffee altogether, so I can do coffee with you this morning."

"Good. I'll make it, then." Hailey climbed out of bed and headed toward her small kitchen.

They had come back to her apartment only to say goodnight, since Emma had driven them to the theater, but Hailey asked her in. They had spent a couple of hours talking about their summer together after Emma graduated, and then Hailey invited her to stay the night. They hadn't gone past kissing yet. Hailey was both happy and unhappy about that, because her body had always reacted to Emma. Every time the woman was near, Hailey's pulse quickened, her body tensed, and most of the time, she even got wet. She had also gotten turned on last night, while they were nearing the fooling around status, and she wanted more. But she had heard Eva, and had gotten much the same from Ember later, about how they should get to know one another more before they started up again. So, while her body craved those touches she knew Emma could provide, Hailey's brain and heart were telling her to take things slow until she knew they could fall in love with who they were today and not who they were back then.

***

Charlie awoke to Lena lying next to her, and smiled. She thought about waking her first, but decided to make them coffee and bring it back instead. She slid out of bed in the way she had practiced with Hailey and headed out to the kitchen. Eddie was entertaining himself with a toy Ember had purchased for him a year ago, that was surprisingly still intact, but he lifted his head and wagged his tail when he saw Charlie enter.

"Hey, bud. Can you wait until I make us coffee before you go crazy?"

He tilted his head to the right and then returned to his toy. Charlie silently laughed at her character of a dog. If there was anyone on the planet that made her feel like an idiot, sometimes, it was Eddie. The way he looked at her, when she talked to him, made her feel like he thought she was nuts and was definitely judging her for it. Charlie loved him like crazy.

"Good morning." Lena made her way into the kitchen, wearing a pair of Charlie's pajama pants and a black T-shirt with the UC logo on it.

"Morning. I was going to bring this in." She lifted a coffee mug, then placed it in her machine, inserted the pod in the top, and pressed the button.

"I heard you, so I got up." Lena looked over at Eddie, who'd heard her enter and started walking toward her, with his claws making a tap tap tap noise against the hardwood. "Hey, little guy," Lena greeted him.

Eddie's tail went crazy before he started moving his front paws back and forth.

"He needs to go out."

"I can take him," Lena volunteered.

"It's freezing out there. You get this one." Charlie pointed at the mug. "There's sugar on the counter and cream in the fridge if you need it. I'll be right back."

"Let me take him. Seriously, I want to. I haven't had a dog since I was a kid. I miss it."

"You miss taking them on walks in fifteen-degree weather?" Charlie lifted the now full mug out of the machine and placed it on the island.

"He's cute." Lena patted the dog's head. "You take that one. I'll put on some shoes and be right back." She stood, slid the mug back over to Charlie's side, and then walked toward the door.

***

"Thanks for squeezing me in for lunch today," Emma said as Hailey sat down in the chair across from her at the restaurant.

"Of course. I'm sorry, I've been so busy this week," she apologized. "My boss just turned in her resignation, so things are a little crazy right now. She's asked me to be the transition person for whoever gets the job after her."

"Transition person?" Emma questioned. "I ordered you a Coke."

"I'm a Diet person now," Hailey revealed.

"Oh, sorry." Emma took a sip of her water. "I'll have her bring a Diet one, then."

"It's fine. I'll drink it."

"What's a transition person?"

"Oh, you know, that person that kind of has to learn everything you do so they can pass it along to the next person so that they can do it."

"Are you applying for the job?"

"Me?"

"Yes, Hails." Emma smiled at her as the waitress approached with Hailey's drink. "I'm sorry, can I get you to bring her a Diet one? I'll take that one, though."

"Sure," the waitress replied and set the Coke in front of Emma instead.

"Thank you," Hailey told the waitress and then returned her attention to Emma. "I don't really want her job. I like my job."

"You don't want to move up?"

"Not really. Maybe someday. She's a VP. That's a lot more responsibility, and they generally require a master's degree for those roles, anyway."

"Wasn't that a part of your plan back then? Grad school?"

Hailey laughed a little.

"Yeah, I guess. I thought I would go, but I got the

entry-level position at the bank right out of school, and I never looked back." She met Emma's eyes then. "What happened with you and vet school? You never told me."

"Oh, I got to Rutgers and took a lot of electives my first year. One was in public policy. I got really into it and started thinking about health administration after that."

"Do you have any pets now? I haven't asked."

"No. I did, though. I got a dog right after I moved back, but he died a few years ago."

"I'm sorry, Em. What was his name?"

"You're going to laugh."

"Why?"

"Because I named him Frogger."

Hailey did laugh.

"You named him Frogger?"

"Yeah." Emma smiled at her.

"Because of–"

"Yeah," Emma interrupted with the confirmation.

They had returned to their pond numerous times after that night. And more than once, they had made love on top of a blanket under the stars, while listening to the ribbits of the frogs hiding somewhere around the water. It was always Hailey's idea to return there. She considered it their pond; their special place. Emma had jokingly called her Frogger one day, and said that she must loved the frogs more than she loved her. It hadn't turned into a nickname or anything after that, so Hailey was surprised Emma even remembered it at all.

"Sorry, I guess I did laugh."

"You're forgiven." Emma winked at her. "What are you doing tomorrow morning? I don't have to be in the office right away. Do you want to stay over tonight, and we can grab breakfast tomorrow?"

"I can't," Hailey expressed. "I have a work dinner tonight. It's a farewell to the boss thing, and then I have coffee tomorrow."

"Coffee?"

"That Thursday thing I do with Ember and Charlie."

"Oh, right. We can skip tonight, and I can join you guys. I'd like to get to know them more," Emma offered.

"Sorry, no girls allowed." Hailey took a sip of the recently placed Diet Coke and looked up at the waitress.

"I do not understand that logic," Emma returned.

Hailey placed her own order, and Emma followed. The waitress wrote everything down, took their menus, and walked off.

"I mean, no *other* girls. We just say 'no girls allowed' because we're all gay, so there's no girlfriends or dates allowed." Hailey specifically added the part about dates because she and Emma had not discussed their current relationship status, and Hailey knew she wasn't ready for them to be girlfriends yet.

"Ah, I see. Well, never mind. I can get to know them some other time, then."

"I'll be wedding-planning at Ember and Eva's this weekend. We're kind of making a whole thing out of it. Charlie, me, Alyssa, and Hannah are renting a lake house. We are heading up there Friday night and staying until Sunday evening. It's like a wedding workshop, almost. But it will be fun."

"So, I won't get to see you until you get back?"

"I'm packing tomorrow night, but if you're free, you can come over and stay the night. I'm leaving straight after work. Ember is picking me up, and we're driving."

"I'd be happy to help you pack." Emma smiled. "Can I make you dinner?"

"Sure. That sounds nice," Hailey said and returned Emma's smile.

***

Charlie woke up on Thursday morning and sent a quick text to Ember. Then, she checked her messages and found she had a good morning text from Lena. They hadn't seen one another since Sunday morning. Lena was opening a new store in Evanston and had spent Monday through today there. The woman had been at the store pretty much non-stop and had gotten a hotel room instead of making the commute back and forth. They had plans to see one another that night, since Charlie would be out of town for the weekend. Charlie texted Lena back with a smile and a promise to call her later when she could.

The weekend away had been Ember's idea. She'd found a great deal online for a lake house and booked it without telling anyone, because they'd all already told her they were free to plan the wedding. Ember was paying for the place, so no one really had a problem making the commitment. But Charlie had not seen Hailey since last Friday night, and she wasn't sure how it would feel to be around the woman again. She was grateful that the others would be there, but it would still be strange for them, because the other four were coupled off. Charlie and Hailey were the two single girls of the group. Hell, for all she knew, maybe Hailey and Emma were officially back together, and Charlie would be the only single one there.

She liked Lena and wanted to see where it could go, but they'd only had two dates, and they hadn't even kissed yet. Charlie didn't mind that last part. She'd meant what she had said to Lena: she had no problem waiting. But she also wouldn't be calling Lena her girlfriend anytime soon. She knew that was more than okay with the hesitant Lena. Charlie's phone rang as she climbed out of bed, which was strange, because it was Ember calling her. It was very early, and Ember wasn't normally an early riser.

"Did morning sex wake you up early?" Charlie questioned into the phone.

"No, smart-ass," Ember replied. "I was working in my office when I got your text."

"One of those nights?" Charlie turned on the bathroom light.

Ember had nights every so often, where she would hole up in her office and scribble things only she understood on her massive chalkboard walls until someone – usually Eva now, stopped her with food and water. Or, Charlie guessed, probably also morning sex.

"Yeah. But why aren't you coming to coffee this morning? First you, and now Hailey? Did one of you get a cold and give it to the other one?"

"Hailey's not coming, either?" Charlie stopped squeezing toothpaste on her toothbrush while holding the phone between her shoulder and her cheek.

"No. She's respecting your space, I think," Ember stated and sounded a little frustrated.

"She told you?"

"Of course, she told me. She couldn't tell you."

"Em, it's just–"

"I know," Ember interrupted. "I know. You've gotten to the point where you can't take it anymore. I've been waiting for this for a while."

"You have?"

"Charlie, you've loved the girl forever. And you've watched her date woman after woman."

"But, why now?"

"The women she dated before were all wrong for her. You could deal with it because of that. But Emma is someone she's always talked about. Seeing them together, the other night, really freaked you out."

"I'm that transparent, huh? If that's so, why can't she see how I feel?"

"Why can't you just–"

"Tell her? We've been over this, Ember."

Ember sighed, "Hailey can't see it because you've always been in love with her."

"That doesn't–"

"Make sense? Yes, it does."

"Does Eva like it when you interrupt her?"

"I stopped doing that to her a while ago, because I want her to marry me," Ember retorted. "Hailey doesn't know any different, Charlie. You two have always been this close. It wasn't like you weren't into her, and then suddenly you were, and she could see the difference in your behavior even if you refused to tell her. Things have always been like this. Why do you think I keep getting on you to just tell her?"

"So you wouldn't have to keep my secret?"

"I told Eva. I'm good now," she replied. "We'll skip coffee today. I get that you need time, but she'll be there this weekend… Are you going to be okay? I'd say I'd cancel, but it's important to Eva. It's for our wedding, Charlie."

"I know. I wouldn't do anything to mess up your wedding, Em. I'll be okay."

"Even if she comes tomorrow and tells us she has a new girlfriend that is actually her old girlfriend?" Ember asked.

"Has she?"

"Jesus, Charlie! I don't know. I haven't talked to her this week. She's been busy, and so have I. That's why we have the weekly coffees, remember?"

"I know."

"Next week, no excuses."

"Understood," Charlie acquiesced. "I'll be there."

"Good. I'll see you tomorrow."

"Okay. Thanks, Em."

"You two are my friends, Charlie. I love you both."

"I know. I love you, too."

"Goodbye."

"Bye."

Charlie hung up the phone, placed it on the sink, and got ready for her day.

CHAPTER 9

HAILEY arrived at Emma's apartment building with the promised bottle of wine and headed to the third floor via the stairs, since, like Hailey, Emma lived in a walk-up with no elevator. Hailey decided to look into her finances and maybe have Ember take a glance at them, too, by the time she made it up the stairs. She needed a new apartment. She was tired of stairs. Maybe she could afford a nicer place, as Charlie suggested. The upside to living with that many stairs, though, was that her legs always looked really good.

"Hey." Emma opened the door before Hailey had a chance to knock. "Come on in."

"Thanks. This is for dinner." Hailey passed her the bottle and entered the apartment. "I've never been here before. That's weird. I feel like for as long as I've known you, I should have been to your place already."

"Well, I offered to let you come up a few times, but you declined, Hailey Grant." Emma watched Hailey remove her jacket and smiled at the threadbare jeans with holes in the knees and an old green T-shirt with a long sleeve and a white shirt under it. "You look adorable," she shared. "Thanks for coming over. I know you needed to pack. Let me give you the tour."

Hailey took a quick look around the space. The front door led you right into the living room, which was ahead and to the left. Emma had a comfortable-looking couch against the back wall, with a large canvas image of some European city over it. Hailey didn't recognize it, and her eyes moved to the small flat screen on an old TV stand, made for the older-model bulky television sets. There were two bookshelves anchored to the wall. One had actual books on it, and the other had odds and ends, like candles and other more decorative items. Hailey smirked, because Emma had never been a big reader. She was very good in school and studied hard, but she wasn't someone who bought books to read when she didn't have to. That, at least, was still the same. The coffee table looked new. The room was too small for a chair or any other spaces to sit on beyond the couch. Emma set the bottle of wine on the coffee table, and Hailey dropped her coat over the couch, along with her purse, and followed Emma toward the kitchen, which was on the other side of a wall and was a tunnel-style kitchen, with little to no room for two people to work in comfortably.

"Nice," Hailey told her.

"It's small. You don't have to lie." Emma smiled at her and took her by the hand. "I chose the government job, which doesn't exactly make me a millionaire, but I like this place enough to keep resigning the lease. I don't need much room for just me," she explained. "And this is the bathroom." Emma pointed at the room just to the right of the bedroom. It was also small, with one sink, but Hailey admired how the woman had decorated it with different bright colors to make it appear homey. "And this is the bedroom, obviously," she explained and let Hailey's hand go as Hailey walked in past her.

The bedroom was clean. Emma had a nice taste. Her bedroom furniture was something Hailey would have picked out for her own bedroom, had she lived in an apartment with an actual bedroom that had walls. The bed was a queen, and there was an even smaller TV in the corner, resting on a table that was meant for the other side of the bed and matched the one that was on the side that Emma probably slept on. There was a wide, short bookshelf that was on the wall opposite the bed, and it was filled with books of varying topics, shapes, and sizes.

"You read?" Hailey asked her as she took it in.

"Yes, Hailey." Emma laughed. "I do read. Was there some doubt that I was literate?"

Hailey glanced back at her.

"No. You just never used to read anything outside of what was required for school."

"Well, most of those are kind of required for my job. They keep me up to date on the field. But some are just for fun. I got into the habit of buying airport books when I was traveling a lot a few years ago."

"Airport books?" Hailey laughed a little and walked back toward her.

"Yeah, books you would likely not buy, but you have a long layover and need something to do, so you go to the airport store and find a book to read. Probably half of those are airport books."

"And you've read them all?"

"Most of them, yeah." Emma replied, looking very confused at Hailey, and then walked them back toward the living room. "So, what made you change our plans? We were supposed to do this at your place."

"I got done with work a little early and missed traffic, so I was able to get my packing done. I thought I'd come over here, and we could hang out. Then, I'd go home."

"So, you're not staying over?" Emma questioned and grabbed the bottle of wine off the table to carry it into the kitchen to open, while Hailey stayed at the entrance of the kitchen so as not to crowd it.

"No. I'm taking the train in tomorrow. My place is closer to work than your place."

Emma opened the bottle and then turned to stir a pot of something on the stove.

"Okay, next time then," she suggested. "I made beef stroganoff. I hope that's okay."

"Your dad's recipe?" Hailey got excited.

Emma laughed at her reaction.

"Yes, Hails. I remembered how much you used to like it when you came over."

"What can I do to help?" Hailey asked.

"Nothing. It's done. I made it last night and just had to reheat it. Go sit down." Emma motioned with her head toward the four-person round dining room table behind Hailey.

Hailey grabbed the wine bottle and the glasses, which Emma had out already, and carried them to the table. While Emma dished out bowls in the kitchen, Hailey poured them wine. She deposited the bottle back in the kitchen and helped carry in the bread basket that Emma had prepared, while Emma followed her to the table.

"How was work?" Hailey asked as she spooned her food, trying to get it to cool down before taking a bite.

"It's good. I saw Charlie today," Emma revealed and took a sip of her wine.

"You did?"

"We're working on that project together, so… I'll probably see her a lot over the next few months."

"Oh, I forgot about that," Hailey returned and decided to burn her tongue on the food.

Once the initial shock wore off, Hailey was brought back immediately to Emma's father, making this for them on cold nights when Hailey would stay for dinner.

"I don't think she likes me," Emma explained and sat forward, placing her glass on the table.

"Why do you think that?" Hailey glared at her with confusion.

"I don't know. I guess I shouldn't say that. I know she's your friend, but this is a work thing. She's probably just trying to do her job."

"Charlie has this thing at work: she's professional to a fault. She's always been like that," Hailey offered. "It comes from the city planning office. They have all these rules about fraternization and ethics. She just held on to them when she left. It was funny, because when she first joined the firm, it took her months before she'd wear anything that wasn't business casual; and they're jeans and T-shirt kind of a place." Hailey laughed at the memory. "She showed up every day super early, wearing at least khakis and a button-down, or something even more professional. She would be the only person there for, like, two hours, and would be the best dressed. It took forever to wear her down and get her to relax a little."

"Then, I'm sure that's what it is. She was just very focused on the work. I thought that since you and I are together, she'd look at it a little differently." Emma took a bite.

"Together?" Hailey checked.

"Sorry, I didn't mean *together*. I just meant that we are... I don't know. What are we doing, Hailey? Normally, I wouldn't ask. But you and I were more than together before. I know it was a while ago, but it's easy to just call it that now."

"I'm not ready for that, Em," Hailey said quickly. "I like this. I like what we're doing. But I'm not ready to call us a couple."

"Okay," Emma said. "Can I ask why, though? I'm just curious to know why you're not."

Hailey kept her spoon in her bowl.

"Because we're still getting to know one another." Hailey glanced toward the living room. "I was looking at your shelves in there, thinking about how you still weren't a big reader... Then, I walked into your bedroom, and it's filled with books."

"So, you don't like readers? Got it," Emma jested.

"I know it's silly, but it's something that's changed about you. I don't care either way; read or don't read. It's just something different that I want to learn as we keep going with this before we call it serious."

"Okay. That makes sense," Emma agreed. "Can I ask you a question, though?"

"Sure."

"Are you seeing anyone else?" Emma braved and took a drink of the wine.

"No. Are you?"

"No," Emma replied just as quickly.

"I can't guarantee I won't, Em. I don't have any plans to, but if something happens..."

"I get it," Emma told her. "Can you just be honest with me as we go? I'm kind of all in right now. I understand that you need time. I have no problem giving it to you. But I don't think I can see anyone else right now. I just feel like I know what I want, and that's you. But, if you aren't thinking the same thing, I want you to tell me *if* and *when* you figure that out. If you do meet someone, I'd like to know. You don't have to give me details or anything... I know I don't want those."

Hailey nodded at her and then took another bite, admiring Emma's ability to mimic her father's recipe successfully.

"Tell me something else," Hailey said after a moment.

"About?"

"Anything. Tell me something else that's changed since we were together."

"Oh. Well, that's a while ago." Emma thought for a moment. "I changed toothpastes." She smiled.

Hailey laughed at her and continued eating.

***

Charlie wasn't seeing Lena before the weekend away, after all.

"I'm so sorry," Lena told her over the phone. "I'm stuck here until tomorrow, at least. I haven't even had time to eat lunch, and I should be eating dinner now," she revealed. "The store manager we hired needs a lot of micromanaging right now. It's his first store, and he doesn't know what he's doing. I'm considering firing him and starting over at this point."

"It's okay. I understand," Charlie told her. "I'll be back Sunday night. I'll probably be exhausted, but we can play it by ear. I can call you. Maybe we can grab dinner or something."

"That sounds good," Lena replied. "That would be our third date, right?"

Charlie smirked at herself, knowing where this was going.

"Yes, it will be our third date."

Lena had jokingly asked her on the phone one night, if the third date rule applied to lesbians as well. They'd both laughed. Charlie told her she would have no problem if it did, but also that if it didn't, that would be okay, too.

"Thank you for being patient with me and dealing with my newness to all of this. I really wanted to see you tonight."

"I wanted to see you, too."

"Shit!" Lena exclaimed.

"Everything okay?" Charlie checked.

"Yeah, it's just that someone else is calling."

"Work?"

"No, it's not work." Lena let out a long breath. "You know how you're the first woman I ever asked out?"

"Yes."

"Well, there was one woman who asked *me* out," she said and seemed to be waiting for Charlie to say something, and when Charlie didn't, she continued, "Her name is Mara. I met her at the gym a few weeks ago."

"Oh. What did you say?"

"I said no at the time, but then I saw her again, and she asked me again. I gave her my number because I didn't know what else to do. She called once while I was in a meeting, so I didn't answer. She also didn't leave a message, so I didn't call back."

"And she's calling again now?"

"She just hung up, but… I guess."

"Are you going to call her back?" Charlie asked.

"Should I?"

"That's not really a question I can answer for you, Lena. Do you like her?"

"I hardly know her. She's nice. She's a social worker. She has a cat. That's about as much as I know about her, outside of the fact that she goes to the gym four days a week."

"If you want to call her, you should call her."

Charlie didn't know what else to say. Lena was new to dating women, and Charlie wasn't ready to say they had anything exclusive. They had only been on two dates. And while they were great dates, they hadn't even kissed yet, because Lena wanted to take things slow. Charlie didn't think it was fair of her to ask Lena not to call another woman back. Charlie had no intention of seeking other female companionship, but if a woman happened to strike her fancy in her desire to push Hailey Grant out of her heart and mind once and for all, she wouldn't say no to the possibility, either.

"You'd be okay with that?" Lena asked.

"We're just starting out. If you want to date other women, I'd understand that," Charlie stated.

"I might call her, but I don't know."

"Okay," Charlie told her.

"I should go. I have to grab something to eat before I pass out, and then I have a late meeting with a vendor."

"Lena, I don't–"

"It's okay," Lena interrupted. "I'm not upset. You're being completely logical. I understand, I promise. I just really do have to go."

"I'll call you, okay?" Charlie told her. "Sunday."

"Have fun this weekend."

Charlie had no reason to think Lena was upset by it. Her tone conveyed that she really did understand Charlie. Charlie, herself, didn't think she was being completely unreasonable in suggesting Lena call this Mara woman. Charlie remembered that after Julia, she kind of became a bit of a woman on a mission. She didn't sleep around or anything, but she would sneak into some gay clubs, after telling her mom she was sleeping over at a friend's house. She enjoyed getting to know different girls somewhat around her age. She had made out with a lot of them, she had also slept with a few, and she always considered that to be something she needed to do for herself. It sounded silly to her now, but she had been out for a long time. When she had fallen for

Hailey shortly after those experiences, the idea of sleeping around or even going out to meet different women and dating them at the same time just seemed wrong.

Charlie didn't like the idea of Lena dating someone else. She didn't want her to go out with Mara. And she certainly didn't want Lena's first kiss with a woman to be with someone else. But she also knew that this was Lena's journey to go on. If she liked Mara enough, and things went that way with them, then Charlie would have to deal with it. If she and Lena ever got to the point of exclusivity, it wouldn't matter anyway.

That was new. As Charlie sat on her couch, she realized that might be the first time she had even considered being in a relationship with another woman in a long time. Her previous relationships had always been with Hailey still in the back and, often times, the forefront of her mind. This was Charlie's first attempt at a concerted effort to not keep Hailey back there; to not compare Lena to Hailey in every way. She smiled at that revelation. She would be able to move on from Hailey after all.

Her thoughts did drift back to Hailey, though; when Charlie remembered she had seen and worked with Emma earlier that day. She'd done her best to remain professional, because that was what her job called for; but it had been hard, because Emma kept asking her questions about her personal life. She wanted to know about Hailey and their friendship, about Ember, and about Charlie herself. Emma seemed to think they were just two friends, meeting at a dilapidated building to talk about their personal lives, when all Charlie wanted to do was stop thinking about how her working on this project had brought Emma back into Hailey's life. Charlie didn't ask if they were together. She just assumed they were at least dating or trying to figure out if dating was on the horizon. Charlie knew she would hear more about it over the weekend, and she was dreading the drive to the lake house. It would only be about an hour, but Ember and Eva were picking them both up, which meant she and Hailey would be in the back seat. They would be spending the next two nights with their four shared friends. Charlie meant what she said, though. She wouldn't cause any problems for Ember's wedding. She'd put on a brave face, and she'd have fun, too. She had at least the prospect of Lena on Sunday and beyond, to help her through any talk of Hailey Grant and Emma Colton.

CHAPTER 10

HAILEY watched Ember pull up to the curb outside her office and saw Eva wave at her from the passenger's side. She noticed the back door open and saw Charlie get out. Her hair was getting longer. It was still a pixie cut, but it really did appear that the woman was growing it out. Hailey didn't say anything at first. She just watched Charlie take her roller bag and place it for her into the open trunk.

"Hey," Charlie greeted her after she closed the trunk, and Hailey walked to the open back door.

"Hi," Hailey returned unconfidently.

She hated this. They'd never been like this with one another.

"I promised Ember I wouldn't be an asshole this weekend."

"Were you planning on being an asshole before you made that promise?" Hailey questioned with a shy smile.

Charlie smiled back.

"Not technically, no." She then leaned against the side of the car between the trunk and the door, and said, "Hails, I'm sorry. I didn't mean to make you feel bad or anything. I just have some stuff—"

"To work out," Hailey completed for her. "Yeah, I remember."

"I'd like us to just be us this weekend, if that's possible."

"Us?" Hailey asked. "Friends again until you push me away as soon as Ember drops us off?"

"No, that's not..." Charlie was clearly trying to find a way to say something while Hailey just kept glaring at her quizzically.

"It's fine. Let's just be us this weekend. After that, you can go back to figuring things out by yourself."

"Hails…"

"Charlie, I'm fine. I just don't want to talk about this anymore. You've made your point. I'm trying to give you what you asked for. We also happen to be in this wedding, and we can't be a problem for Em and Eva, so I get it. Let's just go." Hailey climbed into the car and, thankfully, heard the radio blaring loudly.

She wasn't sure if it had been doing that before or if Ember or Eva turned it up when they started talking outside. As Charlie climbed in next to her, Hailey scooted over and away from her. Charlie pulled the door closed and stared out the side window.

"Hey, Hails," Ember greeted.

"Ready to get this wedding party started?" Eva turned and asked her with a smile.

"I am totally ready." Hailey smiled back, excited by her friend's upcoming nuptials.

"Then, let's get to it." Ember put the car in drive and moved them into traffic.

Hailey glanced over at Charlie, who appeared to be staring outside. Charlie must have felt her glance and turned to see her staring. Hailey offered her a sideways smile, which Charlie returned, but it clearly didn't meet the woman's eyes. *'And they were great eyes,'* Hailey thought to herself.

"It's not your fault," Charlie whispered to her, while Ember and Eva talked about something in the front seat.

"What's not?"

"What's going on with me; it's not your fault," Charlie explained. "I'm sorry if I made you feel that way."

Hailey leaned over until their faces were close enough to speak a little louder without drawing the attention of Ember or Eva.

"Why can't you tell me? You're the person I tell these things to. I thought I was your person."

Hailey watched as Charlie's dark eyes watched her own, then the woman lowered her gaze before lifting her eyes back up to meet Hailey's green ones again. Charlie's expression was something Hailey hadn't seen on her before. She couldn't identify it, but she loved the little glint of what appeared to be happiness, maybe, in Charlie's eyes.

"Hey, Alyssa and Hannah are already there," Eva proclaimed.

Hailey turned her attention to Eva, who had her phone in her hand and was staring at the message.

"They left earlier," Ember told her fiancée. "Tell them that the key to the place is in the mailbox and to go on in."

Eva began typing her reply.

"This is going to be fun," Eva stated after hitting send.

But as Hailey met Charlie's eyes again, she wasn't so sure.

***

"Okay. So, there are three bedrooms in this place," Ember began when they started removing bags from the car and carrying them inside. Alyssa and Hannah helped. "Eva and I are taking the master. Sorry, ladies," she proclaimed. "Alyssa and Han, you are in a room with the queen and sorry, Charlie and Hails, but you two have the twins." Ember shrugged at them as they entered the house.

It was a large two-story structure that looked like it belonged in any main street suburban neighborhood. It even had the shutters on the windows and the front porch. The foyer opened up to the wide staircase with a small loft at the top. There was a living room to the right that had a large fireplace with a stack of wood ready to go and what looked to be fairly comfortable furniture. To the left was the dining room, with a large oak table and eight chairs. Charlie couldn't see the kitchen initially, but as she dropped their stuff at the door, removed their winter gear, and headed past the staircase, she saw a kitchen with new appliances and old wallpaper with a 70s-style floral pattern. Charlie followed Ember out a backdoor off the kitchen, which led outside to a patio covered in snow. Through it, Charlie could see a covered grill, that probably got a lot of use during spring and summer months. And through some trees, that had long ago shed their leaves, she saw the lake itself. Charlie was cold, but she wanted to enjoy the view for a minute before heading back inside. She watched Eva come out to stand next to Ember and wrap her arms around her friend's body, while Ember put her own arm around Eva's shoulders and pulled the woman in a little to warm her up. Then, Charlie felt hands on her own hanging arms, sliding up and down at a rapid pace.

"You always get so cold." She heard Hailey's voice from behind her as she closed her eyes. This was not helping… "You should get your coat if you're going to stay out here," the woman added. "Remember when you nearly froze to death on that Michigan trip?"

"Yeah." Charlie took a step forward, severing the contact. "I'm going to unpack." She then walked around Hailey and back inside the house.

"Hey, are you two okay?" Hannah asked her when Charlie nearly passed her in the kitchen without saying anything.

"Yeah. Why?" Charlie questioned back.

"Just checking. You guys don't seem like your normal Charlie and Hailey selves."

"What does that mean?"

Alyssa made her way in, carrying a paper bag of groceries, and began removing items.

"I don't know… You're normally all smiles around each other, and there's this…"

"Banter," Alyssa finished her wife's sentence. "You guys banter a lot."

"Yeah, that's what it is," Hannah agreed and smiled at Alyssa.

"I'll give you a pick of the beds," Hailey said as she walked into the kitchen.

Charlie let out a deep breath.

"The one by the window," she returned and glanced over her shoulder at the girl with the green eyes.

"I knew it." Hailey pointed at her and then walked by into the hallway that would lead her to the stairs. "You're going to get cold," she reminded.

Charlie followed Hailey toward their bags, and they carried them up the stairs. They walked past one bedroom, that had a queen bed, and then past the master, which had a nice king bed and, likely, the master bath. On the right was the bathroom they would share with Alyssa and Hannah. The last door was their room. They walked in to see a room that looked like Charlie's grandmother had decorated it forty years ago. There were two ancient twin beds sharing a wall, and above each bed, there were picture frames that were made to look like a window with images of nature in its faux glass. There was an old man doll on one bed, leaning back against the pillow, and an old woman doll on the other. They both had glasses and appeared to be staring at them.

"That is some creepy shit," Charlie said.

"Do you think the place is haunted?" Hailey looked over at her and then at the room again.

"Don't joke about that," Charlie said and dropped her bag in front of the bed nearest the window.

She looked at the wide dresser with three drawers. The old-fashioned TV on top of it was so small, that even if it actually got HD, they wouldn't be able to see anything on it. Charlie wondered if it was more for decoration than anything else.

"You scared of ma and pa ghost dolls?" Hailey had the bed with the old man doll on it, and she held it up to look closer.

"Ghost dolls?" Charlie gulped at the creepy looking creature on her own bed.

Hailey walked over, picked up the doll of the old woman, and carried it over to the closet. She opened the door and set them on the floor before turning to face Charlie.

"I even made them face the wall. Just don't hang anything up in there, and you'll be fine." Hailey winked at her.

"Thanks."

Charlie walked over to the window and pulled back the curtain. Their room didn't face the lake directly, but it did have a nice view of evergreen trees. She could also see a squirrel scamper from one place to another, and that made Charlie smile.

"This place actually reminds me a little of your mom's place." Hailey sat on the edge of Charlie's bed behind Charlie near the window.

"This place is massive. My mom's place is a shack compared to this." Charlie turned to see Hailey there, with her hands clasped in her lap.

"Not the whole house," Hailey explained. "This room. It's a little like her guest room. She even had the twin beds with white bedspreads."

"Because she had this delusion that JJ and I would stay over more if she had a room for us." Charlie sat beside Hailey on the bed. "She kind of forgot JJ has a wife he'd probably bring along."

"It was a nice idea, though, and it worked for us," Hailey said.

"She tries," Charlie said of her mother.

Then, she stood and began unpacking her bag. She placed the few items she had brought for two days into the top drawer in front of her bed. Hailey did the same with the top drawer on the right. A few minutes later, they made their way back down the stairs to hear laughter in the kitchen and headed that way.

"What's so funny?" Charlie asked.

"Nothing," Alyssa said and pointed a baguette at Hannah, as if to keep her from answering the question.

"Babe, it was funny." Hannah laughed more. "When we were on our honeymoon, this one here, tried to dive into the water and ended up belly-flopping. It was hilarious."

"It hurt, Han." Alyssa gave her puppy-dog eyes.

"You had to be the badass diver." Hannah kissed her wife's cheek.

Ember and Eva made their way into the kitchen.

"So, I'm thinking dinner first and then planning fun," Eva suggested while rubbing her hands together quickly.

"Seconded," Ember agreed with her. "I'm cooking, because none of you can, but I'm putting Charlie on table duty and Hails on wine pouring duty. Hannah and Alyssa are in charge of the salad, and my wife-to-be, here, is in charge of cutting this bread."

"Always the restaurant manager," Charlie said in Ember's direction.

***

The six of them went through the motions of creating dinner and keeping polite conversation, but Hailey couldn't focus on the topics being tossed out. She kept glancing in Charlie's direction, wondering what was going through the woman's mind. Hailey then started to wonder more if what she'd said before had even been true. She had thought they'd always shared everything with one another because she'd always shared everything with Charlie. But, now that she was seeing this version of Charlie – the perpetual bad mood Charlie, Hailey considered that maybe more of the bad moods had just been Charlie keeping things to herself. That terrified her. She wanted to be Charlie's person; the one she shared everything with and withheld nothing from. She looked around and knew that Ember had found that person in Eva. Hailey even knew from her short time of being friends with Hannah and Alyssa, that they had found that in one another, too.

"Huh?" she uttered to herself, standing next to Charlie while she put the napkins on the table, and Hailey set the now empty bottle of red wine down.

"What?" Charlie questioned.

Hailey realized she'd said that out loud and looked wide-eyed at Charlie.

"Oh, something for work. I just remembered."

"Okay." Charlie sat down in her chair, and the others followed in.

Hailey sat down next to her and chanced a look in the woman's direction, while Charlie was helping Ember set down their dinner. She was Charlie's best friend and would always be close to her. She would always be important to Charlie. But, eventually, Charlie would find a girlfriend, and then a fiancée, and a wife. That woman would become Charlie's person. Hailey took a long gulp of her water and thought about how that would change their relationship. She then lowered her head as she recalled the fact that Charlie had a date a week ago, and she had no clue how it had gone.

***

"So, we're thinking about simple, flowing dresses, with the same color on both sides," Eva began. "Accents in jewelry, but just simple stuff. Neither of us really wants a big wedding. But we want to give this to our families and have some of ourselves in it, too, obviously."

The six of them sat in the living room. Ember and Eva were sitting on the sofa, while Hannah was sitting on the floor in front of Alyssa, between the woman's legs. Charlie was on the floor across from them, wrapping a blanket around her body.

"Where's Hailey?" she asked when she noticed Hailey was missing.

"Here." Hailey entered the room. "I was looking for the fireplace lighter. Found it in the kitchen." She held up the long lighter.

Charlie watched as Hailey loaded several logs into the fire, along with a starter log that had been provided by the homeowners, and lit it. The fire started off small. Hailey knelt in front of it, supplying it with helpful oxygen until it took hold. She set the lighter on the floor and returned to sit next to Charlie.

"You looked cold," Hailey explained, then smiled a quick smile in Charlie's direction, and returned her attention to Eva.

***

"Should we try to see what channels we can get on this thing?" Charlie proposed as she leaned down and stared at the tiny TV with old antennas.

"I bet we can get American Band Stand on it," Hailey teased and tossed Charlie a hoodie that hit her in the back, causing Charlie to flinch.

"Hey!" Charlie exclaimed and turned to pick it up off the floor.

"You're going to get cold by the window. You always do. You never listen to me. I'd offer you my bed, but you won't take it."

"I'll be fine."

"You're like a broken record. I read this study about prolonged exposure to cold and how it changes the actual structure of your brain," Hailey began.

Charlie tossed the hoodie back onto Hailey's bed and listened to her talk about the study. It had been a while since she had brought one up, and it was oddly comforting. They talked for only a few more minutes before they each decided they needed to get some sleep after their long workdays and their eventful evening of wedding-planning. Charlie turned the light off for them, lay back down, and rolled on her side, facing the window.

***

Charlie woke up shivering in the middle of the night. She hated that Hailey was right and would not admit it to her. She should have accepted the damn hoodie. She wondered if Hailey was asleep. She had her own sweatshirt in her drawer. Charlie could get up, grab it, and climb back into bed. She heard her teeth chatter and hated the lack of insulation that, apparently, was a problem in this house during winter. Although, not many people have likely vacationed on this particular lake during this time of year. Her blanket then lifted behind her, and Charlie felt the press of a warm body against her.

"Hey, it's okay." Hailey wrapped an arm around her stomach and drew Charlie back into her. "I told you this would happen."

"I'm okay. I just need a sweater," Charlie protested, but as she felt the warmth of Hailey's body, she knew she needed it.

"You're too far gone, Charlie. Come on." Hailey used the hand on Charlie's stomach to coax Charlie into rolling over. "You know you either need some body heat or a hot shower. What's it going to be?" Hailey asked.

Charlie gulped and shivered again before rolling over to face Hailey. Hailey smiled at her, concerned, wrapped an arm around Charlie, and pulled her closer.

"Why didn't you listen to me?" Hailey asked.

"Because I'm stubborn," Charlie admitted.

"You always have been," Hailey agreed and ran her hand up and down Charlie's back rapidly, to try to increase circulation. "Put your feet on my feet."

"No way, Hails."

"Charlie, they're freezing. Do it."

"You'll freeze."

"No, I won't. Of the two of us, you're always the one that's cold, and I'm the one that warms you up. I also protect you from the ghost dolls, that I know you're still scared of, and I'm the one that left the hall light on, and the door open just a crack so that you wouldn't be in the dark tonight."

Charlie took in Hailey's green eyes.

"Which one am I? Besides the one that gets cold..."

"You're the one that makes me coffee and buys my cereal. You're the one that opens doors and helps me with my coat. And–" Hailey then stopped herself, and Charlie wondered what was in her changed expression.

"And?"

Hailey considered something.

"The one that always lets me sleep on her couch because it's super comfortable."

Charlie just nodded. She had stupidly hoped for something more and would kick her own ass, if she could, for even thinking that Hailey might say something a little deeper than she's allowed to stay over on Charlie's couch when she wants.

"Right." Charlie pulled back slightly. "I think I'm going to take that shower."

"It's the middle of the night, Charlie."

Charlie pulled back all the way and missed the heat from Hailey's body instantly. She stood and hated herself for doing that, because it was freezing in the room once she was out from under the blanket.

"It's the only way I'll warm up. You should go back to sleep. Sorry I woke you up." Charlie walked off toward the bathroom.

She closed the door behind herself and let out a long sigh before she walked to the shower and turned on the water. She waited until it was near scalding before stripping off her clothes and climbing inside. The heat of the water, combined with her near frozen form, made her feel like she was being pricked with a thousand needles. Charlie wanted to climb out immediately, but she also knew she needed this. Her body was too cold. She should have known better, but she'd been stubborn and would have to deal with the pain. Charlie pressed both hands against the wall and faced the stream. She wished she could take a cold shower, because there were other parts of her body that were plenty hot and in need of cooling down. She could feel that pleasant and common ache between her legs that came with her feelings for Hailey. Charlie wished she could do something about it, like she had done so many times before, but she wouldn't dare do that in this shower, knowing Hannah and Alyssa were on one side of the wall, and the object of her affection was on the other.

So, instead, Charlie just used the water to warm her

body. Once she felt like every bit of the cold was gone, she turned off the water and wrapped herself with a towel. She dried off quickly and put her clothes back on.

***

Hailey stared at the ceiling above her bed. It was one of those waffle ceilings. And with the light on in the hallway, she was able to make out patterns and pictures in it. She saw a face, and a dog, and maybe a kite. She was doing this to try to keep her mind off of what just happened. She had done that with Charlie before. Charlie was the cold one. She always had been. Hailey had warmed her up like that before.

But, this time, there was something different about it. Hailey closed her eyes, formed her mouth into the shape of an 'O,' and then let out a focused deep breath. She was turned on. She was turned on by her best friend in the world; by Charlie. She had felt Charlie's body pressed against her own and saw this look in the woman's eyes that just made her forget what she was about to say in that moment.

"Hey." Charlie entered the room and immediately grabbed at the hoodie that was still on Hailey's bed.

"Feel better?" Hailey managed.

"Yeah, I'll be fine with this. Sorry. Get some sleep."

Charlie slid the sweater over her head, and Hailey averted her eyes, because when Charlie raised her arms, she revealed a small amount of skin between her shirt and her sweats. What the hell was happening?

Charlie closed the door all the way, leaving only the light from under the door, which Hailey thought was a little strange, given Charlie's need for more light than that.

"You can leave it open."

"It's fine." Charlie slid under her blanket. "Night, Hails."

"Night."

Hailey did not fall asleep. It appeared that Charlie did;

but Hailey remained awake for at least the next hour, trying to figure out what had just happened. She finally rolled on her other side, facing away from Charlie, and stared at her phone. She had exchanged a few texts with Emma since she had gotten to the lake house. She smiled at Emma's use of emoticons, like a thirteen-year-old, and tried to focus more on the girl she was dating than the best friend she could not have these thoughts about.

When Hailey woke up, Charlie was already gone from their shared room. She made her way to the bathroom first, to perform her morning routine, and then proceeded downstairs. Ember was in the kitchen, sitting at the table and scribbling something in a notebook. Charlie was pouring a cup of coffee at the old-style machine.

"Morning," she offered them both.

"Hey." Ember didn't look up. "Sorry, in the middle of a thing."

"She's geniusing right now," Charlie offered. "Here." She passed the coffee cup to Hailey.

"I'm okay." Hailey tried to hand it back to her.

"I'm the coffee maker, remember?" Charlie winked at her.

Hailey smiled and nodded, "Thanks."

"Morning." Eva walked into the room and approached Ember. She kissed the top of Ember's head and left her hand on her fiancée's back. "Babe, are you good?"

"Just... like, ten minutes."

"She'll be another hour," Eva said to Charlie and Hailey.

Hailey wondered when exactly it happened that Eva knew more about their best friend than they did.

"Ten minutes," Ember repeated as she scribbled.

"Okay, babe." Eva rolled her eyes and leaned back down. "I love you."

"Love you, too," Ember muttered and went back to work.

"We should probably leave her alone. She'll be done

faster that way," Eva said.

"Hannah and Alyssa said they want to go for a hike. They found a trail and want to bundle up and take it," Charlie announced.

"Babe, do you want to go for a hike when you're done?" Eva asked Ember.

"Sure," Ember replied and finally looked up at all of them. "Oh. Hey, guys," the woman said like she finally just realized they were all there.

Hailey and Charlie laughed.

"I don't think I'd survive. I get cold in the bedroom, so I'd probably die of hypothermia out there," Charlie shared.

"Hails?" Eva questioned.

Hailey considered leaving the house to get a few hours away from Charlie, to try to sort out her thoughts, but she also knew she wouldn't really get the chance to do that, with the rest of them around. She would have to focus on the other four of them and participate in the conversation instead. Charlie had turned back to the coffee pot to pour herself a cup.

"I think I'll stay back, too," she said after a moment.

Charlie stopped moving for a moment, and Hailey thought she'd made a mistake. Charlie had asked her for space. Hailey had been determined to give it to her, but last night, she had woken up to the sound of her best friend shivering to try to keep warm, and she knew how to fix her. This morning, she should have just said she'd go on a damn hike, to give Charlie some time alone. But she'd said no because she wanted to spend time with her. She hoped Charlie would reveal what was actually going on.

"Eight minutes," Ember said.

Hailey noticed she had returned to her notebook and to her scribbling of complex math equations no one else in this house would ever understand.

"I'm going to go sit by the fire," Charlie said and carried her coffee to the living room.

Hailey stood there, watching Eva massage Ember's hunched-over shoulders, before leaving them alone to go back upstairs. She showered, dressed, dried her hair, and then returned downstairs to find that the others were already gone. Hailey was determined again. She would leave Charlie alone the entire time the rest of them would be gone. She headed into the kitchen and grabbed a banana before heading into the dining room. She scrolled through some emails on her phone for a while and then put her headphones in to listen to some music. That got her through about fifteen minutes. She thought about calling or texting Emma but didn't know what to say. She didn't have any updates to provide, and it was somewhat early for the weekend. Emma might still be asleep. Hailey didn't want to wake her up for no good reason. So, she went back up the stairs and found an old collection of *The Baby-Sitters Club* books in the closet she had shoved the creepy dolls in. She loved those books as a kid and picked the one on the top to start reading.

***

"You are avoiding me," Charlie stated as she leaned in the doorway.

Hailey closed the book and looked at her.

"You avoided me first," she said.

"That's fair." Charlie nodded.

"I was trying to give you space, like you wanted."

"I know. It's weird here, though, with just the two of us; I'm down there, and you're up here." She approached Hailey's bed. "What are you reading?"

Hailey smiled and held up the book.

"There were a bunch of them in the closet. I thought I'd time-travel back to my youth."

Charlie made her way over to the side of Hailey's bed and took the book from her to review.

"I was more of a *Hardy Boys* fan, myself," Charlie revealed.

"You didn't read *The Baby-Sitters Club*?" Hailey was almost offended by Charlie's gross oversight.

"No. I pretty much steered clear of those and *Nancy Drew*. I read *Goosebumps* and *The Hardy Boys*, mostly. Is that a problem? Is our friendship over now?" she joked.

"I'll make an exception for you." Hailey mock-glared at her. "Do you want one to read? The rest are in the closet."

"I'm okay." Charlie shook her head no.

"You don't want to go in the closet, do you? You're afraid of those stupid dolls," she suggested.

"They're dolls, Hails. I am not afraid of them."

"Yes, you are." Hailey sat up and hung her legs over the side of the bed and in front of Charlie.

"I am a grown woman. I am not afraid of dolls that look like they were based on real-life people that used to live here, probably died, their spirits moved inside the dolls, and they don't want people in their family home. They spent last night murmuring to one another, trying to plot our deaths."

Hailey laughed loudly and tossed the book aside.

"You *are* scared of the dolls!" she exclaimed and reached out to tug mockingly on Charlie's T-shirt, pulling the woman just a step closer to herself as she stared up at her.

"They're really creepy, Hails," Charlie said.

Hailey thought she sounded adorable. She stopped mocking and smiling and stared up at Charlie's face. Her expression was soft, and her eyes were warm. She lowered her eyes to Charlie's near-full lips and watched Charlie lick them with her tongue. She took in the woman's strong jawline and her throat, and continued moving her glance down to Charlie's breasts, that were slightly larger than her own. Hailey could tell she wasn't wearing a bra, thanks to the chill in the room, and she lowered her eyes even more to Charlie's hands at her sides, which she took in her own without even thinking about it and then linked their fingers together. As her eyes moved back up to Charlie's now surprised expression, Hailey saw a visible gulp in the woman's throat.

'She doesn't want this,' Hailey thought. Charlie was freaking out, because this was different than other touches they've shared, and she didn't want this. Did Hailey want this?

"I'll protect you," she finally said, referring to the dolls in the closet.

"You will?" Charlie asked as if she was really concerned Hailey wouldn't protect her.

It wasn't just about the dolls, though, Hailey surmised.

"Charlie..." Hailey started and stood, keeping their hands linked as she did.

"Hey, we're back!"

Someone's voice came from downstairs, but Hailey wasn't sure which woman it belonged to. She pulled her hands away from Charlie's and watched Charlie step away entirely before the woman turned and left the room without a word.

CHAPTER 11

CHARLIE needed to leave that room. Hailey didn't get it. She just didn't understand what she did to Charlie, and Charlie couldn't be around her right now. She made her way downstairs and found her phone on the coffee table in the living room. She knew there were few places she could go to find privacy in a house with six women in it, so she went out to Ember's car with the keys, and warmed it up while finding the contact she was looking for.

"Hey. I didn't expect to hear from you today," Lena greeted her.

"I know. I just had a free minute, so I thought I'd see how it went, wrapping things up in Evanston."

"Oh, it was fine. I got back last night. I'll have to go back again, for the grand opening, but it should be okay for now. And the pitch is going to be approved, by the way."

"It is?" Charlie asked.

"Should I tell you that? I don't know what the protocol is here. We're kind of seeing each other, but you also work for the firm, and it's my company's decision."

"I honestly don't know. I won't say anything to my boss, though. I wouldn't want you to get into trouble." Charlie smiled.

"Oh, well, thank you." Lena laughed. "So, how are things there? How goes the planning?"

"Well, they have the colors chosen, and cake flavors have been determined."

"Oh, yeah? Which ones?" Lena asked.

"They're going to do red velvet for a layer and vanilla with some kind of filling. But that has yet to be determined. They'll go cake-tasting in Iowa – where the event will take place, to finalize it. But Ember is a sucker for red velvet. Eva said her family is pretty basic, taste-wise, so she suggested just plain white."

"Sounds good."

"Yeah. So, what are you up to today?"

Lena took a moment.

"I called Mara last night on my way home."

"Oh."

Well, that answered Charlie's question she had been avoiding asking.

"I wasn't going to call her, but… I don't know."

"It's okay," Charlie told her. "It's weird, but it's okay. I get it."

"We're going for coffee in a couple of hours."

"See? I already feel better. She just gets coffee. And I got an actual dinner date," Charlie deflected.

Lena laughed an awkward laugh.

"Should I not have told you? I'm new at this, too. Even when I dated guys, I never dated two at once."

"No, it's fine. It's strange for me, because I like you, but I want you to pursue this, if you like her, too."

"I don't know how I feel about her. I kind of feel like I should meet with her and see if there is something. There probably isn't. I'll be able to move on, and things won't be awkward at the gym, where I run into her at least three times a week."

"That makes a lot of sense."

"But… I want to see you tomorrow night."

"I'll call you when I get back. You wanna come over?"

"Yeah, that would be nice."

"Okay. I should get going. They're calling me back to the planning table," Charlie lied.

"I'm glad you called," Lena said.

"Me too. Have a good day."

"Have fun planning."

Charlie hung up the phone but stayed in the car. She wasn't sure how she felt, knowing that Lena was going on a date with someone else, now that it was a reality. It was awkward, to be on the phone with someone you were dating as they talked about dating someone else. She liked Lena, but she had to admit she didn't know the woman all that well yet. The date with Mara wasn't a big deal. It was coffee. They might hate each other when it ended. They also might be in love by the end of the date. Charlie wasn't entirely sure which scenario she preferred.

***

Hailey kept a close eye on Charlie as the woman sat on the opposite side of the room, absorbed in a bridal magazine Eva was pointing to. Ember was chatting with Hannah and Alyssa about something, and Hailey was just observing the whole thing. They'd planned before lunch and then after lunch. It was getting late, and Hailey was tired.

"I'm going to head up." She stood.

"Okay," Ember said.

"Good night," Eva stated and looked up at her.

"Yeah, night," Hannah said, and Alyssa echoed with a nod.

Charlie looked up at her and smiled a goodnight, that Hailey thought felt a little awkward and maybe forced. She assumed Charlie would go up with her, but she had been wrong. She made her way upstairs, took care of things in the bathroom, and then climbed under the blanket to get warm.

"Hey, I'm just going to grab some stuff." Charlie came in and headed toward the drawer where she'd stuffed her things.

"What are you grabbing?" Hailey wondered.

"The rest are going to bed, too, so I'm just going to sleep on the couch downstairs."

"What? Why?" Hailey sat up in bed.

"The fireplace. It's a lot warmer down there." Charlie grabbed a sweater out of the drawer and closed it. "I'll see you in the morning."

Hailey didn't say anything. She just nodded. She heard Charlie in the bathroom for the next several minutes as the other women made their way upstairs, talking and laughing. She didn't know when Charlie headed downstairs, but she heard Hannah and Alyssa talking in the bathroom, so she assumed Charlie was already down there.

Hailey turned the bedroom light back on. She wasn't tired, after all. She took out her phone and sent Emma a quick goodnight message, just to have something to do. They had done that when they were younger. Texting wasn't common when they were dating, but they called each other every night just to say goodnight. It was one of the first things to go when Emma went to school. They had tried in the beginning, but once Emma got busy with classes and then met a new group of friends, the goodnight calls got later and later, and Hailey needed to be asleep for school the next day. After that, they were only on the weekends, and Emma wasn't actually going to sleep. She was just calling to tell Hailey goodnight. Eventually, the calls ended without either of them saying anything to the other about it. It had become understood that neither of them had the time or the desire to try to keep up with them. That was one of the things that had hurt Hailey the worst. She and Emma had talked about everything back then. Yet, something so integral to their relationship like talking for a few minutes every night, had ended without one of them saying a word about it ending. Neither had told the other that they thought they should pick back up again, nor had they just admitted that they were done with that part of their relationship.

Hailey grabbed the book she had been reading earlier and turned to where she left off. She hadn't brought her computer and was regretting that now. She wasn't a fan of surfing the internet or playing games on her phone, because she had read a study about the fact that humans will likely have massive eyes in a thousand years, thanks to evolution and the small screens people stare at all day now. She only did it when she needed to, but avoided it when she could.

Not long into reading did she hear someone moving downstairs and determined that Charlie was still awake.

She held the book in her lap for another moment before deciding to go downstairs and check on her. She wouldn't interfere with her alone time. She just wanted to make sure she was okay. She padded down the stairs in heavy socks, so as not to be heard, and leaned over the railing to see Charlie sitting up on the couch, appearing to be staring at the fireplace, which had nothing more than still burning ashes now.

"I know you're there, Hails." Charlie's voice invaded the silence.

"How did–"

"You always think you're quieter than you actually are." Charlie still hadn't turned around. "Plus, there's a mirror above the fireplace, dumb-ass," Charlie joked.

Hailey lifted her eyes to see that there was indeed a small mirror leaning on the mantle as a decoration, and Charlie could see her, thanks to the angle.

"Oh, right." Hailey looked down, a little embarrassed. "I just wanted some water and didn't want to wake you," she lied, thinking that was better than confessing that she wanted to check on her. "Can't sleep?"

"I'm just not tired, I guess." Charlie still hadn't turned, but their eyes were meeting through the mirror, so it didn't matter.

Hailey walked the rest of the way down the stairs and into the living room.

"Me neither," she shared.

"You're still reading that?" Charlie pointed at the book Hailey was still holding.

"Oh, I didn't mean to bring it with me." Hailey looked down. "I was bored." She shrugged.

"What is it that you liked about those books so much as a kid?"

Hailey sat on the floor in front of the couch, feeling that it would be better to keep a little distance between them, since she had invaded Charlie's requested space yet again.

"I didn't have a lot of friends at that age. I had some, but we weren't close. These girls are all like sisters. I guess I liked that. I didn't even have a sister to be sisters with."

"I used to think I wanted a sister," Charlie offered.

She slid on the sofa, so she was lying down on her side facing Hailey now.

"Yeah?"

"I was like nine or something. JJ was being an asshole. I thought it would have been better if I just had an older sister. Then, I thought that I'd rather have a younger sister that I could be the older sister for." Charlie lowered her head against the small pillow. "Then, I realized that would mean there would be another mouth to feed, and things were already hard for us, so I nixed that idea."

Hailey brought her knees in and wrapped her arms around them.

"You never told me that before."

"What? That I wanted a sister for a day?"

"That you used to think about things like that? The money and stuff."

"Oh, I guess not. When you don't have a lot of it, even when your parents are doing everything they can to cover that fact up, it's kind of obvious – when you go to school and the other kids are wearing brand new clothes on the first day, with their school supplies all bright and shiny, ready for use, and you're in thrift store-bought shirts and jeans, with your brother's old, beat up trapper keeper."

"I bet your mom is really proud of you, Charlie," Hailey offered with a smile on her face.

"Why?"

"Look at all you've accomplished," Hailey said and tilted her head at her. "You put yourself through college; you have a kick-ass job that affords you an awesome apartment. And I know you send money to her every month, and you buy your brother stuff that he needs, instead of sending him money, because he has too much pride to admit that he needs help sometimes. You call them gifts so that he doesn't feel like it's charity and turn it away," she added. "You're an amazing person, Charlie Adams."

Charlie rolled onto her back.

"Will you read me a few pages?"

"Of the book?" Hailey questioned the deflection.

"Yeah, you seem to love it so much. Read me a page or two, and I'll tell you if you're crazy." She smiled at the ceiling.

"I haven't read to you since that time you got sick."

"Yeah, and you did voices for all the characters," Charlie recalled and laughed lightly so as not to make too much noise.

Hailey smiled at the old memory. Back in the day, when Charlie got incredibly sick and could hardly move, Hailey stayed at her place for over a week to help take care of her and worked from there as much as she could. Charlie's eyes wouldn't focus, and she was bored to tears just lying in bed, so Hailey offered to read to her instead of Charlie downloading audiobooks. She had argued that Charlie shouldn't buy an audiobook for a book she already owned, because that was just fiscally irresponsible. They'd shared a laugh about that comment that ended with Charlie in a coughing fit, and Hailey had offered to read the book to her instead. They did it a chapter at a time. Hailey made sure to use different voices for each character, and she loved Charlie's reactions to some of the accents she tried and her embellishments in some moments.

"I'll read you the first chapter. No voices, though. I do *not* have the energy for that tonight," Hailey said after a moment.

She opened the book and began reading. As she continued reading, she would lift her eyes every few minutes to see that Charlie was still staring at the ceiling. When Hailey finished the chapter, she looked up again and saw that Charlie's eyes were closed. She looked so peaceful like that. Her hands were at her sides, and one leg was crossed over the other. Hailey set the book on the table and reached over Charlie, standing as she did so. She pulled the blanket down on top of her, making sure not to wake her. She walked over to the fire, placed two new logs into it, and made sure they caught fire before she turned to see that Charlie had rolled on her side, woken up, and was now looking at her.

"Thank you," she whispered.

"You're welcome," Hailey replied. "You sure you want to stay down here?"

"Yeah, I'm good."

"Okay, then. Good night." Hailey sighed and walked past the couch toward the stairs.

"Hails?" Charlie said a little louder.

"Yeah?" Hailey stopped and turned around.

"Are you and Emma back together?" she whispered again.

Hailey wondered why Charlie's voice had gotten low again. She walked back around the couch so that she could see the other woman's face.

"No," she told her. "We're dating. Or, we're kind of dating... I think," Hailey added and knelt in front of the couch again. "But I'm not ready to call us together."

Hailey wasn't sure why she had felt the need to say that they were *kind of* dating. They were dating. She knew that, but she couldn't just admit that to Charlie.

"Why not?" Charlie asked sleepily.

"Because I'm just not there yet," Hailey answered with shrugged shoulders. "How'd your date go last week?" she asked in return and realized she had been wanting to know that for a while now.

"Good," Charlie replied directly, with a small smile that hurt Hailey's heart a little. "She's nice."

"Nice?" Hailey lifted an eyebrow.

"She's never been with a woman before. We're taking things slow."

"Never?" Hailey checked.

"She just came out. We've been out a couple of times. She stayed over last weekend. It was nice."

"She stayed over?" Hailey sat on the floor completely.

"Yeah," Charlie answered. "We didn't do anything, though. We haven't even kissed yet."

"Really?" Hailey felt relieved, which she knew wasn't fair, because she had definitely kissed Emma, and she didn't know why she cared about who Charlie was kissing.

Charlie had kissed plenty of other women before. Why was she thinking about Charlie's lips right now? How could anyone dating Charlie resist them? They were so perfect, and probably so soft. Hailey's eyes got big at that thought.

"What?" Charlie asked.

"Nothing."

"Emma seems nice," Charlie said softly.

"She doesn't think you like her," Hailey returned.

"Why?"

"She just doesn't know you," Hailey answered. "You were at work. I get it."

"Yeah," Charlie agreed.

Hailey took a moment just to watch her. Thanks to the angle and the now building fire, she could see the flames bouncing around in Charlie's deep, brown eyes.

"Are you warm enough?"

"Yeah. Thanks," Charlie said and pulled the blanket back up to her neck.

"Are you just saying that?" Hailey lifted an eyebrow and glared.

"Yes." Charlie rolled her eyes at herself. "I'll be fine in a few minutes, though."

"I should go back upstairs."

"Yeah," Charlie said that for the third time now.

"I think I've been invading your space a lot this weekend. I promise, I don't mean to, but... Do you want me to stay? You can scoot over. I can just—"

"I'm good," Charlie interrupted.

Hailey swallowed and nodded. She stood, and without

saying goodnight again, she headed back toward the stairs. She was disappointed. She took the stairs slowly, in the hopes that Charlie would call her back and tell her she'd changed her mind. Her heart started racing at the thought of lying next to Charlie and wrapping an arm around her as she had done the previous night. When Hailey got to her room, she saw her phone lit up. She picked it up and saw a goodnight message from Emma. The woman had been out with a few friends and hoped she didn't wake Hailey up. Hailey thought about calling her, to see how her night went, but she knew she wasn't in the best mood right now. She didn't want to put that on Emma. Plus, Emma had always been pretty good at figuring out Hailey's moods. She would likely want to know what was causing this one, and Hailey did not have an answer to that question herself yet.

***

Charlie woke up early. The sun wasn't up yet, thanks to winter, and that just made the feeling of the cold in the room even worse. The fire had long since burned out, and the thin blanket she'd had wrapped around her was no longer proving useful. She stood, rubbed her face with her hands, and then walked back up the stairs. She noticed the door to the bedroom was closed, and she worried she would wake Hailey, but she wanted to climb into the bed and try to warm up. It seemed Hannah or Alyssa was already up and in the shower. And for all Charlie knew, both of them were in there; so hot water wasn't an option. She opened the door slowly and heard a gasp.

"Sorry, it's just me," Charlie said softly and pushed the door opened the rest of the way.

Hailey's eyes were wide, as if she had been caught by her mom with a girl in her bed, and Charlie just stood in the doorway, wondering if she should continue inside or go back downstairs. Hailey wasn't saying anything. Her eyes were glued to Charlie. Charlie's own eyes went big to match

123

Hailey's as she realized what Hailey had been doing. Her heart started pumping blood throughout her body at a rapid pace, but one location seemed to be getting the majority of it. Charlie felt a pulse beat between her legs and knew that she had gotten wet instantly. This was the opposite of what Charlie needed in many respects, but at least she was suddenly no longer cold.

"Sorry," she gulped out.

"I wasn't–" Hailey's body was still.

It felt to Charlie as if she had forgotten how to move, or that her body wouldn't allow her to move.

"Okay. Yeah," Charlie said quickly, closed the door behind her, without understanding why, and walked toward Hailey's bed. "You left this down there."

She placed the book Hailey had read to her last night on the table next to the other woman's bed and then realized her mistake. She was closer to Hailey now, and the tension between the two of them was palpable. At least Hailey had been able to take care of herself – or at least had started to, before being interrupted. Charlie would be stuck with this feeling of longing and desire until she arrived home and could take care of it herself. One of Hailey's hands emerged from under the blanket and clasped Charlie's wrist.

"I–" Hailey still couldn't complete a sentence.

Charlie didn't know what to do. Hailey's hand was on her wrist. Her left hand. Hailey was left-handed. And her left hand was on Charlie's wrist. Hailey probably used her left hand to do what she was doing to herself only moments earlier, and that would explain what else Charlie was feeling on her wrist.

"Oh, Jesus!" Hailey realized the same thing at the same time and instantly pulled her hand away, leaving the now cool wetness on Charlie's wrist. "Fuck. I'm–"

Charlie closed her eyes. She thought about what Ember had said to her more than a dozen times, what Eva had echoed almost as many, and about the fact that she had evidence of Hailey's arousal now on her skin. Charlie could no longer keep herself up. Her legs were shaking. Her body was trembling all over. She practically fell onto the bed but managed to keep herself sitting upright. Hailey moved over slightly, to accommodate her, but neither said anything when it happened.

"Hails," Charlie stated with no intention of adding anything to it.

"I'm sorry," Hailey replied with deep red cheeks after a moment. "I'm mortified, and I'm sorry."

Charlie decided that for once in her life, she could be brave. She swallowed hard.

"Hails, I have to tell you something."

"Now?" Hailey checked.

Charlie turned to face her. She could see the redness of embarrassment plastered on Hailey's cheeks.

"It's why I pulled away."

"Oh."

"What I'm going to say now will change everything," Charlie practically whispered. Her eyes stayed on Hailey's as she watched the other woman's eyes widen in concern. "So, are you sure?"

"Charlie, tell me," Hailey implored.

"I've been in love with you since the moment we met."

There were two feelings that started all at once inside of Charlie. The first was the sense of absolute dread. She was watching Hailey's reaction, and she couldn't read it. She could always read Hailey before, except in the moment she needed to be able to read her the most, apparently. Hailey's eyes were still big, and her lips were still slightly parted, but her jaw hadn't dropped completely open. Hailey hadn't gulped or turned her eyes away. The initial blush from her embarrassment was still present. Charlie didn't know what any of that meant.

The second feeling that hit her was that of freedom; amazing and remarkable freedom. It was over. It was out there. No matter what happened next, whatever Hailey's reaction was going to be, Charlie had at least finally said it.

Her last secret had been revealed. She no longer had to feel like she was hiding a part of herself from anyone. With that realization, she started laughing. It was soft, at first, but it began building up until Charlie was laughing wildly and no longer paying attention to Hailey's reaction.

"Charlie?"

"I'm sorry. I'm sorry," she repeated and tried to calm her laughter, letting it die down, until she felt wetness on her cheeks and realized she was crying. "I've been holding that in for so long. I didn't realize how fucking good it would feel to just say it." Charlie wiped at her cheeks, regained her composure, and turned again to see Hailey staring at her, mystified. "Hails, the first time I saw you was at your interview. You were up after me, remember?"

"I remember," Hailey muttered.

"You had on that red short-sleeved button-down shirt, with the collar and the two breast pockets, and these black pants. Your hair was down. It was shorter back then, but not by much. It was around your face, at first, but you pushed it back behind your ears when Francine called your name. I almost tripped over a chair on my way out. I almost said something to you, and I almost just walked up and introduced myself, but... You were so beautiful, Hails." Charlie smiled lightly at the memory. "And you were trying to get a job. I didn't want to get in the way, but I never wanted to get a job more in my life. And I hoped you got the job, too, because I felt like I had to see you again. And that when I did, I would be brave." Charlie looked toward the window where she noticed the snow falling. "I finally worked up the courage to ask you out one night. Honestly, I had asked the bartender to sneak me a shot, because I needed the liquid courage. I walked up to you, and you started talking about Ember and how you liked her. I was absolutely crushed."

"Ember?" Hailey questioned.

"I liked you, but you liked her. Ember was always better at this stuff. She could get any girl she wanted. I figured that if she wanted you, it would be over for me."

"Charlie, Em and I never—"

"I know," Charlie interrupted and placed her hand on top of Hailey's hand that was over the blanket. She knew it was the hand Hailey had just been using, but she didn't care. "But, by the time you got over her, you were dating someone else. Then, there was someone else, and I just never told you." Charlie let out a breath she had been holding in. "I've watched you date woman after woman. None of them deserved you, Hailey. But, after over a decade of not telling you how I feel, I'm not so sure I do, either." She lifted her hand off of Hailey's and stood. "I pushed you away because I saw you with Emma, and it hurt worse than all the others combined, because Emma was *the perfect girlfriend.* You've actually used those exact words to describe her. I know you two only broke up because of distance. Now, there is no more distance, so it's going to work out this time. And I've just told you that I love you. Things are going to be bad for a while between us, because I can't be around you right now, when you're with her, Hails. I can't. I pushed you away because I need to get over you." Charlie headed toward the door. "I have to not see you with her, okay," she proclaimed and wiped another tear from her cheek. "I want you to be happy, Hails. I want me to be happy, too, though. I'm going to try to get over you, and maybe we can get back to the place we were—"

"I didn't know, Charlie," Hailey interrupted her.

"Hails, I didn't want you to know." Charlie didn't turn back to look at her. "I don't really want you to know now, but I *need* you to know. If I have any chance of making something work with someone else, I just needed to tell you and move on." She opened the door. "I'm going to see if I can catch a ride back with Hannah and Alyssa."

"Charlie!"

"I need it, Hails."

Charlie didn't stop walking until she opened the front door and headed out onto the porch to inhale and exhale rapidly and lean back against the door, before sliding down it and feeling her body absorb the cold, wet feeling of the snow against her pants. The tears she had been somewhat holding in began to fall. Most of them were sad tears, because she had just officially given up on ever being with Hailey Grant. But the rest were happy tears, because at least now that she had told her, and Hailey had Emma, Charlie could finally move on.

CHAPTER 12

HAILEY couldn't move. She sat frozen in the tiny twin bed, with her eyes unfocused but staring at least in the direction of the open door. Charlie bolted out of the room before Hailey could even say anything to her. Hailey didn't know what to say to her, anyway; Charlie loved her. She loved her, and she had for a long time, and Hailey hadn't noticed. How had she not noticed? She spent practically every free moment she had with Charlie and Ember – and mainly Charlie, especially since Ember met Eva. It was as if her entire friendship with Charlie was now replaying in her mind. Charlie even remembered what Hailey wore when Hailey first interviewed at the restaurant.

"Black jeans and a white polo," she said to herself.

"Huh?" Ember was standing in the doorway.

"When did you get there?" Hailey focused her eyes on her friend.

"Good morning to you, too, Hails. I just got here. I was about to go make breakfast, and I saw you were up. Where's Charlie?"

"I don't know," Hailey said.

"Black jeans and a white polo? Are you planning what you're wearing today?" Ember questioned, leaning against the door.

"Huh?"

"That's what you just said."

"Oh." Hailey smiled. "It's what Charlie wore the day

we both interviewed with your mom."

"You remember what she wore that day? That was, like, a million years ago. I don't even know what I wore last week."

"Em, can you check on her, please?" Hailey wiped her cheek and sniffled. "I can't, and I think she needs someone to check—"

"Hailey, what happened?" Ember walked in and sat on the end of the bed, leaning toward Hailey, who was still half under the blanket.

"She's going to need someone, and she won't let it be me." Hailey tried to produce a smile. "It should be me, but it can't be."

Ember kept her eyes on Hailey's glassy ones.

"She told you." She nodded as she said it.

"You knew?" Hailey accused, but in a gentle voice because that was all she could manage.

"She told me a while ago. She was drunk and confessed to me, but I knew before that."

"How?" Hailey wanted to know. "How did *you* know, and *I* didn't?"

"It's hard to see when it's you, Hails. Charlie always played it close to the vest. It took me some time to even notice the little things she'd say or do, but, mostly, it was how she looked at you."

"How she..." Hailey stared at Ember with an expression that must have said she had no idea what the woman was talking about.

"You know how I look at Eva?" She patted Hailey's leg. "That is how Charlotte Adams looks at Hailey Grant."

"I didn't know. I just thought that was how she looked at me. I didn't know the difference."

"Hails, the question you need to ask yourself is what you're going to do about it."

"What do you mean?"

"Hailey, I used to think it was one-sided. Charlie loved you, but you didn't feel it." She took a thoughtful pause.

"But I told her years ago to tell you how she felt because I thought you felt it, too. At one point, you started looking at her that same way. It's been there ever since. I don't know if you've noticed that, but, Hailey, every woman you've ever dated has basically been a dud… Did you ever think there was a reason you kept going for women like that?"

"Em, not every woman," Hailey said. "Emma isn't a dud."

Ember stood and sighed.

"You need to tell Charlie that nothing's going to happen between the two of you if you want Emma, Hailey. Emma is the reason this is all happening right now. Charlie never really worried before, because the women you dated weren't going to stick around. But if Emma is, and you love her and want the life with her you never got back then, you need to tell Charlie. Let her go, because she's been in pain for years. It's been worse, though, since Emma reappeared."

"She told me she's moving on," Hailey announced. "She said she needs to move on."

"Do you love her, Hailey?"

"Hey, breakfast?" Eva walked up to the door. "Oh, I'm interrupting something." She started to back up.

"It's okay," Ember told her and then turned back to Hailey. "You've got some thinking to do. But, now that you know, it's time to figure out what you want, Hails. She's just trying to let go of what she's wanted her whole life. That's not easy. It's especially hard if you keep her on the hook, you know?"

"I wouldn't do that to her. If I would have known, I…" Hailey glanced in Eva's direction.

"And there's where the thinking needs to come in." Ember pointed at her. "I'll check on her. Babe, can you start breakfast? I have to find Charlie." Ember stepped to Eva and placed her hands on her fiancée's hips before leaning in and kissing the woman's forehead. "I love you," Ember whispered it, but Hailey heard it and closed her eyes when she did.

"Sure," Eva told her. "Love you, too."

Eva gave Hailey a half-smile and a shrug as Ember pulled her along, leaving Hailey alone in the room.

Hailey's eyes were unfocused again. She couldn't stop the memories from flowing into her brain. She wondered how she couldn't have seen it, but also how Charlie had managed to put up with it all these years. They'd been so close. Hell, Hailey had heard from a few different people at various functions that they thought she and Charlie were a couple. Once, she had told an old boss about Charlie, and after ten minutes of talking, the boss asked if Charlie was her boyfriend or husband. That was before that boss knew Hailey was gay, but the perception was that Charlie was her other half nonetheless.

She had been thinking about Charlie a lot differently over the past week and a half. Ever since the other woman had asked for space and mentioned that she was going on a date, Hailey had felt differently about Charlie and their situation. When they had arrived at the large yet also seemingly claustrophobic lake house, Hailey had felt things she had never felt before. She had stared at parts of Charlie she had never really stared at that way before. She had touched Charlie several times and wanted to touch her more. In fact, she had followed Charlie outside, when they'd arrived, specifically for the chance to run her hands up and down Charlie's arms, knowing the woman would be cold, and just wanting to feel her. She had tried to warm Charlie up that first night and had the best of intentions, but once she had been lying next to her, it became about more than just keeping Charlie from freezing. Last night, she'd gone downstairs to check on her, sat down to read to her, and wrapped Charlie in a blanket. She had offered to lie down next to her again, because she wanted to feel that press of their bodies, the softness of Charlie's skin.

She'd woken up earlier than usual and felt the all too familiar arousal that sometimes forced her from slumber. It had always been funny to her, when Ember referenced

Eva's fondness for morning sex, because Hailey was also a morning sex kind of girl. Her body had no problem with sex any other time but seemed to prefer it more in the morning. She often woke up with a tingle to do something about it. Normally, she wouldn't dare, being in the same house with five other women. But she had been thinking about Charlie. For the first time, she thought about Charlie and wanted to touch herself, to picture the two of them kissing slowly and gently, while she pressed fingers to her clit and moved them around just as slowly, as she got more and more turned on with the combination of the touching and the images.

She had been smart enough to close the door but hadn't thought to lock it, because it was five in the morning on a Sunday, and even Charlie didn't wake up that early. Hailey had been wrong, though. Just as her fingers started pressing harder and faster, as she imagined Charlie's lips on her nipples – sucking and pulling, while Charlie's hand slid down between her legs to start touching her just as she was touching herself, the door opened. And it was the object of her fantasy standing in the door while Hailey yanked her hand from between her own legs and tried to pretend she wasn't just masturbating to the thought of her best friend making love to her. Hailey considered that thought and re-called the visual. Charlie wasn't fucking her. They weren't just having sex with Hailey's in the fantasy. Charlie was making love to her.

Hailey rolled her head back against the pillow. While Charlie had been in love with her forever, Hailey's feelings were very new to her. She had just discovered that she thought of Charlie as more than a friend. If she told Charlie she'd been thinking about the two of them together, and she wasn't ready for the whole thing – the relationship and the love beyond what was shared between two close friends, Hailey knew it would destroy any friendship between them. She couldn't hurt Charlie any more than she already had by being so clueless.

She also had Emma to consider. Charlie had the new

woman in her life, too. While they were both taking things slowly right now, with the other women in their lives, Hailey needed to figure out what was going on with Emma before she even attempted to think about whatever she may be feeling for Charlie. Hailey knew she liked Emma. She had loved her once, and now, there was a possibility they were on their way back to that. When she kissed Emma, it felt like their lips were in perfect harmony, and Hailey had wanted to take things further, prior to coming on this trip. She wanted to find out if Emma really was the one she was supposed to be with. In fact, as she thought about all of it together, Hailey wondered if the reason she was confused about her feelings for Charlie was because things were real with Emma. That meant they would be a couple soon, and they would settle down together. That was scary. Hailey had dated a lot of women, and she'd thought several of them would be around for longer than they actually were, but she had never thought of any of them as the one for her.

After Emma, it had taken Hailey a long time to open up to the idea of finding someone else. And then when she did, and it didn't work, Hailey thought she'd have to date a lot of women to find anyone that could hold a candle to her first love. She had been wrong on all accounts, of course, but Emma was back in her life. Hailey wanted to see where it was going, but she had been honest with Emma that she wasn't ready for anything serious yet. She planned to keep it that way. She'd push her surprising feelings for Charlie down so that she could focus on Emma. That would give Charlie the chance to move on with her life. Hailey didn't want to confuse either of them by confessing that she had had one fantasy about the woman and wondered what her lips would feel like on her own body.

It would be better this way.

***

"Hey," Ember greeted Charlie with her coat.

Charlie was still sitting outside but moved away from the door when she felt it open. Ember tossed the coat onto Charlie's head and then handed her the boots she'd brought.

"Let's go for a walk," she added.

Ember had already put on her own coat, gloves, and boots. Charlie stood, put the boots on first, and then the coat, removing the gloves she had previously shoved into the pockets. She went to slide them over her hands. The snow had let up, and the sun was rising, so, while it was still cold, it wasn't as bad. And, honestly, Charlie wasn't feeling much of anything at the moment.

"I guess she told you," Charlie said and zipped her bulky winter coat, enjoying the warmth immediately.

"I went to say good morning and kind of figured it out," Ember replied and headed down the porch steps.

"At least now she knows." Charlie followed, placing her hands in her pockets.

"How do you feel?" Ember questioned as they began their walk.

"I feel like I just ruined the best friendship I've ever had," Charlie confessed.

"You didn't ruin it, Charlie. She'll take the time she needs, and you'll do the same, but you guys will come out of this okay." Ember looped an arm through Charlie's.

"Em, I can't be around her right now. I know we have to plan your wedding, and that it's only a couple of months away – and I promise I'll do everything I can to help, but being around her like this hurts so much."

"Okay. Okay," Ember consoled. "We'll figure something out."

"I'm sorry. I shouldn't have told her. I should have kept it to myself, or at least until after your wedding. She'd be with Emma, and it wouldn't have mattered. I wouldn't have said anything, and we'd go on being fine."

"Charlie, you haven't been *fine* since you figured out you loved her. For what it's worth, I'm proud of you. What you did took guts. And I knew you had them all along. Don't worry about the wedding. We'll figure something out. If you don't want to be in it anymore, I'll understand."

Charlie stopped them and turned to face her.

"No, Em. This is your wedding. And you're my best friend, too. Of course, I want to be in it. I can be mature and put my own crap aside. I just don't think I can sit around and plan things, with her in the room, and that makes me a bad maid-of-honor. Can you demote me or something?" she proposed.

Ember laughed and pulled them along.

"No, I'm not demoting you. But you are dismissed from the intense wedding-planning sessions that involve Hailey. I'll make sure you do the fittings and stuff with just Eva and I. Or even just me, okay?"

"Thank you. I'm sorry."

"Hey, it's okay. Let's talk about something else. What do you want to talk about?"

"Anything other than Hailey Grant," she requested.

***

Charlie rode back with Hannah and Alyssa. Neither of them asked questions about why. She hadn't participated in the last round of planning the others had done that morning, claiming she didn't feel well – which was technically the truth. Hailey hadn't gone into the bedroom at all, while Charlie sat on the bed and then curled up in it before she got up and started packing her things. Hailey had waited until Charlie was outside, waiting for Alyssa and Hannah to take her home, before she made her way up the stairs. While they shared a few glances that were sufficiently awkward, neither of them had said anything.

Charlie had said thank you and goodbye to Hannah and Alyssa and made her way into her apartment. Her neighbor had been taking care of Eddie for her while she was away. When she opened the door, he jumped on her almost immediately, happy to see her, and also probably ready to go outside. Charlie took him for a walk and then watched him bounce around as she laughed at him when they returned. One of the best things about having a pet was their ability to make people happy when they were having a bad day.

Charlie tossed her dirty weekend clothes into the laundry pile and made her way to the shower. She decided she wouldn't shed any more tears over Hailey and her feelings for her. She had done what she had always been afraid to do, and it was over now. She called Lena, before getting dressed, to see if she still wanted to come over. When Lena said yes, and that she would bring dinner, Charlie dressed for a casual date and waited for her arrival.

***

"Hi," Charlie greeted.

Lena looked beautiful. She had her hair down, and it was slightly wavy again. Her eyes were bright, and her smile was wide. She held out a bag of food, with a bottle of wine, and made her way into the apartment.

"Welcome back."

"Thanks. I'm glad you're here," Charlie stated and realized she meant it.

The weekend had been a difficult one. Charlie hadn't been sure she should see Lena after it, but when she saw the woman at her door, Charlie knew she made the right decision. Lena walked past her and into the kitchen, where she dropped the food on the counter, turned, and waited for Charlie to approach her before she held her arms out. Charlie smiled a shy smile and walked into them, allowing the hug and the scent of lavender to overtake her senses. She pressed her own hands into Lena's back and her head into Lena's neck. It felt good, to hug her and to be hugged by her. Charlie pressed the same light kiss to Lena's neck that she'd given her before, and pulled back to look into those impossibly teal eyes.

"I'm glad I'm here, too," Lena shared. "I brought food from this little Ethiopian place near my house. Is that okay?"

"Sure."

Charlie rested her hands on Lena's hips and held them in place there. Then, she looked down at them and slid a finger into each of the belt loops of Lena's jeans over the belt.

"Are you okay?" Lena questioned and placed one hand against Charlie's chest, while she ran the other one along her jaw.

"Yeah, I think I am," Charlie stated as she looked up and smiled at her.

Lena's eyes flitted down to Charlie's lips and then back up to her eyes. Charlie kept her eyes on Lena's and felt a thumb slide across the lips that she had just put a small amount of lip balm on. Then, the thumb pulled down on her bottom lip lightly, and Lena moved in another step. Charlie thought about making sure that this was what Lena wanted, but she didn't think she needed to, because Lena was leading.

"I–" Lena started and stopped herself.

Then, she leaned in just enough to make Charlie feel like she could match her lean with one of her own and connect their lips, which Charlie did.

Lena's lips were tentative, and Charlie matched that tentativeness because she thought it might help Lena get comfortable. Within a few moments, Lena's mouth was confident and seeking. Lena's hand was on the back of Charlie's neck, playing with her short hair, while the other hand remained at the base of her back. Charlie opened her mouth, indicating that she wanted to take the kiss further. Lena granted her entrance to explore her hot mouth with her tongue, which Charlie did, earning a moan from the other woman.

Charlie then took a few steps forward, moving Lena back against the counter, and ran her hands up and down the woman's sides slowly and undemanding, while she continued to explore Lena's mouth with her soft tongue that was sliding against Lena's and then swirling around it. Lena moaned again, and her hand on Charlie's back moved to lift Charlie's shirt to slide under. The feeling of her own hand against Charlie's skin caused Lena to pull back from the kiss, breaking their revelry and leaving them both practically gasping.

"Oh, wow!" Lena exclaimed after a moment and then brought a hand up to her mouth in embarrassment.

"Wow is right," Charlie offered and pulled Lena back in.

"Yeah?" Lena checked unconfidently.

"Yes, definitely," Charlie returned. "Want to, maybe, do it again after we eat?"

She could tell Lena wanted more, but given the woman's reaction, Charlie also sensed that maybe Lena could use a little time to let their kiss sink in. Food was probably the best option for them both. Lena nodded, and Charlie pecked her lips gently in reply before moving around her to the counter.

What surprised her the most, was that the kiss *had* been amazing. Charlie hadn't thought of Hailey once since Lena entered her apartment. And given what had transpired between Hailey and her this weekend, that was a good thing. Charlie smiled as she dished out food onto plates and showed Lena where the wineglasses were.

They made their way to the couch and ate together while they put the TV on to mainly provide background noise. Lena told Charlie about her week in Evanston. Charlie talked about her workweek as well while they wrapped up their delicious meal. After the dirty dishes had been moved to the sink, Charlie sat back down beside Lena, and using what was left of her bravery, she asked her a question.

"So, how was your lunch date yesterday?" she chanced.

"It was okay." Lena turned to face her and smiled.

"Okay?" Charlie lifted an eyebrow.

"Is this weird?" Lena lifted an eyebrow in a different way.

"Yes. But I do want to know, if that's okay."

"We had coffee and talked. That was it. She was sweet. I liked her at first, but neither of us committed to another date. I don't think she's likely to call for one."

"Why not?" Charlie questioned.

"I told her I'm new to this, and she asked if I was a baby gay."

"No, she didn't," Charlie said.

"She sure did," Lena confirmed. "I realize that most women are not interested in someone who just figured this stuff out about herself and started dating women, but I don't like being condescended to."

"I don't blame you," Charlie replied. "I apologize on behalf of all lesbians worldwide for her comment."

"Thank you. But I do want to be honest with you about something."

"Okay."

"I like you, and I really liked what we did over there." Lena pointed to the counter. "I am definitely a gay lady." She laughed a little and looked down at her fidgeting hands. "But I'm not ready for a commitment. I think what I found out yesterday was that I do want to go out with women; not just one woman." She looked back up. "I want to do more of what we did, and go further than that, too, if and when it happens with you. I don't plan on asking anyone else out anytime soon, but–"

"If it happens, and you like the girl, you'll say yes," Charlie completed and felt a little down, having to say it to Lena but understanding it all the same.

"I guess... what I want to know is... How do you feel about that? I know you said before you'd be okay with it, but I really want to know how you feel about it. If it's going to be a problem or... God, I don't know what I'm saying. I've never been a dater, you know? I don't know how to do this."

"Lena, you're doing fine," Charlie encouraged. "This is a strange situation. I like you, too. I like what we did in there, and I would like to do more when you're ready. I don't want to be condescending like Mara, but I get the whole coming out thing and wanting to explore a little. I guess, I just want you to be honest with me. I'll be honest with you if I'm seeing someone else."

"Will you?" Lena asked her and seemed a little concerned.

"I might," Charlie admitted. "I'm sort of in this new phase of my life, too. I've cut myself off from stuff in the past. I'm finally trying to move beyond that, and there's a chance I'll meet someone and want to go out with them. But, for now, there's you. And I'm good with that, too."

"Okay." Lena gave her that shy smile again.

"I'm going to kiss you now, if you're okay with that," Charlie said.

Lena seemed surprised, pleasantly so, but nodded, and Charlie captured her lips with no hesitation or trepidation this time.

CHAPTER 13

HAILEY arrived at Emma's place and knocked. She wasn't even sure if the woman was home. She hadn't called or texted first. She had just dropped her stuff off at her own apartment, after a long and awkward ride with Ember and Eva. Hailey just wanted to sit in silence, and they were happy and in love, talking about their upcoming special day. She had changed into something more comfortable, grabbed her keys, and headed over to Emma's.

"Well, this is a surprise," Emma greeted with a smile. "I thought you were going to call me."

"I just came over. Is that okay?"

"Yeah, come in." Emma opened the door all the way for Hailey to walk through. "I see you dressed up for me," she joked.

Hailey had thrown on sweats and a T-shirt under her puffy winter coat.

"Yeah, yeah. It was a long weekend," she replied and unzipped her coat, while Emma closed the door.

Just as she was about to remove it from her shoulders, Emma appeared behind her to help her slide it off. Emma then placed it over the back of the sofa, while Hailey smiled and dropped her purse to the ground.

"You want to talk about it?" Emma asked. "And these are cute, by the way." She pulled lightly on the waistband of Hailey's sweatpants. "Did I ever tell you that I always preferred you like this?"

"Like what? A mess?"

Emma chuckled and wrapped her arms around Hailey's waist.

"No, like this. Just… like, yourself. No makeup, hair pulled back, just comfortable. I find that sexy on a woman."

"You do?"

"Especially on you." Emma kissed her nose with gentle warm lips. "Now, do you want to talk about your long weekend, or do you want to *not* talk about your long weekend?"

"I would like to *not* talk about my long weekend. I'm just over planning a wedding right now."

"Understood. What I heard was that you'd like me to put the Wedding Planner on so that we can watch and take notes. Is that right?" Emma winked at her.

Hailey rolled her eyes at her, finally wrapped her arms around Emma's neck, and pulled her closer.

"I think I'd like you to kiss me now," she said after a moment.

"I can do that." Emma's lips met Hailey's then.

There was a second, at first, where Hailey thought about Charlie, but after that second, it was only Emma on her mind; how the woman's lips felt and tasted, and then, how they pressed to Hailey's neck and just below her earlobe before sucking on that earlobe. Emma's hands stayed still on Hailey's waist, but Hailey's moved on their own to Emma's back and up her shirt, to feel that Emma wasn't wearing a bra underneath. Hailey moaned into the kiss when Emma's lips returned to her own. Then, she was being moved backward so they could lie on the couch. Emma hovered over her and reconnected their lips. It was still so slow and deliberate, that Hailey felt it all over her body and wanted more. Her hands went back under Emma's shirt and then moved to the other woman's sides before settling on Emma's stomach, eliciting a small gasp from her.

"I'm not ready for everything yet, but can we maybe lose the shirts tonight?" Hailey asked when Emma's lips moved to her collarbone.

Emma didn't actually say anything, she just lifted herself up. Hailey moved her hands to her breasts, covering them fully, while Emma pulled her shirt up and over her head. Hailey's hands felt the firm breasts and the nipples that hardened in her hands as she squeezed. Emma stared down at her and placed her hands on Hailey's stomach now, sliding them up slowly to cup the breasts that were also not covered in a bra, because Hailey had forgotten to put one on.

Hailey hadn't felt those hands on her in so long, but they felt so good. Emma seemed to remember what she liked, squeezing the entire breast a few times with hard pressure, before using her thumb and forefinger on Hailey's nipples, causing Hailey's breath to quicken and that feeling to return between her legs. As Emma's hips moved against her body unintentionally, Hailey felt herself getting wetter. Emma's hands continued to play with her breasts. After a few moments, Hailey lifted herself up. Emma removed Hailey's shirt, tossing it to the floor, and reconnected their lips, lying Hailey back down.

"I want you like crazy, Hails," she let out and moved her lips to cover Hailey's nipple. She sucked first, and then played with it with her teeth and her soft tongue. "God, I missed you," she said and continued her assault on Hailey's nipple, while Hailey closed her eyes to try to keep herself from getting to the point where she was so turned on, there would be no turning back.

She wanted Emma. She knew she did. But after the day she had, and the feelings she had experienced for Charlie, Hailey didn't want their first time since high school to be on the same day she had almost gotten off to the thoughts of another woman.

"I want you, too, Emma, but–"

"I know. It's okay. I'm on board." Emma lifted her head and met Hailey's eyes. "I mean, I'm on board with the taking things slow and getting to know each other again thing. I just wanted you to know that I want you."

Hailey smiled at her and placed her hands in soft hair, while Emma went back to kissing her breasts, her abdomen, and then her stomach. When they went to the bedroom later, Hailey returned the favor, exploring Emma's skin with her mouth and hands, and enjoying the sights, smells, tastes, and sounds of Emma Colton beneath her once again.

Hailey didn't stay over at Emma's. She wanted to, but she had none of her stuff there, and she needed to go to work the next day. After midnight, she finally got in her car, drove the short distance back to her apartment, found a lucky parking spot nearby, and went inside to crash onto her own bed, fall asleep, and wake up on Monday not at all rested and in need of a long shower.

***

Hailey's boss had put in her notice and had been phoning it in ever since. This infuriated Hailey, because not only did that mean she had to do her own job, but it also meant that she had to do her boss's job at the same time and learn it as she went. Her Monday was not going well, and she knew she would be working late. Her boss had decided to work from home, which meant she wouldn't really be working. Hailey got a call from one of the other major VPs at the bank's corporate office, that one of their tellers had gone off on a racist rant at a customer that morning.

Hailey had been handling the phone calls from the media outlets that wanted statements from the bank's PR department. She had said, 'no comment,' at first, until she could meet with HR. They informed her that the employee had been terminated, and the customer had been issued an apology from the bank's manager. There's wasn't a need for Hailey to go to the bank itself, but her job did require her to issue a public statement. She spent time crafting one and then had it sent out to the media and anyone else who might be interested in reading it. Normally, her boss was the one they would get on camera when that was required, but with the other woman essentially already moving on to her next job, it was Hailey's turn in the spotlight.

She was now much better at public speaking than she had been as a kid, but she still wasn't happy about having to do it, when it technically wasn't her job. Hailey made sure her hair and makeup looked okay, and knew she would come off somewhat pasty on camera, since she wore only light makeup, but she didn't have anything with her to adjust her look. She stood on the steps of the bank's corporate headquarters and delivered a statement to seven waiting cameras and boom microphones. She made it through the brief statement, ensuring the people that the bank had taken the necessary steps to terminate the employee and to apologize to the customer.

Unfortunately for the bank, there weren't that many things, outside of an apology, that they could offer their customers. Hailey didn't work for a giant retail outlet that could issue a massive gift card. She didn't work for a fast-food restaurant that could offer a year's supply of tacos. She worked for a bank. The customer, who had been the victim of this employee's terrible words, wasn't seeking anything of monetary value. But Hailey knew that the media searched for things like that in issued statements. Instead, she spoke as eloquently as she could and then stepped away from the microphones, because the most important person in this situation wasn't holding a camera. She was sitting at home, wondering how she walked into her bank that morning, expecting to apply for a loan, and when she asked the bank teller if she could talk to one of their loan agents, he had returned that the bank shouldn't give out loans to people like her, and then followed it with racial epitaphs. Hailey returned to her office, let out a deep breath, and picked up her phone.

"Mrs. Vincent?" she greeted when the woman answered her phone. "My name is Hailey Grant," she introduced herself as an employee of the bank's PR department.

"Yes, Miss Grant. What can I do for you?"

"Nothing, ma'am," Hailey replied. "I wanted to call you because I wanted to personally apologize for what happened to you this morning."

"Someone from the bank already spoke with me."

"I know," Hailey returned and let out a sigh. "What happened to you today was not okay, Mrs. Vincent. I wish I had something more to offer you than an apology."

"I don't need any–"

"Yes, ma'am. I understand. And I didn't mean it like that. I mean that I wish I could do something to prevent instances like this from happening at all. I wish these kinds of attitudes and expressions of them didn't exist in the world, because no one should have to go into a place where they're attempting to do their business and have something like this happen to them. You wanted a loan from your bank, and this never should have happened. I wanted to apologize to you myself and ask if there was anything we could do, and not because I am an employee of the bank and this is a part of my job, but because I genuinely want to know if there is anything I can do."

"No, Miss Grant. There's nothing you can do. I'm sorry to say that, but this isn't the first time this has happened. And it won't be the last," Mrs. Vincent replied.

"I am really sorry, Mrs. Vincent," Hailey returned. "I understand you have another appointment with a loan officer?"

"I do. And I do not want any special treatment because this happened. I just want a chance to state my case and get my loan, if I meet the criteria."

"I understand, ma'am. If there's anything I can do, please reach out to me here. I can give you my direct line."

"That's not necessary. But, thank you; I appreciate the call."

They disconnected, and Hailey took a break from work to get some coffee. She needed it if she was going to get through the rest of the day.

***

When Charlie got home, she turned on the TV absent-mindedly and let Eddie go crazy around her, while she opened her mail at the counter. She was reading her credit card statement when she heard a very familiar voice. She looked up at the TV to see Hailey Grant on the news, speaking to reporters. Charlie stopped what she was doing and walked to the couch. She sat down and listened to the snippet of the statement the news provided her with. It was strange, because Charlie thought she needed to not see Hailey for a while, but as she watched her on the screen, doing her job – looking professional and also beautiful, Charlie found herself rewinding the news so that she could watch it again.

***

By Thursday, Hailey sat at Sally's wondering if Charlie was going to show up. She knew Ember wouldn't be there, because she'd texted that she had an appointment with her advisor at Northwestern. Her best friend was blowing them away in her program – which shouldn't have surprised Hailey, but Ember had also hidden her talents from her friends for the majority of their friendship, so it was still something Hailey was getting used to. Ember had been asked to present some findings she had made on something math-related, that Hailey didn't even try to understand, and she had to meet with her advisor one more time before the presentation at an academic conference that was hosted by Northwestern at the end of the month.

Hailey sat and drank her coffee while she observed the others mill about the café. She told herself that she would wait one more minute. If Charlie didn't show by then, she would leave. But just as Hailey resolved herself to stand and deal with the fact that her relationship with Charlie would forever be changed and she'd have to accept that, Charlie Adams walked through the door and gave her a confident smile. Well, that was unexpected.

"Hey," Charlie sat down in front of Hailey.

"Hey there. I didn't think you'd come," Hailey returned honestly.

"I almost didn't. I knew Ember wouldn't be here, so I thought about skipping it, but I changed my mind."

"Why?" Hailey asked.

"I guess I wanted to see if you'd come." Charlie unzipped her coat but left it on. "And I also figured that if I ever want things to become somewhat normal with us again, I need to see you in person."

"So, you're hoping for normal again?" Hailey questioned.

"Yes, Hails." Charlie slid her coat off, and Hailey knew now that the woman was staying. "I thought that, by telling you how I felt, I'd need time away from you, to figure out how to move on. But I think it's the opposite."

"What do you mean?"

"I think I need to be around you," Charlie said. "I feel so much better, now that you know. And I wish I had told you years ago, because this feels good. It feels like there's finally no secrets hanging over my head. I can just be myself now."

"You weren't yourself before?"

"Yeah, but not entirely," Charlie said.

"Charlie…"

"Hails, I wanted you," she admitted. "Every time I was around you, that was on my mind. I was myself, but feelings like that are a big part of a person, too. It's freeing now, to just have it out there so I can move on and see you move on. And if that's with Emma, then I hope she makes you happy. And I can just… breathe."

"So, you've spent ten-plus years in love with me, but you're over me now?" Hailey checked and wasn't sure why she did.

She shouldn't be asking that question. It wasn't fair. She should be grateful that Charlie was happy, because she looked happy.

"Not even close." Charlie seemed almost offended. "Hailey, I'm not even close to being over you. That will take time. But I don't want to avoid you anymore, either. I'm not saying that I'm ready to hear about you and Emma together. And I know I don't want to hear about any of the physical stuff, because that will absolutely break me right now." Charlie lowered her head for a moment before lifting it back up. "I'm balancing on a wire as is. It's like I can see you, talk to you, and feel okay about it, but I'm still in a place where I can't picture you with anyone else. If I do, it might make me have a mild panic attack," she replied with a coy smile.

"Oh," Hailey returned. She then wrapped both hands around her coffee and decided that if they were ever going to get back to normal, she needed to do something that was normal. "You're up."

Charlie nodded with a more definitive smile and headed to buy them both coffee, which was one of the most normal things in their friendship. While she was waiting, Hailey thought about what Charlie had revealed. Charlie needed to be around Hailey to help her get over her, but Hailey was starting to wonder if she, herself, could be around Charlie. She hadn't seen the woman since Sunday. Four days without her, and Hailey missed her like crazy. But seeing her in their normal coffee house was different now. Charlie was the most important person in her world, but Hailey couldn't stop seeing her hovering above her and touching her skin as she had imagined in her fantasy earlier. Hailey tried to push it out of her mind as competing thoughts of Emma's actual lips on her skin came into her mind.

"So, I made sure to ask for that extra pump of vanilla, but I'm not entirely sure he's put it in." Charlie set a fresh cup of coffee in front of Hailey and sat down with her own cup. "He seemed a little pre-occupied with the hot chick behind me." Charlie nodded her head backward without turning around. Hailey saw the young woman she was refer-ring to, as well as the teenage boy, who appeared to be checking that woman out. "There's also a chance he put in, like, ten pumps, too. It could go either way, I guess," she added with a light laugh.

Hailey smiled at her and glanced down at the drink, deciding if she should risk it.

"*Hardy Boys*," she stated to change the subject.

"Is a book series?" Charlie tried to understand.

"I told you about *The Baby-Sitters Club*. You tell me about why you liked *The Hardy Boys*."

"Oh." Charlie laughed. "I liked the mysteries. It was fun. Plus, JJ was reading them, and I wanted to be just like my big brother."

"That's cute," Hailey said and then thought maybe she should take that back, but Charlie didn't seem to be bothered by the comment.

"The town that we lived in was tiny, as was our house. But when he did actually allow me to play with him, he would make little places to discover for us."

"What do you mean, little places?" Hailey took a sip of her old coffee accidentally and then pushed it aside, grabbing her new coffee instead.

"He would put boxes up places and make little forts with pillows and blankets. He would also hide things that we'd have to search for. He was really into that for a while. Then, he turned into a teenager and never wanted to talk to me again."

Hailey watched Charlie as she told the story and saw the light in the woman's eyes at the topic of her brother, who, Hailey knew, was very important to Charlie, despite the fact that they didn't see one another that often.

"Teenage boys are pretty much the worst," she shared.

"Our dad was away a lot," Charlie continued. "He worked over an hour away and pulled twelve-hour shifts six days a week. When he was home, he was exhausted. And my mom worked all the time, too. So it was just JJ and I against the world there for a while."

Hailey took another sip of her coffee and felt like it had just enough vanilla in it. But, more importantly, she felt a little behind somehow. She had known Charlie for years, but this was new information to her. This was something they'd never talked about. This was her chance to get to know more about her best friend.

"What kind of factory was it again?" Hailey couldn't remember ever being told exactly what John Adams had done for a living.

"Tires," Charlie stated as if she was embarrassed by it. "They recycled old tires. Shredded the rubber and then shipped it out to places that knew what to do with it. My dad had scarlet fever when he was a kid. He almost died."

"What?!" Hailey exclaimed.

"Yeah. He got really sick, and it did damage to his brain when he was around three or four. He almost didn't make it, but he pulled through. It just meant that he had a hard time in school, and then he eventually dropped out, because he hated it. He had a hard time reading and could barely pass pre-algebra. So, when he was fifteen, he quit school and got a job at a farm, doing manual labor, until he was eighteen and could work at a factory and make a little more money. He met my mom then, though. And she got pregnant right away," Charlie explained. "JJ came out after. They got married when he was a baby, and I came later. My dad worked at the factory until he died."

"How did I not know this stuff?" Hailey questioned.

"I don't know. I don't really like talking about it that much."

"You should talk about it more. It's your... origin story, Charlie Adams."

"Tell me more about your origin story, then," Charlie pressed. "Tell me why you needed a book series because you didn't have a lot of friends."

"Oh," Hailey stated. "Well, I was a shy kid," she admitted. "I wasn't an outcast so much as I was just invisible."

"How could you ever be invisible?" Charlie practically guffawed.

Hailey lifted the corner of her mouth.

"I liked it, for the most part. I didn't feel like I was missing out or anything. I was invited to slumber parties and things. Sometimes, I went; and, sometimes, I didn't. Even when I did, though, I mostly just stayed out of the way. I'd sit back and watch."

"And you chose PR?" Charlie seemed surprised. "I saw you on TV the other day, Hails."

"It took some practice, but I became a little more extraverted when I needed to be. But I don't exactly enjoy the on-camera stuff. I prefer the behind-the-scenes PR work."

"How are things going with the boss that's leaving?"

"Leaving? You mean checked out? Because that's exactly what's happened. It's just me right now. They're interviewing her replacement, but that person won't start until mid-April, because HR has to go through the application process, the phone screens, the first-round interviews, and it just keeps going... So, I'm expecting I'll be this busy until May, at the earliest."

"Sorry, Hails. That sucks. I would never do that to my people. Even when I was leaving the city planning office, I showed up every day and got my work done."

"Well, I'll just work really hard for a while, and then, things will calm down. They will likely ask me to help interview people so that I can have a hand in picking my next boss."

"You never even considered applying, did you?" Charlie checked and sipped on her coffee.

"How'd you know?" Hailey lifted an eyebrow.

"Just a guess," Charlie replied as the phone in her coat pocket sounded, and she reached in to grab it.

Hailey wanted to ask if it was Lena texting, but she didn't think that was fair. Things were actually going well between the two of them. She didn't want to introduce any topic that would make things awkward.

"I didn't, no," Hailey said. "I don't want that job."

"Sorry, it's one of my guys." Charlie looked at the text message on the screen. "They need me on site."

It wasn't Lena. Hailey let out a deep internal breath.

"Oh, okay." There was a smile behind the coffee cup Hailey lifted to her lips. "Will I see you this weekend, for the rest of the planning stuff?"

Charlie replied to the text and then reached on her chair for her coat.

"I was planning on skipping it."

"Because of me?"

"Because of me, Hails. Look, this isn't your fault. And I *was* planning on skipping it. But I think I can be okay. I don't want Ember to suffer because this is happening right now."

"Me neither," Hailey agreed. "She deserves the best."

"She does."

"So, I'll see you tomorrow night at their place?"

"I'll be there. Do you want me to bring Eddie? He kind of misses you."

"Yes." Hailey's face lit up. "I miss him, too. Tell him that tonight."

"I will." Charlie laughed, stood, and gathered her things. "I'll see you tomorrow."

"Tomorrow."

Charlie then smiled, turned, and walked toward the door. Hailey was happy for many reasons. And the most important one of all was that there was a chance she and Charlie could not only get back to what they had before, but that it could get better; because now, Charlie was able to truly share everything with her. That made Hailey smile into her coffee drink with that extra pump of vanilla that Charlie never forgot about.

CHAPTER 14

CHARLIE had done it, and she was proud of herself for it. It was amazing what came along with this complete honesty with Hailey. God, she felt good. She felt like she could do this. She could actually be a complete friend now, and not just someone who was a friend, but who also secretly harbored intense romantic feelings for her.

She ran home after work on Friday and changed her clothes. She packed a bag as well, because she would likely be at Ember's and Eva's late. If that happened, she would probably just stay in their guest room. Eddie loved going over to aunt Ember and aunt Eva's, because they had a free-standing house with a small backyard, and he had free reign to run around in it. Eddie also liked snow; not the ice-covered sidewalks, but the snow-covered ground. Charlie walked him out quickly and then returned to the apartment to call Lena and check-in. They hadn't had much time to talk this week, and this wedding-planning stuff was taking what time Charlie did have left over after her workweek.

"Hey," Lena greeted.

"Hi."

"What's up?" Lena asked her.

"Oh, nothing," Charlie replied. "Just wanted to say hi, I guess."

"Sorry... I'm still at the office," Lena returned.

"I can let you go," Charlie offered.

"Are you still going over to your friend's tonight?"

"Yeah. And I'll probably be with them most of the weekend. They were both on vacation this week, so they planned some more without us, and now they want to clue us in."

"If you get free, maybe we can have dinner."

"Sure. I'll call you," Charlie returned.

"Okay. Listen, have fun."

"I will." Charlie smiled. "Try to leave your office at a reasonable hour, okay?"

"I will do that." Lena laughed. "Bye, Charlie."

"Bye."

***

"All right, calm down." Charlie's voice was heard through the front door when she let herself in, and then Hailey heard the pounding feet of Eddie rushing toward her, as she sat on Ember's couch, waiting for her friend to come downstairs.

"Hey, buddy!" Hailey greeted him.

Eddie's front paws went up into her lap, and then he barked once, indicating that he wanted Hailey to pet him.

"Sorry, Hails. He's really happy to be here."

"It's okay. I missed this face." Hailey squished Eddie's face between her hands.

When Eddie jumped down, he made his way toward the back sliding door, that Charlie opened for him and watched him rush into the backyard. Charlie reached into her bag and pulled out his favorite rope toy to toss out for him. She watched him hunt for it in the snow, grab it, and then toss it across the yard to go retrieve it.

"He'll be out there for a while." Charlie rolled her eyes at the dog.

"Hey, you two!" Ember's voice rang down from upstairs. "Get up here."

"Hello to you, too, Em," Charlie replied and closed the door.

"We're being summoned." Hailey walked toward the stairs, and Charlie followed.

They made their way up and then into Ember's bedroom.

"Eva's going to be home any minute. Tell me what you think." Ember stood in front of an old-style floor-length mirror, facing it, but then turned when she saw the two of them standing right inside the door.

"Wow!" Hailey took in the sight of her friend in a long white dress. It flowed off of Ember's toned frame and had thin straps that rested perfectly on the woman's shoulders. It also shimmered on the bodice just enough to draw attention. "Em, you look amazing."

"Ember, it's beautiful," Charlie agreed. "When did you pick it out?"

"This week. Eva and I went dress-shopping with Alyssa and Hannah, and I found this one. I went back and bought it today. I just felt like this is the one."

"It is, Em." Hailey thought there had never been a more beautiful bride-to-be than her friend, with her long ash-blonde hair, hat was framing her face, and her light eyes. "That's your dress, girl."

"Yeah?" Ember asked a little shyly.

"November Elliot, that is your wedding dress," Charlie chimed in, and Hailey turned to glance at her. "You're getting married, Em!" Charlie brightened, and her tone lightened at the same time.

Hailey hadn't seen this side of Charlie before. She was never a sappy woman. Hailey found herself wondering how Charlie was with her past girlfriends. Had the woman been a romantic? Had she ever done anything like what Hailey had heard Ember and Eva had done for one another? Or like when Alyssa proposed to Hannah at the top of the Ferris wheel on Navy Pier?

"I know. It's crazy," Ember said. "I'm getting married, guys."

"I never thought I'd see the day when you'd settle down." Charlie sat on the edge of Ember's bed.

"Me neither; until I met her." Ember walked into the master bathroom and closed the door just enough so that she could change in private. "And now, I can't imagine my life without her. That's what it is, you know?" she asked them, but didn't wait for a response. "That's what made it different for me. I couldn't imagine her not being mine. I couldn't imagine myself with anyone else." Ember emerged from the bathroom a few moments later, and after a second of silence, Hailey turned to her and felt Ember's confused expression on her.

"Hey, babe!" Eva's voice came from downstairs.

"I'm putting this away. You two, stall her," Ember rushed.

"Yes, ma'am," Charlie joked, mockingly saluted, and stood.

Hailey waited a moment and then followed her out.

***

"Hey, guys. Is Em upstairs?" Eva asked when they arrived in the kitchen.

"Yeah. She'll be right down."

"She bought the dress, didn't she?" Eva questioned. "I got dinner." She was now in the process of unpacking bags of food.

"Are Hannah and Alyssa coming?" Charlie asked.

"No. Al's brother is home on leave from Germany. It was sudden, and he's only there for four days. They left for Los Angeles yesterday. Al helped me pick out my dress, though, but I haven't gone to actually pick it up yet. Hey, babe," Eva said it all very quickly and then greeted Ember, as she bounded into the kitchen excitedly.

"There is a garment bag hanging in the back of our closet. You are not allowed to open it." Ember leaned in and kissed her fiancée on the cheek. "These two didn't spill any details about it, did they?"

"We didn't even confirm that you had bought the dress," Hailey said.

"Well done." Ember winked at her. "Let's eat. Eddie's outside?" she asked as she grabbed two boxes of food to carry them to the living room, where they would sit around the coffee table and have a relaxed dinner.

"Yeah," Charlie stated, carried some food items along, and then glanced out the door to see that Eddie's nose was currently buried in snow. He lifted up a mound and then shook it off before bouncing around in glee again. "I swear, he's five years old, but he acts like a damn puppy most of the time."

Hailey walked up behind her and said, "He's adorable. I like that he's like that."

"Me too. He entertains himself," Charlie told her and turned around.

When she did, Hailey realized how close she was standing to Charlie. Hailey hadn't done it intentionally. She just wanted to see what Eddie was up to, but Charlie was right in front of her now. She could smell the scent of Charlie's shampoo. It was juniper berry. Of course, Hailey had no idea what actual juniper berries smelled like, but she had taken enough showers at Charlie's to have seen the label on the woman's shampoo. She knew that was at least what the shampoo company thought juniper berries smelled like. As Charlie just stared at her, Hailey saw this new ease to Charlie in those eyes and in her shy smile. Hailey was starting to feel her heart pound inside her chest, and she liked the feeling.

"My dress is currently on hold. Should I pick it up tomorrow?" Eva's voice broke the moment between them.

"Yeah. And let these two see it so that they can tell me all about it," Ember suggested.

Charlie looked over Hailey's shoulder to the two women now seated on the couch next to one another.

"We won't tell her anything," Charlie said and walked around Hailey toward the coffee table.

She sat on the floor, and Hailey let out a deep breath before turning and sitting down next to her.

***

Charlie felt Hailey's eyes on her throughout the entire meal. She had been so proud of herself earlier, but Hailey, staring at her, was making things more difficult than she thought they would be. She felt a bit like a zoo animal that was sitting still, minding its own business, and some kid was staring, waiting for her to play with a giant plastic ball or roll over and yawn. Hailey's eyes kept coming back to her, and she didn't understand why. The only reason Charlie could think, was that Hailey was trying to see if she would be different somehow, or maybe Hailey was just checking on her to make sure Charlie was okay. Either way, it wasn't making things easy on Charlie, and she needed easy right now.

"Dresses are done, and the cake has been chosen," Eva said after they finished eating and the cartons had been disposed of.

Charlie had let Eddie in from the cold, and he had his head resting on Hailey's thigh, while she absentmindedly rubbed behind his ear.

"We have to take a trip to Iowa next weekend, to meet our wedding planner, Anna," Ember said in a light tone about Eva's sister. "She wants to go over decorations."

"If we don't go, she'll just pick out stuff on her own," Eva reminded.

The four of them sat around for another couple of hours, trying to finalize the bridal shower, which neither woman wanted, so they would skip that. But then, the talks of the bachelorette parties started, and several suggestions were tossed out. Eva and Ember both said they were exhausted and that they could pick up the planning in the morning. A little before midnight, they went up to their room, while Hailey and Charlie remained downstairs. Charlie let Eddie out again. When he came bounding back in, she made the decision to stay the night. She was tired, too. She'd had another long week at work and just wanted to fall asleep without having to drive back into the city.

"Are you staying?" Charlie asked Hailey, who was sitting on the couch.

"I was thinking about it," Hailey shared. "You are, too, aren't you?"

"I was thinking about it," Charlie echoed with a smile.

"I can sleep on the couch. Take the guest room with Eddie."

"Eddie is probably going to stay with you," Charlie admitted. "He likes you more than me."

Hailey laughed and stood.

"They have a four-bedroom house with two offices and one spare room. That was great planning," Hailey said sarcastically.

"It works for them, though," Charlie reminded her.

"Take the guest room. It's colder down here." Hailey stared at Charlie.

Charlie gulped and then surprised herself.

"Hails, you can come up with me," she stated, then almost took it back but decided to stand her ground, after all.

This was okay. She could do this. Hailey was with Emma. Charlie, herself, was dating Lena. They could just share a bed as friends, like they'd done before. And, this time, it would be better, because Hailey knew. Charlie didn't have to worry anymore about saying or doing something in her sleep that could give her away.

"We can share the bed. I'm okay. We've done it before," she added.

"Are you sure?" Hailey asked and seemed sincerely concerned.

"Yeah, I'm good." Charlie nodded as if to assure herself. "Come on."

Eddie followed the two of them upstairs. Charlie completed her bathroom routine first so that she could get him situated with his blanket in the corner, while Hailey took her time in the bathroom. By the time Hailey came back into the room, the woman was wearing a borrowed shirt and pants from Ember. Charlie saw her gulp before moving to the bed and sliding under the blanket next to Charlie, who was answering a work email on her phone to keep herself distracted. Charlie felt the dip in the mattress and knew Hailey was staring at the ceiling. She placed her phone on the table next to her and turned on her side to face Hailey.

"What was your favorite *Hardy Boys*?" Hailey asked to the ceiling.

"What?" Charlie laughed out. "I don't remember. I read, like, a bunch of them over twenty years ago."

"You *do* remember." Hailey rolled to face her. "You and your brother acted them out. Which was your favorite?"

Charlie thought back to the mini-forts they'd made, their favorite book-inspired capers, and sighed.

"*What Happened at Midnight.* The bad guys were thieves. Diamonds," Charlie clarified softy. "JJ would hide marbles and pretend they were the diamonds. I was the bad guy, of course. I would try to steal them, he would stop me, and we would do it all over again."

"What did you want to be when you grew up?" Hailey was smiling at her.

"What? Hails, where's this coming from?"

"We've known each other forever, but there's still so much I don't know about you. I want to now. Is that okay?" Hailey asked softly.

"A diamond thief," Charlie told her with a smirk.

Hailey pushed at her shoulder, causing Charlie to laugh as she rolled onto her back.

"I'm serious." Hailey's laughter made those words ring false, but Charlie knew they were true.

"I don't know, Hails. We didn't do that stuff." Charlie was still laughing.

Hailey moved slightly closer and rested her head on her elbow, looking down at Charlie.

"What do you mean?"

"JJ and I, we didn't grow up like that. It wasn't about dreams, or plans, or anything. Our parents had no money. We both saw school as the thing we had to do until we grew up and moved out. I wasn't the little girl that thought about being a teacher or a nurse."

"What did you think about, then?"

"Hails, I don't know," Charlie said. "I didn't think

about much until we moved here, and then it was different, because there were possibilities here. My dad and JJ were gone, and that was hard, but the city was a lot bigger than Elkhart. I could maybe see myself graduating high school and going to college. Was it different for you?"

"Yeah, I guess." Hailey seemed taken aback by the switch. "I always thought I'd go to college. I was working on that for a while before I thought about PR, though. I didn't think I'd do anything like that in high school. I actually thought about accounting most of my junior and even into my senior year."

"Accounting? You?" Charlie seemed surprised and gave a small laugh.

"Yeah, accounting. What's so shocking about that? I had great grades in all my math classes in high school, and I had to take a few at Northwestern, too. I did all right. I'm no Ember, of course, but I did okay."

"Hailey, it's surprising because you aren't Ember. You are you." Charlie turned to face her again. "You're Hailey Grant – a PR maven, who shouldn't be hidden behind spreadsheets and calculators. You should be doing what you do because you're great at it; even when you don't think you are. I can't see you as an accountant; just doing taxes for people in some office with barely any light, squinting *those* eyes at a computer screen. I mean, those eyes should not be squinting at a computer screen," Charlie said it before she had a chance to think about it.

She then averted her own eyes from Hailey's now darkened green ones. This was not supposed to happen. She was supposed to fall asleep, wake up tomorrow, plan the wedding some more, and keep everything relaxed and not at all about her still lingering feelings for her best friend.

"Hey, Charlie?" Hailey gave a soft question.

"Yeah, I know. I'm so–"

"I'm scared," Hailey said that even more softly, which, in combination with the words, caused Charlie's eyes to re-connect with hers.

"Of what, Hails?"

"I don't know what to do." Hailey shook her head. "Never mind. Let's just—"

"Hailey, just tell me," Charlie pushed. "What are you scared of? Me? Do you think I'll do something?"

"God, no! I don't want to be selfish. And I think I'm being selfish, and that's not fair to you."

"Selfish? No, Hails, I told you this was okay. I'm okay."

"It's not about that." She inhaled a deep inhale that Charlie imagined took several minutes. "Last weekend, and a little before that, too, I think, I started thinking about things," Hailey said and then added, "about you."

"Me? What about me?"

"You, Charlie. I've been thinking about you. I've been feeling things. Then, you told me how you felt, after you found me doing what I was doing. I was so embarrassed, and then so shocked by your words, that I didn't say anything. You left, and I thought I shouldn't say anything, because you deserve better than me, Charlie," Hailey said it all very quickly. "You finally put me behind you, and you have this new person you're dating. I have Emma. And I didn't want to tell you, because you are, like, years ahead of me. I don't know that I can ever make up for that or feel everything that you feel, Charlie, and that's what scares me. It's not that you have feelings for me. It's that I have feelings for you, but they're so new and scary, and you're already there. You're there. You know, and I don't know. And... this is wrong. I shouldn't be telling you this. I hate myself right now, Charlie. Because you're trying to get over me, and I'm telling you that when I was touching myself last weekend, I was picturing you. And this is not fair to you."

Charlie stared at her with her mouth open. Her heart was racing. Her breath was coming in short bursts, and she was beginning to see small stars in her eyes due to the lack of consistent oxygen to her lungs.

"You were... me?" It wasn't a complete sentence or even a complete thought, but Charlie could barely focus on the green concerned eyes that were staring back at her.

"I'm sorry," Hailey apologized.

She then reached out and placed a gentle hand on Charlie's cheek. Charlie didn't know why, at first, until she felt Hailey's thumb under her eye, sliding away, and felt the wetness that came with the tear Hailey had wiped away for her.

"Hails…"

"I'm going to go." Hailey went to pull back. "I've made it worse. And will never forgive myself if this ruins what we have. I'm going home, and I'll give you whatever you want. If you want time and space, I'm gone. If you want to–"

"Hailey!" Charlie nearly yelled and pulled Hailey in by her waist, forcing Hailey to remain in the bed. Charlie wanted to kiss her. She wanted more than anything to run her hand under Hailey's shirt and pull her in ever closer, to taste her lips, and to touch her everywhere. She wanted everything with her. "Go out with me?"

Hailey pulled her face back slightly to check Charlie's eyes.

"What?"

"I should have asked you out when we were nineteen, but I didn't. I'm asking now. Will you go out with me?"

"But… I just told you I'm not where you are yet. I don't think I am, at least. I've been trying to figure things out. I haven't been able to yet."

"I'm not asking you to marry me, Hailey. I don't need you to love me. I've been trying to be braver lately, and I want us to go on a date." Charlie's hand slid away from Hailey's waist.

"What about Lena?"

"Lena and I aren't close to being exclusive. Emma?"

"No, we're just dating. I don't know what's going to happen. That's why I've been so confused."

"Do you want to go on a date with me?" Charlie asked and was certain that she had never been more nervous in her life. "An actual date where–"

"I pick you up," Hailey interrupted. "And we go to dinner, and maybe a movie?"

"Yeah." Charlie smiled at her.

"And then, I take you home."

"Yes."

"And we stand awkwardly at your door for a minute, while I wait for you to maybe invite me in?"

"I'm not inviting you in," Charlie returned.

"You wouldn't invite me in?" Hailey asked, surprised.

"No. Not on our first date, Hails. If we do this, we're taking our time."

"Okay." Hailey smiled shyly.

"Okay?" Charlie checked as her heart skipped about five beats.

"Yes. I want to go on a date with you," Hailey confirmed.

"Then, I should go sleep on the couch," Charlie said.

"What?" Hailey laughed.

"If I'm here, and you're here, I'm worried we won't–"

"Take our time?" Hailey smirked and lifted an eyebrow.

"Don't do that." Charlie pulled back. "That's your sexy look. Don't do that."

Hailey laughed wildly before asking, "I have a sexy look?"

"That's enough." Charlie stood, causing Eddie to lift his head.

"Stay in here," Hailey insisted. "You'll be cold down there." Hailey stood.

"You sure?" Charlie considered what to do for a moment.

"I like taking care of you. I always have," Hailey said. "I'll leave the door open a little for you so that you have the light. Good night." She walked toward the door.

"Yeah, good night." Charlie sat on the bed and smiled a goofy smile.

She then looked at her phone and pressed the home button. The screen read that it was exactly midnight. *'What happened at midnight?'* Charlie laughed silently as she recalled the title of the book before she climbed back into bed. When she did, she heard Eddie whine softly.

"Oh, go ahead," she told him and heard the metal tags on his collar clang together as Eddie nosed his way through the door, following Hailey downstairs.

CHAPTER 15

THERE was absolutely no chance Hailey was sleeping. Eddie, it appeared, had no problem passing out, though, and had been snoring all night. By four in the morning, Hailey had officially given up on sleep after hours of rolling over, and then back and over again. She had gotten a snack from the kitchen, tried reading on her phone – which she hated doing and thought it might knock her out, but it didn't. Hailey knew it was because she was thinking about the woman upstairs.

She was going on a date with Charlie. Charlie Adams, who was her best friend. They were going on a date together as two adult women who liked each other. Hailey had no idea how it would go, or what it would mean if it didn't go well. Maybe that was what they needed. Maybe they just needed to go on a date to know that it wouldn't work between them. Then both of them could move on with someone else and get back to being friends. Of course, the other side of the coin left the possibility that the date would go well... And that would lead to another date.

Eddie lifted his head at the sound of Eva moving down the stairs toward the kitchen. Hailey checked her phone to notice that it was 5:30. Eva came into the living room and saw that Hailey was awake.

"Hey. You're up early," she said to Hailey and then put her headphones in.

"Yeah. Going for a run?"

"Yeah. Em's still sleeping. I'll probably be back before she wakes up, and then I'll make breakfast for us."

"Okay. Have a good run." Hailey waved her off.

"Thanks." Eva smiled at her, and then Hailey heard the front door close behind her.

Eddie followed Eva, at first, and then walked back over to where Hailey was on the couch and started doing his dance.

"Let's go, buddy." Hailey stood slowly and made her way over to the sliding glass door.

She watched him burst outside and into the snow as soon she opened it. She smiled and laughed as the dog went immediately to his rope toy, tossed it as high as he could, and then tried and failed to catch it in his mouth. He lost interest after, and in the dim lighting of the backyard, she watched him do his business and then run around in the snow for a few moments before making his way back to the door, which Hailey re-opened to let him back inside. He shook his head and his tail to get the snow off, and then made a dash up the stairs. Hailey's eyes got big as she realized he intended to go into the guest room and would, likely, wake Charlie up. She followed the dog upstairs, whispering after him to try to get Eddie's attention, but he beat her into the room and made his way over to his blanket. He then turned to glance in Hailey's direction, decided he didn't care that she was calling him, and flopped down onto his makeshift bed, appearing content.

"I'm awake, Hails," Charlie greeted her in the moonlit room.

"I'm sorry… He wanted out, so I let him. But then, he just came up here. I couldn't stop him," Hailey returned.

She could only make out Charlie's shape, since it appeared Eva had turned off the hall light when she had gone for her run.

"It's okay. I was already up," Charlie admitted.

"Couldn't sleep, either?" Hailey chanced.

"No." Charlie reached for the lamp by the bed and flipped the switch, giving them a little light to see one another and also to cause Eddie to lift his head hopefully. But when Charlie didn't move to get up, he lowered it again. "I failed miserably at sleep. Thanks for letting him out," Charlie added softly.

"Of course," Hailey replied. "Eva went for a run. Em will probably be up soon. Eva said she'll make breakfast when she gets back. I'll go back downstairs. Maybe you can get a little sleep before the day starts."

"I doubt that," Charlie shared.

"It's weird, huh?" Hailey suggested and sat on the edge of the bed.

"We're going on a date… Yeah, that's weird." Charlie sat up and nodded.

"When?"

"Huh?" Charlie finally looked at her.

"When are we going out?"

"Oh." Charlie widened her eyes as if that would help wake her up before making them normal size again. "I don't know. I hadn't thought about that. I've been lying here the whole night, trying to figure out if I imagined the whole thing or if it really happened."

Hailey smiled and shook her head from side to side.

"You are very sweet, Charlie Adams. It's cute, and I don't know how I've missed it before."

"What about tonight?" Charlie suggested.

"Go on a date with you tonight?" Hailey repeated because she needed a moment.

"Or not. We can do it another time," Charlie backtracked.

"Tonight," Hailey stated. "Yeah."

"Yeah?"

"Tonight, but I think I need to wrap up this little planning fest with these two so that I can head home and take a nap." Hailey stood. "And I want to plan it."

"Plan the nap?" Charlie was clearly tired.

"Plan the date," Hailey corrected.

"You want to plan our date?"

"Yes," Hailey told her. "I would like to plan our first date."

"Okay." Charlie seemed relieved and, also, somewhat surprised.

"So, let's make enough noise to wake Ember up, then pretend like we didn't do it on purpose, go downstairs, eat breakfast with them, and then head out."

Charlie nodded her assent with a coy smile.

***

Charlie made it downstairs after changing, let Eddie back outside for one last round of fun in the snow, and made her way into the kitchen, where she saw Ember standing next to the coffee maker, rubbing her sleepy eyes. She found Hailey standing at the counter, stirring coffee with a spoon. Hailey slid the cup across the counter in Charlie's direction, and as Charlie took it with a smile, Ember passed the next full cup to Hailey, who added her own sugar, while Ember made a cup for herself. This all happened silently and worked like an amazing assembly line. When Eva came into the room after her short shower, Ember passed her a cup as well. Once they all had their coffee, Hailey and Charlie leaned over the counter and watched Eva attempt to make them omelets. She had told them she had been working on her cooking. They tried not to mock the woman too much, when the first one she made flipped half out of the pan. Ember said she'd eat it anyway, though.

Charlie felt a hand on the small of her back. She turned to see Hailey nod in the direction of the window, where Eddie was standing, tilting his head. Charlie headed over and let him in, but she still felt the touch of Hailey's hand on her back even after she returned. Ember seemed to be staring at them and moving her eyes back and forth, as if she felt like she understood something, but wasn't saying anything about it, because she wasn't sure. Eva finished up their omelets. Charlie marveled at how quickly Hailey was consuming the food, because she knew how Hailey's brain worked. The woman was probably already trying to figure out what they would do on their date, what she would wear, and about a hundred other things.

Charlie had to admit that, despite her slightly more butch appearance – thanks mostly to the pixie cut hair she got because a hairstylist years ago told Charlie that it would work for her shape, people assumed – especially the women she dated, that Charlie was likely to be a more dominant woman in a relationship. The women she dated expected her to want to be a top in bed, to plan dates, and pull out all the romantic stops. While Charlie had no problem with any of it, she still secretly wanted someone to recognize that she wasn't like that. She wouldn't mind a little romance being thrown in her direction, and having someone else taking the lead, at least once in a while.

"So, I think I'm going to go," Hailey said after the dishes had been cleaned.

"Oh, I thought you were staying. I was going to check out my dress later," Eva announced.

"I'm not really feeling well," Hailey replied. "I didn't sleep well. I think I just need to go home and get some rest."

"You do, huh?" Ember squinted her eyes in Hailey's direction.

"Yes, I do."

"I'm going to go, too. I have some work to do this weekend," Charlie added.

"Where was this work yesterday?" Ember questioned.

"It was at my apartment, where it is now, Ember." Charlie practically gritted her teeth until Ember stopped squinting at her. "So, I'm going to go do it now, then."

"Fine. Go do your work. And you, go feel better," Ember told Hailey.

"Okay," Hailey said.

"I have no idea what's going on, but you two can go whenever you want. And I think maybe you need some more sleep, babe," Eva joined in and placed a hand on Ember's shoulder.

"Yes, sleep," Charlie suggested. "Get some sleep, Em."

"Call me later, Charlie," Ember told her. "You too, Hails."

"We will," Hailey stated, and then her eyes grew three sizes. "I mean, I will, and she will. We will, but separately."

"Okay. Bye." Charlie stood and moved quickly to grab her things and to get Eddie ready to go.

They made their great escape out to Hailey's car. Charlie had ordered herself an Uber while inside the house.

"Are you sure you won't let me drive you? This is ridiculous," Hailey asked.

"Yes, I'm sure," Charlie replied.

"Fine, weirdo." Hailey chuckled at her. "I'll call you later, okay?"

"Yeah."

Hailey smiled and then climbed inside her car. Charlie watched her head out of the driveway as her own, ordered car arrived.

***

Hailey went to work as soon as she got home. She knew exactly what she wanted to do and needed her computer to find out if it was possible. She spent about one hour researching and finalized the plan. Then, she called Charlie and made plans to pick her up at six for their date before she climbed into bed. Hailey was excited and had a hard time falling asleep. But, eventually, the exhaustion overtook her. She got a couple of solid hours of sleep before she had to get up to get ready. After her shower, Hailey searched for something to wear that would be appropriate for the evening and heard her phone ring in the kitchen. She saw Emma's name on the screen when she picked it up. And for a moment, Hailey wasn't sure how she felt. She had never dated two women at once. It was strange. She didn't know if she should answer a phone call from Emma when she was about to go out on a date with Charlie. She had promised to be honest with Emma, though, so she leaned toward telling her about the date, but she also didn't know if it would even be worth mentioning.

If the date went wrong, or either of them determined

they weren't interested in pursuing it, it wouldn't matter. And if it went well, she could tell Emma then. Hailey also didn't want to lie to her about her plans. She knew if she answered, it would come up. Hailey wasn't the type of person to tell Emma she was still stuck wedding-planning when really, she was out with Charlie. And if she said she was free, Emma would likely want to come over or for Hailey to go over to her place. Hailey ignored the call and went back to getting ready.

She settled on her outfit and pulled her hair back. Once she felt ready, Hailey stared at herself in the mirror for several minutes, finding non-existent lint on her sweater and trying to get a flyaway piece of hair in place. She checked the time and knew she needed to leave if she didn't want to be late. Hailey decided she looked as good as she was going to be, grabbed her coat and purse, and went to pick up Charlie for their date.

***

Charlie paced in her apartment. It was 5:53 p.m. If she knew the woman well, and she did, then she knew Hailey would be at least five minutes early. That gave Charlie two minutes to find a way to get rid of the nervous energy that had prevented her from sleeping all day and last night, despite how unbelievably tired she was. Eddie was restless, too, and didn't seem to know what to do with himself, so he just kept walking around the apartment in his own brand of pacing.

"Shit." Hailey walked into the apartment and saw Charlie's surprise. "I used my key." She held up the key card she'd had ever since Charlie moved in. "I meant to knock, and I used my key... I'm sorry." Hailey closed the door, leaving herself in the hallway.

Charlie stood still about ten feet away from the door, not sure what just happened or what she should do about it. Then, there was a knock on the door, and she rolled her eyes at Hailey before walking to it and pulling it open.

"Better?" Charlie questioned with a smile.

"Hey, I'm trying to make this a real date here, and not just me coming over to hang out."

Charlie nearly melted at the sentiment.

"Sorry," she replied.

"You ready? Does Eddie need to go out?"

"No. I knew you'd be early, so I already took him," Charlie shared and took the other woman in.

Hailey looked beautiful. She was dressed somewhat casually, in a pair of form-fitting jeans and probably a sweater under her tweed jacket.

"You look nice," Charlie complimented softly.

"So do you," Hailey complimented back. "Let's go."

Charlie pulled on her coat, checked her pockets to make sure she had everything – as a stall, because the nervous energy hadn't yet gone away, and she hoped that the extra few seconds would make it evaporate and leave her feeling confident and ready for this. It didn't.

"So, where are we going?" Charlie asked once they were in Hailey's car and had been on the road for about ten minutes.

Neither of them had spoken since they left the apartment. Charlie knew they were likely both nervous, but she also wondered if this was a good sign, because people typically talked on first dates.

"It's a surprise." Hailey turned to her with a smile. "I just hope you like it."

"I thought we were just grabbing dinner and, maybe, going to a movie. I even checked some movie times just in case."

"Of course, you did. I told you I was planning this date. I came up with something else," Hailey told her. "Do you want music?"

Hailey turned on the radio. Charlie saw her hand tremble a little as she did. Charlie wanted to take it and pull it into her lap, but she wasn't sure if she should. They hadn't discussed any of the physical stuff. Charlie didn't know what was okay to do at the beginning of this date and didn't want to ruin it before it even began. Twenty minutes later, they pulled up in front of a building that looked like a small warehouse. In fact, Charlie knew it was a small warehouse, because they were in the warehouse district. They were clearly parked in the back, because there were no windows on the building. There were, however, a few more cars there, so there was definitely something going on.

"Hails?"

"Come on." Hailey got out of the car without explanation, and Charlie followed her. "So, this is a little crazy, and it's really made for more people, but I called and made sure we could get a room all to ourselves."

"A room?" Charlie was confused until she saw an old-fashioned sign hanging above a door. "Trapped Cipher Room?" she asked and looked at Hailey.

"Yeah. Come on, diamond thief. Let's see how you are when you're the good guy."

Hailey tugged on Charlie's coat and opened the door for them. When they entered, they were in a small lobby, with benches lining two walls and a giant chalkboard hanging on the third wall, with the names of teams and times next to them. A short girl with a nose ring stood behind a counter. Hailey walked up to her.

"I'm Hailey Grant. I have a 6:30 reservation," she told the girl.

"Sure. You wanted the diamond caper room to yourself." The girl typed something into a computer.

"Yeah." Hailey turned to see Charlie behind her. "Are you coming?" She questioned with a smile.

Charlie couldn't believe it. Hailey had reserved them an escape room.

"I can't believe you did this," Charlie told the woman when she stood next to her in front of the counter.

"Follow me," the girl stated and walked them back to a room where there were lockers for their belongings. "Ernie is going to walk you two through the rules. You can put your coats and purses in the lockers and keep the keys with you. You don't have to lock up your phones, but we just request that you don't use the phone for spoilers while in the room, and that you don't ruin the fun for everyone else by ruining the magic," the girl said in a monotone voice, as if she had delivered the same message a thousand times and hated her job.

"Hey, ladies, I'm Ernie." A stocky guy, probably in his mid-twenties, approached as they were stuffing their belongings into tiny lockers and tucking keys into their pockets. "I'm going to be your outside man tonight. You are insurance investigators, known worldwide for your ability to prevent the theft of priceless artifacts and jewelry. Through an interview with a known high-end jewelry thief, you know there is a two-hundred-and-fifty-carat diamond located inside the auction room of a century-old building. The potential thieves are on their way, and you need to prevent them from stealing the diamond to save your company the high payout and to save the client from a major loss. The only problem is that the diamond is so important to the auction house, that they've not only secured it, they've hidden it. The auction house and the diamond are owned by an eccentric old man, who's been a victim of theft too many times and has vowed to never let it happen again. His name is Anthony Miller. He's recently had some problems with his memory, so he left himself clues to ensure he wouldn't forget where the diamond is hidden and the location of the safe. Your job is to simply find the diamond and remove it from the auction house before the potential thieves arrive. Mr. Miller is currently on a plane and is unreachable, so you'll have to do this on your own to prevent the theft. The good news is that I've got some information that can help you, and I'll be right outside in the van, keeping a lookout."

Ernie seemed really into his job. Charlie was trying to absorb the whole story but was having a difficult time, because she just kept thinking about how Hailey had done this for her based on a silly story about her favorite book and a memory from her childhood.

The guy handed Hailey a walkie-talkie. "I'll radio in anything I find on my own, and if you need me, just radio. You can use the radio three times before the thieves will be able to tap into our frequency and know we're here. We also need to catch them in the act, or they'll just try it again later. So, we'll call the police when I see them outside and..." He just kept talking.

Charlie tried not to think about how ridiculous the scenario itself was and just enjoy the moment. Ernie finished up by telling them they would be locked inside the room and would have sixty minutes to find the diamond. If they didn't, the thieves would arrive, and all hope would be lost. Ernie walked them to a door, opened it, and walked them in. He showed them the timer hanging above the door and told them to hit the button on the wall if they needed to evacuate; or, in reality, just needed to give up, or there was an emergency. He wished them luck, set the timer, and closed the door behind them.

"Hailey, I can't believe you did this for me," Charlie shared.

"You better get to it. We only have an hour." Hailey winked at her. "Come on *Hardy Boy*, let's find the diamond."

The room wasn't as big as Charlie pictured. It was an office that looked old in nature, which fit with the eccentric old man's character the guy had described. On the walls, there were old paintings, maps, and a wall-length bookshelf, filled with books and other random items. There was a door that had an electronic lock on it that Charlie guessed was a part of the puzzle.

"Let's get to work." Charlie rubbed her hands together and began taking it seriously.

The two worked together in near silence, only communicating when they needed to exchange clues. They found a flashlight that illuminated numbers on the paintings and tried those to open the door, but failed. Ernie radioed in that the lock had a two-minute reset, so they'd have to wait two minutes after three failed attempts to try again. Hailey found what she thought could be a code in a few books. That code led to a key, which opened a drawer, and on and on it went... Until they got the code to open that door, but that door led to another room with more objects and more clues. There was a safe, and with twenty minutes left, Charlie thought they'd found it, but the safe only had an old-fashioned transparency in it that she had no idea what to do with. It was Hailey that figured out that the letters written on it seemed to fit a keyboard, and there was an old typewriter on a desk. She placed it on top and found that each letter represented another letter. Another piece of paper with random letters they'd found earlier now made sense, and they worked together to translate the code, which then gave them the name of a city on the map and a direction. The map had push pins in it, with numbers written on them. They started at the first city and moved east, which gave them six numbers.

"We have two lockers," Hailey said and then looked at the timer. "And thirty seconds, Charlie."

"Read me the numbers," Charlie told her and grabbed a padlock on the locker to her left.

"Three, two, one, four, two, eight," Hailey read them quickly. "It could be thirty-two, fourteen and twenty-eight. Or, three, two, one, and then four, two, eight are for the other locker," she suggested.

Charlie turned the dial back and forth once and tried to open it, but nothing happened. In spy thrillers, they could get close enough and hear the soft clicks, but Charlie didn't have time for that. She tried three, two, one, while Hailey gripped the other padlock and tried a combination of numbers to try to double their odds.

When Hailey's combination failed, she looked up at the timer and noticed that they only had ten seconds left. Charlie prepared herself for the failure and for feeling guilty for not being a better fake insurance investigator with a really ineffective way of catching jewel thieves. Then, she heard the click and the sound of the padlock unlocking. She pulled it away and opened the locker to see a giant and a very fake diamond inside.

"Congratulations, you have..." Ernie's voice came over the radio.

But Charlie didn't hear it. She was too busy staring down at the diamond and then into Hailey's eyes that were shining at her along with the woman's wide smile.

"You did it," she congratulated Charlie and wrapped her arms around Charlie's neck to pull her in for an embrace.

Charlie wrapped her arms tightly around Hailey's waist, and after a moment, when they pulled away, she leaned in and captured Hailey's lips without even thinking. It took a second before she realized Hailey wasn't kissing her back. Charlie's heart started racing, and not for their victory, but because she had done something so incredibly stupid. Then, Charlie felt soft lips begin to move in harmony with her own. She gripped Hailey's waist tighter, needing to hold her closer.

***

Charlie's lips had parted, and Hailey knew that her tongue was sliding inside Charlie's mouth and that this new sensation was remarkable. As their tongues began a tentative dance, Hailey splayed her hands on the small of Charlie's back and enjoyed the depths of Charlie's eager mouth, and the small, almost imperceptible moan she heard coming from the woman. Then, she heard a throat clear and realized they had been interrupted. Hailey pulled back, trying to give Charlie a reassuring glance as she did so, but it wasn't possible, because Charlie's face registered utter disbelief, mixed with absolute joy. And Hailey wasn't sure anymore. She was terrified.

CHAPTER 16

"LET'S get your picture for the wall," Ernie told them the moment they exited the room and stood back by the lockers against a bright-green wall that had the name of the escape room on it in big black and white letters. Charlie's arm went around Hailey's waist, and Charlie pulled her into her side. Ernie snapped a picture and congratulated them again. They pulled their items from the lockers and threw on their coats. Charlie couldn't stop smiling. She knew she looked like a giggling schoolgirl, but this date had already been the best date of her entire life, and it wasn't even over.

Hailey was silent as they walked toward the car and climbed inside. Charlie wasn't sure how to take that, because she thought their kiss had been amazing. Maybe Hailey had thought the opposite. Her facial expression, when they broke apart, was hard to read. Charlie wasn't sure if the fear she saw in Hailey's eyes was because she liked the kiss so much, it was a little scary; or that Hailey felt nothing and would have to tell Charlie that this wasn't going anywhere after tonight.

"That was awesome, Hails. Thank you," Charlie broke the silence.

"I have a confession to make," Hailey stated while staring out the window.

Charlie gulped, hoping that the confession Hailey was about to make wasn't that she was taking Charlie home because she didn't want the date to continue after that kiss.

"Okay," Charlie replied with severe trepidation.

"I asked them to alter the room," Hailey started and then turned to Charlie. "The real scenario is that we're the diamond thieves, trying to steal the thing. But, I knew that JJ always made you the bad guy. I thought it would be nice for you to be the good guy, for a change. So, I called them earlier today and asked if they could change it up a little."

"You did?" Charlie let out a sigh of relief.

"That's kind of why it made little sense. They threw it together for me, like, three hours ago."

"Hails…"

"I just wanted it to be something special for you."

"Hailey, it was," Charlie began and then turned in her seat to face her. "It was amazing. I don't know how you thought of it, but no one's ever done anything like that for me before."

"Because you give off this vibe to people," Hailey offered and then proceeded, "that you don't want or need those kinds of gestures."

"Yeah." Charlie lifted the corner of her mouth, taken aback by how well Hailey knew her.

"But… I know you, Charlie. I probably know you better than you do." Hailey laughed. "Which is why I'm taking us to the Rainforest Café right now."

"We're going to the Rainforest Café?" Charlie asked with excitement she couldn't contain.

"You are such a kid, sometimes." Hailey laughed and turned the car into a parking garage. "I know you've always wanted to go there but haven't, because you only admitted to me that you wanted to check it out in passing, and then pretended like it didn't matter. You've lived here forever, and you've never gone."

***

"Hails, I can't believe you did all this for me."

Hailey pulled them into a parking spot and turned off the car.

"Yeah," she stated and then climbed out.

Charlie had gone from smiling to dumbfounded and confused. Hailey's delivery had gone from happy and laughing, to just plain matter-of-fact. Charlie climbed out of the car. Hailey waited for her so that they could walk to the restaurant together.

The Rainforest Café was a theme restaurant with rainforest sights and sounds amongst the tables. It also came complete with a gift shop. It was a tourist trap, which was why a lot of locals avoided the place. But Charlie had always wanted to check it out, because it seemed like something fun to do while you were eating dinner; look at fake rainforest animals, listen to the water running around you, and watch everyone's childlike excitement as they ate and explored.

They made their way inside, and, thankfully, Hailey had made a reservation, because the place was packed. Charlie couldn't recall if another woman had ever made reservations for her before and smiled, despite worrying about Hailey's change in demeanor. She'd seen it happen twice already, and both times were after they shared their first kiss. Well, first, but maybe the last, too, given the lack of any confirmation that Hailey had enjoyed it since. They were sat immediately and provided with menus. Charlie wasn't yet interested in the food, because she was taking in the ridiculousness of the room around her. Trees hung all around them, and she could hear the sounds of forest birds chirping and cawing. A fake snake coiled in a tree over Hailey's head. Charlie made a note not to call her attention to it, because Hailey hated snakes, real or otherwise. And just turning around and seeing the thing would likely cause her to freak out.

"Well?" Hailey asked her after several moments of Charlie's gazing around.

Charlie returned her eyes to Hailey's and noticed that the lightness had returned to them, which made her relax slightly.

"It's cheesy. I love it," Charlie stated and earned a smile from Hailey in return.

There was a moment of shared awkwardness before their waiter approached and took their drink order. Hailey insisted Charlie order a fruity umbrella drink, that was the house special, while she stuck with iced tea, since she was driving. Charlie agreed, because Hailey had already gone through so much trouble to put this all together for her. When the waiter returned with a bright blue concoction, with not just an umbrella but giant chunks of pineapple, oranges, and cherries all skewered on a stick and deposited into the giant bowl-sized cup, Charlie decided that Hailey would have to at least help her drink a little of this thing. It was huge, and it would get her drunk very quickly if she didn't pace herself. Hailey laughed at her while Charlie tilted her head to try to look at it in more detail.

"You look like you're trying to figure out where to start," Hailey commented on the drink after their waiter left with their order.

"I am," Charlie stated. "This thing is nuts."

"It looked a lot smaller on the picture." Hailey leaned over the table, getting closer to Charlie as she did so, and stirred the skewer around into the liquid before lifting her eyes to meet Charlie's. "Tell me something I don't know about you," she said softly and a few inches from Charlie's face.

"Something *you* don't know? That's probably a short list."

Charlie took a sip and was met with immediate sweetness and only a small hint of alcohol, which didn't mean it wasn't there or that it was in short supply. It meant that the drink was mixed with sweet liqueurs, and it was dangerous for someone like Charlie, who didn't drink mixed drinks like this often. She would pace herself. She took the straw and moved it around in the glass to pass to Hailey, who placed her hand on top of Charlie's for a moment during the exchange. Charlie's breath caught as she watched Hailey take a small sip of the sweet drink and smile once she pulled away.

"Tell me something about your friends in high school before we met," Hailey suggested. "I don't think you've ever mentioned anyone specifically."

"Oh, I guess I don't mention it because I don't think I had real friends back then," Charlie shared.

"You were popular, though, weren't you? You've talked about having a lot of friends, and I know you had a boyfriend, Charlie Adams," Hailey mocked.

Charlie laughed and chanced placing her hand on top of Hailey's as they both rested near the center of the small two-person table. Hailey looked down at their hands, one resting atop the other, and Charlie saw an almost imperceptible smile reach her lips before it reached her green eyes, that looked even brighter now, given all the dark-green fake foliage around them.

It took a moment, but Hailey pulled her hand out from under Charlie's. She didn't move it away, though. She just pushed it back into Charlie's hand so that they could link their fingers. Hailey stared at the hands for several long moments, while she apparently contemplated either how it felt, or what she would do next. Charlie wasn't certain what Hailey would do, but she was certain about how good it felt to hold her hand like this. She had held Hailey's hand a few times before, but never like this. And this was definitely the best way to hold hands with someone.

"I had a boyfriend, yes. But I think we both know that was more of a beard-type situation."

"I've never kissed a guy," Hailey stated something Charlie already knew about her. "What was it like? Did it feel strange, since you already knew you liked girls?"

Charlie considered it for a moment and thought back to the few kisses she'd had with the only guy she had ever kissed, before deciding she wouldn't use another guy to hide her sexuality and also before she was brave enough to do anything about the fact that she was gay.

"It felt wrong," Charlie finally said and took a drink, holding the straw with her free hand, because she didn't dare to let Hailey's hand go. "Every time, it just felt wrong. Looking back on it, I remember feeling like I was having an out of body experience. It felt like it wasn't me kissing him. I was watching – looking down from the sky or something, at two people kissing one another, but it didn't feel like me."

"And when you kissed Julia for the first time?" Hailey asked, knowing the story of Charlie's first time.

"Well, that was different."

"Well, yeah," Hailey agreed.

"No, not just because it was with another girl. It did feel good. It felt like I was at least kissing the right gender."

"But not the right person?" Hailey questioned.

"No way." Charlie laughed at that thought. "It was also different, though. Because we didn't kiss and then took the time to savor it or to even think about it. It was a kiss that immediately led to more. And when it was all done, I knew for sure that I was a gay. But I also wasn't disappointed when nothing else happened with Julia." Hailey's facial expression was unreadable. "What?"

"I don't know." Hailey seemed to be thinking a lot tonight. "I just feel like you deserved better than that for your first time."

"What? Like rose petals, candles, and soft music?" Charlie laughed lightly. Hailey didn't say anything, but she pulled her hands back. "Hails, I'm sorry."

"No, it's okay," she returned. "I did have the cliché first time experience," Hailey reminded as Charlie now had thoughts of Emma entering her mind.

And Emma Colton was the last person Charlie wanted to be thinking about while sitting across from Hailey on their first date.

"But it was what we both wanted, and I'm glad it happened that way," Hailey added.

"I'm sure," Charlie returned and placed her hand on her own lap, realizing that their moment of hand-holding had passed. "I didn't mean anything by that. I just know what I was like back then, Hails. I didn't think I'd ever find a way to express that part of myself. I was so closed off. That's why I don't think I had any real friends back then. I had people that I spent time with, and I had fun sometimes, too, but not one of them knew me. Not one of them understood that I was hiding a very important part of myself. And because I had pushed it down so deeply, I'd given up on ever expressing it. Then, I met Julia. I had an instant crush, and I still thought that would be it. But she surprised me, and we had a brief but pretty remarkable encounter, because, even though it wasn't planned or even that good – now that I know what good sex can be – it was what I needed at the time. It happened. I don't regret it or even wish that it happened differently. It gave me confidence a couple of years later – when I met two crazy girls in a restaurant, to tell them that I was gay," Charlie confessed. "It gave me the best friends I've ever had, Hails. And for that, I'll always be grateful to Julia."

"Me too," Hailey agreed. "There's something different about you now. I don't know if it's because I started seeing you differently or–"

"It's because I told you," Charlie shared confidently. "It's the same thing as with Julia. There's something that comes with fully recognizing yourself."

"You're freer, somehow; lighter," Hailey added.

"No more secrets. It feels that way to me, too," Charlie agreed.

They ate in relative but comfortable silence for several moments before the conversation picked up naturally. Charlie felt at ease as they talked more about their lives before they met one another and even a few funny memories they shared together. They talked about their worst experiences waiting tables and some of the parties they went to after work.

"Oh, my God! I remember her," Hailey exclaimed as she took a drink. "She followed you around for weeks until she got fired."

"Dana Gifford," Charlie said the woman's name out loud and then set her fork on top of her plate, signaling that she was done eating. "She would not give up."

"We went to that bar every Friday night, after work, and she would wait for you, even when you were closing. You played pool, and she'd stand behind you while you were lining up your shots. She tried to get you to teach her how to play."

"She did," Charlie admitted. "I can't blame her, though."

"Why? Because you're so hot?" Hailey mocked with a small laugh.

"No, because we hooked up," Charlie admitted.

Hailey's smile disappeared from her face.

"You hooked up with her?"

"It was after you told me about your little crush on Ember."

"What?" Hailey questioned.

"I liked you, but you were into Ember. Dana was nice. She hadn't turned into the annoying version of herself yet. We talked one night after work. I walked her home, and she invited me up. We hooked up, and I figured that would be the end of it, but she started hanging around all the time and wanted to date. I didn't want to date her, so I was thankful when she got fired."

"Who else did you hook up with that I know?" Hailey asked.

Charlie wasn't sure why Hailey was asking. Was she asking because she wanted to know as Charlie's friend who knew these people, or was Hailey asking because she was trying to find out all the women Charlie slept with as someone she was on a date with now?

"This is a weird topic for a first date, Hails."

"You're right. Sorry."

They stopped talking while the waiter removed their plates. Charlie's drink was only half gone, but she knew she wouldn't finish it. Neither of them was interested in dessert, and when the check came, Hailey insisted on paying. When they stood to leave, Charlie helped Hailey with her coat, like she always did, and then turned her body so they could walk out.

"This way," Charlie directed.

"Why are you pulling me this way?" Hailey asked and then went to turn her head.

Charlie was there, and she covered Hailey's eyes for a moment while she kept a hand on the small of her back.

"Hailey, fake snake." It was all Charlie needed to say. "It's fake," she whispered into her ear.

Hailey's body tensed and then relaxed as Charlie repeated the word 'fake.'

"Okay," Hailey replied.

Charlie removed her hand from Hailey's eyes and couldn't stop herself from a quick glance down at Hailey's lips. She resisted doing anything in a crowded restaurant. Hailey kept her eyes on hers. Charlie kept her hand on Hailey's back and ushered her toward the way out of the restaurant. In order to leave, they had to walk through the gift shop. This gave them time to pause and laugh a little at the souvenirs on offer. The gift shop had items one might use if they were taking an actual rainforest voyage, like toy compasses and water bottles with the name of the restaurant on them. There were shirts and sweaters, of course, and when Hailey held a particularly garish one up to Charlie, Charlie nodded a definitive no. Hailey laughed at her and bought the shirt anyway. They carried the bag out and headed toward the car, continuing their shared laughter.

***

Hailey drove them toward Charlie's apartment as they talked and simultaneously got closer to where she would drop Charlie off for the night. Hailey started getting more nervous. Her plan had worked, but it had come at a cost. She wanted to get to know Charlie in a new way. Because Charlie had been in love with her for so long, Hailey needed to try to catch up; or at least, that was how it felt. She had known Charlie as her friend for years, but the past couple of weeks, Hailey had been starting to see her differently.

Some of it was physical. She began enjoying the shape of Charlie's face and her nicely cut jawline. Hailey took in just how well Charlie's short hair worked for her. She had thought about running her hands through it, and how Charlie's lips would feel pressed to her own. She had started to notice how sexy Charlie looked, sometimes, when she was just wearing sweats and a T-shirt at bedtime. She liked how Charlie's dark eyes seemed to get lighter now than Hailey had ever noticed before. She guessed that Charlie was right. Charlie felt free now, and that made her feel happy, which was evident in the woman's entire being. Hailey found that she liked the changes in her, and she wanted to explore this more.

Hailey's plan had worked. She had discovered that she had feelings for Charlie. But she still worried that those feelings wouldn't compare to whatever Charlie felt for her. If they didn't, and then they went away, or Hailey spent more time with Emma and found that Emma was who she wanted, she would hurt her friend. She couldn't do that to Charlie. Earlier, when they kissed, Hailey felt a tingling sensation spread throughout her entire body. She wanted more of that. She wanted more of Charlie. She wanted to know what it was like to be with her. But the thought of disappointing Charlie, or not being who the woman thought Hailey was or expected her to be, nearly ate her up inside.

If someone had been in love with a person for over a decade, they must have had a certain view of them. They must have thought about what it would be like to be in a relationship with that person. It was, likely, something she could never live up to. That might have been the scariest of all Hailey's thoughts.

She pulled them up next to Charlie's building and parked. Hailey then also turned the car off, because she didn't know what else to do as Charlie turned to face her.

"Come up," Charlie stated.

"To your place?" Hailey stalled with a stupid question.

"Yes." Charlie laughed. "I have to take Eddie on a

walk. Walk with me?"

Hailey knew Charlie was trying to help her with the tension she undoubtedly recognized the closer they got to the apartment.

"Sure," Hailey agreed.

They made their way upstairs. Charlie allowed her to use the keycard to unlock the door, supplying them both with a moment of levity.

"You told me *I'm* such a child sometimes." Charlie laughed at Hailey's smile.

After they readied Eddie for his walk, they made their way back down the stairs. Hailey linked arms with Charlie as they walked and watched Eddie sniff here and there before finally settling on a place to do his business. Then, they headed back toward the apartment. Hailey grew nervous again, because this would be where they'd say goodnight and, likely, share another one of those heart-stopping kisses.

They arrived at the building's entrance. Eddie started to head up the stairs, thinking they would both be going up. But Hailey stopped, and she was the one holding his leash, so he stopped as well and turned back.

"So, I should go," Hailey said into the cold night air, while Charlie kept her eyes locked on her.

Charlie leaned in closer, and Hailey's lips parted, expecting what was to come the moment Charlie's hand landed on her cheek. A soft buzzing came from Charlie's coat pocket, which Hailey could feel more than hear, thanks to their proximity.

"Don't answer it," she told Charlie and connected their lips.

The buzzing continued, but Hailey pushed it out of her mind as Charlie's lips parted and allowed her tongue to play with her own. Hailey's hands found their way into Charlie's hair, and she pulled Charlie closer. She felt Charlie's hands trying to make their way under her coat and pulled her lips away, feeling them instantly grow cold again.

"Now, I should really go," Hailey repeated with her

eyes closed and forehead pressed against Charlie's.

"Why? Hails, come upstairs," Charlie repeated her invitation. "We don't have to do anything. Just come up."

"Next time," Hailey said softly.

She smiled at Charlie and pecked her lips gently while pressing her own hand to Charlie's cheek. "Good night." She kissed the opposite cheek.

Then, Hailey walked back toward her car and climbed inside. She took a last look at Charlie, gave her a shy smile, and drove off. When she got home, Hailey couldn't focus on any one emotion. She changed into some comfortable clothes and sat herself in front of the TV, not turning it on, though.

She felt Charlie's lips against her own as if they were still attached. She tried her best not to consider Emma's lips against her skin. She tried to think about how good it felt to take Charlie out and see the smiles the woman had been delivering in Hailey's direction all night long. She tried to think about the two of them together.

Hailey pictured them as a couple, waking up next to one another each day, double-dating with Ember and Eva, and taking all those important relationship steps together. She tried not to allow the fear to take over her again as she made her way to her bed for the night.

Hailey's phone rang just as she had resolved herself to try to sleep and stop thinking. She rolled over to see who it was and smiled at the thought that it would be Charlie. She smiled still, though duller, when she saw it was Emma calling instead.

"Hey," Hailey answered.

"Hi, sorry. I know it's late," Emma replied. "I just called earlier and hadn't heard back, so I wanted to make sure everything was okay."

"Sorry. Everything's fine. I've just been busy." Hailey rolled onto her back.

"How's the wedding-planning going?" Emma asked. "Yeah, I'll be right there," she then said to someone else, and Hailey could now tell there was background noise wherever Emma was.

"Where are you?" Hailey questioned.

"Oh, I'm at my friend's; Eli's," Emma shared. "I would have invited you, but I knew you were busy this weekend."

"Yeah," Hailey stated. "Who's Eli again? Do you work with him?"

Emma laughed a little and said, "Eli is short for Elizabeth. We met a few months ago through another friend. Today's her birthday. She had a few people over," she explained.

"Fun," Hailey stated with no real emotion.

"So… How's the wedding-planning going?" Emma asked again.

"We can talk about it later. You're busy, Em."

"No, it's okay. This thing is winding down, and I wanted to talk to you."

Hailey had tried to find a way out, but Emma was persistent.

"The wedding-planning was fine, but I wasn't with Ember and Eva tonight. I had a date," Hailey said it quickly, as if, by doing that, it wouldn't register to Emma.

"Oh." Emma let out a sigh. "Good."

"Good?" Hailey checked.

"I knew that was a possibility, right?"

"Em, I wanted to be honest with you. You said that's what you wanted."

"I do. I'm glad you told me," Emma shared. "Yes, I'm getting off now. Hold on," she said that away from the phone. "Hails, Eli wants us to play a game or something. I should let you go."

"Oh, okay."

"Can I call you tomorrow?" Emma asked.

"Sure," Hailey returned.

"Okay. Good night."

"Night," Hailey said, and they hung up.

CHAPTER 17

CHARLIE fell instantly asleep Saturday night. In part, sleep came easily because she hadn't slept in over thirty-six hours; and also, because Charlie felt like she could. She felt at ease. She slept soundly and woke to a bright Sunday morning, realizing she had slept a lot later than she normally did, and also, recognizing the early signs of Chicago spring and welcoming it with open arms.

She completed her morning routine and considered calling Hailey, but then thought it might be too soon. She also thought about calling Ember, but she didn't know what Hailey would be comfortable sharing with her. Instead, she sat herself in front of the TV and decided to catch up on some recordings. Her phone rang later, and she answered it without looking at the screen.

"Hello."

"Hey," Lena greeted. "I'm in the neighborhood and wanted to know if you wanted to grab coffee with me."

"Oh." Charlie looked down at the cup of coffee in her hand. "Sure. Just let me get ready. Ten minutes?"

"I'll pick you up," Lena said, and they said goodbye.

Charlie got ready quickly and was finished by the time Lena knocked on the door.

"Morning," Charlie greeted her and motioned for her to come inside.

"Morning." Lena leaned in and gave Charlie a brief kiss.

Charlie's lips reacted on their own and returned the kiss.

"So, coffee?" Charlie asked after a moment.

"Yeah, let's go." Lena smiled and ran her hand through her wavy hair.

They walked down the stairs and to the café a couple of blocks over, enjoying the relatively warm weather for this time of the year. Charlie ordered for them and joined Lena at the table at the somewhat crowded café.

"How was your weekend?" Charlie asked.

"It was good," Lena shared. "I got a lot of work done. I'm actually a little ahead, which I haven't been able to say in a while."

"That is good. I still have some stuff waiting for me at home."

"How was the wedding thing?" Lena asked and blew on her steaming coffee.

Charlie took a drink, nearly burning her tongue in the process.

"It was good. I think they're pretty much done. They'll finalize everything with Eva's sister, who is acting as their wedding planner in Iowa, where Eva's from."

"So, you can relax now?"

"Kind of, yeah. I think the major part of it all is done."

"When is the wedding?"

"June," Charlie returned.

"Nice." Lena smiled. "A June wedding."

"Yeah, it should be fun. The six of us are going to head up a few days before that, to help get everything set up. And then, there's the wedding, of course."

"Six of you?"

"Eva and Ember, obviously. Hannah and Alyssa – Eva's best friends. They're married already. And then Hailey and I."

"What about dates?"

"What do you mean?" Charlie questioned and took another drink.

"Are you and Hailey bringing dates?"

"Oh, I don't know," Charlie answered. "I haven't really thought about that yet. I just figured Hails and I would go together."

Charlie hadn't meant that they'd go as a couple. When

neither of them was with anyone else, she and Hailey just always went places together as friends.

"So, she's not seeing anyone?"

Charlie almost said something and then stopped, but she proceeded when she realized Lena was still waiting for a response.

"She is, yeah," Charlie said. "She reconnected with an old girlfriend a few weeks ago, but they're not a couple. They're dating."

"Like, how we're dating?"

"Yeah," Charlie answered.

Lena took a drink of her coffee, looked around the room, and then met Charlie's eye.

"I have to tell you something," Lena said after a moment. "It's kind of why I asked you out for coffee."

"Okay."

"We said we'd be honest, so I want to be honest."

"What's wrong, Lena?"

"I don't know if something's wrong exactly, but I did something last night."

Charlie leaned back in her chair.

"You went on a date?" Charlie asked and hoped that it would make things easier when she told Lena she had been on a date as well.

"I did, yeah. My friend Arden took me out to a bar last night. She's straight, but she's trying to be supportive." Lena looked anywhere but into Charlie's eyes. "She's a lot better at meeting people than I am. She started introducing me around, and there was this woman there. She and I hit it off."

"Okay." Charlie wouldn't have been concerned, except that Lena appeared to be concerned.

"I went back to her place, and we..."

Charlie knew what would happen next.

"You slept with her?" she guessed.

"It happened fast, Charlie. I had a few drinks with her at the bar, and then we went back to her place."

"You don't have to explain anything to me. We're not exclusive. You can sleep with whomever you want."

Charlie denied the feeling of frustration in the pit of her stomach. She'd been patient with Lena, because Lena had never been with another woman. In fact, Lena hadn't been with anyone other than her ex-husband. Charlie had understood and told her they could wait until Lena was ready. She knew there was a chance that Lena would meet someone else, of course. And, maybe she'd been wrong to assume that if they ever got to that step, Charlie would be Lena's first.

"I feel terrible, Charlie. You've been so understanding, and you've waited for me to be ready. I thought it would be you."

"Why was it her?" Charlie asked, pushing her coffee toward the middle of the table, no longer interested in it.

"I worried I would be bad at it. I thought about how much more experienced you are at this than I am. I told her about that. We talked about my ex-husband. I also told her you and I were dating, but that I was nervous. It didn't help that Arden kept telling me that I just needed to get laid, and then I'd feel a lot better about being with you. I let it all get to me. It's no excuse," Lena shared. "I know it's no excuse, but it kind of also worked."

"It worked?"

"I woke up this morning and let out this sigh of relief. I've been holding on to this idea that I needed to wait and make things perfect. That put all this pressure on me, and it would've probably put pressure on whoever I was with. But after it was over, and I got dressed, I just felt like I was ready for something real now. I doubt that makes any sense to you."

"It does, actually." Charlie thought back to her first time with Julia. "I felt the same way my first time."

"You did?" Lena was surprised.

"Yeah, I did."

"So, you're not mad?"

"I'm not mad," Charlie confirmed and realized that she wasn't.

She wasn't mad at all. She wasn't even hurt by the fact that Lena had slept with someone else.

"Can we go out tonight?" Lena asked. "Not just morning coffee, but on a real date?"

"I went on date last night, too, Lena," Charlie revealed.

"Oh." Lena seemed taken aback. "I thought you were with your friends."

"I was. But then Hailey and I talked."

"It was with Hailey?"

"Yeah, it was with Hailey." Charlie leaned forward. "We've been friends forever, but that was our first date."

"How long have you had feelings for her?"

"Forever," Charlie returned, not wanting to lie. "I'd just given up all hope when I met you," she continued. "I like you, Lena. I think you're great."

"But you're going to be with her now?" Lena set her coffee cup down.

"No. Well… I don't know. We didn't make any officials plans or declarations. Things are kind of weird, because we've been friends for so long. And she is dating someone, too."

"But you want to be with her?" Lena nodded, as if she was answering the question herself.

"No matter what I feel for Hailey, it doesn't change what I felt for you. But, Lena, I don't think we should keep dating, either." Charlie tried to soften her voice as much as possible. "Do you really want to be in a relationship? I mean, with anyone? Is that what you're looking for right now?"

"I thought we were just dating."

"I just meant in general. It seems like you're ready to go out and… mingle; like you want to meet women and explore. I think that's great. I want you to do what you want to do and find the right person for you. But I find myself at a different place." Charlie inhaled deeply. "I have no idea what's going to happen with Hailey and I, but I know that I want a relationship now. I want one person to come home to one day." She paused again. "Whether it's Hailey or she tells me that after one date she doesn't see it happening with me, and then I need to move on – I know I don't want whoever I'm with to be sleeping with someone else. I don't think I want to do the whole go out and bar scene anymore, either."

Lena nodded along as Charlie spoke.

"I think you're right," she agreed after a moment of silence was shared. "As much as I like you, I think I'm at a place where I want to meet women."

"Not woman," Charlie said.

"I wanted to. I wanted to with you. I thought I wanted a commitment, but… I think you're right. I think I want to just search around a little more, now that I'm actually comfortable in my own skin."

"How about you do that, and we try to stay friends?" Charlie proposed.

"I think I can do that," Lena returned with a smile. "And good luck with Hailey."

"Thanks." Charlie pulled her coffee cup back toward her and lifted it to her lips.

"So, if we're friends, do you want to tell me how your date went last night?" Lena asked.

"You sure?" Charlie lifted an eyebrow.

"I'm sure."

"I've been dying to talk about it, but I can't with Ember, because she's our friend, too. But I don't want you-"

"It's okay, Charlie. Spill," Lena encouraged.

Charlie smiled at her and set her cup back down to begin the story that seemingly started so long ago.

***

Hailey sat across from Emma at lunch and listened to her talk about her workweek. Hailey took bites of her salad, while Emma talked about some problems she was having with a co-worker. Hailey laughed when Emma told her she had considered putting laxatives in the guy's coffee because he had been such an asshole. They finished their meal and decided to take a walk to the store, to pick up a few things for Hailey, because she had failed to go shopping over the weekend, given all the other things she had done. Emma looped her arm through Hailey's. It reminded Hailey of doing that same thing with Charlie the previous night.

"Do you want to pick out some wine for tonight?" Emma suggested as they made their way toward the checkout counter with the few items Hailey needed to get her through until she could really go shopping.

"Tonight?" Hailey turned to her.

"I was thinking... we could stay in and watch a movie," Emma returned and held up a bottle of red. "Merlot?"

"Oh, I don't know about tonight," Hailey said. "I'm exhausted from this whole weekend. I think I just want to be alone. Is that okay?"

"Sure, I guess." Emma was clearly disappointed.

She placed the wine back and fell in line with Hailey, who paid for her purchases before they headed back out onto the street.

"Hails?" Charlie nearly knocked her over as the two women left the store.

"Charlie, hey." Hailey looked up to see her standing there and then looked at Emma and back to Charlie.

Then, she noticed another woman standing next to Charlie, that she didn't recognize.

"Hey, Charlie." Emma waved a hand in Charlie's direction.

"Emma." Charlie didn't take her eyes off Hailey.

Hailey could see there was both confusion and worry there.

"Oh, this is Lena," Charlie remembered her manners and motioned with her hand to the woman with wavy blonde hair and these intensely blue eyes, standing to her right.

Lena was definitely attractive. She was also standing close to Charlie. They were either finishing up a date or just starting one.

"Lena, this is Hailey, and this is Emma," Charlie continued.

"Nice to meet you," Emma replied. "Are you guys out enjoying the change in the weather, too?"

"Yeah," Charlie told her but kept her eyes on Hailey. "Just heading home now, though. I need to let Eddie out."

"Oh, I almost forgot." Lena reached into her large purse and pulled out a bag of small dog bones treats. "I got these for him. I forgot to give them to you before."

"He loves these." Charlie looked at them and then at Lena. "You want to give him one? Just know that if you do, he will always assume you're carrying bones with you at all times and expect you to deliver."

Lena laughed at that, and Hailey cleared her throat.

"Well, we'll leave you to that," she proposed.

"Hails just had to pick up a few things, and then we're heading to the Lincoln Park Zoo. It's nice enough to go, finally, and it's one of my favorite places," Emma said.

Charlie looked down at the bag in Hailey's hand.

"Milk and cereal?" she asked with a smirk.

"Yeah," Hailey replied. "I was out at home."

"Because you usually have it at my place," Charlie shared and then glanced at Emma, who looked a little confused. "Have fun at the zoo."

Charlie walked past them. Lena followed her, after delivering a quick *'nice to meet you,'* wave, and a smile.

"You want to drop that stuff at your place first?" Emma asked, apparently unfazed by the meeting.

Hailey *was* fazed, though. It was strange, seeing Charlie with Lena. It was even stranger, considering they had just gone on their first date, and the next day, Charlie was out with Lena. Hailey hated herself because she had done the exact same thing with Emma. She couldn't exactly be mad at Charlie when she, herself, was standing next to another girl, planning the rest of their afternoon.

"Can we skip the zoo? Let's just go back to my place and hang out instead," Hailey suggested.

"Yeah?" Emma lifted an eyebrow. "I'm definitely okay with that."

They got back to Hailey's apartment. She put her things away while Emma got settled on the couch and turned on the TV. Hailey sat next to the woman and then felt Emma take her hand and place it in her lap. Hailey stared down at them clasped together and felt Emma's eyes on her.

"Yes?" Hailey lengthened the word and then looked over at her.

Emma didn't say anything, though. She leaned in and pressed her lips to Hailey's neck just below her earlobe.

"Can we, maybe, move this hang-out session to your bed?" she asked and lifted her eyes to check Hailey's.

Hailey nodded in response and then stood. Emma followed her. Neither said anything as Hailey slid back on her bed, allowing Emma to climb on top of her.

"I've missed you," Emma said before connecting their lips.

Emma's lips felt how they always did, like they craved Hailey's mouth with the intensity that often comes with first love. Hailey kissed the woman back and ran her hands up and down Emma's sides. Then, she rolled them over and kissed Emma harder and with more determination as she slid her hands up Emma's shirt.

"I think you've missed me, too," Emma said with a laugh.

Hailey stopped to look down at her and asked, "Do you want kids?"

Emma's eyes went wide before she replied, "Sorry?"

"Do you want kids, Em? Do you want the wedding, and the house, and the kids, and everything that comes with it?"

Hailey backed off Emma and knelt in front of her, causing the other woman to sit up and back against the pillows.

"Hails, we were just making out. What the hell?"

"We still haven't done it, Emma."

"It? Sex? You wanted to wait."

"Not sex, Emma. I still don't know you now. I don't know what you want."

"And you need to know it right now, while we're in your bed, about to… *Were* we about to?" Emma shrugged her shoulders and then offered Hailey a near desperate expression. "Because I know I want that, Hailey."

"But what about the other stuff?"

"You want to know if I want kids? Hails, this is weird. We're not even together, because you aren't ready, but you want to talk kids?"

"No, Emma. I want to know if you want them one day. I'm not asking you to have mine now." Hailey was growing frustrated and took a second to calm herself. "I'm sorry. You're right. Let's just go back to what we were doing."

She went to move back on top of Emma, but Emma pressed her hands to Hailey's shoulders to hold her back.

"No. You want to do this; let's do this. If you're asking me if I want kids someday, the answer is – I don't know. But I don't think so."

Hailey sat back on her heels.

"You said you wanted three."

"When I was eighteen, yeah. I did want three. I thought I would have at least one or two by now already, but I'm thirty-two, Hails. I don't think that many is in the cards for me. Even if I adopted, or my girlfriend or wife had one or all of them, I don't think that's what I want."

"Oh."

"You do, don't you?"

"I do, yeah. I always have. I thought I'd have them by now, too. But I know I want at least one or two, and I want to have them if I can."

"Okay, then we can talk about it," Emma proposed. "Later. We can talk about the kid thing if we get there."

Hailey looked at her own hands in her lap and then back up at Emma.

"Is your favorite color still purple?" Hailey asked.

"What? Yes, Hailey. My favorite color is still purple. My favorite food is still that pizza my dad used to make, with the chicken on it, and that I can't seem to get right. My favorite place in the whole world is still that little pond behind my high school's football stadium." Emma sat all the way up and hung her legs off the side of the bed. "It's the place where I had my first real kiss with this girl I fell in love with and dated for over a year, before we both let life get in the way." Emma glanced over at Hailey. "It's a place I hoped to bring that girl back to, one day; to, maybe, ask her to be my girlfriend, or maybe, if things kept going well, then I'd propose to her there while we listen to the frogs croak and laugh." Emma's eyes were now glassy with tears. "You don't see that, though, do you, Hailey?" she asked softly and with worry in her tone.

"Em, I don't know." Hailey felt her own eyes well up with tears. "I feel like I shouldn't want to take things slow with you if it was meant to be, you know?"

"Hails, you wanted to take things slow so we could get to know each other again. Let's do that. Let's get to know each other again. All these years later, we keep coming back to each other. We've stayed in touch for a reason. And don't think I didn't notice that every time I started dating someone, you disappeared. Then every time you dated someone, I couldn't stand to see it, so I'd disappear."

"I went on a date with Charlie last night, Em," Hailey said and let out a massive breath she had been holding in.

Emma stood and turned to face her.

"So, *that* was what I noticed earlier."

"What do you mean?" Hailey moved to hang her legs over the edge of the bed and face her.

"There was something up with the two of you earlier.

I could tell. I guess now I know what it was, and also, why Charlie seems to hate me."

"She doesn't hate you," Hailey defended.

"Oh, yes, she does. I get that she's professional at work. But, Hailey, Charlie is not my number one fan. It makes sense now." Emma paused and then knelt in front of Hailey. "How long have you two been dating? I thought we said we'd tell each other if we—"

"Just last night," Hailey told her as Emma placed her hands on her knees. "It was our first date."

"And will there be another?"

"We haven't talked about it," Hailey shared. "I don't know."

"Yes, you do, Hails." Emma stood again. "Do you want to go out with her again or not?"

"Yes," Hailey stated and then stood as well. "But she's dating Lena, too, like I'm dating you. It's just complicated, Emma. I don't think I want complicated." Hailey went to take her hand, but Emma pulled back.

"I'm not simple, Hailey." Emma took a step away.

"That's not—"

"I know," Emma stated. "That wasn't fair. I'm sorry." She sighed. "Hails, I thought I'd be okay with you dating someone else, but I'm not. I don't know what's going on with you and Charlie, but I don't want to be someone you date until you figure it out. I thought we were heading in the right direction. I thought you needed time to get to know me again, I'd get to know you again, and we'd find our way back to one another. But now, I'm wondering if you even want that."

"Em, these feelings for Charlie are very new," Hailey offered. "It just happened one day. I started thinking about her as more than just a friend, and it happened to coincide with you coming back into my life. I didn't plan it. I don't want to hurt you."

"I know, Hails. You're a good person. No matter what else has changed since high school, I know that's still true,"

Emma complimented. "How does she feel about you? Have you guys at least talked about that?"

"I know how she feels, yeah."

"Then, you need to figure out how you feel, Hailey. You need to do it for yourself, and not for me or for her; but for yourself. I can't guarantee I'll be waiting around, because I don't know if I will. But, take the time to do what you need to do. If you decide that I'm a part of that picture, let me know." Emma walked toward where her jacket rested on the couch.

"Em, I'm sorry. I really am."

"I know." She slid the jacket over her shoulders and turned back to Hailey, who was still standing in front of the bed. "I meant what I said all those years ago. A part of me will always belong to you, Hails. It's still true."

Emma left the apartment, and Hailey sat back on her bed, wondering what she had done.

CHAPTER 18

CHARLIE let Lena out of the apartment after they talked for a while and Lena gave Eddie his treats. Charlie made her way over to her computer and dove into the work she had left on Friday. When Eddie started going stir-crazy toward the front door, she turned and got up to take a look. Normally, he only got excited like that when he sensed someone there. It was Sunday, so there weren't any delivery guys coming by. Charlie checked the peephole and saw a nervous-looking Hailey standing there. She pulled the door open, and Hailey turned from nervous to surprised.

"Oh, hi," she said.

"What are you doing out here?" Charlie asked.

"I wanted to come in, but I didn't know if I should use my key anymore. I wasn't sure if you had company. I thought I'd just knock at first, and then I thought I should text you, to see if you were even here. Then, you opened the door, so none of that mattered," Hailey explained in rapid succession.

"Why wouldn't you be able to use your key, Hails? You love using the key." She smirked at her and then motioned for Hailey to come inside. "What's going on?"

"Is Lena here?" Hailey asked as she appeared to be checking the place over with her eyes.

"Lena? No. Why?" Charlie closed the door and walked over behind her. "Hails?"

"We went on a date last night, Charlie," she said in a soft and adorable voice without turning around to face Charlie.

Charlie smiled as she approached Hailey and placed a tentative hand on the woman's back.

"Trust me, Hailey; I remember every single thing about last night. No matter what happens next, I always will," Charlie revealed.

"What do you mean, *no matter what happens next*?" Hailey asked again without turning around, and her head was hung low.

Charlie wasn't entirely sure what to make of her posture. She couldn't tell if Hailey was struggling with wanting to take things further between them, or if she was struggling to tell Charlie that it wasn't going anywhere at all.

"Hails, just tell me. I can take it."

Hailey turned around at that.

"Take what?" She looked just as confused as Charlie felt.

"Did you come here to tell me that you're with Emma, and we're not going on another date?" Charlie assumed.

"What? No." Hailey placed her hands on Charlie's waist and held them there. "We left it so open-ended last night. I wondered where we stood."

"Hailey, I would love to go on another date with you," Charlie said with a smile and placed her arms around Hailey's neck. "Is that an option?" She lifted an eyebrow.

"I don't know if I can do this, Charlie," Hailey then proclaimed, and Charlie immediately stepped back and out of Hailey's arms. "No, wait… That's not what I meant." She pulled Charlie back. "I mean that I don't think I can do this if you're with Lena."

"So, you can date Emma, but I–"

"I'm not dating Emma," Hailey interrupted and pulled Charlie closer.

"You're not?"

"We didn't go to the zoo. We went back to my place and talked. I told her that you and I went on a date. She can't be with me if I'm also dating you, and I can't not date you, Charlie." Charlie's eyes must have shown her surprise.

"I don't know what's going to happen, but I want to try. I don't think I can do this halfway, though, Charlie. I can't date you if you're with someone else."

"I'm not."

"You're not?"

"Not anymore," Charlie told her. "Hails, are you sure?"

"About what?"

"You and Emma? You two were just starting up again."

"Are you trying to convince me to date Emma now?"

"No. I just know how important she is to you. She was the perfect girlfriend, and—"

Hailey's hand went to Charlie's cheek.

"She doesn't know me how you know me, Charlie." Hailey lifted and then dropped her shoulders. "I don't think anyone does, or can, honestly."

"So, we're going to try this? We're going to date?" Charlie gulped audibly.

Hailey leaned in and pressed her forehead against Charlie's. It took a moment before Charlie recognized that Hailey's hands were sliding up the back of her T-shirt. It then took her another moment before Charlie felt the press of Hailey's soft lips. It took only another minute before Hailey had her pressed against the counter, and her hands were roaming over Charlie's back and then sliding around the front onto Charlie's stomach. Hailey pulled back for a second and looked down. She smiled.

"This is my shirt." Hailey tugged on the shirt Charlie had no idea belonged to her.

"It is?" she asked and pushed Hailey's hair back behind her ears. "How did I get it?"

Hailey looked at her like that was a stupid question.

"Do you know how many of your shirts I probably have at my apartment?" Hailey leaned back in and pressed her lips to Charlie's jawline. "I've wanted to kiss you here for a while," she stated confidently and applied her lips a little lower, making Charlie gasp out. "And here." Hailey pressed warm lips to cool skin, and Charlie shuddered.

209

"God, Charlie. I'm sorry it took me so long." She pulled back and met Charlie's dark eyes.

Charlie felt like she was about to burst into tears, but they'd be happy tears if she did.

"It's okay. You're here now." Charlie buried her hands into Hailey's hair and pulled the woman back into her, reveling in the sensations that were taking her body by storm.

Hailey's lips were on her neck, and then Hailey's tongue was dragging up and toying with Charlie's earlobe, while her hands were sliding down. Charlie gasped as Hailey's fingers grazed the button of her jeans without attempting to undo them. It was as if she was testing the waters. Charlie's brain was muddled. She didn't know what the right thing to do was. Should she stop this so that they could talk and take things slowly? Should she let it continue because she'd waited so long and because it seemed that Hailey wanted it, too?

She felt Hailey's hands grip her waist, and then Charlie was placed on top of her counter. Her legs were spread, and Hailey was now standing between them. Had she helped Hailey get her up there, or was Hailey that strong? Charlie heard a moan and realized that it was Hailey who was making the sound. Hailey's hands were lifting at Charlie's shirt, and they disconnected so she could remove it, but the moment the shirt was pulled over her face, Charlie heard the familiar sound of a key card in her front door.

"Shit." Hailey stood away from her.

Charlie lowered her shirt and then her body off the counter. Ember Elliot walked through the door as Charlie scurried over to a cabinet to pretend she was pulling something out of it.

"Em? What are you doing here?" Charlie asked in an attempt at nonchalance. "Hails, here's that... bag of rice you wanted." Charlie shook her head at herself, as the item she had pulled down from the cabinet without looking, was a bag of rice she didn't even know she had.

She tossed it onto the counter in front of Hailey, who

picked it up and stared at it for a moment.

"Oh, right. Yeah, thanks." Hailey turned to Ember. "I was going to make stir-fry tonight," she lied.

"All right… What the hell is going on with you two?" Ember wiggled an accusing finger at both of them. "And Hailey, when have you ever made stir-fry?" Ember set her bag on the counter and crossed her arms over her chest.

"It's a new recipe I'm trying." Hailey's voice got even softer as she tried to continue the lie.

Charlie just laughed because she couldn't help it. That caused Hailey to give her the *'are you kidding me right now'* look. Ember sat on the stool next to Hailey.

"You guys have been acting weird since yesterday. What happened?" she asked and looked back and forth between them again. "Oh, my God. Just tell me already!"

Hailey smirked and rolled her eyes. Charlie stared at her impatient friend.

"We're dating," Charlie said after a minute.

"I knew it!" Ember stood and then pointed at each of them in turn. "I knew it. I told Eva you two were doing it, and she didn't believe me." Ember pulled her phone out of her back pocket.

"What are you doing?"

"Texting her that I was right, obviously," Ember replied.

Hailey took the phone out of her hand and placed it on the counter.

"We're not *doing it*," she delivered. "I mean, we haven't, yet. We haven't done that *yet*."

Charlie lifted an eyebrow with the word *'yet'*, and somehow put it together just in that moment that dating Hailey would mean they would have sex. She knew that before, but this comment from Hailey was the first confirmation Charlie had that Hailey wanted that, too. Knowing that Hailey had touched herself the previous weekend, thinking about it, had been nice to hear. But this was bigger than that. This was after their first date, after their first kiss, and Hailey wanted more.

"Oh… I just assumed that since Charlie's wanted it forever, and you've been acting crazy lately, that you would have just gone right for it."

Ember meant that in a teasing tone, but Charlie wasn't looking at Ember. She was staring at Hailey, who's face showed something only for a moment before she smiled again. Charlie wasn't sure what to make of that.

"Well, we have self-control," Hailey returned.

She couldn't hide the smirk on her face from Charlie, though, because they hadn't had self-control just a minute ago, when Hailey lifted her onto the counter and spread her legs to stand between them. Just the thought of that had Charlie turned on and feeling a pulse between her legs.

"We've been on one date so far. That's why we left yesterday," Charlie explained. "And Hailey just got here, right before you did, to talk about the second date."

"I'm really happy for you guys," Ember stated. "This has been a long time coming. I worried for a while that it wouldn't happen. But I'm so glad it is." She paused at a realization. "This is going to be great, guys. Alyssa and Hannah on one side of the aisle – as the old married couple, Eva and I getting married in the middle, and then you two on the other side – just starting out." Ember seemed genuinely happy for them. "I guess we don't have to worry about giving either of you a plus-one for the ceremony." Ember then grabbed her phone and looked back at Charlie. "Actually… I don't think we've even planned on that, because we just figured you two would go together." She looked at Hailey. "Wait… What about Emma?"

"We're not…" Hailey dropped off, and Charlie saw a little flicker of pain there.

"And you, with that woman you met at work? Lena?"

"We never really got started, but we're not going to now. I think we're going to be friends," Charlie explained.

She looked back at Hailey, who was smiling again. Damn, that girl could go from one emotion to the next so quickly, Charlie had no idea what any of it meant. Ember smiled wide and typed out a message, presumably, to her fiancée.

"I'm bragging to Eva right now, because I told her you two would make this happen before the wedding. She said that if you ever did it at all, it would be after, so I win the bet," Ember said and tucked her phone away.

"You bet on us?" Hailey probably didn't mean it the way it sounded initially, but then she glanced over at Charlie and lifted a corner of her mouth, telling Charlie silently that she realized how it sounded after she said it.

"Can I be honest for a second?" Ember offered and stood between the two of them. "I've been waiting for one of you to tell the other forever. I knew how Charlie felt. That was obvious to everyone other than you, Hails. But that's not all your fault. Charlie didn't want you to see it, so she hid it from you. I don't even think Charlie wanted to see it herself there for a while. But then, while I was off dating woman after woman, you two always seemed to be together without being together."

"We weren't—" Charlie started.

"We're all best friends, right?" Ember challenged.

"What? Of course, we are," Charlie replied.

"When was the last time you bought me my favorite cereal for when I stay over? Hell, when was the last time I even stayed over?" She turned to Hailey. "How many times have you stayed at this apartment since she moved in? How many times has either of you sat next to *me* at Sally's? How many times have you two just gone places together, instead of finding dates? When you are both attractive, successful, and pretty awesome women, who would have no trouble finding them." Ember paused. "I've kept this to myself this whole time. I'm glad I don't have to anymore." Ember's phone beeped in her pocket, and she pulled it out to look at it. She smiled and swiftly typed back another message. "She conceded. I win."

"What exactly do you win?" Charlie questioned.

"You probably don't want the details." Ember winked.

"Well, I only stopped by because neither of you was calling me, like you said you would." She glanced at Hailey. "*Separately*, right?" Ember recalled Hailey's inability to lie well the day before. "Now that I know you're safe and together, I will leave you alone."

"And because you want to go collect your prize," Hailey stated with a laugh.

"And collect and collect." Ember smiled and backed away toward the door. "Really happy for you guys."

She made her way toward the door, petting Eddie as she went, and then closed it behind her.

"So…"

"Yeah, so." Charlie nodded in agreement.

"Rice, huh?" Hailey looked down at the bag of rice on the counter.

Charlie followed her eyes and then reached for it to put it back into the cabinet.

"It was all I could think of," she replied and then tossed the bag into the cabinet unceremoniously. "I don't even remember buying a bag of rice. Why the hell would I do that?"

Hailey walked around the island counter to stand in front of her.

"You didn't. I did," Hailey shared. "You don't remember?" she asked, and Charlie shook her head no. "I was dating–"

"That woman who just moved here from Tokyo," Charlie recalled almost immediately. "You bought a bunch of stuff to try to cook dinner for her." Charlie returned to the cabinet and pulled out a bottle of Asian hot sauce. "She broke up with you before you got the chance, and you couldn't look at the stuff, so I brought it over here, and I completely forgot about it."

"I can't believe you still have it," Hailey said.

"It was food. I wasn't going to throw it out. Plus, at that time, you seemed convinced that she was going to come to her senses and tell you she wanted you back. I kept it in case that happened, and you needed it," Charlie revealed, and as Hailey took a step back, Charlie watched her obviously taking her in. "What?"

***

Hailey just stood there, looking Charlie up and down. This woman was wearing Hailey's shirt; she had her cereal in her apartment. She had also stayed over more times than she could count, only to wake up to Charlie making her coffee, and then, they'd go about their days. Some nights, she even came straight here from work. They'd eat dinner together and watch a movie or just talk. She would see Charlie fall asleep in her room, as she walked past it to go to the bathroom, and she would turn Charlie's TV off for her, or make sure Charlie was covered up, because she often fell asleep above the blankets on her bed.

"What?" Charlie asked her.

"Can we order in dinner and watch a movie tonight?" Hailey asked her.

"That sounds nice," Charlie answered. "I still kind of have some work I need to get done, though. It shouldn't take too long."

"Work on it. I can order food and occupy myself," Hailey said.

"Okay." Charlie smiled at her and took a step forward.

Hailey felt the press of now familiar lips on her forehead.

"Chinese?" Hailey asked.

"Yes, but get extra egg rolls," Charlie told her, slid her hand along Hailey's stomach over her shirt briefly, and headed toward her desk. "You ate them all last time."

"You ate all the shrimp last time," Hailey called after her.

"Then, get extra shrimp, too," Charlie suggested and sat down in her chair.

Hailey watched Eddie doing his dance by the front door.

"I'll take this guy out first." She walked to Eddie, who sat down for her so that she could attach his leash. "He'd never eat all of my shrimp." She rubbed behind the dog's ear.

"He would *absolutely* eat all of your shrimp," Charlie stated without turning around.

Hailey stood upright and glanced around the space. Charlie was working. Hailey was taking the dog out. They were going to eat dinner together and have a simple night in. Maybe Charlie would invite her to stay over, and this time, she would sleep next to the woman; and not just as friends. Hailey was beaming as she walked Eddie around the block and ran into another dog he must have known, because they sniffed and then danced around one another, while Hailey and the other dog's owner just watched before pulling them apart. She called the Chinese place while she walked back and ordered them their dinner. Knowing it would take over thirty minutes for the food to arrive, she headed back upstairs, let herself into the apartment, and allowed Eddie to run around the room.

Charlie had turned to see that Hailey was back and delivered a smile in her direction before turning back to her computer. Hailey didn't want to distract her, but she also felt like she just needed to touch her. It was a strange feeling, this need to be this close to Charlie, after she had known her for so long. But she felt this desire to touch Charlie's back, her neck, her shoulders, and it wasn't sexual. It was sweet how she wanted to touch her. The pull was too strong. She walked over to Charlie, placing a hand on one shoulder while she leaned down against the other.

"Food's on its way," she said into Charlie's ear.

"Thank you," Charlie replied and wrapped a hand around Hailey's neck to pull her a little closer. "This is nice," she said.

"It is," Hailey agreed and kissed Charlie lightly on the neck before pulling back. "Will the TV bother you?"

"No, go ahead," Charlie returned.

Hailey made her way to the couch, sat down, and

turned on the TV. She quickly found something to entertain herself while she waited for the food and for Charlie to finish her work.

"Well, this is going to be weird," Charlie said after several minutes.

"What is?" Hailey turned to see that Charlie was making her way to the couch to sit next to her.

"I got an email from Emma," Charlie stated with a concerned look.

"What?" Hailey turned to face her.

"She sent it on Friday. It's for the work I'm doing for the Health Department. It's not personal, but it's going to be weird. The project is still ongoing. I'll have to see her."

"I hadn't even thought about that," Hailey said. "I forgot you guys were working together."

"It shouldn't be too much longer, but I will have to meet with her at least a couple more times," Charlie started. "The building was in pretty good shape, and the contractor we use is really good. They'll be finished with the major alterations in a couple of weeks. We're already starting on the interior, structural stuff. Then, it's just moving things in and around and making sure electric is good, but that's not mine to worry about. My team can handle the final inspection with her, and then we'll be done."

"So, like a couple of months?"

"Probably. Will that be weird for you? Me, seeing her?"

"I think it will be weirder for her, but she's a professional. She'll be fine."

"Why do you think that?" Charlie asked.

"She still hopes that one day…" Hailey faded out.

"That one day you'll get together?" Charlie checked. "I thought you said it ended."

"It did, Charlie." Hailey took her hand and then heard Eddie scamper toward the door a second before the doorbell rang. She stood and went to grab her purse. "It's over, but she still has feelings for me." Hailey paid the delivery man and then set the food on the counter, while Charlie still sat on the couch, staring off into space. "Charlie, you just ended things with Lena, too. Do you think her feeling just went away?"

"Lena isn't Emma, Hails." Charlie stood and walked to the counter, where Hailey was busy pulling out the food.

"What's that mean?"

"I dated Lena for a couple of weeks. We kissed a few times, but that was it. You and Emma were together for a long time. She was your first girlfriend. You loved her and compared every girlfriend after to her. That's a lot to live up to, Hailey," Charlie offered.

Hailey stopped with the food and met Charlie's eyes.

"Charlie, I'm not comparing you to Emma."

"Why not? You did it with every other woman," Charlie returned.

"You're not every other woman," Hailey explained, wondering where this was all coming from. "Charlie, you're not every other woman, okay? I'm not comparing anything about you to anything about Emma." She paused. "Besides, what do you think it's like, living up to the fact that you've had feelings for me since we met?"

"Living up to it?" Charlie looked upset and confused. "What do you have to live up to, Hails?"

"That version of me you have in your head."

"Version? What are you talking about?"

"Charlie, you've pictured us together for years, right? You've had this image in your mind, whether you wanted to or not, of us together. And fantasy rarely lives up to reality."

"So, you're worried I'm comparing the actual you to some image I have of you in my head?"

"How can I not, Charlie? How can I not do that? You've been in this a lot longer than I have. I've just figured out that I like you as more than a friend and want this with you, but you're in love with me and have been forever. Apparently, everyone else figured it out. But I was so deaf, dumb, and blind, that I didn't. I looked around, earlier, and realized that it's been obvious. It's so obvious, that we've been doing this without really doing anything this whole time."

"Doing what? Hails, why are you getting upset?" Charlie took a step toward her.

"We've been dating without really dating, Charlie, and I can picture it. I can picture all of it with you. I can see us living here together one day. It feels good to think about it, but I'm still scared." She felt tears welling up in her eyes. "I'm terrified that now that you have me, you won't want *this* me; you'll be reaching for the one you've been in love with all these years. And I'm scared that I'll never be able to catch up to what you feel for me, because I was too oblivious to see it before."

"Hails, what…" Charlie seemed to be out of words.

"I'm going to go."

"What? Hailey, don't. Come on." Charlie reached for Hailey's hand, but Hailey pulled away.

"I'm sorry. I thought I could, Charlie. I thought I could, but… I don't know. I feel all this pressure," Hailey said and realized it at the same time. "Pressure to be who you want me to be, and pressure from Emma to try to get back what we had, when I don't think we ever can. I'm hurting both of you, and I don't want to do that. I think it's better if I pull myself out of the picture."

"Hailey, no. That's not what I want. I'm not trying to put any pressure on you to be different than who you are. I love who you are."

Hailey could hear the worry and concern in Charlie's tone.

"Charlie…"

"Please don't do this, Hailey. We can just talk. I don't want whatever you think I do. I want–"

"I need some time, Charlie," Hailey interjected. "I'm sorry, but I need some time to reconcile all this." She grabbed her stuff and headed toward the door. "I'm so sorry," she said again and then left the apartment.

CHAPTER 19

"HEY, Charlie." Andrew, a VP at the firm, entered the conference room where Charlie had just wrapped up a meeting but was now alone. "I have kind of a last-minute request."

"What's up?" Charlie asked and closed her computer.

"David's group was going to head up our first project in Detroit, but he's getting pulled to work on our rollout plan for the rest of Michigan, because he's a better project manager than an architect. Don't tell him I said that." He pointed at her in jest. "Here's the request part... Can you take over Detroit and farm the Health Department thing out to your team?"

"Yeah, that shouldn't be a problem. It's already under-way."

"You'd have to be up there for a couple of weeks, at least. It's a big deal. There's a tech start-up that's trying to revitalize a whole city block by expanding their office there and then adding some outdoor green spaces, too."

"A couple of weeks?"

"We just got the bid approved, so you'd be starting right at the beginning. But, yeah, it'll be at least a couple of weeks up there, and you'd have to check in every so often while the work's happening. We'll put you up in a nice place, of course."

Charlie considered the offer that wasn't really an offer. It was a boss *asking* an employee to do something when they really just kind of *had to* do it.

"When do I need to leave?"

"As soon as possible. Tomorrow, if you can. I can have Kay book your room and flight now. We'll get you a rental up there, so you don't have to make the drive."

"Yeah, okay," Charlie replied. "But I'll drive instead of

flying. I'd rather get the rental here. I have Eddie. I don't want to leave him for that long."

"And a hotel that takes dogs; got it," he returned and left the room.

Charlie was actually grateful. She needed to get away. She needed to not see Hailey at coffee on Thursday, or not be in her apartment, where everything just reminded her of Hailey, despite the fact that it was Charlie's place. It had been two days since Hailey fled her apartment, and Charlie had left her two voicemails and countless texts, asking the woman to talk to her. Hailey had sent one text back, saying again that she was sorry but that she needed time. Charlie recognized the need for time, because she'd asked for it herself. But, thanks to Hailey's poor job at respecting it, Charlie had finally confessed how she felt, and they'd had a chance. They'd had an amazing date and the promise of more. But now, Hailey was the one asking for time, and Charlie didn't know what to do.

She got home and started packing immediately. She didn't want to wait until tomorrow. She gathered what she hoped would be enough stuff, made sure Eddie was good to go, picked up the rental car, and hit the road. Charlie had asked Kay to book her a room for the night so that she could get a head start on the project, but she really just needed to get out of Chicago. She was heartbroken and couldn't stand to walk around the city as if nothing life-altering had happened to her recently.

She had kissed Hailey. They'd made out and were about to do more before Ember's interruption. She now knew what it felt like, to have Hailey in her arms; what it was like to kiss Hailey and be kissed hungrily by her in return. Charlie could never go back from that.

The drive was relatively easy once she got through city traffic. Charlie waited until she was more than halfway there before she texted Ember and told her friend she would be out of town for the next couple of weeks. Then, she turned off her phone and finished the drive.

***

Hailey arrived at Sally's earlier than most days, because, and only because, she had promised Ember she would be there. For the past several days, Hailey had spent every moment at work or working from home, just to try to keep her mind off Charlie Adams. She had failed miserably, though, because Charlie was either at the forefront of her thoughts, or hidden just beneath.

Hailey had been so close to having what she wanted, but her fear got in the way and obliterated her chances of making it work with Charlie. She had been holding that in since she first found out about Charlie's feelings for her. The constant replay of their shared memories, mixed with her new and intense feelings for Charlie, got the better of her.

"You want to tell me why Charlie fled the state the other day?" Ember said the second Hailey sat down.

"What?" Hailey returned in surprise.

Ember slid a coffee cup in Hailey's direction.

"She's in Michigan for the next two weeks or something."

"She is? Why?"

"She said work, but I doubt that. You, not returning my calls, and, apparently, not knowing that the woman you're dating is in another state, leads me to believe there's more to it than that."

"Em, come on," Hailey implored.

"Hailey, what the hell happened? Neither of you will talk to me about it, and Charlie won't even return my calls anymore."

"I freaked out," Hailey admitted.

"About what? You and Charlie?"

"Yes." She rolled her eyes at Ember. "It's too much, Ember."

"What is?" Ember tried to understand.

"What she feels for me."

"Huh?"

"I can't be who she wants me to be."

"Hails, I'm pretty sure she wants you to be *you*. That's kind of the point… So, what are you talking about?"

"You don't know what it's like, Em. You met Eva. You two started dating right away, and now you're getting married. Charlie and I have known each other for so long. This is just now starting, and it's scary, because what if I'm not the person she thought I was this whole time? What if I'm not enough, and it ends, and we can't get our friendship back?"

"You always do this, Hailey. You're frustrating beyond belief, sometimes." Ember glared at her across the table and grunted her frustration. "You either pick the wrong woman, and then *she* leaves, or you finally pick the right damn one, and *you* leave."

"Hey," Hailey said to defend herself.

"I love you, Hailey, but I've seen Charlie suffering for far too long. She looked so damn happy last weekend. She's been different since she told you. I like this new Charlie, because she's happier. But you're pushing her away when you've just started figuring out how you feel… Why? Is it really just you freaking out about Charlie? Is there still something going on with Emma?"

"No, Emma and I are over," Hailey shared. "But, yeah, I was confused between the two of them. Emma's just always been around, and she and I worked so well before."

"But, Hails, Charlie has always been around, too. And you two work so well now. You always have," Ember said. "I'm not going to try to talk you into anything. You have to decide what you want. But I think no matter what you decide to do, you need to take the time to figure it out before you talk to Charlie. Don't do that again to her, Hails. Don't give her hope, if you're just going to take it away again. Know what you want, that you can do it, and if you can't, then talk to her and try to see what you guys can salvage of your friendship. Because I'd like both of my friends back and, preferably, talking to one another, too."

Hailey knew Ember was right. She needed to give Charlie the time and space she hadn't given her before. Hailey needed to take her time and space to figure out what the hell was going on inside her head and why she couldn't just allow herself to be happy with Charlie.

**

Charlie had been in Detroit for over two weeks when she made her first appearance at the hotel bar. She had been working practically non-stop to get the project going, as well as checking in on the Health Department project, which was ahead of schedule. She had exchanged a few work-related-only emails with Emma and hated doing even that, because it reminded her of Hailey. And Charlie was trying to do anything else but think of Hailey.

Hailey had always been the one she would never have. Now, she was the one that got away, and that was an adjustment in Charlie's thought process.

"Hey."

Charlie looked up to see her main contact for the Detroit project standing next to the booth she was sitting in, sipping on her wine.

"Hey. Glad you could make it," Charlie replied.

Summer Taft was about twenty-five and was one of the co-founders of the tech start-up Charlie was working with. She was a millionaire several times over, thanks to the app she developed with her brother, and had successfully built offices in three locations around the globe. The first was in Silicon Valley, where they started. But the other two were in places that needed jobs and a kick to help out the economy; in India and the Philippines. They had now chosen Detroit for that very reason, and Charlie thought it was a great idea. She was helping them bring a little Silicon Valley to Detroit, while also trying to maintain that Motor City vibe.

"Thanks for the invite." Summer sat across from Charlie, and the bartender approached to take her order. "Can I get scotch and soda?" she asked

The bartender nodded and walked off.

"Scotch and soda?" Charlie questioned with a long drink of her wine.

"It was a long day; on top of a lot of other long days," Summer replied.

Charlie had really taken to Summer when they met on her first day in the city. The woman was bright, funny, and had dark-brown hair, with matching eyes. Her lips were thin and typically coated with a light sheen of gloss with no color, and she usually wore very casual clothes, even to the office, which Charlie appreciated.

Charlie had invited her out for the drink because Summer had just been dumped the night before and told Charlie about it that afternoon. She figured a drink and some time away from the project might help cheer her up. She also thought that her *strictly professional* rule could be a little more relaxed, given the circumstances.

"It's coming along, though," Charlie said.

"Yeah. But you'll be leaving soon, right? It will probably slow down once you leave. You know how to get things done," Summer complimented.

Charlie smiled at her as the bartender delivered her drink. Summer didn't waste any time and took a big gulp before she placed it back down.

"I still can't believe he broke up with me," she shared. "I was going to break up with *him*."

"Then, the problem isn't that you still have feelings for him… It's that your ego is bruised?" Charlie suggested.

"I guess. I didn't want to be with the guy anymore, but I also wasn't ready for him to dump me and tell me he's already seeing someone else."

"That is hard." Charlie nodded.

Summer took one more gulp, and her drink was gone.

"It's strange. You're in a relationship with someone

one day, and then you're not the next. You get used to considering their opinions and needs. Then, you don't anymore. I almost called him to tell him that I was meeting you here before I realized I didn't need to do that anymore."

"I've been there myself," Charlie said. "Being here has been strange for me, because it's just Eddie and I, and I'm used to considering my friends in a lot of my plans."

"So, you're single, then?" Summer asked, and it was the first time she'd asked Charlie a question like that.

"Yes, I'm single," Charlie answered after a moment of consideration.

She hadn't spoken to Hailey since she had arrived in Detroit, and had no plans of doing that when she returned until Ember and Eva's bachelorette party in a couple of weeks. It was just better this way. If Hailey didn't want her or couldn't see that Charlie just wanted her, then they needed more time apart. Despite Hailey trying to assure Charlie that Emma was nothing to worry about, Charlie still had her doubts. After all, she'd spent countless nights hearing Hailey talk about their endless love, while Charlie kept hearing Sinéad O'Connor singing in her head that *'nothing compares to you'.*

"When do you leave?" Summer asked her as the bartender brought her a refill.

"I don't know yet. I just had the hotel extend my stay until next week, because your brother still wants to talk about the living roof."

"That's his pet project," Summer started. "He's a big fan of environmental design."

"It's a little more complicated here than it was in California. The weather here is much harsher, so it will take some time. I've got a consultant coming in next week, to try to figure out how to make it work," Charlie explained.

"I'm heading home in a couple of days," Summer told her. "I'll come back in a few weeks to check on things, but my actual job is in California, and I need to get back to it. My brother, apparently, loves building offices, though, so he'll stay here and give you whatever you need." She took another drink. "At least my now-ex and I weren't living together. Being dumped over the phone is hard enough. I'd hate to have to go back and find him with his new chick," she joked.

Summer finished her second drink. Charlie even had another glass of wine herself. By the time Summer had finished her third drink, Charlie could tell the woman was drunk, or at least very close to it.

"It's getting late, and I have Eddie in my room. I should let him out," Charlie said.

"You have a guy in your room? I thought you were gay," Summer said with a playful wink.

"He is technically a guy. And yes, I am gay."

Charlie knew Summer was aware that Eddie was a dog and was just playing with her.

"Can I meet him? We weren't allowed to have pets as kids, because my brother is allergic. I started working in college and haven't stopped long enough to consider getting one for myself. My dad got one once Seth moved out, and Seth now takes allergy pills whenever he goes to the house, but I've never had my own."

"Sure, come on," Charlie said.

Summer stood and placed a hundred-dollar bill on the table to cover their check and a nice tip for the bartender. They made their way down one hall and passed through the lobby and down another hall to Charlie's first-floor room. Eddie jumped on her the moment she walked into the room, and then began sniffing Summer, once he realized Charlie wasn't alone. The hotel accommodated pets well, and Charlie had a room with a patio out back and a sliding glass door. She attached Eddie's leash to his collar and walked him outside. They didn't go for a walk, but Eddie had gotten used to that since they'd been in Detroit and went back in without fighting with her. Charlie let him go, and he headed immediately back to Summer, who was sitting on the small couch to the left of the bed.

"Hey, Eddie." The woman rubbed his head, and Charlie handed her a bag of treats. Summer gave him one, and he rushed off to enjoy it on his blanket. "He's so cute," she said.

"He has his moments," Charlie agreed and then sat on the edge of the bed to pull off her shoes.

"His owner's pretty cute, too," Summer said, causing Charlie to turn around and check to see if she'd heard right.

Charlie didn't say anything, though. Summer stood, moving around the bed to stand in front of Charlie.

"I'm kind of glad that I'm single now," she said and placed her hands on Charlie's shoulders, while Charlie stared up at her.

"Summer, we can't…" Charlie's words faded. "You're straight."

"I'm bi, Charlie. I've been out for years," she revealed. "My longest relationship to date, by the way, was with a *woman.*"

"We're working together, Summer." Charlie felt Summer push her back on the bed and then climb on top of her. "Summer, come on. You're drunk."

"Charlie, I've been thinking about doing this with you since we met," Summer explained and leaned down, holding her lips just above Charlie's. "It has nothing to do with the alcohol, and it won't get in the way of us working together." She leaned down the rest of the way and pressed her lips gently to Charlie's before removing them. "You're so sexy when you work. You wear those button-down shirts and those jeans. They look really good on you." She paused again and checked Charlie's eyes. "Do you want to stop?" she asked.

"What is this?" Charlie asked, her hands still at her sides.

"Just tonight, if you want," Summer offered. "If it keeps going, though, I wouldn't mind."

Summer smirked down at Charlie, but it wasn't a confident or cocky smirk. It was a genuine smile that told Charlie she was leaving it up to her. The woman waited patiently as she hovered above, bit her bottom lip, and appeared at least a little bit nervous all of a sudden.

"But, just sex?" Charlie stared into deep brown eyes.

"I like you, but I don't think we can have anything more than that. I'm not normally like this, I swear. I'm not a friends with benefits kind of person or anything, but I think that's all this could be, given where you live and where I live. I just really like you."

Summer ran a slow hand up under Charlie's shirt and looked down at it. She lowered her hand and placed it over the button of Charlie's jeans. She then looked back up and waited for Charlie to tell her to stop or go. When Charlie didn't indicate either, Summer popped the button and leaned down to capture Charlie's lips in a heated kiss, that told Charlie this woman had been waiting to do this for a while now.

Prior to that, Charlie had had no idea that Summer was bisexual, or that she was interested in her in this way. She didn't want to dwell on it, though. Summer was sexy in general, but, like this, she was even sexier. Charlie kissed her back hard and with passion. Her hands slid up Summer's back and rested there before she felt Summer roll them both over so that Charlie was on top. She started working the buttons on Charlie's shirt and went to pull it over and down her shoulders, but Charlie's lips stopped moving. She lifted herself up and tried to catch her breath to try to clear her muddled thoughts.

"No," she then stated.

"No?" Summer asked quietly as she leaned up on her elbows. "I thought…" She sat up and pressed her lips to the skin of Charlie's revealed abdomen. "I thought you wanted-"

"I'm sorry, Summer," Charlie apologized and pulled back. "I'm sorry, but I can't do this with you."

"Okay." Summer slid her legs out from under Charlie. "I'm sorry. I thought you and I were having a fun night, and—"

"We were. You do not have to apologize to me. I

should apologize to you," Charlie insisted as she buttoned her shirt and stood. "I'm not in a place where I can be with anyone. And I've never really been good at casual sex. I'm sorry. I shouldn't have let it get this far."

"Why did you, then?" Summer climbed off the bed.

"I don't know. I'm sorry," Charlie replied.

"It's okay," Summer said after a moment. "I came on a little strong there. I probably should have warned you or something."

"I had no idea, by the way," Charlie pointed out. "You kept talking about breaking up with a *boyfriend.*"

"I know," Summer stated and rubbed Eddie's curious head, as the dog approached now both standing women. "I should have told you before that I was bi. I've just been crushing on you for the past couple weeks. And I was going home to break up with the boyfriend in person, since I'm a good person." Summer laughed a little again. "I thought when I got back, if you were here, I'd ask you out. We were having fun tonight. I jumped the gun, but I am sorry." She headed toward the door. "Luckily, I'm staying in the same hotel, so I don't have to worry about driving anywhere." She turned to Charlie. "I'm going to go sleep it off. Are we okay, though? I swear, I've never done anything like this."

"Yes, we're okay," Charlie offered her a reassuring smile.

"When I see you tomorrow, let's pretend that this night ended with me heading to my room after meeting Eddie, and that I didn't stick my tongue down your throat and try to get you naked," she suggested.

Charlie just nodded and laughed.

CHAPTER 20

"HOW have you been?" Emma asked Hailey as they sat next to one another on the couch in Emma's apartment.

"Confused," Hailey admitted.

They hadn't spoken in a while. She had called Emma to try to explain what had happened before. Emma agreed to meet. And now, Hailey wasn't sure why she thought this was a good idea, to begin with, because she was still searching. She felt as if she had figured nothing out. When she was away from Emma, it was easy to remember that they weren't the same people that had fallen in love all those years ago. When she was near her, though, those thoughts and feelings came rushing back.

"About me?"

"About *me*," Hailey replied.

"Hails, what's going on?"

"When we met, Emma, I thought I'd found my soulmate at seventeen," Hailey shared with a shy smile. "You made me feel safe and loved. We kept coming back to each other, and this time, I thought that it was supposed to happen."

"Hailey, if you're trying to dump me again, you've already done that. This is just cruel." Emma turned to face her but offered a smile with her words to show Hailey she wasn't being serious.

"Em, that's not what I'm doing." Hailey turned to her, too. "I screwed things up. I kept thinking that if you and I spent more time together, it would feel like how it felt for me back then."

"I know."

"Do you really still feel that way about me?"

"The way I did when we were kids?" Emma stared down at the floor for a moment. "No, I guess not."

"I don't think we're meant to be, Em."

"Well, you're with Charlie now, so I'd hope not. Or that would be really mean of you, Hails."

"I'm not with Charlie," Hailey said.

"What? What happened?"

"I messed it up. But I don't want to talk about Charlie with you, Emma. That's not fair."

"Hailey, I'm dating someone," Emma blurted out. "It started after you told me about Charlie, but we've been dating since, and it's going well."

"Oh, wow."

"Probably shouldn't have just announced that... I just didn't want you to think I had been sitting around here crying or something," she added. "I think I got caught up in it all; in what we used to have. And I thought we'd get back there, like you did. But then, I met Eli and–"

"Eli? Your friend Elizabeth from the party?"

"Yeah. She's really great, and I like her, Hails."

Hailey recognized the woman's wide smile. Emma used to smile at her like that. Then, it clicked.

"Oh, my God! You really like her!" Hailey laughed.

"Don't make fun of me," Emma said. "I like her. She's funny and sweet."

Hailey continued her laughter.

"I'm sorry. I think it's great," Hailey stated as her laughter died down. "Emma, it is. So, you've been dating for, like, three weeks?"

"Yeah."

"And you guys have..."

It amazed Hailey how much she wanted to know and how much she wasn't at all hurt by the idea of Emma sleeping with someone else. Then, it *really* clicked.

"You really want to know this?"

"Only if you want to tell me."

"Yeah, we have," Emma revealed with a coy smile. "It was good, too. Well, it's been good. We've done it multiple times now, obviously." Emma sighed. "She's ready for what I'm ready for, Hails."

"That's important."

"She's a few years older than me. She doesn't want kids and is fine if she never gets married, but wouldn't mind it if the woman she settles down with wants the ceremony and the whole thing. She's successful in her career but doesn't work too much to where she can't make time for me."

"Like me?" Hailey accused herself.

"Well, yeah. But I understood, Hailey. Your boss just quit and left it up to you. I still don't know why you didn't apply for her job."

"I told you; I don't want it. I like what I do."

"Sorry, I'm just used to the people I work with. It's all cutthroat. Everyone is just trying to get the next big promotion."

"I'm not saying I don't ever want a promotion, but I don't want one now. I'm really good at work, Em. It's my personal life that needs fixing right now."

"What happened with Charlie, Hails?"

"I got scared. I got really scared, Em. I told her I couldn't do it. And then, she went out of town for work. I haven't spoken to her since. She's been gone for close to a month on another project."

"I knew she was out of town. One of her people told me."

"This is the longest I've gone without talking to her since we met. I had forgotten what it was like, not having her in my life. She's been in it for so long… I haven't seen her in close to a month, Emma."

"Have you tried to call her?"

"I did, after the first week. But she didn't call me back. I felt like I should give her the time she wants. I needed time to figure things out, too."

"What have you figured out?"

"That I am terrified of not living up to what she thinks."

"Hailey..."

"She's had these feelings for me for a long time. And I have this history of sucking at relationships."

"You didn't suck at our relationship."

"I hadn't developed that skill yet. With you, it was different. You were the first and the only there for a while. Then, I crushed on Ember for a minute, realized that was crazy, and I started falling for the wrong women. Just, every time, they were wrong. And even if they were right, I'd run away after a while."

"Did you ever stop to think that you did all that because none of them were right for you?" Emma asked her. "Hails, I'm not going to lie and tell you that I'm over this, because I'm not yet. Eli's nice. We're getting to know one another. But I'm still working through this. I'm not telling you that to make you feel bad, but I want you to know, I don't have any reason to want you to be with Charlie other than the fact that I want you to be happy."

"She's got this head start on me, Emma. I'm not used to that."

"So?" Emma challenged. "So what if she does? Why does that change anything? I had a head start on you."

"What? No, you didn't."

"Hailey, in high school, I was totally into you before we talked that day in the bathroom. You knew that."

Hailey moved her head back and lifted her eyebrows in surprise.

"You said you'd seen me around," Hailey said.

"I was playing it cool. I told you later, though."

Hailey laughed, "No, you didn't. I would have remembered that."

"Oh, shit! Maybe I just thought I told you. Yeah, Hails, I'd seen you around, but we had the same lunch period for two years. I'd noticed you since you were a freshman. I was a much more sophisticated sophomore, of course." Emma winked.

"Oh, of course," Hailey mocked.

"I'd see you around in the halls, but I kind of lunch-stalked you there for good two years." Emma laughed at herself. "I remember, the first day of my senior year, I was so excited for lunch. I looked for you the entire time, but you weren't there."

"Why me?"

"Hailey, you were beautiful. You seemed quiet; and smart, I guess, because you were usually studying at lunch while you ate and, sometimes, instead of."

"Why didn't you talk to me before that day?"

"Because I wasn't ready to admit to myself that I wanted you as more than just a friend. I still wasn't ready that day, but it seemed like time was running out. I was in my last year, and then, I'd graduate. I felt a little bit better about the whole likelihood of me being gay thing. And then, you gave that speech, and it was so cute. You were so cute up there, and I saw you go into the bathroom. I stood outside for a few minutes and then pretended that I had to pee, because when I saw you, I lost my nerve. I had no idea if you were gay, straight, or bi. I just thought I would talk to you, and if nothing happened, then at least I would know."

"You never told me any of this," Hailey offered.

"I guess I never thought it mattered, given that we got together after that. Plus, I still wanted you to think I was cool."

"Oh, you were. You were *so* cool, you wore that super cool purple dance uniform."

"Hey, I couldn't control the school colors."

Hailey leaned back against the sofa.

"So, what you're saying is that you were clearly obsessed with me," Hailey teased and turned her face toward Emma.

"What I'm saying, Hails, is that the head start doesn't mean anything," she replied seriously.

"What if I can't live up to what she thinks of me?"

"You didn't live up to what I thought."

"Hey!"

"What? You didn't. Hailey, you were *better* because you were *real.*" Emma leaned back to match Hailey's posture. "Have you thought about what it would be like to be with Charlie?"

"Yeah," Hailey answered softly at the recollection of touching herself to that very idea.

"And, I'm assuming you guys have…"

"Oh, not yet," Hailey told her. "We've kissed and almost… We were interrupted."

"So, which was better: imagining you were kissing her, or actually kissing her?"

"God, actually kissing her," she answered immediately.

Emma laughed at her and asked, "Why do you think it's not the same for her?"

"I guess, I don't know."

"Look, you and I didn't work out. I don't know if you and Charlie will, but I hope that you do, because I think she's the reason you've been holding back with everyone else; and I'm including myself in that."

"Can we be friends? And not like the friends that see each other once a year, Em. Can we be real friends?"

"Yeah, we can be friends, Hails." Emma shot up. "Actually, you can do me a favor."

"We've been friends for ten seconds, and you already need a favor?" Hailey jested.

"There's this party I need a date for, and Eli's out of town. Can I borrow you instead?"

"I'm your replacement date?" Hailey poked her shoulder.

"It's this Friday night. Eli's visiting her sister's family. She just had twins."

"I'm free on Friday."

"I was dreading going alone. It's a work thing… At least if I have you there, I'll be able to keep from being bored to tears."

"Well, I'll take that as a compliment."

***

Charlie arrived at the hotel just as Summer did, and she pulled the woman into a hug.

"Hey. Thanks for coming," she said.

"No problem. I'm glad I was in town." Summer pulled back.

Since the incident in the hotel, Charlie and Summer had continued getting to know one another. When Charlie returned to Chicago and got settled back in, Summer had a trip scheduled there, with some potential investors, so they agreed to meet up. They'd shared a drink and laughed about the time they almost hooked-up. Charlie asked Summer to join her at the party she was attending as a guest. Lena wasn't available, because she was doing a round of speed dating at a local lesbian hot spot. Summer being in town meant that Charlie didn't have to go alone. She had thought about asking Ember, but they hadn't talked beyond a few text messages since Charlie had left the city. She wasn't ready to let it be known that she was back until she had some time to readjust.

"Well, this is for work, so I can't guarantee we'll have a good time... But if it sucks, we can leave after, like, an hour," Charlie told her. "Well, you can leave whenever you want, actually. *I* have to stay for at least an hour."

"I wouldn't leave you at a boring party; even if I'm not getting laid after." Summer winked at her.

They'd established that they would be friends. Charlie had spent a lot of time talking to Summer about Hailey, and it was nice to have someone that didn't know them well weigh in on the situation. The big theme in all of Summer's advice had been to give Hailey time. Charlie was exhausted from giving Hailey time. Of course, it wasn't fair of her to add the ten-plus years she'd been in love with Hailey to that ticking clock, but Charlie did anyway, because she had wanted the woman for so long, that she couldn't not.

So, Charlie was exhausted and considered going back

to the whole part about getting Hailey out of her heart and mind and moving on with someone else. But she knew this time, that it would take a lot longer than she'd anticipated, because now, Charlie had had a chance with Hailey. They had been on a date. She had kissed Hailey. Hailey's hands had been on her body. They had laughed and talked like they'd never talked before. It would definitely be a lot harder this time.

They made their way into the hotel and toward the event room, where their hosts had already started the evening. Charlie had opted to arrive an hour late so that the party would be in full swing already. She would be able to make the rounds and then head out. It wasn't a party she'd been that excited to attend. She had received the invite the week prior, while she was wrapping things up in Detroit, and considered not coming back for it. Unfortunately, her company was hosting, so she had no choice.

Charlie made her way around the room after getting drinks for both herself and Summer. She mingled and introduced Summer as her friend to her boss and then to a few members of her team. A couple of them, at least, gave her the impression that they doubted the two of them were just friends.

"Hey, Charlie!" Emma's voice came from behind her.

"Shit, she's here," Charlie muttered to herself.

"Who?" Summer turned around with Charlie.

"Hey, Emma," Charlie returned. "Nice to see you again."

"You too. Your team told me you've been out of town."

"Detroit, yeah," Charlie offered and turned to her guest. "Oh, this is Summer."

"Summer?"

Charlie didn't have to look to her right to know whose voice that was, but she did. And when she did, Charlie saw Hailey standing there, dressed impeccably in a light-blue cocktail dress, with white strappy sandal shoes. Her hair was pulled back away from her face, but it was down. Her eyes were bright green, as always, and she'd brought them out even more with the dark-green tint of her eyeshadow.

"Hails."

"I didn't know you were back."

"I didn't know you'd be here." Charlie then glanced back at Emma. "I knew you'd be here," she said to Emma. "I'm glad the project worked out."

The Health Department project had wrapped early. Charlie's firm was hosting the party as a thank you to their local clients for their business, and also, of course, to drum up new business. It had been put together somewhat last minute, when they lost a huge client to a competing firm. This was less about saying, *'thank you,'* and more about saying, *'please, give us more business to make up for that loss in the upcoming quarter.'*

"It turned out really well. Your team did an amazing job."

"Thanks. I'll make sure to let them know," Charlie replied.

***

"So, Summer?" Hailey questioned as she stood next to Emma, and now in front of Charlie and a woman she didn't recognize but who was, apparently, named after a season.

Charlie looked amazing. Her hair looked like it had been cut, and it looked really good. She had chosen a pair of straight black slacks, with a white button-down that she had tucked into them, revealing that she had a flat stomach beneath just by the way it tucked straight down. Hailey found herself staring for a moment before she turned her attention to the other woman.

"Hailey, this is Summer. Summer owns the company I've been working with in Detroit."

Summer glanced at Charlie with some kind of recognition and then turned back to Hailey. She reached out her hand for Hailey to shake.

"It's nice to meet you, Hailey."

"You too." Hailey shook it and then looked at Emma for help.

"Hails was kind enough to be my guest tonight, since I would've had to come solo otherwise," Emma explained.

"I see," Charlie said. "We should probably go mingle a little."

"Yeah, you do that," Hailey stated in an aggravated tone she wished she'd hidden better. "See you around, Charlie."

Hailey walked away, pulling Emma along with her.

"Hailey, come on. This is stupid."

"You didn't tell me she'd be here!" Hailey waited until they were just outside the room before she practically yelled it.

"I didn't know for sure that she would."

"But you thought there was a chance?"

"Her company is the host, Hails."

"And you didn't think that was worth mentioning to me?" Hailey challenged.

"I thought that if she was here, you two could talk."

"Well, we can't exactly talk now, since she brought a date. Did you see that girl? How old is she anyway? She looks like she could still be in high school," Hailey said as she continued to walk toward the lobby.

"That's Summer Taft. She's one of the biggest up-and-comers in the tech industry. She's like, the next Mark Zuckerberg or something, along with her brother. They created this app that—"

"I don't care what their app does, Em. She's dating Charlie."

"I don't think Charlie said that."

"She brought her to a party. What else would—"

"Hailey, I brought you here. And we're not dating."

Hailey stopped walking, allowing Emma to catch up to her. Then, she let out a deep sigh.

"I'm jealous," she said after a moment.

"Yeah, that's obvious to everyone. Hails, go back in there and talk to her like an adult. Tell her how you feel."

"She came back to town and didn't tell me, Emma. It's not just about the arm candy."

"Hails, come–"

"I'm sorry. I'm going to go. Will you be okay on your own in there?"

"Yeah, I'll be fine. But I drove you."

"I'll catch a cab or take the train. I'll be fine."

***

Charlie sat at the table with Summer while others milled about the room. She was sure she'd said hello to some of them, but she couldn't focus on anything other than the thought of Hailey with Emma. Hailey was at the party with Emma. Emma had to know that Charlie would be there. Charlie's company was hosting the damn party. The woman had to know, and she still brought Hailey to rub it in.

"Hey, are you okay?" Summer asked after a moment and placed a hand on top of Charlie's.

"I'm pissed off, actually," she answered honestly.

"Yeah, I guessed that," Summer said. "Do you want to go?"

"Hey, Charlie." Emma approached cautiously. "Can I talk to you for a second?"

"No," Charlie stated and turned away from her.

"Charlie, please. It's not what you think."

"You didn't bring Hailey to a party you knew I'd be at?" Charlie turned back to her.

"I brought her *because* I knew you'd be here." Emma sat down in front of her. "She and I are not together. I'm dating someone else," Emma said. "I don't know what's going on between you and Summer, but Hailey is single. I brought her because I thought it would force you two to talk. It was wrong, and I'm sorry. I'll apologize to her later, if she ever talks to me again."

"We're not together. We're just friends." Summer attempted to lighten the mood with, "I tried, but she's unavailable."

"She's been trying to figure stuff out, Charlie. I thought she could come here, see you, and maybe you guys would talk. But I didn't expect you to bring a date." Emma stood back up. "I'm sorry. I didn't mean to make things worse." Emma waved at Summer, then turned, and walked away.

"How are you doing over there?" Summer asked.

"Honestly, I have no idea," Charlie replied.

CHAPTER 21

"WE didn't want to do it right before the wedding," Eva told her younger sister, Anna, as they all sat around the living room.

"You should have done the bridal shower, like I suggested. You get much better gifts than at a bachelorette party," Anna suggested.

"My baby sister is giving me wedding advice and planning the whole thing. Who would have expected that?" Eva kissed Anna's forehead. "I'm glad you made the trip. Thank you."

"Of course. Who else will make sure this thing goes off without a hitch?"

"I think the whole point is that we do actually get hitched," Ember suggested as she walked up behind her fiancée, wrapping her arms around Eva's waist. "Right?"

"Yes, babe," Eva answered with a smile.

Hailey was standing in the small backyard, listening through the open sliding glass door. Thankfully, spring was finally in Chicago, and all remnants of the snow had gone with the winter. Most of the guests were inside, but Hailey felt like she'd only bring the party down if she was around people. She would have skipped it entirely, but Ember and Eva deserved better than that from her. This was their joint bachelorette party, and Hailey had helped Anna throw it together at the last minute, because Ember's aunt had taken a turn for the worse. The doctors weren't sure she'd make it to June and be able to travel at that. So, Ember and Eva's wedding would be moved up to the following weekend. New invitations and apologies had been sent out to the guests. The backyard had been decorated with white and dark-blue lights and other decorations. There were four rented round tables in the yard, with white tablecloths and blue accents. There were already about fifteen women in the living room, including Alyssa and Hannah, who trickled outside to chat with Hailey.

"Hey there," Alyssa greeted and hugged her.

"Hi. Haven't seen you two in a while." Hailey hugged Hannah next.

"We've been crazy busy lately," Hannah said.

"Hey, my friends." Eva made her way toward them and gave the women a giant group hug.

"She's had a couple of glasses of champagne already," Ember said as she took Eva's hand following the hug. "She's starting to feel it."

"It's my bachelorette party," Eva excused.

"Please tell me you and Anna did not hire a stripper," Ember said.

"What? No way," Hailey told her with a laugh.

"Thank God," Ember replied.

"We don't need one, anyway. She can just dance for me later." Eva took another sip of her champagne, apparently not realizing that what she'd just said would cause them all to burst into hysterical laughter.

"You need a drink, Al," Ember told her, noticing that Alyssa wasn't holding a drink.

"No, I'm okay," Alyssa replied. "I'll grab water in a minute."

"It's a party, Alyssa," Hailey added.

Hannah and Alyssa looked at one another in that way that only married couples seem to look at one another.

"There's something we need to tell you, guys. We were going to wait, because this is your night, but since you'll probably figure it out anyway, we'll just tell you," Hannah said.

"Oh, my God!" Eva pointed at Alyssa and exclaimed, "You're pregnant!"

Alyssa nodded and smiled. Hannah wrapped her arm around her wife's waist.

"You are? Congratulations," Ember said.

"That's amazing, guys," Hailey added.

"How far along are you?" Eva asked after hugging both of them.

"Twelve weeks. We haven't even told my mom yet, but the not drinking wine tonight thing probably would have given it away," Alyssa answered.

"What did I miss?" Charlie stood in the open door at first but then was ushered aside so that two women Hailey didn't recognize would move through it and past her.

"They're pregnant." Eva pointed at her friends.

"What?" Charlie walked quickly toward them. "That's awesome." She hugged Alyssa first and then Hannah.

When Charlie pulled back, Hailey felt Charlie's arm against her own and realized how close they were standing to one another. The hair on her arm stood up, and she recognized the goosebumps and the nerves that went with them.

"And where have you been?" Ember reached over and pulled Charlie into a hug. "I wasn't even sure you'd be here tonight."

"I wouldn't have missed this." Charlie returned the hug, but her eyes were open and on Hailey. "I had to go to Detroit for work, but I'm back for the next few weeks."

"Few weeks?" Hailey asked before she had a chance to think.

"It's an ongoing project. I'll go back and forth for a while." Charlie answered her and then hugged Eva next. "I'm sorry I went radio-silent. Things were just really busy."

"Eva, the food's ready." Anna emerged from the house and motioned for Eva to help her.

"I've got it." Hailey headed inside.

She needed to be away from Charlie. She needed a minute to put on a brave face, get herself together, and then have fun at her best friend's party.

***

A few hours later, Eva and Ember looked entirely way too happy, which also made Hailey happy, because they deserved it. Alyssa was sitting on Hannah's lap on the sofa. Anna had already gone upstairs to the guest room, to call her husband and say goodnight. The majority of the other party-goers had already headed out. Hailey caught sight of the elusive Charlie Adams, sliding the door closed behind herself after bringing in some of the trash and dishes from outside. Hailey hadn't spoken to her since the woman had arrived, and she wasn't sure what she'd say if she did. She watched Charlie say goodnight to Ember and Eva, and then Hannah and Alyssa. After that, she glanced in Hailey's direction and nodded a farewell before she went to the front door, opened it, and left.

"I'm not going to ask," Ember said to her as Hailey washed the glasses in the kitchen. "Because we've already talked about how you two are being idiots… But we're leaving on Thursday for this wedding. So, please–"

"Em, we'll be fine," Hailey told her. "We're just not really talking at the moment. We'll pull it together by then."

"Good. We're going to borrow my dad's van so that the six of us can fit. Anna's driving back tomorrow, to help set up whatever she can in advance, since this is happening faster than we thought."

"Okay. So, meet you where? Here? The restaurant?"

"Meet us here."

"I'll be here."

"Good." Ember glanced at her. "How are you, Hails?"

"Well, I'm not great," Hailey said. "I haven't talked to my best friend in over a month. And Emma and I were just starting to figure our friendship out, when she tried to pull an intervention on me, so I'm not exactly talking to her right now, either."

"I'm sorry, Hails."

"I know."

"I should get back out there. Eva's exhausted. Anna is a real piece of work. She had us up so early this morning, to finalize things."

"I know. She called me to make sure I tried on my dress one more time, in case – and I'm not paraphrasing here – I put on too much weight to fit in it."

"I'm going to put my love to bed now. You good to get home?"

"Yeah, I'm good."

Hailey stopped for a moment to think about how inaccurate that statement actually was.

***

"Okay, but why aren't you talking to her if she's single now?" Lena asked.

"Because I don't know what to say. It's never been about whether or not Hailey was single. It's been about whether or not she believes me when I tell her I just want her, and not some fantasy. It's been about me trying to get past the fact that Hailey had the world's most perfect girlfriend, and that woman re-entered her life recently."

They were sitting on the couch, drinking the coffee that Lena had brought her. Charlie's phone buzzed on the table. She lifted it and saw the name.

"Her?" Lena asked hopefully.

"Summer," Charlie answered. "She's just texting that she got back to Detroit okay."

"So, nothing's going on there? Really?"

"No. She's nice, though," Charlie said. "We had an almost-thing happen, but I'm–"

"Into Hailey?"

"That's always been my problem."

"How are you going to get through this whole wedding thing? It's hours in a car with her, and then, like, three days of festivities. You're both in the wedding party."

"We've gotten pretty good at avoiding each other. I

guess we'll just keep that up."

"That's a pretty terrible plan."

"Well, it's the only one I've got."

***

"So, your plan is to simply ignore her?" Emma questioned.

"Yes," Hailey replied. "What else did you expect me to do?"

"I told you, she's not with Summer. She's single."

Hailey was driving to Ember's, preparing to hit the road for likely, a very awkward trip. She had finally returned Emma's many calls and texts, after getting over herself and her stupid problems to think about what a nice thing Emma had tried to do for her. Given the fact that Emma had wanted to be with Hailey only a short time ago, it was pretty selfless of her to try to get Hailey to repair her relationship with Charlie.

"I know that, Em. But that doesn't mean I'm just ready to jump back into things with her."

"Not even your friendship?" Emma asked. "I'm not saying you need to start a new relationship with her, Hails. But you two haven't talked in a long time. I know how important she is to you."

"I know," Hailey said softly. "I'm here. I should go. I'm sorry I didn't call you back sooner. I've been blaming you for something that you had nothing to do with. I know you were just trying to help."

"Have fun this weekend. Try not to let anything that's going on between the two of you get in the way of everything else."

"I won't let Ember and Eva suffer because–"

"Not them. I mean, yeah, don't be an asshole, because it's their wedding. But it's also your best friend's wedding, Hails. You should enjoy it. It's only going to happen once."

Hailey hung up the phone and pulled up onto Ember's

street to park. An old catering van was parked in the driveway. Ember was currently loading things into the back while Hannah helped.

"Are Alyssa and Eva inside?" she asked when she arrived at the back of the van and placed her roller and garment bag in Ember's hands to load up for her.

"Yeah. So is Charlie."

"Oh." Hailey glanced up and down the street, as if Charlie would somehow be there.

"We picked her up," Hannah said. "We had a doctor's appointment in the city, so we just grabbed her and brought her over."

"Everything okay?" Hailey asked.

"Oh, yeah. Al's great, and so is the little one," Hannah answered with a smile. "Just a regular appointment."

"When will you guys learn the sex?" Ember questioned and loaded Hailey's stuff into the back, hanging the garment bag next to several others.

"We don't know if we're going to," Alyssa offered when she joined the group outside. She carried a bottle of water and passed it to Hannah. "My mom said she had fun not knowing what I was going to be, so we're kind of thinking we might go that route."

"*She's* thinking that," Hannah said and opened the water bottle.

Hailey watched as she didn't take a drink of it. She passed it back to Alyssa, who did, though. It was pretty remarkable, watching stuff like this between couples. They hadn't even exchanged words about the water bottle. Hannah just knew that it was for Alyssa and that Alyssa needed help opening it.

"You want to know?" Ember asked Hannah.

"I do." Hannah looked at Alyssa and then placed a hand over her stomach. "I can keep a secret," she said to Alyssa, who glared at her and delivered a smirk. "What? I can."

"Not from me, you can't. You're terrible at that."

"That's true." Hannah removed her hand and glanced into the van. "So, this thing is for the restaurant?"

"It was, yeah," Ember began. "We used to use it for catering, but we have the food truck now. My dad had two rows of seats put in this, instead of just buying a new van. I think his plan was to give it to Zack and Grace, to use when they have kids, but who would trust this van with their kids?" She pointed to the van that was likely about fifteen years old. It was the color of an eggplant and had the restaurant's name and logo on the side.

"You realize we're about to get in this thing for, like, a six-hour road trip, right?" Charlie questioned.

Hailey felt Charlie's presence before her words even came out. Despite the fact that Hailey hadn't seen the woman due to her position behind the opened back door of the van, she felt her there, in that way that she always somehow felt Charlie's presence when they were close.

"You want to strap a baby's car seat into self-installed van seats?" Ember jested.

"We will not be doing that," Alyssa added with a hand over her stomach.

"Are we ready?" Eva emerged from the house.

She approached the back of the van to see everyone standing around.

"Why are we all climbing into this thing?" Charlie motioned to the van. "I remember doing catering jobs in this, back when we first started at the restaurant."

"You never could drive it," Hailey said with a smile and then caught Charlie's eyes.

"You weren't any better," Charlie retorted.

"Which is why I'm driving," Ember stated. "Also, we're doing this instead of taking separate cars, because this is kind of like our wedding gift to each other." She nodded toward Eva.

"Us in a van is your wedding gift?" Alyssa examined Eva.

"We've all been so busy lately. Charlie's been out of

town, Hailey's been pulling all-nighters at work, you two have been off getting pregnant." Eva looked around at her group of friends. "We thought it would be fun to take this trip together."

Fun' wasn't exactly the word that came to mind first for Hailey, as she stood a few feet away from Charlie, but she did smile after the initial concern faded away, because she loved her friends.

"Let's do this." Ember pulled Eva into her. "Wanna ride shotgun?" She winked at her.

"Next to you? Always." Eva leaned in for a sweet kiss.

Ember and Eva took the front. Hailey couldn't exactly argue with the married pregnant couple that wanted to sit next to one another. That meant that she and Charlie were stuck in the back row next to one another. Once everyone got settled in, Ember put the van in reverse, and they all headed down the road to get her and Eva married.

***

Charlie stared out the side window for the first hour, while participating in conversation only when necessary. She could feel Hailey's eyes on her periodically, but for the most part, they were both clearly on the same page. They would ignore and pretend the other didn't exist for the entirety of the drive and, likely, the event itself. During the next hour, Charlie talked about Detroit and how the new project was going, while Hannah and Ember both seemed interested and asked her questions.

At hour three, they made a pit stop for gas and a bathroom break. When they climbed back in, Hailey was in the middle seat, and Hannah slid into the back. She appeared to want to know more about Charlie's work – turning older historical buildings into modern structures while still maintaining their original aesthetic. Hailey and Alyssa were in deep conversation, and Charlie found herself listening in whenever she and Hannah experienced a lull in their own.

"How many do you think you'll have?" Hailey asked her.

"We're just starting with this one. If we don't screw him or her up, we'll consider another. But if we only have one, we'll both be okay with that. Right, babe?" Alyssa turned back to Hannah, who just smiled at her. "Are you going to have any?" Alyssa asked Hailey.

"I want to one day, yeah," Hailey said with a lowered head and a soft voice. "Not sure if I will, but I think I'd like at least two."

"Yeah?" Alyssa glanced back at Hannah. "Han, wanna try for another?"

Hannah rolled her eyes at her, and Alyssa just returned to her conversation with Hailey.

"I love that woman like crazy," Hannah leaned in to share with Charlie. "She's carrying our baby. It's like this incredible thing. You think you can't love someone more, and then you do, and then you think that again, and again, and then you do."

"Yeah, I can understand that," Charlie replied and looked at Hailey, who – though wasn't looking back at them – was listening in all the same, Charlie suspected.

By hour four, Charlie had started to lighten up a bit. She was having fun with her friends, talking about the up-coming wedding and potential names for Hannah and Alyssa's baby. They had tossed out several that were definitely not going to happen, and some potentials, but the best names were the ones they shouted just as jokes.

"What about Rainbow?" Eva suggested. "For obvious reasons."

"Yeah, that won't get our kid mocked," Alyssa returned.

"How about Aardvark?" Ember suggested. "Works for a boy and a girl, and they'd always be first in the alphabet."

"Sure. Aardvark Granger," Hannah said out loud and then laughed. "Sounds great."

"Well, we could always go with Hermione, if it's a girl," Alyssa then stated. "Our last name gives us the perfect opportunity."

"Is that the real reason you took her name, Al?" Eva turned around and asked.

"No," Alyssa said. "It's just an added benefit."

The other benefit, Charlie surmised, was that Alyssa Masters was a well-known name everywhere in the country, thanks to a tragic incident that had happened years prior. Alyssa had been able to move on from it, and the world moved on to its next tragedy, but it was still out there, and every now and then, something would happen that would bring it all back up again. Becoming Alyssa Granger wasn't just done because she loved her wife and wanted her name, or for the possibility of having a baby girl named after a *Harry Potter* character. It was one more way for Alyssa to put that part of her past behind her.

"I'm thinking, you should name her after one of us," Ember stated. "Come on. There should be more Novembers in the world."

"Why are you so sure we're having a girl?" Hannah asked her.

"If not, you could name him Charlie," Hailey suggested.

Charlie perked up at the sound of Hailey's voice and the mention of her name. She met Hailey's eyes and gave her a shy smile, which Hailey returned.

***

By hour five, they had to stop for another bathroom break, thanks to Alyssa's pregnancy bladder, and Charlie had gone inside as well. Hailey went around to the back of the van to try to find her chapstick, which she had packed and then forgotten to remove before stowing the luggage away. Ember joined her in the back while the gas pumped into the van. Hailey had to push a few plastic bags aside.

They'd brought snacks for the trip to Iowa and the trip back. Since Ember and Eva's honeymoon wouldn't take place until June still, as planned, they'd all ride back together. Hailey pushed one bag to the side and pulled out her small bag. She then removed the chapstick out of it and slid it into her pocket before placing everything back. But, as she moved the plastic bag back on top of her roller, she saw something inside that caught her eye.

"Em, did you bring this?" Hailey asked and pointed.

"No. I thought you did," Ember replied, and then heard the gas pump stop with a thud and walked to finish up.

Inside the bag was a box of Hailey's favorite cereal. There was only one other person in the world that knew that and would bring it. Charlie walked out of the gas station with Alyssa and Eva, and she was laughing.

***

They arrived at Eva's family's farmhouse and began unpacking. Eva's mom and dad helped them get situated into the rooms they would occupy for the remainder of their trip. Since Anna had moved out and was the last child remaining at home, they had two guest rooms upstairs, along with Eva's childhood room. Hannah and Alyssa would share Anna's old room, which had a relatively new full bed. Ember and Eva would be in Eva's old room with the full bed her parents recently purchased to update the room. It no longer contained the remnants of Eva's past, but instead, was a fully functional guest room they used for visiting friends and family members. That left the last room for Charlie and Hailey to figure out how to navigate. That room had also been updated with a full bed, which would make things incredibly awkward for them, considering they still weren't talking. Ember, knowing this, dug out an old twin-sized air mattress from the garage and told Hailey to figure out who would sleep on it.

Charlie had disappeared shortly after the arrival, and so did Ember, the moment after she handed Hailey the air mattress. Hailey wondered if they were off talking about her, and hoped that she wouldn't lose both of them in this mess. She made her way into the bedroom and set about blowing up the mattress and covering it with the sheets and a blanket Ember had also provided.

Dinner was around the picnic-style kitchen table for the six of them, since Eva's parents had already eaten. Her mom had left them plenty of home-cooked food, and they all enjoyed it along with their shared laughter. Charlie and Ember disappeared once again after the meal, and while Eva and Hailey were helping with the dishes, she thought to ask what was going on.

"Oh, I don't know. Em just told me she would be busy tonight and that she had asked for Charlie's help," Eva responded to her question. "Are you two okay?"

"Who?"

"Really?" Eva rolled her eyes.

"No, we're not. But I promise, we'll be okay for you guys," Hailey replied and dried the last dish.

Hailey showered after Hannah and Alyssa wrapped up in the bathroom, and then retired for the night. She climbed on the air mattress and rolled onto her side. Charlie and Ember were still missing in action, and while Hailey found herself curious about what they were up to, she let the exhaustion of the day carry her away into sleep.

CHAPTER 22

WHEN Charlie walked into the bedroom, she first noticed that the lights were out, meaning Hailey was likely already asleep. She went to use her phone to provide light so that she could get ready for bed herself, and then noticed that Hailey had taken the air mattress. Charlie also noticed that she didn't need her phone after all, because there was a night light plugged into the wall. She hadn't seen it initially, because it was on the other side of the bed. It hadn't been there before, when they dropped their stuff. Thanks to the location of the outlet and the placement of the air mattress, the light illuminated the top of Hailey's head, her closed eyes, and soft features. Charlie stared for long moments before Hailey went to scratch her nose. The woman didn't wake up, but Charlie smiled at her and then turned away so she wouldn't get caught if Hailey did wake up. She changed her clothes, finished her nightly routine, and climbed into the bed.

***

When Charlie woke up, Hailey was already out of the room. Charlie showered, dressed, and walked downstairs to find that there were muffins on the table along with some bacon that had been fried earlier. The old-fashioned coffee pot was full and sitting on the table as well. Charlie filled a cup and took a walk around the house to see if she could find anyone.

She found Alyssa and Hannah in the living room, talking to Anna and Eva's mom. She decided not to join in on the conversation and headed outside, where she saw Ember and Eva sitting on the porch swing. They looked to be a little occupied and attached at the lips. She let them have their private moment and took her coffee along for a walk around the property. She had finished it by the time she found Hailey staring up at the tree house in the backyard. Hailey turned just in time to see her place the empty cup on the back porch and then walk over.

"It says, *'No admittance.'*" Hailey pointed at a sign that had been taped to the ladder that was attached to the tree.

"So, you better not go up, then," Charlie warned.

"Is it falling apart or something?" she asked.

"No, it's actually the opposite."

"It's falling together?" Hailey lifted an eyebrow and turned to Charlie.

Charlie laughed and then said, "No, it's what Em and I have been working on. It's her present to Eva."

"A tree house?"

"She started making some modifications when they came back a few weeks ago. She and I have been finishing it. We're trying to get it ready for tomorrow night."

"What's tomorrow night?" Hailey asked.

"She's going to show Eva after the wedding. They're going to stay out here."

"They're going to stay the night in a tree house?" Hailey questioned the logic.

"They had their first kiss up there. It's important to both of them. You can go up. We just put this here so no one else would. Eva's dad told her they're thinking about taking it down because of the damage it sustained during a winter storm, which is a total lie Ember convinced him to tell her. And he even said that the sign was a legal requirement, in case kids came on the property."

"I can go up?"

"Sure."

Charlie watched as Hailey climbed into the tree house and then climbed after her. When Charlie got inside, she watched Hailey look around.

"You guys did all this?" Hailey asked.

The tree house had been pretty bare when Charlie arrived. Ember had worked on the structural stuff during her last trip and had even stained all the wood to prevent further warping and damage. She'd told Charlie that the house used to have a bean bag chair, some blankets, and random bookshelves for Eva's collection, but not much else.

"Yeah," Charlie replied.

She and Ember had created a honeymoon suite of sorts, thanks to Ember's genius and Charlie's architectural and design skills. The room now housed a bed – that was really just a nice mattress on a six-inch wood frame that matched the wood of the house itself. They hadn't made the bed yet, but the sheets, pillows, and a comforter were all resting atop it.

"Charlie…"

"It was Ember's idea. We brought up a space heater, but she wanted that cheesy, fake fireplace thing." Charlie pointed at what looked like a thin black box. "Turn it on," she told Hailey.

Hailey walked over and looked for a moment until she found a switch and flipped it. The front of the box illuminated in fake flames, as if it was an actual fireplace.

"We ran electricity last night. The speakers are all connected," Charlie added.

She then pointed to the ceiling, where Hailey's eyes followed four ceiling-mounted small speakers that Charlie had connected to a central speaker. Ember or Eva could attach their phone and create whatever musical vibe they wanted for their night. They'd placed a small two-person table in one corner, and on it, rested the gift Eva had for Ember, wrapped and ready for delivery.

"That's the gift Eva told me to hide," Hailey shared and pointed at the box.

"I know. Ember won't open it. She knew about it already. We just thought it would be nice to put it up here. They could open it together after everything. Do you know what it is?" Charlie asked her.

"Eva told me last night. It's a first-edition signed copy of *To Kill a Mockingbird*."

"That seems like a gift Eva would get for herself; not Ember," Charlie stated.

"It's the book that brought them together," Hailey explained. "Eva gave her a copy of it that day at Windy's. It was the first book Em read before she read the rest of Eva's entire collection in, like, a weekend or something."

"Oh." Charlie watched the glow on Hailey's face at the story of her two friends meeting and falling in love.

"A mini-fridge?" Hailey pointed at the small appliance.

"It's got snacks in it, mostly. Ember heard that the couple usually never eats on their wedding day because they're so busy. She wanted something in here for them later. Plus, my guess is, they'll want to keep their energy up, too." Charlie laughed at her own comment. "And we put windows in." She pointed at the once square cutouts that now housed makeshift windows. "They're plastic, but they'll do."

"This is great, Charlie. Eva will love this." Hailey turned around to face her.

"I hope so," Charlie stated and then motioned for Hailey to climb down. "I'm going to finish up. I'll meet you back down there."

"Do you need any help?"

"No, I'm good." Charlie lowered her head and walked around the bed. She didn't look back up again until she heard Hailey's footsteps fading away.

***

Hailey went to the neighbor's property, where the

wedding would be held, and helped Anna and the others make the last-minute preparations for both the rehearsal dinner, and the ceremony that would take place the next day. Charlie and Ember had remained behind. Hailey felt much better, now that she at least knew that what they were doing was to bring Ember and Eva joy and not to exclude her. She helped Eva's mom with the cooking – or mainly with the carrying the things the woman had cooked outside to the tables that had been placed between the main house and the barn.

The rehearsal was less a rehearsal and more a dinner between friends and family. Ember and Eva practiced their walk down together with their fathers on either side; after Charlie and Hailey, each paired with a Granger, made their way down and stood in front of the reverend who would conduct the ceremony. It took ten minutes at most, to get through, and then came the time for the meal and some speeches.

Hailey had been placed at one of the round tables on the opposite side of Charlie. While she'd thought it a good idea at the time, because it meant they wouldn't be side-by-side, she now realized that being across from Charlie just meant she would be looking at the woman all night long. They exchanged shy smiles throughout most of the night, until the meal was done and the speeches had all been delivered.

Then, Anna got the idea to have a practice round at the first dance. Ember and Eva were more than game, and after a few moments, others joined in. Eva's parents were first. Ember's followed. Hannah and Alyssa stood, too. Hailey watched how all of the couples seemed to fit together so nicely. Anna and her husband stood along with Eva's brothers and their wives; until the only people left at the table were children, Hailey, and Charlie.

"Do you want to dance with me?" Eva's nephew asked Charlie while Hailey looked on with a smile.

"Oh, wow. Thank you. I would love to dance with

you," Charlie replied and glanced at Hailey with a knowing expression.

Hailey watched on as Charlie allowed the small boy to stand on her feet while they moved slowly in a circle. She laughed silently along with everyone as he attempted to hold Charlie about the waist. Hailey had turned around in her chair to watch the whole spectacle. After a few moments, Ember headed to the table to snag a drink, while Eva danced with her father.

"Having fun?" Hailey asked her.

"The time of my life, Hails. I'm marrying that gorgeous creature tomorrow." She pointed at Eva. "Are you having an okay time?" She took a drink and looked down at Hailey.

"Yeah, it's great." Hailey was less than convincing as her eyes drifted toward Charlie, still dancing; but this time, with one of Eva's other nephews. "She's a hit," Hailey teased and laughed.

"She's always been great with kids," Ember reminded her. "You know, Eva and I had our first dance in this barn."

"What?" Hailey's eyes returned to Ember.

"Yeah, it was pretty amazing. I think tomorrow's first dance as a married couple might beat it, but it will be close."

"I saw the tree house. It's amazing, Em."

"It was Charlie's idea," Ember said.

"What? She said you came up with it."

"I told her about how we had our first kiss there, and how Eva used to spend a lot of time up there, but Charlie actually gave me the idea to fix it up. She helped me draw up the stuff I had to do on my own, and then, she was helping me finish it since we got here. Don't tell Eva, though. I want her to think it was all my idea." Ember winked at Hailey.

Hailey laughed and watched her best friend walk over to dance with her father, who she'd gotten close to since Eva entered her life. She saw Charlie whisper something into the ear of one of the boys. He ran over, looking adorable in his little bowtie and suspenders.

"Would you like to dance?" the little boy asked Hailey

and held out his hand.

Hailey nodded, gave him a smile, and accompanied him to the dance floor.

***

Charlie found Hailey outside the barn. She'd noticed her missing a few minutes before, and after a quick glance outside, she saw the woman around the back. Hailey was lit by the light of the barn, emanating down from the loft inside. She had worn a beautiful yellow dress for the occasion, along with that same pair of white strappy sandals Charlie had seen her wear at the party. Hailey's hair was pulled back into a braid but had loosened throughout the night. Charlie found that she liked the imperfections even more than the perfections she found in Hailey Grant.

"Hey, what are you doing out here?"

"You brought my cereal," Hailey said without turning around.

"Yeah, I set it out for you this morning," Charlie stated. "I figured you'd forget it." She stood beside Hailey now. "You brought me a night light."

"I thought it might be rude to leave the hall light on in Eva's family home." Hailey turned to face her.

Charlie heard the music still playing softly inside, even though nearly everyone had already left. Ember and Eva were still around, as was Anna and her husband. Hannah and Alyssa had gone back to the house. A few more stragglers had been leaving every couple of minutes, but still, the music played.

"Hails, do you... maybe, want to dance with me?" Charlie let out the breath she had been holding in and awaited Hailey's reply.

"Sure." Hailey gave her a small smile.

Charlie placed her hands on Hailey's hips and held them there for a moment while connecting with green eyes. Hailey placed her own on Charlie's shoulders and then wrapped them solidly around her neck. Charlie slid her arms around Hailey's waist and pulled the woman closer. They hadn't been this close since that day in Charlie's kitchen. Holding Hailey like this made Charlie feel like her world was back in balance.

***

Hailey gripped her hands tightly around Charlie's neck. She was fidgeting with her fingers and staring at the ground around their feet as they began to sway. Charlie's hands ran slowly up her back and pulled her just slightly closer. Hailey calmed and rested her head on Charlie's shoulder, relaxing her hands.

"I missed you," she said after a moment.

"I missed you, too," Charlie replied.

"Hey, I–" Ember started. "Shit! Sorry."

Hailey and Charlie pulled apart slowly.

"What's up, Em?" Charlie asked.

"I just wanted to let you know that Eva's parents are being really old-school about this thing… They don't think we should sleep in the same room tonight."

"Oh."

"So, I'm going to bunk with one of you, and Eva will be with the other. Is that okay? I wouldn't actually do this, but I think her mom might check in the middle of the night, and I kind of fear her."

"It's fine, Em," Charlie told her.

"I'll pull out the other air mattress, and we'll flip a coin to see who gets it, Hails."

"So, you're bunking with me, then?" Hailey checked.

"Yeah. Eva doesn't mind the light. I'm not a fan… Sorry, Charlie." Ember then pointed at both of them. "And sorry for… yeah. Oh, and we're heading out in, like, two minutes. So, get to the van if you don't want to walk," she called out without turning back around.

"Well, I guess we should go, then," Charlie suggested.

"Yeah, I guess."

***

Hailey slept on the air mattress again, leaving the bed to Ember, because it was the night before her wedding. Sleep was hard to come by, though, because she kept thinking about how good it felt to be in Charlie's arms, to feel her pressed against her, and then, what it felt like to have it taken away so quickly.

When she woke up the next morning, after getting only a couple of hours, Ember was already up and on the move. Hailey went over to Eva's room to check on her and see if she needed anything, while Ember was in the shower. Eva wasn't there, though. Charlie was. She was standing in front of a floor-length mirror, holding up Eva's dress, as if she wanted to see how it looked. Hailey caught the whole thing through a crack in the door and swallowed hard.

"Hails, can you grab my stuff in there for me?" Ember asked, leaving the bathroom and heading back into the guest room where she would be getting ready.

"Yeah," Hailey returned and then opened the door to see Charlie hanging the dress up on the closet door.

"Morning," Charlie greeted.

"Hey. Ember's going to get ready in that room."

"Okay. I'll hop in the shower and then head in, if that's okay."

"Sure."

Hailey gathered up Ember's things – including the woman's dress, since she wasn't allowed to see Eva's dress, or even Eva herself today – and carried everything back to the guest room. Hailey and Charlie spent the day with Ember, helping their best friend get ready alongside Francine, Ember's mom. Eva was being taken care of by Hannah, Alyssa, and her own mother, while Anna floated between the two rooms trying to make sure everything was perfect.

After makeup and hair were done for all of them, Hailey watched as Charlie began to change into her dress. She didn't mean to, but she just couldn't avert her eyes. Ember's mom had left the room to go get ready. It was just the three of them. Ember was focused on putting on her jewelry. Hailey was looking into a mirror, pretending to apply more lip gloss, while Charlie stood over by the closet, sliding out of the sweats she'd worn all day and revealing white underwear beneath. She pulled her T-shirt over her head, showing off an equally white bra. The dresses Ember and Eva had chosen for the bridesmaids were navy-blue. Hannah and Alyssa would be wearing the same color, to support the symmetrical theme. Ember's dress had a navy-blue sash around the waist that matched, and Eva's accent was a one-inch wide ribbon at the top of her strapless dress that wrapped around the back and tied into a neat bow.

Hailey watched as Charlie pulled the dress up her legs and then over her torso. She slid the straps over her shoulders and then turned to the mirror to see how it looked, while Hailey turned her eyes away. Her heart was going crazy, and she knew her breath was coming in short bursts.

"Can you help me?" Charlie stood next to her and turned around, facing away from Hailey.

Hailey saw the zipper and the skin of Charlie's back under it. She wanted to reach out and touch the woman. She wanted to wrap her arms around Charlie, but now wasn't the time. Instead, Hailey pulled the zipper up slowly and allowed Charlie to walk away.

Hailey needed some space and some air. She headed downstairs and into the kitchen. She grabbed a glass of water, practically chugged the whole thing, and then stared at the box of cereal on the counter. It was something so stupid, so silly, but she sat the glass down and stared. Her eyes got big, and she thought back to her last argument with Charlie, about Hailey not being able to live up to Charlie's expectations or fantasies. Then, Hailey thought about the cereal, and it made sense. She thought about the wedding dress she had seen Charlie holding against her body earlier, and it made sense. She had been so confused this whole time. She had thought Emma was the one for her, only to realize that

Emma couldn't be the one, because neither of them was who they used to be. And then, Hailey thought she could be with Charlie, but she'd gotten scared, because Charlie had been in this for far longer.

But, things were clear now. Hailey had finally achieved the clarity she had been trying to find forever.

**

Charlie stood just outside the barn and tried not to look at Hailey, who looked perfect in the bridesmaid's dress Ember had picked out. The guests were already inside. The music had started playing softly. Anna motioned for Hailey and Alyssa to walk first, and a few seconds later, Charlie and Hannah followed them down the aisle. Charlie made it toward the front just in time for Hailey to turn around and catch her eye. Charlie smiled at her and then took the spot next to her.

A few moments later, she watched her best friend, Ember, and the love of her life, walk down the aisle together with their fathers at their sides. They were all smiles. Charlie listened as the reverend began the ceremony. She stared at Ember's back and Eva's smiling face, while they stood facing one another hand in hand.

It was a beautiful ceremony. Anna had made the barn look rustic yet classic at the same time, although Charlie doubted Ember and Eva cared at all about the décor. They likely wouldn't remember the details of the accents in the flowers that were hanging along the rows of chairs. They probably wouldn't remember that the wind from outside blew open a shutter in the loft and caused a slight knocking sound in the middle of the vows. Charlie knew though, that they would remember the color of each other's eyes, the happy tears that streaked down their cheeks, and the feel of sliding a ring on a shaking finger.

Charlie felt something, too, and looked down to see that Hailey's hand was behind her, reaching for Charlie. She looked out at the guests first, but their eyes were rightfully on the brides. So, Charlie took a step closer to Hailey and placed her hand into the other woman's hand. As she felt Hailey's hand tighten around her own, Charlie laced their fingers together. She wondered if her hand was shaking; and if it was, if Hailey could tell. They stayed that way until the reverend gave permission for the new wives to share their first kiss as a married couple. Only then did Charlie pull her hand back to applaud. She followed Hailey back down the aisle and outside, where everyone took turns hugging the two newly-weds.

"Picture time." Anna began pushing them over to the side yard before anyone could really say anything more than, *'Congratulations.'*

They took probably over a thousand pictures in every configuration; some with the wedding party, some with just Ember's side, and some with just Eva's. Then, there were the family pictures, and then just some of the two of them, while Anna took her pictures as part of Eva's family first, and then returned to the barn to help the small staff they had hired move the chairs around and replace them with tables. There were caterers also setting up a buffet line as the pictures went on.

"Hey, Charlie." Hailey and Charlie stood off to the side by Hannah and Alyssa, while Ember and Eva took the final pictures.

"Yeah?"

"I know it's technically half over already, but…" Hailey's words faded, and Charlie turned to face her with a quizzical look. "Will you be my date at this wedding?"

CHAPTER 23

"WILL you be my date at this wedding?" Hailey asked her.

"What?" Charlie questioned after a moment of trying to make sure she had heard Hailey correctly.

"At the reception, technically," Hailey added. "And I don't mean my friend date. I mean my actual date."

"Hailey, we—"

"We've been trying to ignore one another. I hate it, Charlie. I hate it," she said.

"You two; let's get one of just the two of you with Ember, and we should be good." The photographer pointed at them.

"Please." Hailey shrugged.

"Yeah, okay," Charlie agreed and smiled.

They were ushered over next to Ember, who was glowing. They stood on either side of her, and after a few more clicks of the camera, they were dismissed to join the party with Hannah and Alyssa. Ember and Eva would make a grand entrance in a few minutes. As much as Charlie wanted to just be alone with Hailey right now, she had obligations as her best friend's co-maid-of-honor to fulfill. She did make sure to stick close by Hailey, though, whenever she could.

While they weren't exactly alone and couldn't share too much, there was a new ease with Hailey that Charlie could feel, and it felt great. When they stood in line for food, Hailey pressed a hand to the small of Charlie's back to usher her along. When they sat at the table to eat, Hailey's hand went to her thigh and rested there like it was meant for that very spot all along. Charlie found herself staring at it for a while before she placed her own hand on top of it and linked their fingers under the table. They carried on conversations with everyone at the reception and occasionally said a few words to one another, but the touches between them were enough to sustain Charlie until they could really talk later.

When the dancing started, Charlie caught Hailey's eyes watching Ember and Eva sway to the music. They both looked beautiful, but Charlie was staring at the new gleam in Hailey's eyes and wondered what exactly had brought it on.

"Dance with me?" Hailey turned and caught her staring.

"Okay," Charlie said without thought.

Hailey pulled Charlie up and onto the dance floor that was now crowded with couples. Hailey's arms went around her waist this time, and she pulled Charlie tightly into her. She felt Charlie's stiffness at the new touch and lifted Charlie's arms around her own neck before placing her hands back where they were.

"It's okay," she whispered into Charlie's ear. "I promise."

Hailey then kissed her just below that ear, and placed one hand on the back of Charlie's head, encouraging the woman to rest it against her shoulder, which Charlie did. Hailey kept her hand there, grazing her fingers over Charlie's short hair and neck, and then, cupping the back of Charlie's neck tightly as if to tell Charlie to stay there before she slid her hand back down to meet her other one. The song carried on, with them remaining in that position until well after it finished and the next song began. They returned to their table and rejoined conversations. Ember gave them both a lifted eyebrow and a smile, but her attention was diverted to Eva, who placed her hand on Ember's shoulder and asked for another dance.

***

It was several hours later when nearly all the guests had gone. Ember had taken Eva off to enjoy their night in the tree house. Charlie was looking forward to hearing Eva's thoughts on it tomorrow, when they drove back. Hannah and Alyssa had just left, and the hired staff was cleaning up the remnants of a great party.

When she saw Anna calling it a night and paying the two staff members that were still there, Charlie realized that she and Hailey were relatively alone in the barn. It was after one in the morning. Hailey said goodnight to a woman Charlie hadn't gotten around to meeting, and then turned around to see Charlie standing near the table, grabbing the sweater she had brought, but hadn't needed.

"You ready?" Hailey asked her.

"Yeah," Charlie said, and they headed out toward the long driveway, where Ember had left them the van to drive back.

"I'm driving. I don't trust you with this thing," Hailey teased and took the keys from Charlie's hand.

"No argument here." Charlie climbed in beside her.

The drive was short, and they pulled into a spot right in front of the house.

"Have you explored this place yet?" Hailey asked while leaning back in the driver's seat.

"Not really. I spent most of my time in the house or helping Ember with the tree house. Why?" Charlie asked.

"I did," Hailey began. "Yesterday, I walked around. And, apparently, about twenty years ago, they had this family that needed work and a place to live. They let them stay in the caretaker house a couple of acres away from the main house, and the family helped with the farm."

"Okay... Where are you going with this, Hails?"

"It's been empty for a while now," Hailey told her. "I checked with Ember tonight, and she said that if we wanted to stay out there tonight, we could."

Charlie then watched Hailey swallow hard with nervousness.

"You want to stay out there?"

"I do, yeah." Hailey turned to her. "I asked Hannah for a little help earlier, too. It's one of the reasons she and Alyssa left so early. Will you come with me?"

"Okay," Charlie agreed with a gulp of her own. "Should we get our stuff?" She nodded toward the house.

"It's already there," Hailey said.

She opened her door and then walked around to the other side of the van to open Charlie's for her, because Charlie had yet to do it herself. Charlie climbed out and closed the door behind herself. Hailey took her hand immediately and then began walking them around the side of the house and around the back, where the driveway got thinner but continued along the property. As they passed the tree house, they both looked up at the sound of laughter and the sight of muted light in the room. They laughed before looking away to give Eva and Ember their privacy.

"Eva's parents decided not to stay here tonight. Did you know that?" Charlie asked her after several moments of silent steps.

"No. They're not there?" Hailey turned her head around, as if expecting to see Eva's parents there.

"No, they stayed at the farm we were on, with Anna and her husband. I guess they didn't want to be in the house while their daughter was getting defiled by Ember."

"Pretty sure Eva was defiled a long time ago." Hailey laughed alongside her.

"True. But would you want to hear someone having sex with your kid right outside your window?" Charlie asked.

"God, no."

"Yeah, neither would I. I think I'd probably shoot whoever it was."

Hailey nearly cackled at that, and Charlie just stared at her, confused but smiling.

"You'd shoot someone trying to have sex with your kid?"

"Depends on the situation, but, yeah."

"That's cute, Charlie," Hailey said. "It's cute that you'd be that protective."

"With my kid, hell yeah," Charlie replied and smiled.

Then, she saw a small house that she would describe more as a cottage coming into view. It was painted white but looked like it could have used a fresh coat about ten years ago. There were shutters on the two windows, and the front door matched their dark-green color, or at least they looked dark-green in the dark. There was light inside, but it was muted and flickering. Charlie glanced at Hailey.

"Come on." Hailey pulled her along.

Hailey opened the door and allowed Charlie to walk in first. The house was definitely small, but it appeared to be in good condition. There was a small kitchen to the right, with old appliances, and a living room of about the same size to the left, with a love seat that had seen better days. Hailey flicked on the light switch next to the door. Charlie heard it close behind her.

"When was the last time someone lived here?" Charlie asked as a stall, because she still wasn't entirely sure why they were there.

"This way." Hailey took her hand and pulled Charlie through the small hallway.

Charlie saw the bathroom on the right and then, straight ahead, was the bedroom. The nervousness suddenly overtook her. Hailey pushed the door open, and Charlie gawked at the room.

"Hails..."

Hailey had seen to it that the room was lit with candles. They were everywhere. They were on the small table by the bed and on the dresser that lined the wall opposite the bed. They were on the top of the headboard. There were even some on the hardwood floor. The bed was a full, which was, apparently, the norm around here, but Charlie could tell there was new bedding. The candles, providing the flickering light, allowed Charlie to notice the rose petals strewn about the bed, and the speaker Hailey's phone was attached to, that was presenting them with slow jazz music.

"You never got to have this, Charlie."

Hailey was behind her, but Charlie couldn't turn to look at her, because she suddenly felt shaky and more nervous than she had ever been.

"Hailey, we should talk and–"

"We will." Hailey's arms were around her waist, and her head was pressed against Charlie's shoulder. "We can talk all night, if you want to. I want to know about what I've missed since you left and since you got back." She kissed Charlie's neck, and Charlie trembled at that. "I want to know about work, and Eddie, and I want you to tell me how your friendships with Lena and Summer are going. I want to talk to you about the wedding we've just attended, and how our best friend is now married, and our other friends are about to have a baby." Hailey turned Charlie around in her arms. "I want to talk about all those things, Charlie. But I want to start by telling you that I am sorry." She pressed her forehead to Charlie's. "I am so sorry that I pulled away from you. I was scared of losing you because I couldn't be what you wanted me to be. But then, you went away, and I did lose you, and I hated it. I hated myself for making that mistake."

"Hailey, it's–"

"It's not okay, actually," Hailey interjected. "Cereal, Charlie."

"What?" Charlie opened her closed eyes at that and pulled back a little.

"You always make sure you have that stupid cereal I like so much in your apartment. And you brought it here, even though we weren't talking."

"I don't understand, Hails."

"You love me. You love me even though I eat a stupid cereal, made for kids; and even though I try to lecture you with studies about cold and lack of sleep. And you love me when I take thirty-minute showers, because I think better in the shower than I do when I'm actually trying to think. It's your shower that I'm using, and you're running late for work. You even love me when I date all the wrong women and try to convince myself that they're right. I get it now. You just love me." Hailey put her hand on the back of Charlie's neck. "I'm sorry. And, tonight, we can talk all you want; we don't have to do anything. But, Charlie, I want to. I want you. I want us." Hailey squeezed Charlie's waist with her hand. "Am I too late?"

***

Hailey waited for Charlie's reply, but she didn't let go of Charlie's neck or her waist, despite the trembling in both of her hands that she knew Charlie could feel.

"No," Charlie said.

Hailey watched the smile on Charlie's face grow wide, and she ran her hand along Charlie's cheek.

"I'm not?" she repeated for confirmation.

"No, you're not." Charlie pressed their foreheads back together. "Hails, you could never be too late. I've been waiting for you my whole life."

Hailey pressed their lips together. Before, a comment like that would have scared her to death, but not anymore. She was ready for this. She was ready for Charlie. Charlie's lips moved with her own, as if that was what they should have been doing all along. Hailey felt Charlie press her body closer and she walked them back toward the bed. She had to finally admit to herself that she had wanted this for a long time. Her body was already starting to react to Charlie's pleading gasps and frantic touches, as Hailey pressed the woman against the bed. They stopped there for a moment, and Hailey moved her lips to Charlie's neck. She slid her tongue up and then back down, while her hand slid around to Charlie's stomach and stopped there.

"Do you want to stop?" Hailey asked, knowing they had things to talk about and wanting to give Charlie a chance to tell her they should do that first.

"No," Charlie replied instantly.

Hailey pushed on Charlie's stomach enough to tell Charlie what she wanted. Charlie sat on the side of the bed before she leaned back and rested on her elbows. Hailey bent down and removed her shoes for her and then undid her own strappy ones, kicking them aside. She knelt down in front of Charlie and pulled her legs gently apart, while Charlie watched with darkened eyes. Hailey slowly slid her hands up and down the outside of Charlie's thighs, listening to the woman's intense breathing, before moving to the insides. Charlie's dress was slid up her legs, revealing the same white underwear beneath it that Hailey had seen earlier. She leaned down and pressed her lips to the inside of Charlie's thighs, over and over, moving back and forth as her hands slid up and down Charlie's calves, feeling the muscles tense and relax as she did.

When Charlie dropped back on the bed, no longer able to support herself on her elbows, Hailey looked up at Charlie's chest rising and falling faster than she had seen it before. She moved her lips back to where they were just seconds prior, and applied more kisses to new spots of skin she was dying to touch. Hailey used her teeth to graze over spots and then her tongue to sooth them, leaving light-red marks in their place. Her hands were on Charlie's hips, that were lifting slightly off the bed with nearly every touch of Hailey's mouth.

Hailey moved one hand to the inside of Charlie's thigh, then took her thumb and slid it over Charlie's underwear that she could now see were already soaked through. She smiled at the sight and flicked her thumb back and forth, hearing Charlie's gasps as she did. She felt the throbbing between her own legs intensify, and she squeezed her thighs together involuntarily while she leaned her head in farther and pressed a kiss just above Charlie's clit, earning herself a raise of Charlie's hips and a need to see and feel more.

Hailey stood up and watched as Charlie watched her. She pulled Charlie back up by the hands and reached around her back, while she kissed the woman and allowed their tongues to play with one another. She pulled down on Charlie's zipper and pressed their lips to one shoulder, while she slid the strap of the dress down and then did the same with the other strap. The dress didn't require much else to fall to the floor, leaving Charlie only in her underwear. Hailey then took a step back and stared at Charlie's perfect form. Her skin was flawless. Her abdomen was toned. Her legs were long and lean. And Hailey couldn't be that far away from her anymore.

Her lips were back on Charlie's. She felt Charlie's hands around her back, hastily attempting to slide Hailey's zipper down. Hailey stepped back slightly, only to allow it to fall to her feet. She stepped back into Charlie's body, pressing her thigh between Charlie's and earning a near grunt. Hailey pushed the woman down onto the bed and climbed on top of her. They moved, while their lips remained attached, until they were at the head of the bed. Charlie had rose petals attached to parts of her arms and, likely, her entire backside. But Hailey would pull those off her later, one by one, and possibly with her teeth, Charlie thought as Hailey took her hands in her own and placed them above their bodies, while Hailey's lips moved down to her collarbone.

"God, Charlie," she uttered when her lips made it to the tops of Charlie's breasts.

Hailey's hands disconnected with Charlie's, but she noticed that Charlie kept her own where they were. Hailey moved her hands around Charlie's back, not wanting to waste any time. She quickly undid the clasp and moved her hands back around and under the cups of the bra, grasping at firm breasts without even removing it all the way.

Charlie's hips lifted. Hailey pressed her own thigh between them again. She rolled down into Charlie without even thinking about it, and knew that her body was more than ready for more. Charlie lifted herself up, and Hailey used that as an opportunity to remove the bra entirely. She then stared down at Charlie's chest. Her hands went back, and she clutched Charlie's breasts in both hands, while she continued to slowly assault Charlie's neck with her lips and tongue.

"That feels good," Charlie said between rapid breaths.

Hailey used her thumb and forefinger to play with one of Charlie's nipples. The sensations this action brought out in Charlie were wonderful, but even Hailey, herself, was reacting. She was now certain that she had never wanted someone, or something, more than she wanted Charlie Adams in this moment. She leaned down and captured the other nipple between her teeth, and she was the one that moaned when Charlie's hips lifted up and pressed against her. She sucked on the nipple, and when Charlie's hands moved to the back of her head, Hailey used her free hand to move them back where they were, above both of them. Once she knew Charlie would keep them there, she slid down lower and met Charlie's abdomen with her tongue, feeling the muscles underneath ripple as she dragged it up and then blew on the wet spots as she moved back down. Charlie's skin broke out in goosebumps. Hailey swirled her tongue around Charlie's belly button before dipping it inside, causing Charlie to jerk.

Hailey slid down farther first, but then, she sat up, straddling Charlie's legs. She pulled her own bra off and cast it aside. Her chest was heaving, and she saw the desire in Charlie's eyes take over. Charlie sat up and pressed her hands to Hailey's breasts while she kissed between them. Hailey moved her hand to the back of Charlie's head, encouraging her to continue. She gasped when she felt Charlie's teeth pull at her nipple before the woman started sucking on it.

"God!" Hailey exclaimed and felt herself losing control.

Charlie's arms were around her and moving up and down her back. Hailey felt her own center press against Charlie's body, and she slid against her.

"I can feel you," Charlie said and then moved back to

watch Hailey's hips roll against her body. "Oh, Hails!" She held on to Hailey's hips, as if she wanted to feel what Hailey's body was feeling and holding on to her would allow that.

"Lie back," Hailey told her.

Charlie looked up at her pleadingly, but Hailey stopped moving, and Charlie moved back against the bed. Hailey climbed off her and slid Charlie's last remaining article slowly down her legs. Her eyes never left Charlie's. She tossed the underwear aside and then tore at her own ungracefully to be able to climb right back on top of Charlie.

Charlie gasped when she felt Hailey's thigh between her own again, and Hailey felt how wet Charlie really was for the first time, while allowing Charlie to feel her own wetness against the other woman's thigh.

"Hails, I–" Charlie stopped herself as her head rolled back against the pillows.

Hailey watched her from above until she felt Charlie's hands on her back, and then, Hailey was being rolled over, and Charlie was above her, kissing her first and then kissing her neck. Hailey's hands went to the back of Charlie's head as the woman lowered herself down to take Hailey's nipple back in her mouth. Hailey felt Charlie's hand begin to slide down her stomach and land on her thigh, as if Charlie was waiting for permission or courage. Hailey was ready. She knew she'd come quickly if Charlie touched her, but she didn't want to come like this.

"Hey, come back up here." Hailey tugged on the back of Charlie's head and encouraged her to meet her eyes. "You're so beautiful, Charlie."

Hailey lifted her head to connect their lips and used the distraction to roll Charlie back over. Charlie pulled back from her lips and smirked at Hailey with a lifted eyebrow, knowing what Hailey had just done. Hailey leaned back up again, but she practically yanked Charlie up with her this time and kissed the woman hard. She held Charlie's head in place while Charlie's hands were on her hips.

"Hailey, I want you," Charlie gasped out as she moved her own mouth to Hailey's neck.

Hailey took Charlie's hand in her own and held them clasped together for a moment before she guided Charlie's hand between her legs.

"Oh," Hailey gasped audibly at the first touch of Charlie's hand to her wetness.

She held Charlie's hand there and then pushed on it, giving Charlie the hint. Charlie slid her own hand down through Hailey's wetness, and Hailey felt one finger circling her entrance. Her hips began to move again. Charlie slid one finger inside her, causing Hailey to press down into Charlie's body and then start rocking against her. Charlie slid it out, and then slid two fingers back in, while her palm pressed to Hailey's ready and swollen clit.

"Yes," Hailey moaned and rocked slowly against Charlie's pressing hand.

She reached around her own body with her left hand and pressed her body farther into Charlie's while holding on to the other woman tightly. She wanted Charlie inside her whole body. She wanted them to be one in every way. Her hand made its way behind herself to reach between Charlie's legs. She wouldn't be able to thrust inside Charlie this way, but she would still be able to touch the woman. Hailey needed to be touching her. As she pressed two fingers into Charlie's wetness, which she had been unprepared for, Charlie jerked her body before relaxing into the touch, while she continued to work inside and outside of Hailey's body.

Hailey's fingers slid up and down while she pulled Charlie's face up with her free hand, allowing herself to see Charlie's eyes. She pressed her fingers against Charlie's clit and felt how ready the woman was for what was about to happen. Hailey flicked her fingers gently against it, barely grazing it, as Charlie began moving faster inside her, curling her fingers and pressing her palm harder. Hailey's hips were moving faster, and she felt herself getting closer just as she started pressing harder to Charlie's clit.

"I'm–" Charlie's mouth was wide open, but no words came out.

Hailey knew Charlie was close, and she kissed her. She kissed her hard and knew she would likely bruise Charlie's lips, but she kissed her hard because she wanted to be kissing this woman when she came; and with one more thrust and a hip roll down into Charlie, Hailey came. Her body rocked and was uncontrollable as she jerked into Charlie's hand, only being held in place by Charlie's protective hand on her back.

Hailey's movements caused her own fingers against Charlie's clit to press harder. She rubbed them up and down, and up and down, until Charlie's eyes shot open and then closed again. Hailey wrapped her arm around Charlie's shoulders and pulled Charlie even closer. She rocked and pressed until the woman came in her arms. Then, she kissed Charlie just as hard and lowered them both down to the bed, keeping herself straddling Charlie, since Charlie's fingers were still inside her. She pressed herself against Charlie's chest and listened to her heartbeat while she felt her own, intense rhythm match it.

They shared a moment of calm silence before Hailey pressed her hands into the mattress so that she could hover over Charlie. She watched Charlie's closed eyes and cheeks reddened, thanks to their activities, and she smiled. She pressed her lips to Charlie's neck again and then went lower still, causing Charlie to pull out of her.

"Beautiful," Hailey muttered against Charlie's skin as she made her way down.

"Hails, what–"

Hailey slid all the way off the bed and pulled on Charlie's legs until they were hanging off.

"I can't wait," Hailey finally said; and she didn't.

"Oh, Hailey!" Charlie exclaimed as Hailey's mouth met her center.

Hailey's tongue slid around, tasting Charlie, before she decided to land on Charlie's clit. She licked up and down, while Charlie's hips rose and fell. Charlie pressed both hands to the back of Hailey's head, and Hailey took her between her lips and sucked on the woman's already swollen and sensitive clit. She felt Charlie's hips lifting while her hands pressed Hailey's face down into her more, and Hailey wanted all of her. She wanted to feel Charlie inside. She then took her left hand, that had been helping to hold down Charlie's eager hips, and placed it on the inside of Charlie's thigh, waiting for the right moment before she thrust two fingers inside Charlie.

"Oh," Hailey gasped out as she pulled back for a second.

She watched as her two fingers pulled out, bringing Charlie's arousal with them, and then pushed back inside. She kissed the inside of Charlie's thigh and continued to focus on the sensation of feeling Charlie like this.

"Baby," she said and slid her own fingers in deeper before returning her lips to Charlie's clit.

**

Charlie came in Hailey's mouth after a few perfectly timed thrusts of the woman's fingers. She felt her entire body trembling as Hailey moved back on top of her and then slid back on the bed. Hailey hovered over her and pressed a hand to Charlie's heart.

"Are you okay?" she checked as Charlie was visibly shaking.

"Yes," Charlie confirmed and pulled Hailey down into her. She then ran a hand into Hailey's hair and pressed Hailey's sweat-covered body down against her own. "How could you ever think I'd want anything more than this?" she whispered into Hailey's ear.

She felt Hailey lift herself up and look down at her. Hailey's lips pressed to her forehead.

"Charlie, I love you," Hailey said when she pulled her lips back and looked into Charlie's eyes with her perfect green ones.

"Hails, you don't–"

"Shh," Hailey quieted her, and Charlie felt the press of Hailey's lips and the taste of her own arousal on them. "I love you," Hailey repeated. "I love you as my best friend." She kissed Charlie again. "And I love you as more than just my best friend." Hailey lowered her head to Charlie's neck. "I want you to be mine, Charlie."

"Hailey, I've been yours for years," Charlie reminded.

"And I want to be yours," Hailey revealed. "I love you."

"I love you, too," Charlie told her, and she felt the sudden relief that came along with finally having the woman you love more than anything in your arms, saying she loved you back.

They remained that way for a long while as the soft music continued to play in the background and the candles began to die down. Charlie felt her own body pulling her into sleep, but she resisted, because she had Hailey in her arms, pressed against her body. She didn't want to fall asleep, in case this was a very vivid dream. Hailey lifted herself up after a while and rolled onto her side, facing Charlie. She began pulling rose petals off of Charlie's body and tossing them onto the floor.

"I'll deal with those tomorrow," Hailey said and then pulled some off her own body. "I had thought about taking them off you with my teeth, but I don't think I have the energy for that."

"I can't believe you did this whole thing," Charlie said and looked at Hailey's nude body for the first time that she could just focus on it.

"I wanted to do something nice for you."

"This was definitely nice," Charlie replied and kissed her shoulder as Hailey finished removing flower petals from their bodies.

"Yeah?" Hailey checked.

"Hails, this was the fantasy. *You* are the fantasy," Charlie told her and ran a hand over Hailey's stomach. "I've always just wanted you."

"I get that now," Hailey offered.

She encouraged Charlie's arm around her so that she could lie on the other woman's shoulder and wrap her own arm around Charlie's waist.

"So, are we…"

Hailey leaned up to look at her.

"Together?" she questioned amusedly. "Yeah, Charlie. I think we can safely say we are finally together."

She then leaned down and kissed Charlie gently.

"Do you want to get ready for bed?" Charlie asked, realizing it was likely close to three in the morning, and they were supposed to be in the kitchen for breakfast at an early hour before they would hit the road.

"I'd love to get ready for bed with you."

CHAPTER 24

HAILEY woke up with Charlie pressed against her back. She smiled and held Charlie's hand tighter against her stomach.

"Morning." Charlie kissed the back of her shoulder.

"You're awake?" Hailey questioned.

"I usually am before you." She kissed Hailey's shoulder again.

"How long?"

"About twenty minutes," Charlie replied. "I didn't want to move."

"What time is it?" Hailey rolled over in her arms.

"About 7:45," Charlie stated. "I slept in, technically."

"And we have to be in the kitchen in fifteen minutes?" Hailey asked and held Charlie close.

"Yes."

"So, we don't really have time?"

Charlie laughed. Hailey felt the rumbling in her own body.

"Not really, unfortunately." Charlie kissed Hailey's forehead. "But, I'm free tonight, if you are."

Hailey pulled back, slapped her own forehead, and said, "I made plans with Emma."

"Oh." Charlie pulled back.

"No, no! Not like that. We're over, Charlie; way over. We're just trying to be friends. And I didn't know this was going to happen between you and me…"

"It's okay."

Charlie rolled onto her back. Hailey knew it wasn't

okay, the way Charlie pulled her entire body away from her own so that they were no longer touching at all.

"Hey," Hailey said and placed a hand on Charlie's stomach. "See this?" She tugged on Charlie's shirt. "Whose shirt is this?"

"It's your shirt, Hails," Charlie stated and glanced at her.

"And whose shirt am I wearing?"

"My shirt."

"And neither of us is wearing anything else, Charlie," Hailey said. "I do not love her. I love you. I'm with you. I will cancel my plans with Emma because she is a friend, but *you* are my love, Charlie. You're my person, remember?"

"I remember." Charlie lightened.

"We should get dressed and head back," Hailey said and pecked her lips.

"You know everyone is going to know we did this, right?" Charlie asked as she sat up.

"Yeah, because I'm going to tell them." Hailey moved to straddle Charlie's thighs.

"You're going to tell them what we did last night?" Charlie lifted a curious eyebrow and held on to Hailey's hips.

"I'm going to tell them that we're together. That's okay, right?"

"That is very much okay." Charlie kissed Hailey's neck and pulled the woman down on top of herself as she fell back on the bed, causing Hailey to scream and then giggle.

***

Charlie felt lighter than she had ever felt before as she and Hailey walked back toward the main house, pulling and carrying their bags. When they arrived at the back door and left their stuff outside, they found Hannah and Alyssa already at the table. Both women looked up in their direction and grinned a mile wide.

"Okay," Charlie said. "That's enough."

Hannah laughed first, but Alyssa joined in right after.

Ember and Eva entered from the back door, and Charlie turned around to see that the two of them also had matching grins.

"Good morning, Hails," Ember said. "And, Charlie."

"Morning, newly-weds," Alyssa offered over Charlie and Hailey.

"Hey, oldly-weds," Ember joked and pulled Eva along to sit down at the table. "Coffee, babe?"

"Yeah, thanks." Eva lifted her head to kiss Ember as Ember moved to the coffee pot.

"So, how did you two sleep out there, in the old place?" Ember asked and then turned to look over her shoulder.

"Good," Charlie said.

Hailey took Charlie's hand and then placed the other hand over their clasped ones.

"We slept well, thank you," she said in Ember's direction. "And, thank you," she delivered sincerely to Hannah and Alyssa.

"So, it finally happened?" Eva asked. "You two…"

"Yes," Hailey confirmed. "We're together." She looked over at Charlie, who could only smile.

"Finally!" Ember offered the room.

"Ignore her. She's a little excitable right now," Eva excused her wife. "And, Charlie, thank you. The tree house is perfect. You guys put in so much work. It was amazing."

"I was happy to help. It's really cool up there. What are your parents going to do with it now?" Charlie asked. "Hails, coffee?"

"Yeah, thank you." Hailey let go of Charlie's hand.

Charlie made her way over to the counter, where Ember was pouring cups for all four of them now. Ember lifted an eyebrow in her direction and then bumped her shoulder.

"I'm happy for you," she whispered.

"I'm happy for you." Charlie nodded back to Eva.

"I'm happy for me, too." Ember turned to deliver Eva her coffee and carry her own over as well.

"I don't know," Eva answered Charlie's question. "I don't think they thought that far ahead. They'll probably leave it like that until winter. They can take the mattress out and turn it into a cool hangout for the grandkids."

"Your parents will likely burn that mattress," Alyssa said and got a laugh.

Charlie turned around and carried Hailey's coffee to the table, to where the woman was sitting next to Hannah. She also set down a bowl of cereal, earning a glance upward from Hailey and a wide smile. Charlie took advantage of the moment and leaned down to kiss her gently.

"Oh, guys. It's so cute," Ember said.

"Okay. Calm down," Charlie returned and went to grab her own coffee.

***

Hailey drove the van back home so that Ember and Eva didn't have to. They took the prized back seat and spent most of their time smiling at one another and sharing sweet moments. Hailey caught each of them staring at their ring while the other wasn't looking. She was pretty sure that during the entirety of the six-hour drive, they were never not touching one another in some way.

Hailey found herself glancing in Charlie's direction several times and wishing they could have private moments like that, but thanks to the wide gap between them up front, they couldn't even hold hands. It was a small price to pay so that the two married couples in the car could have their time together, but Hailey still didn't like being that far from Charlie when they'd just shared so many intimate moments. Charlie appeared to be deep in thought most of the drive, and Hailey wished more than anything, more than the touches she so desperately wanted again, that she could know the other woman's thoughts.

"Are you okay?" she asked Charlie.

"I'm good." Charlie turned to her, smiled, and then

turned around to see that Alyssa was lying in Hannah's lap asleep, while Hannah was playing with her hair and looking out the window. "I want that, Hails."

Ember and Eva both had their eyes closed, and as Hailey looked through the mirror at them, she could tell they were asleep. Eva's arm was around Ember's shoulder, and Ember's head was pressed into Eva's neck.

"Want what?"

"What our friends have," Charlie said.

Hailey smiled out at the windshield and wished they didn't have a little under an hour left in their drive, because she wanted to be alone with Charlie more than anything right now.

"Tell me which parts, specifically," Hailey said.

"The marriage and the kids," Charlie stated without reservation.

"Yeah?" Hailey turned and saw Charlie's confident free expression.

To most people, after sharing one night together, the idea of talking about marriage and having kids would be terrifying; but, apparently, not to Charlie. Charlie Adams was afraid of the dark, but she was finally unafraid of sharing her whole self with Hailey.

"Yes," Charlie confirmed.

"With me?" Hailey asked.

Charlie didn't answer right away. She turned back to see a field of high grass pass by the window. Her eyes squinted in deep thought, it seemed.

"I never thought about that," she finally said.

"You never thought about having that with me?"

Hailey was more than surprised. She had assumed that if someone loved you for more than a decade, and they wanted those things, they would think about you being the one they shared them with. It actually jarred her a little bit, to know that Charlie hadn't considered it.

"It hurt too much," Charlie said and then leaned over the center console. She pulled Hailey's right hand off the wheel, brought it to her lips, and kissed it. "Whenever I thought about those things, I'd picture this nameless, faceless woman. Because if I pictured it with you, it just hurt."

"Oh, baby," Hailey replied sweetly and pulled Charlie's hand onto her thigh.

"It's okay now. Do you want that stuff, though?" Charlie asked her.

"You know I do," Hailey said. "You heard me in the van the other day. I could tell you were listening. A super spy you're not, Charlie Adams. Besides, we've talked about this stuff before."

"Not since we started this," Charlie said. "Not since I told you how I felt, and we went on a date, and definitely not since last night." She smirked. "And yes, I was listening in, but things are different now."

"Well, nothing's changed, Charlie. I still want all that," Hailey said.

"Nothing's changed?" Charlie checked and pulled her hand back.

"That's not what I meant," Hailey argued. "You know that."

"Yeah," Charlie returned in an unbelieving tone.

"Charlie, don't do this."

"Do what?"

"You always do this." Hailey glanced at a sign that said Chicago was in twenty-seven miles.

"I always do what?" Charlie asked.

"You spend all this time working toward what you want. Then, when you get it, you start pulling back and question it."

"I don't do that," Charlie stated in her defense.

"Yes, you do," Hailey retorted. "You always have. You spent two years in college trying to figure out what to major in, when you knew you wanted architecture and design. When you finally declared, you spent weeks fighting it. You even went to UC's counseling center and took that aptitude test to see if you were right about what you wanted to do;

which is ridiculous, because it was exactly what you wanted to do, and you were good at it. The test agreed, and even then, you kept reading the course catalog to see if there was something else out there for you. The job you have at the firm took you forever to decide on, and you needed Ember's math to help push you in the right direction. Right after you took it, you still reached back out to your old boss to see if your position had been filled already, in case the firm didn't work out. You wanted a contingency plan. Your apartment!" Hailey exclaimed as she remembered and then continued, "I was there when you first saw that place. You loved it, and you wanted it right away, but you went all around Chicago looking at other places, until you finally picked it. And then, as soon as you signed the lease, you started talking about how it was only a six-month lease, just in case something went wrong or you didn't like it. You proceeded to point out that it wasn't as close to work as another place we saw, or that key cards could be hacked, and maybe that didn't make it more secure. I had to show you that study on RFID to get you to calm down about that and not ask the building owner to call a locksmith. You love that apartment. You love your job. You fight with the things you love right after you get them." Hailey looked toward Charlie for the longest moment she could chance while driving. "I'm asking you not to do that with me. Don't have a contingency plan for me, Charlie."

***

The downside to just starting to date a best friend, after over ten years of friendship, was that she knew all the secrets. Hailey knew everything Charlie kept from everyone else. She knew Charlie's familiar trepidation and her hesitation when it came to major life decisions. She also hated when Hailey was right, and Hailey was right about this. Over the course of the drive, Charlie had started to feel uneasy and couldn't understand why. She had finally gotten everything she had ever wanted. She had spent an amazing night with the woman she wanted to spend her life with. Why couldn't she just enjoy it? Why couldn't she push these feelings of inadequacy away?

"Charlie?" Hailey asked after Charlie failed to say anything.

"Yeah, I won't," she said and could tell by Hailey's expression that the woman was unconvinced.

"Hey, beautiful," Alyssa must have woken up and greeted Hannah.

Charlie turned to see her sit up in her seat and give Hannah a kiss.

"Hey, sleepyhead," Hannah replied.

"Are we almost there?" Alyssa asked and sat up straight, placing her arm over the back of the seat so that Hannah could slide over and rest against her side.

Charlie watched as Hannah's hand pressed gently to Alyssa's stomach. Alyssa smiled and looked down at it before covering it with her own hand.

"Still in there, babe," Alyssa reassured her wife.

"I know. I just like touching you. Is that a problem?" Hannah looked up and teased.

"No, not a problem at all." Alyssa returned her smile.

"And we're about half an hour away," Hannah told her.

"Remind me to call my mom when we get back." Eva had woken up. "I promised I would let her know we got back okay."

"Okay." Ember kissed her temple.

And just like that, Charlie and Hailey's moment of pseudo-privacy had been broken.

***

When they arrived back at Ember and Eva's, everyone unloaded their stuff; with the exception of an annoyed Alyssa, because Hannah wouldn't allow her to carry or lift anything.

"I'm not broken, Han. I'm pregnant," she argued.

"What's your point?" Hannah returned with a smile.

Alyssa gave in and hugged each woman goodbye one at a time before climbing into the passenger's seat of the car.

"I think we got everything," Ember called as she walked toward them. "Now, I love all of you for everything that you've done for this wedding and for us, but I'm going to need some privacy with my wife."

"Babe!" Eva came up from behind her and wrapped her arms around Ember's waist. "You guys can come in, if you want," she said.

"We need to get home. Al's pretty worn out," Hannah replied.

"No, I'm not," Alyssa disagreed through the open window and earned herself a laugh from everyone.

"Charlie, are you riding back with us?" Hannah glanced from her wife to Charlie.

Charlie looked over at Hailey, who was closing the van door. Hailey's phone rang in her pocket. Charlie watched the woman pick it up and look at the screen. Charlie knew instantly who was calling. Her nerves and hesitation got the better of her.

"Yeah. Let me put my stuff in the trunk," Charlie replied and hastily shoved her bags into Hannah's trunk.

Hailey just watched her in disbelief as she put the phone to her ear.

"Hey," she greeted the person on the other side of the phone call.

Charlie looked at Ember, who shook her head from side to side in disappointment at her. Eva seemed to pick up on it and glanced pleadingly at Charlie.

"Congrats again, guys. I'll see you later." Charlie climbed into the back seat and closed the door behind herself.

Alyssa turned around immediately, while at the same time pressing the button to roll up the window.

"Not that I'm not happy to have you along for the ride

or to drop you off, but… Do you want to tell me why you're not driving off into the sunset with your brand-new girl-friend?" she asked.

Charlie didn't say anything, and after a moment, Alyssa got the hint and turned back around to see Hannah climbing in beside her. Charlie saw Hailey walking toward her own car with the phone to her ear. Charlie lowered her head in shame at her inability to just ride off into that sunset with her best friend in the world.

***

Hailey sat on her couch in her apartment. She had showered, changed, and hadn't moved since. It had now been over an hour. She couldn't figure out where they'd gone wrong. She had finally told Charlie how she felt. She told the woman she had nothing to worry about and that Hailey had finally got beyond her own worries of not being what Charlie really wanted. It hadn't worked. They were in separate homes now.

Hailey made the mistake last time by running away. It appeared, Charlie was doing the same thing now. Hailey re-played their night together, trying to figure out what she'd said or done that made Charlie not trust her or pull away. It was after seven that night when Hailey realized that this would not happen. She wasn't about to let Charlie make the same mistake she had, that caused them not to speak for over a month.

***

"Okay…" Hailey entered Charlie's apartment. "Hi, Eddie," she greeted Eddie and saw Charlie on the couch.

"Hails?" Charlie turned to see Hailey trying to get Ed-die off her.

"Yeah, it's me." Hailey walked quickly toward Charlie. "Your girlfriend. You know, that woman you slept with last night, after we danced around this thing between us and she told you she loves you. You said the same thing, and then you ran off today–" Hailey stopped herself when she noticed Charlie had her iPad on the table, and there was a half-naked woman on the screen, pulling a shirt to her chest to cover her bra-covered breasts. "What the fuck?!" she exclaimed and felt her heart begin to race.

"Hailey, it's not what it looks like."

"Summer?" Hailey glanced more closely at the screen.

"Hi, Hailey." Summer waved. "Really, not what it looks like," she confirmed. "I have a date tonight. I was just asking Charlie to help me find something to wear. Sorry."

"You're half-naked in front of my girlfriend, so yeah, you *should* be sorry," Hailey chastised.

"Summer, I've–"

"Yeah, I'll figure this out for myself." Summer waved and then pressed the screen to make herself disappear.

"What the actual fuck, Charlie?!" Hailey nearly yelled.

"I swear, I wasn't–"

"I'm not talking about her. I don't give a shit about Summer fucking Taft." Hailey flopped down onto the couch next to Charlie, leaving at least a foot of distance between them.

"You never curse," Charlie said.

"You bring it out in me, I guess." Hailey glared at her.

"You really thought I'd be doing something with Summer?"

"What the hell am I supposed to think, Charlie?" she implored. "You left today after you pulled your usual crap in the van."

"My usual crap?" Charlie turned to face her.

"Yeah, your usual crap. You pulled it, and it pissed me off, because we're here now." Hailey slid closer on the couch, facing the other woman. "Charlie, it's me. Talk to me."

"Hails…"

"Don't 'Hails' me." Hailey wasted no time. She leaned forward, captured both of Charlie's hands, pushed her back down on the couch, and then climbed over her. "Talk. Now."

"Last night was the best night of my life."

"And?"

"And this morning was the best morning of my life." Charlie met Hailey's eyes and continued, "And then, we got in that van and started driving back, and... I don't know."

"Yes, you do," Hailey said. "Just say it, baby."

"You call me *'baby'* like you've been doing it forever. It sounds normal."

"It is normal, Charlie." Hailey moved to straddle her hips fully. "Say it."

"I'm scared, Hails," Charlie admitted.

"Why?"

"Because I spent so much time trying to convince you that I just wanted you and I didn't care about a fantasy, that I never thought about how *I* might be as a girlfriend to you," Charlie let out.

Hailey released Charlie's hands and sat all the way up.

"Charlie, you've been my girlfriend basically our entire friendship." She chuckled. "The things you do for me, how you show me you care – that's what I need. This new part of our relationship – the part where I get to touch you, kiss you, and be with you like this – it's exactly what I want." Hailey slid her hands under Charlie's shirt and kept them on the woman's stomach. "This is my fault. Last night, we should have talked more. We should have talked about what this meant and how we would handle it, being together. But, I had waited, and you had waited. I couldn't wait anymore. Last night was the best night of my life, too."

Charlie swallowed. Hailey could tell she had still not assuaged her worries.

"What about that first night with–"

"If you say Emma, I swear to God, Charlie!" Hailey slapped Charlie's stomach lightly. "I do *not* love Emma Colton. I love you. I *want* you."

"Okay. I'm sorry. It's just been a long time. I've been hearing you talk about her since we met. It's going to take some getting used to now."

"What do I have to do to convince you?"

"Nothing," Charlie said after a moment. "It's not about that." She placed her hands on Hailey's waist. "It's this feeling that I have, that hasn't gone away yet. For twelve years, it's been Emma this, and Emma that; and then you two started dating, and I thought that was it, Hails. I thought I had lost my chance, because you'd finally make it work with the woman you had been in love with your whole life. I would be stuck standing next to you at your wedding to her, pining after the one that got away." Charlie paused. "I saw you with her that day you guys were supposed to go to the zoo, and at the party, and then you talked about having plans with her tonight... It just seems like even though you and I are finally here, Emma is this always-present force that I can't seem to reconcile in my mind. That makes me nervous."

"I understand." Hailey leaned down and pressed their foreheads together.

"You do?"

"Yes. It's not that you're worried about me doing something with Emma, when I'm with you; you need the time to pass to see that I'm really here with you, and that this is what was supposed to be all along." Hailey pressed her lips to Charlie's forehead. "Tell me I'm your person, Charlie." Hailey's lips now hovered just above Charlie's forehead.

Charlie placed her hands on Hailey's back and pulled Hailey down to her.

"You're my person, Hails."

Hailey hugged her and rested her head on Charlie's shoulder. Her hand drifted to Charlie's cheek, and she grazed her fingers and thumb across it.

"Next time, just tell me that you're scared. Don't just leave, okay?" Hailey asked. "You're not the only one in this anymore. It hurts when you do that."

"Okay," Charlie replied.

Charlie's arms were around Hailey, holding her close. Her hand was on Hailey's back, dragging up and down.

"Now, do you want to tell me about Summer and her breasts on your iPad?"

Charlie laughed, and Hailey felt the reverberations throughout her own body.

"You want to tell me about the plans you had with Emma tonight?" Charlie returned with a laugh.

"Yes, I do." Hailey lifted herself up to stare down at the woman. "She wanted to introduce me to her girlfriend, Elizabeth. We were all going to meet up at Windy's. Did you hear that part, Charlie? Emma has a girlfriend, and, by the way she talks about her, she is very happy with her."

Charlie smiled up and placed both hands on the sides of Hailey's neck.

"Okay. I get it." Charlie rolled her eyes more at herself than anything.

"You do?"

"Yes."

"I told her we would have to do it some other time, because I had to figure out what the hell I was going to do with you." Hailey took in Charlie's dark eyes. "I also told her that you and I had an amazing night, last night, and that I was in love with you."

"Hails?"

"Yes?"

The doorbell rang.

"Hold that thought," Charlie said and got off the couch, leaving Hailey there so she could answer the door. "I ordered food before you got here." She opened the door, paid the delivery guy, and closed the door to stop Eddie's barking, before she set the bag onto the table next to the door and stood still for a moment.

"Hey, what's wrong?" Hailey stood and walked over to her.

When she arrived, she placed her hands on Charlie's waist.

"You know how last night, we took things really slow, and it was incredibly romantic?" Charlie asked, and Hailey nodded with a smile. Charlie gripped Hailey's waist and turned her until she was pressed back against the door. "Tonight, I was thinking we could do fast and hot."

"What about the food you ordered?" Hailey laughed.

"I don't want the food. I want you," Charlie said and attached her lips to Hailey's neck.

"You're wearing my shirt again." Hailey pulled on the shirt until it was over Charlie's head and on the floor.

Charlie's fingers were already working on Hailey's jeans. She stood topless and used her other hand to pull down on Hailey's shirt, signaling that she wanted it off. Hailey complied and tossed her shirt onto the floor. While her back was lifted away from the door, Hailey unclasped her bra and tossed it aside before Charlie thrust a hand into her jeans, and she was pushed back hard against the door. Charlie's fingers were sliding around without purpose at first. Hailey's hips didn't seem to notice that she hadn't actually started trying to make her come yet. They bucked forward into Charlie's hand. Charlie pressed Hailey harder against the wall, while nipping at the woman's neck.

She then started working her fingers deftly against Hailey's clit and felt her girlfriend's heavy breathing against her own chest as their breasts pressed together. She could also feel Hailey's nipples, tight and hard, against her own, hardening ones, and the wetness that now coated her hand. Hailey tried to tug down on Charlie's shorts, but Charlie pulled her hand away and placed both of Hailey's hands above the woman, on the door, and held them there with her hand. Turnabout was fair play, after all.

"That... there," Hailey managed as Charlie's fingers flicked the tip of her clit fast, over and over again.

"Yeah?" Charlie asked with a gasp against Hailey's ear. "There?" She slid her fingers down and then into Hailey with one hard thrust.

"Yes!" Hailey shouted against Charlie's shoulder.

Charlie felt the woman's teeth dig into her bone but pushed the pain out of her mind. Hailey was tight and wet around her fingers. Her muscles contracted against her, while Charlie pressed her palm to Hailey's swollen clit like Hailey had done to her the night before. Charlie used her thigh to push her hand in harder and faster, and let go of Hailey's hands when they began to protest, to allow Hailey to grip Charlie's ass and bring them even tighter together. Hailey's hands slid into Charlie's underwear and squeezed, causing Charlie to grunt and want more. She kept sliding in and out, until she felt Hailey's walls begin to collapse around her fingers. Hailey came with a scream and then gave in to Charlie's body completely. Charlie held the woman up with a hand on her hip, while the other hand remained inside Hailey, and then pressed their bodies closer together, because she wasn't sure Hailey could stand if she didn't.

As they both began to catch their breath, Hailey started to stand on her own again. Charlie slowly pulled out of her. She started kissing down the front of Hailey's body, taking her time on one nipple and then the other, sucking each into her mouth, and being rewarded with sounds of pleasure emanating from Hailey, as the woman placed a hand on the back of Charlie's neck, encouraging her to explore. Charlie slid down Hailey's body slowly and then pulled on the jeans until they were at Hailey's feet, along with her underwear. Hailey kicked them away. Charlie knelt on the floor and looked up at Hailey, who was staring down at her, with desire still in her eyes.

Charlie had said before that she'd tried not to picture Hailey in those images of her future. But Hailey had sometimes managed to sneak her way in. One of those fantasies, that allowed Charlie to touch herself and have very intense orgasms, involved her having Hailey up against a wall like this, while Charlie took her with her mouth and tasted her. She felt Hailey's sultry stare on her even as she began to drag her tongue through the woman's folds and tasted Hailey for the first time. God, it was better than any fantasy. Hailey gasped each time Charlie found a particular spot she liked, and Charlie memorized each one of them and what she did to elicit the sound, so that she could do it again. She gripped Hailey's ass while the woman's thrusting hips pulled Hailey slightly away from the door. Charlie pressed her face against Hailey hard, and then felt her lift one leg off the ground. Charlie knew what she wanted, so she placed her hand on Hailey's calf and encouraged it up and over her shoulder. Then, she did the same with Hailey's other leg.

"Charlie!" Hailey exclaimed, as Charlie's hands went back around to her ass, and she was lifted off the floor; held in place by Charlie's strong hands and shoulders, and that face that was buried between Hailey's legs. "Oh, my God!"

Charlie sucked her clit hard and fast, and used her tongue to flick against it every so often, earning moans and gasps from the woman above her. She muttered her own moan against Hailey's clit, as Hailey's hand pressed her head closer. Charlie chanced a look up and saw that Hailey's head was rolled back against the door, and her hand was pressed to the door. Charlie watched Hailey's breasts rise and fall with every short, fast breath, and every thrust of Hailey's hips into her mouth. Charlie closed her eyes again and reveled in Hailey's scent and taste while she shook her head sideways quickly. At that, Hailey jerked so hard, Charlie thought she might drop her, but she held on. Hailey came pressed against the door, being held off the floor, and into Charlie's greedy mouth. Charlie didn't let her go. She couldn't yet. She still wanted more. Just as Hailey began to come down, and Charlie felt the hand on the back of her head start to loosen, Charlie pressed herself harder into Hailey again and licked around Hailey's clit.

"Again," Charlie ordered and kissed Hailey's clit before sucking it into her mouth.

"Oh, I don–" Hailey didn't finish her sentence. "Fuck!" she exclaimed.

Charlie loved the sound of that word coming out of Hailey's mouth while she was doing just that. With Hailey off the ground, Charlie could slide her tongue inside her and pull it out just as quickly, before doing it again, and again. She slid it back up to the still swollen hard clit and sucked the woman again, until she felt Hailey's body jerk again, indicating another orgasm. Charlie held Hailey in place, allowing her to ride it out, and then slowed her sucking until Hailey tapped her shoulder, indicating she needed to stand on solid ground.

Charlie helped her lower one leg and then the other one, but kept her mouth between Hailey's legs. She placed her hands on the inside of Hailey's thighs, to keep them apart, while she made sure she brought Hailey all the way down from her high. When Hailey's breathing slowed, and her legs stopped trembling, Charlie stood and wrapped her arms around her. Hailey collapsed against her again and allowed Charlie to pull her back toward the couch. Charlie slid onto the couch first, lying down and pulling Hailey down on top of herself. She held Hailey there, pressed to her skin, until Hailey's heart finally slowed to a normal rhythm.

CHAPTER 25

HAILEY felt liquefied. It was as if she had no bones in her body as she pressed into Charlie. She felt the hands dragging up and down the other woman's back and closed her eyes, listening to Charlie's breathing. It took Hailey some time to gain back the strength she needed. She took one of her still tingling arms and slid it quickly down between Charlie's legs under her shorts.

"Oh!" Charlie gasped as Hailey lifted herself up.

"Hi." Hailey peered down at her girlfriend.

She then rolled her hips down as her palm cupped Charlie's center.

"Yeah," Charlie got out while her own hands went to Hailey's hips to guide the woman back down into her.

Hailey's movements were slow and paced, as she took her pleasure from giving Charlie pleasure. Charlie's hands eventually tugged at her own shorts and underwear to push them down, and once Hailey figured out that Charlie wanted to see what she was doing, Hailey lifted herself up to allow it. She then felt Charlie's legs kicking the articles off her feet, but she didn't turn back to look. She reached between Charlie's legs and opened her, before reaching between her own legs and opening herself, pressing down into Charlie and allowing their centers to meet.

"Hailey," Charlie let out in a soft breath as Hailey rolled into her, feeling her own wetness mix with Hailey's.

"I love you." Hailey pressed her lips to Charlie's chest

between her breasts as she slowly rocked against her.

"I love you." Charlie gripped Hailey's ass and pressed her down.

The feel of Hailey's relaxed clit against Charlie's hard and throbbing one, made Hailey rethink that relaxation, as she felt herself starting to climb again but forcing the feeling out of her mind. She wanted Charlie now. She wanted to hear Charlie come as she rocked against her.

"Tell me what you want," Hailey ordered gently as her lips met Charlie's.

"That feels pretty good, actually," Charlie encouraged.

"Slow, like this?" Hailey asked and kissed her jawline.

"Yes," Charlie let out more like a breath than anything.

Hailey attached her lips to any part of Charlie's skin she could reach without interrupting her hips. She felt the familiar climb again, and while she tried to hide it so that Charlie would know that this was about her now and not Hailey, Charlie's helping hands on her hips caused Hailey to let out a small moan against Charlie's neck. She felt Charlie's hands tighten on her hips and started moving faster against her.

"Come with me," Charlie said in Hailey's ear.

"It's your turn," Hailey smirked as she lifted her head up to fixate her eyes on Charlie's.

Charlie was persistent, though. She guided Hailey's body back and forth, as they both grew wetter, and the friction was too much for Hailey; her body started to tremor. Charlie's eyes were on her breasts.

"Yes," Charlie said in a short burst. "Right there," she encouraged.

Hailey knew Charlie was close. Hailey was close, too. And she held it back until she felt Charlie's hands grip her tighter, and they ground against one another faster until Hailey felt her orgasm taking over. Her hips were moving on their own now while her hands were pressed into the couch on either side of Charlie's head. She wanted more, though. And while Hailey listened as Charlie's orgasm overtook her, she slid her own hand between their legs and entered Charlie, pressing her palm and hips down against her. Charlie let out a startled but grateful cry, as Hailey pushed her over the edge once, and then again, never allowing her to fully come down from the first one.

"God, Charlie," Hailey muttered softly into Charlie's ear, still lying on top of the woman minutes later. "I never knew it could be this good." Hailey pressed her lips to Charlie's neck just below her ear.

"Neither did I," Charlie concurred. "Stay over tonight."

"Okay," Hailey replied, exhausted. "Do you want to eat your dinner now?" She laughed into Charlie's neck. "Or have you had your fill?" Hailey laughed again.

Charlie laughed as well.

"Oh, trust me, I have not had my fill. But I will share my dinner with you, and then, maybe we can take a shower and watch something together before bed," she suggested.

"That sounds pretty perfect."

***

Charlie woke up to the sounds of someone moving in her kitchen. She looked to her left and saw that Hailey wasn't in bed. They had fallen asleep late, after eating dinner and watching a movie together, while Charlie lay across Hailey's lap. They had also showered together, and as Charlie stood in front of Hailey, watching her standing under the rushing water with her head back, trying to get shampoo out of her hair, Charlie wondered how her life could get any better. Sleep came easily after the long and surprising weekend. But then, it was only 6 a.m., and Hailey wasn't usually up this early. Charlie got out of bed, threw a pair of shorts on over the underwear she had fallen asleep in, and headed to the kitchen.

Charlie watched as Hailey navigated her kitchen with ease. In fact, she stood in the doorway, leaning against it with her arms over her chest, watching Hailey slide in socks around on the hardwood, opening cabinets and pulling out items while she hummed something Charlie didn't recognize. Hailey was wearing one of Charlie's old T-shirts and her underwear.

"I'm going to be really cheesy right now and ask if this is heaven," Charlie said after several moments of watching Hailey move around.

"Aren't you a charmer?" Hailey returned.

She only looked at Charlie over her shoulder and kept working. Charlie moved up behind her and wrapped her arms around Hailey's waist.

"Good morning." Charlie kissed her neck. "What are you doing in here?"

"Making you breakfast, for once," Hailey replied. "Eggs and bacon."

"I didn't have eggs or bacon." Charlie lifted her head up.

"Yes... But we live in a world where there are apps for that."

"You had food delivered here?"

"Yes, at 5:30 in the morning. It cost extra, but it was worth it."

Charlie held on to Hailey's hips but stood back and allowed her to work. Eventually, they sat at the counter and shared the breakfast Hailey had prepared for them.

"This is great, Hails."

"Hey, I noticed something last night," Hailey said as she sipped on her coffee.

"Yeah? What's that?"

"You fell asleep without the light on last night."

Charlie looked at her with a piece of bacon hanging out of her mouth in surprise. Hailey laughed.

"I did?"

"Yes." Hailey laughed out. "I turned it on for you later; but you were out, and so was the light."

Charlie finished the bacon and thought about that.

"I never fall asleep without the light on," Charlie said mostly to herself.

"Which is why I'm bringing it up," Hailey said and stood.

She placed her dishes in the sink and walked back around the counter to where Charlie was still sitting but wrapping up her breakfast.

"Do you think it means something?" Charlie asked.

Hailey brushed her hand across Charlie's cheek.

"I think, it means you're happy." She leaned in and pressed her lips to Charlie's. "And I think, it means you feel safe."

"I do," Charlie said.

Hailey wiggled her eyebrows at her.

"Good. I have to go home and then rush to get to the office on time."

"Okay," Charlie said, and Hailey kissed her again.

"Hey." Hailey turned around after walking toward the bedroom.

"Yes, Hails?"

"I'm kind of crazy about you." Hailey winked and didn't wait for a response.

***

"Okay. Before Charlie gets here, fill me in," Ember requested as she sat down in front of Hailey at Sally's. "Also, where is Charlie? Shouldn't you two be glued to the hip, now that you're officially together?"

"Didn't you just get married? Shouldn't you be glued to your wife's side?" Hailey rolled her eyes at her friend.

"I am," Ember said. "This may be the first time I've put on clothes in four days," she replied.

"God!" Hailey laughed at the details she had not asked for. "And Charlie had a conference call with Detroit this morning, so she said she'd just meet us here."

"Did you stay there last night?" Ember asked and took a drink of her coffee.

"Yes."

"And how is it?"

"The apartment?" Hailey asked, confused.

"Yes, Hailey. I want you to tell me all about the apartment I've been to a million times; and not about the fact that you and Charlie are together and having copious amounts of sex," she returned sarcastically.

"Em, I'm not going to talk about our sex life," Hailey told her.

"Why not? You've never had a problem telling me about it before."

"Because Charlie's not like that. When was the last time she talked to you about her sex life?"

"I don't know."

"She doesn't do that. She's private about stuff like that."

"You never have been," Ember pressed.

"It's different this time."

"Because Charlie doesn't want you to talk about it?"

"Because *I* don't want to. Because it's something just between the two of us, and it's amazing."

"The sex?" Ember lifted an eyebrow.

"Yes, Em." Hailey rolled her eyes at her best friend again. "That's all you'll get out of me about it, too. It's amazing. It's the best–"

"Hey." Charlie had been walking behind another customer, so Hailey hadn't seen the woman until she was already at the table. "Hey, you," she said to Hailey.

"Hi." Hailey smiled.

"Okay... This isn't fair now," Ember said while Charlie sat next to Hailey and offered her a quick kiss.

"What isn't fair now?" Charlie questioned.

"You two are together. Our *'no girls allowed'* rule doesn't apply to you, but it still applies to me?" Ember questioned.

"Oh, I guess that's true," Hailey offered in response. "I think she's seeking our approval to invite Eva to our Thursday morning coffees," she then said to Charlie.

"Yes, I would like to invite my wife to our coffees, now that you two are official."

"Foursome?" Charlie seemed to consider. "I think we'll allow it."

"Yeah, we can allow that," Hailey agreed.

"You two are so annoying now; I doubt she'll even want to come," Ember said as she laughed.

***

"You seem happy," Lena said to Charlie.

"I *am* happy," Charlie told her.

They had met at The Lantern, a lesbian bar in the city, because Lena had struck out at the speed dating and was still hoping to find a lady. The Lantern was a regular bar, not a club, and was populated with a pretty standard mix of lesbian types for a Saturday night.

"It's been, like, two weeks, right?"

"Yeah." Charlie couldn't help but smile.

"Don't look now, but that woman is definitely checking you out," Lena said, and Charlie didn't look.

"So?"

"So, how is it they're all looking at you? No offense. I'm the one that's available, and here specifically to meet someone, and I'm not even getting a glance." Lena glared at Charlie. "You must be giving off that vibe that happens when people are in relationships. Other people are drawn to it or something."

"Well, I am happy to direct any attention your way. I'm good with what I've got."

"Hi." A woman, wearing way too much makeup, approached and stood very close to Charlie, practically blocking Lena from view. "I'd like to buy you a drink," she stated confidently.

"Oh, thanks, but no. I'm okay." Charlie lifted her untouched wine.

She looked over the woman's shoulder to Lena, as if to see if she wanted the drink, but Lena shook her head no.

"Hey." Hailey walked up next to Charlie and observed

how close the other woman was to her. "I swear, I do not remember you having girls all over you before we were dating. Did I miss that, too?" she questioned and then leaned down to kiss Charlie on the lips.

"Sorry." The woman turned and walked off.

"You sure you aren't interested, Lena? I can probably get her back," Charlie teased.

Hailey sat down next to Charlie and leaned in, offering her a kiss on the cheek this time.

"You two are cute together." Lena pointed between the two of them.

Hailey placed her arm over the back of Charlie's chair.

"You're possessive tonight," Charlie joked.

"Well, I have Summer stripping in front of you, and now women in bars are all over you... So, I've got to do something," Hailey replied.

"Summer stripped in front of you?" Lena asked. "Summer Taft, the one you almost hooked up with? The hot one?" Lena shook her head. "Why can't I get someone like that to strip in front of me?"

"You can. They're called strip clubs, Lena," Charlie told her.

"You almost hooked up with Summer?" Hailey questioned and slid her arm away from Charlie's chair. "When?"

"What?" Charlie turned to her.

"And that's my cue to go get another drink." Lena stood while mouthing the word *'sorry'* to Charlie.

"When did you almost hook up with Summer?"

"Hails…"

"Charlie, when?"

"Hailey, it wasn't like that. We didn't almost hook up."

"What happened, then? Because I've only heard about your *friend* Summer. I haven't heard anything about the Summer you almost *slept* with."

"Hailey?" Emma stood in front of their table.

"Jesus Christ!" Charlie exclaimed. "Of course, you're here."

NICOLE PYLAND

"Sorry?" Emma said.

"Hey, I got you a gin and tonic." Another woman approached and wrapped an automatic arm around Emma's waist.

"Eli, this is Hailey. And that's Charlie, her girlfriend." Emma pointed at each of them. "This is Elizabeth, my girlfriend," Emma introduced. "We just got here. I saw you and thought I'd come over, but I think I interrupted something."

"I'm going to call it an early night," Charlie said.

"It's nice to meet you, Eli," Hailey said and placed a hand onto Charlie's thigh, as if to keep her there.

"You too," Eli replied and looked at Emma. "So, this is *your* Hailey?"

"Yeah, this is *the* Hailey," Emma replied with a blush on her cheeks that Charlie kind of wanted to smack off.

"That makes me sound important."

"You were important," Charlie stated and stood. "I'm going to get some air."

Charlie walked past the bar, where Lena was talking to an attractive woman, and headed outside. When she got there, she inhaled deeply and then exhaled again as she stood with her back against the wall.

"Okay, that was rude," Hailey stated the moment she saw her.

"Hails…"

"No, Charlie. That was rude," Hailey repeated. "I can't believe you just acted like that. She introduced us to her girlfriend; and you freak out like I'm going home with her and not you."

"I see her and I can't–"

"Charlie, stop." Hailey stood in front of her. "I mean, this is crazy. You know I love you."

"I know."

"So, what is it?"

"Now that I have you, Hails, I hate even thinking of anyone else with you. I'm sorry. Seeing her blush when her

310

girlfriend called you *her* Hailey just bothered me. I don't think I'm ready to spend time with your ex-girlfriend and first love."

"Okay. We don't have to. I didn't know they would be here, Charlie. But, are you planning on answering my question about Summer anytime soon?" Hailey pushed.

"Jesus, Hails. It was when I was in Detroit, okay? She had just been dumped. We had a drink and then she wanted to meet Eddie, so she came to my room, and–"

"And you almost fucked her?" Hailey using that word in this context made Charlie realize how serious the situation was now.

"No." Charlie reached for Hailey's hand but found her unwilling. "She kissed me. It didn't go much further than that."

"You kissed her back?"

"Yes."

"And there was more?"

"We were on the bed, but nothing happened, Hailey."

"Charlie, this was after you and I went on our first date," Hailey stated, clearly hurt.

"This was after you ran out on me, Hailey."

"You ran out on me after the wedding. I didn't go making out with some random woman," Hailey argued. "You kissed someone else, Charlie. After…"

"Hails, we weren't together then. I thought it was over. You didn't want me."

"I messed up, Charlie. But I never even thought of being with anyone else until I could figure out how to get past all my crap so that I could be with you."

"And I didn't think about being with Summer," Charlie replied. "Let me go inside to tell Lena we're taking off, and then, we can go home and talk about this."

"I think I need a night to myself. I'm going to stay at my place. I haven't really been there the past two weeks, anyway."

"Hailey, don't do this again. We talked about this. I

told you I wouldn't pull away, and you said it would be okay. You promised that night," Charlie reminded her of the promise she'd made right before they had made love for the first time.

"I'm not running away, Charlie. But I need the night, okay?" Hailey asked. "I'll call you tomorrow."

Hailey walked off, and Charlie let her, because she could tell that even if she followed, it would do nothing for her case. She stood with her back against the wall and flung her head back, hitting the brick hard enough to hurt and probably give her a headache for the rest of the night.

CHAPTER 26

"WHERE'D Hailey go?" Lena asked.

"Thanks for that Summer comment," Charlie remarked. "She left. I'm going home. I just came back in here to let you know."

"Shit… I'm sorry, Charlie. I didn't mean to cause a problem."

"It's not your fault. I just have to go."

"I understand," Lena replied. "I really am sorry."

"She's upset because I kissed Summer."

"No, she's not," Lena began. "She's upset because you kissed Summer *after* you kissed *her*."

"It wasn't like that."

"I know. You gave me all the details. Did you give them to her, though?"

"No. She just left and said she wants to be alone tonight."

"Charlie, you two have got to stop doing this to each other."

"Doing what?"

"You're afraid of both being together and losing each other. Both of you!" Lena explained. "At some point, you'll have to figure out which of those fears wins."

***

Hailey arrived home and threw herself onto her bed. She hadn't slept in it since she and Charlie started dating. She had only been home every few days, to gather some things to take over there. As she lay face down, Hailey wondered how exactly they'd ended up in this place again. It felt like just as they had found their rhythm, they had lost it again. This time, Hailey couldn't just blame herself, and she also couldn't just blame Charlie. They'd both done it. Charlie continued to react to Emma, and Hailey couldn't do anything about that. They shared a past. And yes, it was a great past, but Hailey couldn't go back and re-write. And even if she could, she wouldn't.

Emma was, at least in part, responsible for the person Hailey was today, in that way that all first loves are responsible for their paramours. A heart, broken in one way, leads a person down a path, while a heart, broken in another, can alter someone's life entirely. Emma had altered Hailey's life entirely. She gave Hailey the courage to be herself with another person and the courage to come out. She gave her a relationship filled with love and excitement, and it lasted over a year. When it ended, it made an indelible mark on each of them. Hailey couldn't change that any more than she could change the color of her eyes.

Now, Hailey couldn't seem to get over this vision, appearing in her head, ever since Lena revealed that Charlie and Summer almost slept together. She pictured Summer naked underneath Charlie's body, now well known to Hailey. Charlie's hand was working between Summer's legs, and their lips were connected. Hailey shook her head and yelled into the comforter of her bed. She knew she had probably made a bigger deal out of it then it was. They hadn't slept together. They'd kissed. Hailey had kissed Emma after she and Charlie went on their date. Why was she so bent out of shape that Charlie had kissed someone, too?

Probably because when Hailey kissed Emma that day, it wasn't really Emma she was kissing. In her mind, it was no one. It could very well have been anyone. Hailey knew that was wrong. She shouldn't have done that to Emma. But she had wanted Charlie, and she had been too scared to admit how far into that she was. Somehow, it felt different to Hailey, because at least she'd been dating Emma at the time.

She had also known the woman practically her entire life. Charlie had chosen someone she'd just met, someone young, hot, and rich; and she made it to the bed with her before she had stopped it. *Why did she stop it?* Hailey wondered to herself and knew she couldn't supply the answer. She hadn't given Charlie the chance to explain, either.

They were doing it again. They were pushing and pulling at one another, which Hailey really shouldn't be surprised about. They'd always pushed and pulled at one another. It was one of the reasons their friendship worked so well. They would challenge one another to be better or to try to reach their full potential. Charlie would take forever to make decisions, while Hailey tended to make them quicker. They would both balance the other out by pulling them just a little toward their side. Now, it appeared that, the very thing that worked well for them in their friendship, was getting in the way of this new part of their relationship. Both of them were pulling away instead of pushing one another together or applying that push/pull balancing act that made them both better people in the end.

***

"Are you kidding me?!" Ember exclaimed.

"Em, come on."

"Charlie, this is exhausting! First, you guys are together, and then, you're not. Then, you're together again, and now, you're not?"

"We didn't break up," Charlie replied.

"So, it was just a fight? You don't look like it was just a fight. You look like shit," Ember told her.

Charlie hadn't slept at all Saturday night. She had tossed and turned for a while before giving up entirely and just working at her desk until the sun came up. Then, she took a long walk with Eddie around the city, returned home to change, and called Ember to see if she could come over and talk to her about what had happened.

"I didn't sleep," Charlie offered.

"I wonder why. Could it be because you and the love of your life are fighting about something stupid? You're getting jealous over Emma, when Hailey has made it more than clear that she doesn't want her. It's just stupid, Charlie."

"I know. I'm trying."

"Trying what?" Ember challenged and finished the sandwich.

She had made them both lunch and even delivered a plate to Eva's office, since her wife was working on her speech for the upcoming conference they'd go to before their honeymoon.

"Trying not to think about her. Trying to forget the fact that Hailey talked about how amazing she was over and over again, for a hundred years."

"You know what I remember?" Ember took a drink of her iced tea.

"What?" Charlie dropped her own uneaten sandwich to the plate and leaned back in the chair.

"I remember all the times Hailey talked about you," Ember replied.

"Em..."

"I'm serious," Ember offered. "You remember pining away for her while she dated all the wrong women. You remember her talking our ears off about them and mentioning Emma in the mix as a comparison. But I remember more. I'm the objective third party – or I'm at least as objective as I can be, given that I want you two together, and I've always thought you should be."

"You have?"

Ember gave her a look that told Charlie that was a stupid question.

"Charlie, she talked to me about you way more than she did about Emma Colton. She'd tell me about how talented you were at your job, and how she was always blown away when she'd see your sketches or pictures of the finished product. She'd tell me how funny you were, and how you always made her coffee in the morning, or how you let her stay over, and how sometimes, you'd put a blanket on her when you thought she was sleeping. She would talk about how pretty you were and how she didn't know how you were still single. She'd go on and on about you, and how lucky she was to have you in her life. Did you really go over to her apartment and fix the leaky sink when her super said it would be another two days?"

"That was, like, five years ago."

"And somehow, I remember it. You know why? Because Hailey does," Ember said. "I think she's loved you all along. She just didn't realize it. I'd see it, too. I've seen it a lot more recently, obviously, but I've seen it for years in how she is with you. It's not how she is with me, and we're all supposed to be best friends. She touches you, Charlie. She hugs me, sometimes, but she touches you. She always has. She'll put her hand on your back or touch your neck and rub your shoulders. You're the only one she does that with. You don't see it because you've never felt like you deserve her. But the reality is – you both deserve each other, because you're right together."

Charlie sighed and considered everything Ember had said.

"What do I do about the Summer thing?"

"Who is Summer to you, Charlie?"

"No one," Charlie answered automatically. "She's someone I met through work. She was a stupid distraction, and I stopped it before it went anywhere, because I love Hailey."

"Hails will see that eventually."

"Eventually?" Charlie began. "Do I have to wait another ten years before she and I try again?"

"Why are you waiting at all?" Ember glared at her. "Charlie, you told me all about the amazing first date you guys had that Hailey planned. I know about the night on the farm and how perfect that was because Hailey told me all about it."

"She did?"

"Not the sex stuff, unfortunately," Ember joked. "She knows you're private about that. But Hailey also told me that it's just something for the two of you, and I understand that. Because, as much as I joke about how Eva is a morning person, when it comes to our bedroom activities, I wouldn't share those details with anyone, because they belong to us. Hailey knows that, too. And she told me about how she gave you the cheesy romantic stuff, and that what you had there was perfect. She said *perfect*, Charlie."

"It was perfect."

"So, why wait? Charlie, that girl couldn't be any more obvious about how she feels about you if she wore a damn shirt that said, *I'm in love with Charlie Adams. Ask me how amazing she is.*'" Ember then leaned back and crossed her arms. "You've kept how you felt hidden for so long. Don't you think it's time you put on the shirt, so to speak?"

***

"I think all my stuff is now at her apartment," Hailey said to Emma on the phone. "I have pretty much nothing to wear to work tomorrow, because I've basically been living there."

"So? Just go over and get it," Emma replied.

"I can't. She's probably there."

"Hailey, you are being ridiculous. Just go get your stuff, or maybe just talk to her about this so that you can move on."

"She kissed some random girl, Em."

"You kissed me."

"Yeah, but I was thinking about her while–" Hailey stopped herself. "I'm sorry."

"It's okay. I kind of figured that part out after we broke apart. And I also kind of guessed it was about her."

"Still doesn't make it okay."

"No, it doesn't, but *I* am okay, Hailey," she explained.

"And did you even ask her about Summer? Maybe she was thinking about you the same way you were thinking about her."

"No, I didn't. She freaked out about you, and I just got upset again."

"I'm not helping. I get it from her side, Hailey. I talked about you to Eli a lot, in the beginning. She had a hard time with it when she and I started dating. I can only imagine what it would be like for someone like Charlie to hear you talk about me."

"I know. But I've told her that I love her. I love her. I want everything with her. I think, I always have. Why can't she get that part?"

"She does, Hails. I'm sure."

"Then, why am I talking to you and not her?"

"That's a question you shouldn't be asking me."

CHAPTER 27

"Em, why are we at Charlie's? I thought we were going to dinner," Hailey asked as Ember pulled her car up to Charlie's building.

"Because you have stuff here you need to grab, according to what you said on the phone, and I have to pick up Eddie."

"Why are you picking up Eddie?" Hailey turned to her.

It was Monday, and Ember had picked her up from the office unexpectedly, to see if she wanted to go to dinner. Having not heard from Charlie after sending her a text that morning, Hailey had said yes, because she needed to get her mind off of the whole thing.

"She went back to Detroit, Hails," Ember said.

"Without telling me?" Hailey questioned in a small, heartbroken voice.

"I think it was last minute. I'm sorry. I just thought you could get what you needed without having to run into her. Eva and I are taking care of Eddie for her while she's gone."

"How long?"

"I don't know. She said she would be back before we leave for our trip, though."

Ember opened the door and got out of the car. Hailey opened the door on auto-pilot, unable to process anything other than the fact that her girlfriend had left town without telling her. Was Charlie even her girlfriend anymore? Was this her cowardly way of ending things between them?

"Em, I don't–"

Ember held her phone to her ear.

"Hey, it's my mom." She pointed at the phone. "Do

you want to get started up there? I'll come up in a minute and help."

"Tell your mom I said hi," Hailey replied half-heartedly.

Ember nodded and walked a little down the street, while Hailey headed into the building. She went up the elevator and walked down the hall. Just four days prior, Charlie had Hailey pressed against the wall right outside of her apartment before pulling her inside, where they made love on the floor of the kitchen, being unable to wait until they made it to the bedroom. Hailey didn't even get the same feeling of childlike joy when she heard the beep after swiping her keycard and opening the door. As soon as she did, Eddie greeted her with a jump onto his hind legs.

"Hi, buddy. I missed you." Hailey patted his head and then noticed something attached to his collar. It appeared to be a rolled-up piece of paper. "What the…"

Eddie dropped to the floor but remained sitting in front of Hailey, with his tail wagging across the hardwood. She reached down and decided to take a look, pulling at it until it came off. The paper itself was only an inch wide and had a light-pink ribbon holding it in its scroll form. Hailey looked around the room, and seeing no one, pulled at the ribbon until the paper unfurled in her hand.

"I love how you push me to make decisions." The piece of paper said in handwritten text.

Hailey recognized the handwriting and looked around the room again. Eddie was now uninterested and ran off to his pile of toys on his blanket to play. Hailey then noticed a box on the kitchen counter that had a giant bow on top of it. She walked over to it.

"Charlie?" she half-yelled, but nothing happened.

The box had *'For Hailey'* written on the top. Hailey smiled and then pulled the lid. Inside were possibly a hundred of similarly rolled bits of paper, with the ribbon holding them together. On top of the pile was a small card that read:

'In a recent study from the National Bureau of Economic Research, findings show that people explore friendship as a mechanism which could help explain a causal relationship between marriage and life satisfaction, and find that well-being effects of marriage are about twice as large for those whose spouse is also their best friend. This is not a proposal, Hailey Grant, but this is a promise. Inside this box are one-hundred reasons why I love you. I could write one-hundred more. In fact, I did. Look up.'

Hailey, still smiling, looked up at the counter to see a box of her favorite cereal with yet another bow on top of it. She approached it and saw another card on the side.

'Open me to find the other hundred reasons and then go into the bathroom.'

Hailey pulled the box open and saw that it was also filled with small scrolls. She felt tears begin to fill her eyes and then headed toward the bathroom. She saw a note on the floor and then looked at the light-activated night light she had bought for Charlie that the woman had never used. Hailey read the card to herself, *'I don't need the hall light on anymore. I do feel safe with you, Hails. Go into the bathroom.'*

Hailey held the note and walked into the bathroom. The shower curtain was pulled back, and there was something in the bathtub. First, she noticed a family-size bottle of Charlie's shampoo, with a post-it on the front. *'Because you always use mine.'* Then, Hailey saw the real prize. There were at least twenty paperback books and yet another note. *'I tracked down as many as I could. I thought you could read my favorites, and I could read your favorites. Go to the bedroom, Hails.'*

Hailey looked down and saw different books from *The Hardy Boys* series, and also some from her favored *The Baby-Sitters Club* series. Hailey's heart was racing as she turned in place and then headed down the short hall and turned into the bedroom, where she saw two T-shirts lying on the bed, but no Charlie. One shirt read, *'I love Hailey Grant'* with a bright-red heart, indicating the love, and the other read, *'I love Charlie Adams'* with the same red heart. There was yet another note that read, *'Turn them over.'*

Hailey did as the note instructed. On the back of the shirt that proclaimed her love for Charlie, it read, *'Ask me how stupid she is for almost letting me go,'* and on the back of the shirt, indicating that Charlie loved her, it read, *'Ask me how amazing she is.'*

By now, Hailey's tears were falling freely from her eyes. She wiped them away and sat the shirts back down to search for another note, but there wasn't one.

"You were so good with all those romantic gestures; I thought I should try one myself."

Hailey turned to see Charlie standing in the doorway, holding a small bouquet of flowers.

"Charlie…"

"The white tulip is supposed to say that I'm sorry." Charlie walked into the bedroom. "And I am, Hails. I'm sorry. I'm sorry for kissing Summer. I did it because I thought I'd lost you, and it hurt so much. I stopped it because her lips weren't your lips, her arms weren't your arms; and I felt nothing for her, Hailey. I've never felt for anyone what I feel for you. And I'm sorry that I keep trying to put Emma between us. I've done a lot of thinking these past two days, and I get now that it's stupid. Thus, the shirt." Charlie pointed. "I won't make that mistake again." She paused and handed Hailey the flowers. "The red rose is for love, Hails; but it's for the forever kind of love I feel for you. I'm done running. I'm done pushing you away. I'm done hiding how I feel now, because this is all that I want. You and me; that's it. It's all I need. And I will write you a hundred more reasons why I love you and build you a tree house, if you want. I'll give you a hundred more reasons if that's—"

Hailey didn't let her finish. She pressed her lips to Charlie's, holding the flowers down at her side and then tossing them onto the bed so she could wrap her arms around Charlie's neck and pull her closer. Charlie's mouth was hot and greedy. Hailey felt the familiar tongue reach out for her own, while Charlie's hands were on her back. Hailey pulled back after a moment and stared into Charlie's eyes.

"I love you," she said.

"I love you, too." Charlie wiped at the tears on Hailey's cheeks. "I'm sorry."

"Me too," Hailey replied. "I get the Summer thing. I shouldn't have gotten upset about it."

"Lena told me that you and I were both scared of the same things."

"Yeah?"

"Yeah. We're both so scared of losing the other person, but we're also scared to just be together."

"I think she's right."

"I'm still scared, Hails," Charlie revealed and moved Hailey's hair behind her ear. "I don't know what I'd do if I ever lost you, but I'm not letting that fear keep me from being with you like this, because this is it for me."

Hailey placed her hand on the back of Charlie's neck and grazed her fingers lightly across the skin there.

"This is it for me, too, baby." Then, Hailey seemed to remember, "Wait! Em is outside. She drove me here and said you–"

"She lied." Charlie laughed. "I put her up to it. She's probably on her way home already. In fact..." Charlie reached inside her pocket where she had her phone. She pulled it up and pressed the home button. "Yup." She showed it to Hailey.

"Update ASAP!" Ember's message read.

Hailey laughed loudly and sniffled a little to encourage her tears to go away.

"Should we update her?" Charlie asked.

"She can wait. *This* can't." Hailey tossed Charlie's phone onto the bed and then pulled the woman down on top of herself, on top of the note, on top of the shirts, and pressed their foreheads together. "So, you'd build me a tree house?"

Charlie laughed and pressed her lips to Hailey's forehead.

"That's what you remember from all that?" She kissed Hailey again. "Yes, if you want."

"Nah, build me an actual house instead."

"What?" Charlie asked.

"One day, build me a real house," Hailey requested. "We can design it together. Well, I'll tell you what I want, you draw it and include what you want, and then build it for me. It will be our house."

"Yeah?"

"Yeah."

"I can do that." Charlie kissed her lips. "I already know a few things we'll need."

"Like what?" Hailey questioned with a smile and ran her hands up and down Charlie's back.

"Well, a keycard front door, of course." She kissed Hailey's neck as Hailey laughed wildly. "And at least two extra bedrooms."

"Why is that?"

"You know why, Hailey."

Charlie lifted herself up and pressed a soft hand to Hailey's stomach. Hailey did know why. She smiled and nodded up at Charlie, who leaned down and kissed her. The phone buzzed again, indicating that Ember wanted her update, but they let it buzz and buzz. Nothing else in the world mattered in that moment, because that moment was everything.

EPILOGUE

"I can't believe you had two at once. You two are classic overachievers," Hailey said as she held the tiny baby in her arms.

"We talked about having two before. I guess we just got lucky," Hannah replied while she ran her hands through Alyssa's hair as the still exhausted woman lay in her lap.

"So, no more after this?" Charlie asked and let the little boy try to tug at her finger, even though his small hand was in its little baby mitten to keep him from scratching himself. "You got two; and you got the boy and the girl."

"They're so small," Hailey remarked as she looked down at the little girl.

Charlie smiled at her girlfriend and wrapped her arm around her, pulling Hailey into her side.

"I literally just had these two. Let's give it some time before we consider adding any more." Alyssa looked up at Hannah, who smiled down at her.

"Fine by me," Hannah agreed.

The infant in Hailey's arms started to fuss.

"Here. I'll take her." Alyssa sat up, and Hailey passed her the baby. "Come here, little Lizzy." Alyssa kissed her daughter's forehead and rocked the baby back and forth.

"Where are my grandchildren?" Judy, Alyssa's mother, walked down the stairs.

"They're right here, Mom. They can't exactly walk off."

"Can I see my baby boy?" Judy approached Charlie. Charlie passed over the quiet child. "Tyler, are you ready for a nap?" she asked.

"I'll take Lizzy up." Alyssa kissed Hannah on the cheek. "Be right back."

326

Alyssa walked off and then up the stairs with her mother and the babies.

"She is a great mom," Hannah said to no one in particular.

"I think you're both great moms," Hailey offered.

"Guys, this one made me late, I swear." Ember entered in through the front door, with Eva close behind.

"She's right. My fault." Eva raised her hand. "I was reviewing her paper, and since I don't understand the half of it, it took me a while."

"Why were you reviewing it, then?" Charlie asked.

"I check for typos, mainly. But it makes her feel better when I read them first, for some reason," Eva explained.

"I just think she's hot when she rocks out those new reading glasses," Ember said and sat on the couch next to Hannah. "Where are the babies?"

"Al and Judy just took them up for a nap."

"What? We only came here to see *them*," Ember said with a sad face.

"She's kidding." Eva sat on Ember's side and smacked her shoulder lightly.

"It's true. But, can I just go say hi before they fall asleep?"

"Sure. But if they say hi back, let me know," Hannah returned.

"That would be Ember's kid," Charlie stated. "She'd pop out a little genius that could talk from birth."

"Babe, a little you." Eva looked awestruck by the idea.

"We'll talk about *that* later," she said to Eva. "*You*, stop it." Ember pointed at Charlie as she stood and headed up the stairs.

"She puts on a big show, but she's a softie," Eva told the room.

"She wants them, doesn't she?" Hailey asked and leaned in closer to Charlie, placing her hand on Charlie's thigh.

"She does," Eva said. "She just wants to get her Ph. D first. Then, we'll start figuring that out."

"We're going to have more little nieces and nephews." Hailey kissed Charlie's cheek.

Charlie smiled and rolled her eyes.

"You two all settled in now?" Hannah asked.

"I am officially out of my old studio and moved into Charlie's apartment. Well, our place now."

"It's been our place for a while. She just still had the lease," Charlie added.

"How does it feel, to be officially living together now?" Eva questioned.

"Weirdly, the same," Hailey said.

"Yeah, Hails was pretty much always at my place, even before we started dating."

"And that didn't tell you anything?" Ember bounded down the stairs and back next to her wife. "They're asleep. I was in the way, so I was told to leave before Alyssa murdered me for waking them up."

"Where's Al?" Hannah asked.

"Judy told her to try to get some sleep while they're out. She's in the process of resisting," Ember relayed.

"That Judy is a smart woman," Hannah returned. "I'm going to go check on my wife and try to convince her to sleep." Hannah stood.

"Do you want us to go so you can get some, too?" Hailey checked.

"No, you don't have to," Hannah answered. "We're doing this shift thing from one of the books. We pretend like we actually know what we're doing."

"I read this study that mentioned–"

"Hails, 78% of studies turn out to be wrong," Ember said.

"What study was that in?" Hailey asked.

Ember just laughed silently and shook her head. Charlie kissed Hailey's temple and pulled her girlfriend closer.

"Hannah, why don't you, Al, and Judy take a nap? Em and I can keep watch over the little ones," Eva offered. "It will give us a little practice." She took Ember's hand.

"You sure? I think I've had, like, six hours of sleep in three days. It could be a long nap," Hannah said.

"Go for it," Ember said and leaned into Eva.

"You guys are awesome," Hannah replied. "I'll tell Al and Judy. There's food in the fridge, I think." She shrugged.

Hannah disappeared quickly up the stairs, apparently believing Eva and Ember might change their minds.

"We'd stay, too, but we have plans tonight." Hailey looked at her watch. "We should probably go, actually."

"Oh, yeah." Charlie turned Hailey's wrist so that she could see the time. "Sorry."

"No problem," Ember said. "Have fun," she said to them as they stood. "Want to order a pizza? You know there's no food in that fridge."

Eva smiled and rolled her eyes.

***

Charlie and Hailey headed out to Hailey's car and then back to their apartment. Charlie let Hailey *'do the beep,'* as Hailey called it, and they walked in. They had to get ready for the event that was in exactly two hours.

"Do I have time for a shower?" Hailey asked. "I'll make it fast, I promise."

"Only if I can join you," Charlie requested and followed Hailey in the direction of the shower.

***

"Do I look okay?" Hailey asked as she stood in front of Charlie in the kitchen.

"Hails, you always look okay."

"I'm really asking. This isn't some girlfriend trick question," she replied.

Hailey was wearing a new dress she had bought for the occasion. It was a pale-pink one and had a pencil skirt shape about it.

"And I answered you, Hailey. I've been in love with you for my entire adult life, and thought you were hot since the moment I first laid eyes on you. I'm not exactly the one you need to talk to about what looks good on you. I think you're hot when you're eating chicken wings and wearing my old sweats and a T-shirt." Charlie then thought for a moment. "That white tank top in particular; it's kind of see-through."

"You are no help," Hailey said seriously. "But that was very sweet. You look nice, too, by the way."

Charlie had chosen a dress for herself that was off the shoulder in green, and she had worn it because Hailey said it went well with Charlie's dark eyes.

"Thank you. You ready?"

"Let's go."

***

The party was nearing full swing by the time they arrived and walked into the room hand in hand. The event was to celebrate both the completion of the project in Detroit for Summer's company, and the launch of the new Chicago office. Charlie's team would be heading up the project and, thanks to Charlie's success, she had been promoted.

"Ladies, welcome," Summer greeted when she saw them and delivered two glasses of champagne to them. "Glad you're here."

"Thank you," Hailey told her, took the glasses, and handed the other to Charlie.

"How long are you staying in town this time, Sum?" Charlie asked.

Hailey let go of Charlie's hand but looped her arm through Charlie's arm instead. She had gotten accustomed to Charlie's friendship with the younger woman and was no longer bothered by their brief history in Detroit.

"I'm going to stay until the project's finished. It's too much, flying back and forth from Cali. It's just easier if I'm here, since the brother has decided to go on sabbatical. He's twenty-seven. He's not old enough to go on sabbatical... What does he need a sabbatical from?"

"You guys have been building a massive company since you were twenty years old. I can imagine being in need of a break from that," Charlie replied.

"I guess. He's going to tour around Asia for a while, and has yet to provide me with a date for his return. I'm going to stay here and try to get actual work done."

"It'll be nice having you around more," Hailey stated and found that she really meant it.

"I actually wanted to talk to you tonight, if I can," Summer said in Hailey's direction.

"Me?"

"Yeah, can I borrow her for a minute, Charlie?"

"As long as I get her back," Charlie replied with a wink in Hailey's direction.

"Always, baby." Hailey kissed her on the cheek and walked off with Summer, while Charlie went to find her team to congratulate them.

Since her promotion, Charlie had picked up another ten employees and now had a supervisor between her and her overall team. It meant more responsibility, and she'd had some long days at the office while she wrapped project after project. But, Charlie had come home to Hailey every night even before the woman had officially moved in, and it made everything better. There was always this moment for Charlie, where she'd be right outside her front door – she would take a deep breath in and then out, and open the door. Hailey was there every time. Sometimes, she'd make them dinner, or she'd order food in. Other times, they would cook together, or Charlie would cook for her, while Hailey worked on her own stuff on the counter.

Charlie's favorite nights were when they'd lie in bed together and whisper things to one another, as if they would be overheard otherwise. Hailey would share things about her day or just something about one of those studies she had read. They would talk about the books they had read and reread, in some cases. Hailey had even gotten them a few *Nancy Drew* books to go alongside those old *Hardy Boys*. She had also told Charlie that Kristy had been her favorite babysitter, while Charlie told her she liked Dawn the best. It had all been silly and ridiculous, and Charlie loved every minute of it. She felt like she was getting to know a part of Hailey no one else knew. That made her love Hailey even more.

***

"Hey." Hailey returned, stood behind her, and placed her hands on Charlie's hips.

They were at a work party, so she wouldn't take it further, but she definitely wanted to. Hailey loved the feel of Charlie pressed against her. Whenever they were together, Hailey found it difficult not to touch Charlie in some way. It had taken Ember pointing that out to her a few months ago, that made her realize she had always been like that. She had always liked touching Charlie. Even when they were twenty-year-old kids, waiting tables, Hailey had always somehow found a way to sneak a touch. She had often approached the other woman from behind, as Charlie filled cups with soda, and touched her waist just like this, causing Charlie to jump in surprise. Hailey recalled she had been so young and so stupid back then.

"Hey back." Charlie turned around to face Hailey first and then turned back for a second. "I'll see you guys later." Charlie waved at a few members of her team she had been able to locate. "What did Summer want?"

"She offered me a job," Hailey said and took Charlie's hands in her own, allowing their fingers to play.

"She what?"

"She needs a new head of her PR department. They've gotten so big, that there's an actual department now; and she doesn't have anyone in charge of it right now," Hailey explained.

"Wow," Charlie replied, happily. "What does that

mean? Are you interested?"

"She said she would call me, and we can set up a time to talk formally. It sounds pretty interesting, though. I'd have a team under me. I could determine how the actual department works. Plus, she told me the potential salary, and, my God, Charlie! It's like, three times what I make now," Hailey exclaimed.

"That's amazing, Hails." Charlie took a long drink of her champagne, and Hailey recognized it for what it was.

"Tell me what you're thinking. Where'd you just go right now?" Hailey always recognized her mood shifts.

"Their main office is in Silicon Valley, Hails," Charlie stated simply.

Hailey was grateful, because in moments like this, in their past, Charlie had often just pulled away and said nothing about it.

"Oh," Hailey replied. "She said we could talk about that. They have multiple offices now, so I could likely just pick one to work out of and travel if I needed to."

"Really?"

"Yeah. I don't know if I'll take it or anything. We talked for, like, five minutes before she got grabbed by someone else. But, now that she's not sticking her tongue down your throat, I really like her. I'm willing to at least hear her out."

"That's great, babe," Charlie said.

Hailey still liked the way Charlie called her that. It was an interesting transition for them, because Hailey had had no problem calling Charlie 'babe' or 'baby' or other terms of endearment, but Charlie had stuck with 'Hails' for a while. The woman had only recently started calling her 'babe,' and Hailey loved it.

"It could be." Hailey took Charlie's glass and took a sip. "If I do take it, though, and we combine that with the nice raise you just got, we might be able to put a down payment on a house, when the lease is up on our place." She looked wistfully at Charlie.

"A house, huh?" Charlie teased her a little.

"It might be nice to have a place of our own, with a guest room for when people need to stay. Your mom has been wanting to visit. And, if Ember and Eva come over and stay late, they could crash."

"That's true," Charlie agreed. "Plus, I love you, and would like us to have a house together one day."

"I know you're usually little *Miss Professional*, and this is a work event, but can I kiss you? Totally PG."

Charlie leaned in and gave Hailey a sweet and all too brief kiss on the lips. Hailey stayed on Charlie's arm most of the night, only breaking off a few times to get them drinks or chat with someone while Charlie moved on to talk to someone else. Summer found her just as the party was starting to die down. They confirmed plans to talk about the job the following Monday. Hailey had to admit to herself that she was excited at this possibility. She liked her job at the bank, but the past few months there had been difficult. They'd taken over three months to find the replacement for her boss. And when they finally found it, Hailey didn't like the guy. When he made a snide comment about the picture she had of herself and Charlie on her desk, with Eddie in the grass between them, she lost what little respect she did have for him and had considered finding something else anyway. She would sit down with Summer and see if this was the opportunity for her.

When they made it home at the end of the night, both of them were exhausted and ready for bed, but Hailey's hunger came first, as she changed into pajamas alongside Charlie. Then, she went into the kitchen to grab a snack before sitting on the couch. Charlie joined her moments later, with something in her hand.

"What's that?" Hailey asked her and pointed to the item after crunching on a chip.

"It's for you. I've finally finished it."

"It?" Hailey checked. "Wait... That's *it*?" She dropped the bag to the table and took the tube from Charlie.

"It's the house, yeah," Charlie said and turned to face Hailey on the couch.

Hailey smiled at her and wasted no time in pulling the top off of the slender tube and then sliding a few pieces of rolled-up paper out. Charlie removed the tube and watched as Hailey leaned forward to unroll the pages onto the coffee table. The top page held the exterior front, side, and back views of the two-story home, and Charlie placed a hand on Hailey's back as she examined the architectural drawings.

"Charlie…" Hailey ran her fingers over the page and then glanced over at her. "It's beautiful."

"Look at the inside stuff." Charlie nodded toward the pages beneath the top one.

Hailey removed the first page and revealed the first story of the house on the next one. The house would have an open floor plan, with a spacious kitchen, living room, and an office for Charlie. There was a dining room with enough room for a table that would comfortably fit eight people, and the deck off the back of the house led to rows of trees they would plant, that would eventually grow and provide shade and cover from the rest of whatever neighborhood they'd build this house into. Hailey then lifted to reveal the final page, which was the second story of the house. It was four bedrooms, and exactly what she had asked for, with a large walk-in closet for them to share off the master bedroom. The master bathroom had dual sinks and a separate shower with a spacious bathtub, also per Hailey's request. She stared back at the first page and turned to Charlie.

"You drew everything," she said.

"That was the idea, right?"

"You put a swing set in the backyard."

"You said you'd want them to have somewhere to play back there." Charlie shrugged.

"It's perfect, Charlie." Hailey leaned forward and kissed the woman gently. "I can't wait until we can have this one day."

"Hails, we can have it now," Charlie said.

"What?" Hailey pulled back slightly to take a look at her.

"Hailey, I've been saving up to buy a place for the past five years. I've been squirreling away money as I could, because I knew I would get tired of renting. Especially now that Ember and Eva have their place, and Alyssa and Hannah have their place, and they're both kind of in the suburbs, I thought it made sense to start putting more away for it. The job with the firm made that a lot easier, and with my promotion, I won't have any problem with a mortgage."

"So, you want to do this now?"

"We have a year on our lease here," Charlie explained and took Hailey's hand, placing it into her lap. "I had an agent scout some potential properties for us, and there are two that I think might work."

"What? When did you do this?"

"A couple of weeks ago, when you were in meetings all day."

"Why didn't you tell me?"

"Because I wanted this to be a surprise. I want to take you to them to see if you like any. I made sure they wouldn't take too long for either of us to get to work, that they're in safe neighborhoods – or as safe as you can get in Chicago, and they're in pretty good school districts. There's even a private school near one of them, if we went that way."

"Baby..." Hailey placed her free hand on Charlie's cheek.

"I know a lot of the good contractors in the city, thanks to my job, and I've reached out to the one I like working with the most. Their work is always good, and they meet deadlines. I'd like us to meet with them about this. They'll likely give me a pretty good discount, too, because I've thrown them some good accounts over the years."

"So, you want to build our dream house now?"

"Why buy something we like, when we can have something we designed ourselves, Hails?" Charlie proposed. "We can afford this. And it's what we both want, right?"

"You still do that, you know?" Hailey said.

"Do what?"

Hailey laughed silently at her and then pushed Charlie backward onto the couch so that she could hover over her.

"You still check to see if I want things with you," Hailey said. "I've basically been living in this apartment since before we even started dating; and when my lease was coming up, you asked me if I was sure about moving in. When you had to go to Detroit for work for two weeks, and I asked to come along, you asked if I was sure I wanted to spend two weeks with you in Detroit. Like the location makes any difference to me; I just wanted to be with you." Hailey paused and stared down into Charlie's brown eyes. "Charlie, I love you. I want this with you. I want this house with you, and everything that comes with it. I even want the mortgage with you," she joked.

"I'm sure I'll stop doing it, eventually. It's only been, like, six months. I'm still getting used to it." Charlie's hands went to Hailey's back and lifted the T-shirt that read, '*I love Charlie Adams.*' Hailey wore it to sleep at least once a week.

"I think it's cute," Hailey said.

"Oh, you do?" Charlie gripped Hailey's ass and pressed the woman down into herself firmly, causing Hailey to laugh. "You think my inability to grasp that you chose me is cute?"

Hailey kissed her neck and then pulled herself back up.

"I still think sometimes, about how you chose me over all those girls who went after you."

"All those girls?" Charlie laughed. "All what girls?"

"I don't know, Charlie. How about Lena? Then, Summer? And then, the girl at The Lantern that night? Oh, and then, there were those two women at Windy's a few weeks ago."

"Oh, I guess," Charlie agreed, though she rarely noticed other women hitting on her, and she had not really paid attention to it before she and Hailey got together.

Charlie had always had blinders on for this woman on top of her.

"You guess?" Hailey laughed and lifted Charlie's shirt up a little to run her hands up and down Charlie's stomach.

Charlie watched the movement and felt the familiar pulse between her legs.

"Hails, I've only ever seen you," she confessed and slid Hailey's hair behind her ears so she could more easily see her eyes. "So beautiful."

Hailey took Charlie's bottom lip between her own, and her hands moved up under Charlie's shirt to encapsulate her breasts in a firm grip. Charlie's nipples reacted immediately, and Hailey probed her mouth with her tongue.

"Can we–" she started.

"Yes," Charlie interrupted, knowing the question.

"Bed," Hailey stated and was standing in an instant, pulling Charlie up with her.

They stumbled as they walked, doing their best to keep their lips connected while clothing was tossed aside; first, in the living room, and then, in the hall to the bedroom. Charlie ended up on top, but Hailey rolled them over quickly.

"You are such a top, sometimes," Charlie teased.

"You love it," Hailey replied with an eyebrow wiggle.

"I do." Charlie returned and felt Hailey's lips on her collarbone.

It always surprised Charlie how quickly Hailey could get going like this, even after claiming she was exhausted from a long day at work. It seemed to take no time at all for the woman on top of her to get turned on. Charlie could already feel it on her thigh, as Hailey pressed herself down onto her leg. She could also sense Hailey's impatience, and she loved that it was her that made Hailey that way. She lifted her own thigh up a little, to give Hailey something to move against.

"Is that okay?" Hailey asked as she rubbed herself harder and used her hands to hold herself up as Charlie toyed with her nipples.

"Definitely okay," Charlie confirmed, watching as Hailey's hips moved a little faster, and she felt Hailey's own thigh press a little more firmly into her center. "Yeah, definitely okay," Charlie repeated.

Hailey smirked and reconnected their lips.

***

Charlie woke up wrapped around her girlfriend. Hailey's breathing was even, and her heartbeat beneath Charlie's hand – which Hailey held in her own clasped to her chest – was paced evenly as well. She glanced at the clock over Hailey's shoulder and noticed it was 6:30 a.m. on a Sunday, which meant Hailey would likely want to sleep in. However, Charlie also knew her girlfriend well, and that included her morning mood. She felt Hailey move a little, as if she was in the beginning stages of waking up. Charlie smirked and kissed her shoulder while sliding her hand out of Hailey's grasp. Hailey moved a little, but no more than before. Charlie placed her hand over Hailey's breast, squeezing it lightly and feeling the woman in front of her stir. She moved her hips against Hailey's ass, while at the same time, continuing the squeezing motion on her breast. Hailey let out a soft moan. Her hand moved slowly to Charlie's hip and pressed down, encouraging Charlie to continue that movement. Charlie did and injected her thigh between Hailey's. The angle allowed her center to press lightly into Hailey's ass, and Hailey gasped when she felt the wetness Charlie had felt the moment she woke up.

"Oh," Hailey gasped out.

Charlie played with her nipple while slowly rocking herself into Hailey from behind.

Charlie's hand slid down Hailey's abdomen and between her legs. She kissed the back of Hailey's shoulder, cupped her, and felt Hailey's hips rock in both pleasure and anticipation for what was about to come. Charlie's hand didn't stay long. She rolled Hailey over onto her back and drove her hips down into her when she did. Hailey gripped Charlie's hips to have her repeat the action, while Charlie's lips engulfed a tight nipple and sucked it into her mouth.

"Good morning," Charlie greeted her unnecessarily, after disconnecting her lips from Hailey's nipple with a pop.

She repeated the action on the other one nipple, while continuing to rock into Hailey, who was now thrusting upwards.

"Impatient?" Charlie teased and kissed her lips, bringing her tongue to Hailey's eagerly.

"You started it," Hailey pointed out when their lips parted.

Charlie smiled and lowered her head to kiss Hailey's neck, her breasts, and her abdomen, where she felt muscles beneath her lips twitch with desire. Then, Charlie placed both hands on the inside of Hailey's thighs and spread them apart, relaxing herself between them.

"I plan to finish it, too," Charlie smirked and lifted a playful eyebrow.

She wasted no time before dragging a velvety tongue up her girlfriend's center, stopping at the tip of Hailey's hard clit that she flicked back and forth, earning a loud moan from Hailey and a hand on the back of her head, asking Charlie to continue. Charlie tasted the woman and felt her own arousal in the pit of her stomach, begging her for some form of release; but this *was* part of Charlie's release. They had spent over an hour the previous night making love. She had fallen asleep sated, as had Hailey. But Charlie had woken up with a mind and body that wanted Hailey again and again. Charlie wondered, as she licked Hailey up and down, if this was because she had gone without Hailey for so many years, while she had wanted the woman in secret. She knew that was, likely, at least a small part of her everpresent need to make love to Hailey and have Hailey's hands and mouth on her own skin. But she also knew that sex with Hailey was remarkable.

Six months in, and Charlie still craved her. She was certain that would never go away. Hailey was a part of her, in the same way that Ember and Eva were a part of one another, which had led them to building a life together because of it. She would be building a life with Hailey, and she knew now that, no matter what or whom tried to get in their way, they wouldn't allow obstacles to overtake them. They had worked way too hard to get to this place where they could be fully open to one another and risk their hearts no matter the consequences; because it was too important not to.

"There! There," Hailey repeated in rapid succession.

Charlie had come to recognize that rapidity as Hailey's indicator that the woman was almost there. Charlie circled her tongue several more times around Hailey's swollen clit and felt Hailey's hips move up and down faster, until Charlie heard her cry out as she came. Charlie slid two long fingers into her then. Hailey gasped out as Charlie's lips continued their work on her clit, while the fingers slid in and out, seeking deeper and deeper recesses to explore. Charlie knew Hailey's second orgasm was always more intense when her girlfriend came back to back like this, and she wanted to deliver. Hailey yelled out as she came again a few minutes later and rolled over almost to her side, forcing Charlie to lift up and out of her and then roll her over onto her back.

"You okay?" Charlie smirked and then climbed on top of Hailey again.

"I'll let you know in, like, five minutes."

Hailey's breathing was ragged, and her body looked languid and relaxed. Charlie leaned in for a kiss and enjoyed the feeling of Hailey's breasts gliding softly against her own. She realized at that, that the reason her breasts were gliding was that her hips were moving against Hailey. Charlie hadn't planned on that, but her body wanted more. Hailey gave her a look that told Charlie that she understood and would help however she could. Hailey's hand slid down between Charlie's legs, and in one fluid motion, her fingers were inside. Hailey's palm was pressed against her. Charlie leaned back to sit up and pulled Hailey closer. She rocked her hips against Hailey's body, as Hailey held on to her with her free hand and coaxed Charlie to take her pleasure.

"Hails, I want it like our first time," Charlie uttered and moved her hand behind her own body to slide fingers against Hailey's still firm clit.

"I don't know if I can again," Hailey said.

"Yes, you can."

Charlie took two fingers and alternated them up and down on either side of Hailey's clit. They'd reversed their positions from their first time together, but the movements were the essentially same; and, yet, they were somehow different. They knew one another now. They understood the sensations that drove the sounds and the other person toward their peaks. They found heightened pleasure with every encounter like this, thanks to that familiarity.

Charlie knew that Hailey would take a little longer to come this time, since the woman had just come twice only moments before. Charlie also knew how turned on she was, and that her body wanted its first orgasm of the day, but she slowed her rolling and, instead, focused on the feeling of Hailey's lips on her neck and her own fingers dancing in Hailey's arousal. Charlie heard the tell-tale signs of Hailey's climb and felt her girlfriend's teeth grazing and nipping at her skin, indicating that Hailey was ready for Charlie to come. Charlie pulled Hailey's face up to kiss her lips, and while their tongues played together, Charlie moaned into Hailey's mouth when Hailey's fingers curled inside her, beckoning her forward into her palm. Hailey could tell Charlie was close now, and she used her free hand to tweak a nipple in the way she knew would likely push Charlie higher.

When it did, Charlie felt a jolt of electricity thunder through her body, and she jerked forward and back, trusting Hailey to hold her up and in place, while her fingers still moved against Hailey's clit. Charlie rode out her orgasm, and as she was then coming down, she recognized that Hailey was on her way up. She immediately refocused her efforts on getting her girlfriend there. Hailey came hard, as

Charlie massaged her clit between her two fingers, and then, she fell back, bringing Charlie with her.

"Baby, you are really good at that," Hailey told her with a deep, throaty laugh.

***

Sundays were their favorite days. Throughout the week, they were usually both so busy, that they never had the feeling of just being able to relax together. Hailey's arms were around Charlie's waist, pulling the woman back into her, while Charlie attempted to make them coffee.

"Did you need something there, Hails?" Charlie smiled at herself and felt Hailey's hands slide up under the T-shirt Charlie had just thrown on.

"Just thinking about how I'm going to even the score," Hailey explained and grabbed two breasts in her hands.

"Even the score?"

"Well, I feel completely satisfied right now, thanks to the intense round of orgasms you just supplied me with. I want to make sure you also feel just as satisfied." Hailey kissed the back of Charlie's neck just below her hairline.

"Oh, I'm feeling pretty damn satisfied right now, Hails."

"Yeah?" Hailey kissed her again.

"Let's eat breakfast and then, talk more about this house we're going to build," Charlie proposed.

"That sounds like a good Sunday." Hailey planted another kiss in the same spot and pulled back so that Charlie could turn and pass her a cup of coffee that Hailey already knew would be perfectly mixed for her.

They ate in near silence, as Charlie watched Hailey read the back of the cereal box, which had puzzles for kids on it. Charlie thought to herself about what a wonderful mom this woman would be one day. Hailey crunched on her cereal, while Charlie ate the oatmeal she had prepared for herself. And the entire time they sat, side by side in silence, Hailey's right hand was somewhere on Charlie's body, as if reassuring herself that Charlie was there and wasn't going anywhere.

Charlie watched her in awe, the same way she always found herself watching Hailey – adoring the woman's messy bed head and the fact that she was only wearing a T-shirt and underwear while eating breakfast. She knew she could do this forever with Hailey, and she knew now that they would. Hailey pulled out the box, that once had a bow on top of it, and took out a small scroll, setting the box aside, as they each took their usual spots on the couch. Charlie was lying in Hailey's lap, while Hailey unrolled the scroll.

"Because you always make sure I'm warm enough," Hailey read out loud.

She smiled, rolled the paper back up, and sat it, along with the ribbon that held it together, on the arm of the couch, before looking down at Charlie.

"You do," Charlie said.

"You know how sometimes, you're too busy living your life to really notice things enough?"

"I guess," Charlie said, placed Hailey's arm over her stomach, and then placed her own arm on top of it.

"I think that's what I was doing all those years. Now that we're together, I can go back in my mind and realize that all those things, they added up to me loving you and not knowing it yet."

"What do you mean?" Charlie asked.

"The first time I realized you were cold," Hailey started saying and then looked up and ahead, as if drawing the memory back into her mind. "You were living in that crap apartment, remember?"

"Oh, yeah, I remember," Charlie recalled the first apartment she had gotten after moving out of her mother's house and arriving at UC. "Four-hundred square feet, with the bed about ten feet from the stove and the door to the building that never had a working lock."

"We were hanging out one night. I think it was just a

few months after we met. Ember had been there initially, but she had gotten a call from some girl she was hooking up with."

"Sometimes, I forget what a total player she used to be," Charlie said. "She's changed so much; it's crazy."

"It was just you and me. We were sitting on the floor in front of your bed. You were studying for a class. I was scrolling through my computer, checking out internships. It must have been the dead of winter, because it was cold inside even with your old heater on. But then, it went out. We called that guy to fix it, but he couldn't get there right away."

"You made me pack up my stuff and stay with you until it was fixed," Charlie added to the story.

"You were so stubborn. You wouldn't say yes right away. You kept saying that you could fix it yourself, which was ridiculous because you had no idea what you were doing. It was at least two hours before you finally gave up and came with me, but neither of us had cars back then."

"And we had to walk to the train," Charlie said.

"It was freezing, and then we walked to my place, and even though I turned the thermostat up as high as it would go, you were shivering like crazy." Hailey placed her hand on Charlie's cheek. "I got you in the shower and thought that would warm you enough, but even that didn't work all the way. I think, that night was the first time we slept in the same bed together. And I held on to you all night."

"I fell asleep," Charlie said. "You held on to me all night?"

"You'd shiver every now and then. I had my hand on your back the whole time, just to check on you. And when you'd shiver, I would wake up and roll over. I wrapped my arms around you and just held on. You actually scared me that night."

"I did?"

"You couldn't get warm no matter what I tried. I'd never seen that before. I even thought about taking you to the hospital at one point. But by – I don't know, two or three in the morning, you finally warmed up and stopped shivering. I knew then that I would always do whatever I had to do, to keep you warm. I just wanted to protect you and keep you safe. I had interpreted that as close friendship back then, but I think it was more. It just took me forever to realize it."

Charlie smiled up at her girlfriend and then placed her hand over Hailey's on her cheek, closing her own eyes to just feel the skin on skin contact.

"Well, I'll forgive you for taking so long, as long as I can have you like this forever," Charlie said.

Hailey didn't say anything for a moment, so Charlie opened her eyes.

"Because you designed our dream home," Hailey finally stated with a smile.

"What?"

"That's one of the reasons why I love you," Hailey explained, and Charlie rolled her eyes at her, sharing that smile. *"Because you don't get frustrated with me when I use the last of the milk,"* she continued. *"Because you always wash my hair when we shower together."*

"Are you just going to keep saying things about me?" Charlie asked.

She then sat up and patted her lap for Hailey to slide onto. Hailey did and wrapped her arms around Charlie's neck.

"No, I'm going to make you a box, like the one you made for me, and I'm going to write them all down. You'll pull them out one by one, like I've been doing. We'll do it every day, and then we'll start over." She kissed Charlie's lips. "I've got some catching up to do, as usual." Hailey lifted her eyes skyward in jest. "But I'll add an extra two-hundred in there."

"Hails, you don't have to do that."

"I want to, babe. I want you to know all the reasons, Charlie. I want to make sure you never forget them."

"Okay," Charlie agreed, loving the thought of them

sharing in this new tradition together.

"You know, I'm running out of these," Hailey said as she turned to pick up the now unfurled scroll and held it out for Charlie to see.

"That's okay. I'll just make more."